APOSTLES OF LIGHT

Books by Ellen Douglas

APOSTLES OF LIGHT

A NOVEL BY

Ellen Douglas

With an introduction by
Elizabeth Spencer

BANNER BOOKS

University Press of Mississippi / Jackson

First published in 1973 by Houghton Mifflin Company
Copyright © Ellen Douglas
Introduction Copyright © 1994 by
the University Press of Mississippi
Manufactured in the United States of America

97 96 95 94   4 3 2 1

The paper in this book meets the guidelines for permanence
and durability of the Committee on Production Guidelines for
Book Longevity of the Council on Library Resources.

Library of Congress Cataloging-in-Publication Data

Douglas, Ellen, 1921-
    Apostles of light : a novel / by Ellen Douglas ; with an
introduction by Elizabeth Spencer.
        p. cm. — (Banner books)
    ISBN 0-87805-737-4 (unjacketed cloth). —
ISBN 0-87805-738-2 (paper)
    1. Nursing home patients—Southern States—Fiction.
2. Nursing homes—Southern States—Fiction. 3. Family—
Southern States—Fiction. 4. Aged—Southern States—Fiction.
I. Title. II. Series: Banner books (Jackson, Miss.)
PS3554.0825A87 1994
813'.54—dc20   94-32158
                                            CIP

British Library Cataloging-in-Publication data available

For my mother and my sons

For such are *false apostles, deceitful workers, transforming themselves into the apostles of Christ.*

And no marvel; for Satan himself is transformed into an angel of light.

Therefore it is *no great thing if his ministers also be transformed as the ministers of righteousness; whose end shall be according to their works.*

2 Corinthians 11:13-15

BRICKS AND PEOPLE

"*Apostles of Light* is a good and courageous book."

I stated the above in a review of the novel written in 1973 when it first appeared ([Greenville, Miss.] *Delta-Democrat Times*, 11 March 1973), and I am glad to re-affirm it more than twenty years later.

The remainder of my remarks, written with the first reading of the book still echoing in my thoughts, can to advantage be restated here. They may give the new readers Ellen Douglas will certainly find with the present edition some idea of the impact the book will have for them.

Apostles of Light "addresses itself without apology [I said] to one of the knottier problems of our society: the plight of the aged. Yet Miss Douglas has by intelligence and talent avoided writing the sort of social protest novel in which the characters have no life outside the author's purpose. The people in it, for the most part, are real in themselves, and she has given us at least two splendidly realized figures who will not fade when her story ends.

"Her title is savagely ironic, as is made plain by the opening quotation from the Bible. These 'apostles' are disguised emissaries of Satan. They are those do-gooders we all know so well, spiritual Snopeses whose 'helping' others is always mixed in with helping themselves. In this story we observe how they treat the old and for what reasons. There is every shading of attitude toward age here; no line is arbitrarily drawn, and it would be a conscienceless reader indeed who did not at times find his own guilt in these pages. Much of this, Miss Douglas is fair enough to make plain, relates simply to the human predicament. Who wants age, who wants to die? The old make all too plain to the young a disagreeable reality. So, little at a time, damage, like flood water, finds its crevices. Pretty soon we are up to our necks. We are seeing at first hand those who put the old away, tidily tranquilize their human anguish, deny them their dignity, their right to decision, their identity; who do not in the long run even hear them, for to say a person is getting 'senile' is a way of saying that nothing he utters is of any validity.

"For all her deceptively quiet manner and muted tone, Miss Douglas's own perception is fierce. If purists complain that novels should not be used to express social problems, let them first dismiss Dickens and Zola; they will have, I think, to come to terms."

The overleaf blurb on the original edition stated: "Miss Douglas's work lies in the main tradition of the English novel from George Eliot to Eudora Welty." But I for one questioned this statement and asked for a closer look. For, as I noted at the time, "there are similarities in literature, but family trees, though often claimed, are seldom seen. We long, as in a children's game, to make everybody freeze for better determining what they're up to." When this novel after some early hesitant pages, "strikes free and runs on its own, the method is that of Greek drama." The story shows us this when "it finds its true protagonist, Lucas Alexander, a local doctor long known as an eccentric, principally, it seems, because he isn't interested in money. A 'home' for older citizens has been made from the lovely old family residence of Lucas's lifelong sweetheart, a retired schoolteacher, Martha Clarke. He goes there himself to live, mainly to be near her. Thus he learns firsthand what is going on and it is the gradual unfolding of this situation to his fine intelligence and conscience that generates both pity and terror. True, a sense of doom has been everywhere from the very beginning, though at first only in normal forms—in Martha's sister's death, for instance, in the human plight of aging at all, in Martha's haunted dreams. But it becomes specific and even Satanic in the sinister intrigues and outrageous cruelties of the nursing home scene. So the net is woven. It is finally Lucas's choice, after his long losing battle to expose the truth, to accept doom supinely and to choose his own death, and his decision is heroic.

"Set against Lucas for dramatic contrast, a method which is obvious, but which works effectively in this writer's hands, is a selfeducated black man, Matthew Harper. Harper was once Martha Clarke's butler, later a servant in the 'home.' As an intellectual hobby, Harper has devoted himself through the years to finding out all the ways in which human beings have slaughtered each other down through the centuries. This long passage is brilliantly done. It gives a needed dimension, a sort of backdrop, to the book, and it even shines at times with a peculiar charm and humor. . . . No fictional diversion is this pursuit of Harper's; he, a despised member of society, just as are the old, has figured out what to do when the time comes and they are trying to get rid of you; survival is all; forget the 'community'; go and hide. Seeing Lucas's plight at the end leads Harper to try to persuade Lucas to see life in the same way—the old, like blacks, are discards. Mere survival for Lucas and Martha seems in Harper's terms, to be all that is possible. He offers to help them escape and hide. This scene is dramatically fine, perhaps the finest in the book. It maintains an impeccable intellectual tension—its pathos is almost unbearable."

So now this remarkable novel is being brought to us again, after three additional novels have followed it— namely, *The Rock Cried Out*, *A Lifetime Burning*, and *Can't Quit You, Baby*. Those who know Ellen Douglas's fiction will also remember the ones that came before: *A Family's Affairs*, a first novel prize winner, and *Where the Dreams Cross*, plus the short stories in *Black Cloud, White Cloud*.

It has been noted many times that despite a thoroughly Southern background, Ellen Douglas bases her fiction in a world that is modern, subject to the changes and attitudes that all Americans experience. That she has done so may seem a paradox, for she has seldom strayed from her home turf of Mississippi. Paradox, but not defiance. We all live here, is the implication. We are all affected by these events. So, as has been said elsewhere, "she has dared to explore in depth the problems of family, race, and sex with a thoroughly modern awareness, knowing that tough, knotty issues may come to light but knowing too, that life is full of great surprises."

From an interview we learn how she admires those grounded and rooted writers whose separate visions, drawn from their own time and place, continue to move and enlighten us today: Conrad, Proust, the Russians, Joyce and Faulkner, Emily Brontë, George Eliot. As for the question of "Southern-ness," which might seem limiting to some, she has herself answered it firmly and reasonably:

"I don't think *regionalism* is important," she has said. "I think *place*, in the sense of the specific, is absolutely essential, but I don't think *a place* . . . is what I'm talking about when I say 'place.' If I had grown up in Birmingham or New York City, the place would still have been immensely important because novels are specific and they are made out of bricks and people. . . . I'm a craftsman, *a maker*."

This credo moves me, as does this writer, her roots going deep into an accessible past which we all can share, but with her own distinct vision, looking forward.

Elizabeth Spencer

APOSTLES OF LIGHT

CHAPTER 1

"It doesn't look any worse than most of the other houses in the neighborhood," George Clarke said. "Not as bad as some." He gestured toward the freeway that cut across the end of Clarke Street two blocks away and diverted four lanes of roaring traffic around the outskirts of Homochitto. "It's no surprise to me that this part of town has gone down."

"But it reflects on us, you know. On us!" Newton said. "We're supposed to be looking after them — responsible for them."

"People in Homochitto make allowances for Elizabeth and Martha," Louisa said. "They've never behaved like ordinary people and no one expects them to. And now that they're old and sick . . ." She shrugged. She and her husband and son had discussed this subject so often that she did not bother to finish her sentence. A step or two ahead of the men, she emerged now from the deep shade (they had been walking along a green tunnel between a row of ancient dense-leaved laurel trees lining the neutral ground on their right and a wall of cane surrounding the house on their left) and paused at the foot of a short flight of worn brick steps leading upward through an opening in the cane. The yard beyond lay in shade; but here the wavering, leaf-patterned sunlight shone on Louisa's neatly curled gray hair and round pleasant face and struck from the diamond pin on her lapel a glittering spectrum of color.

"Looks like we never bother to get the grass cut — much less go inside. Like we don't care whether they're dead or alive." Newton looked about him with an expression of fastidious distaste in his bright blue eyes. He was a tall, sandy-haired young man with the long, big-chinned face that one sees in advertisements for expensive whiskey or British shoes; and he wore just the sort of tan poplin suit and tan buckled shoes that such a man might be expected to wear. He spoke with a blurred, stammering rapidity, mumbling his words and repeating or recasting his phrases as if aware that what he said might not be intelligible.

"But that's not the case," George said. "And anyhow, what difference does it make what people think?" He opened the iron gate and the three of them climbed the steps, overarched by tall cane, and started along a curving brick walk at the end of which stood the house where the two old ladies lived. "They're the ones we have to think about," he said. "Aunt Elizabeth can't see the yard anymore and Aunt Martha likes it the way it is. Her idea of a garden has always been to naturalize."

"Ruling passion strong in death, as Mama used to say," Louisa said.

"Aunt Martha is *not* dying," George said. "She's as healthy as she was twenty years ago."

"That's just a manner of speaking about old age, George," his wife replied.

"Naturalize!" Newton said. "Yes, it's natural, all right. Looks like the Catahoula swamp. The swamp! And probably crawling with snakes." Leaning down, he picked up a dead branch from the walk and threw it out of the way. "Just *look* at the place. You two are so used to it, you don't know — don't even notice — how bad it's gotten."

All around them, within the walls of cane, was an old-fashioned Southern garden gone wild — a jungle of Spanish daggers, neglected japonicas festooned with white webs of scale, mounds of lavender and orange lantana, and mazes of wisteria vines choking the life out of the oak trees. Jonquils and swamp iris had multiplied until the bulbs were too crowded and starved to produce blooms, and, although it was June, the winter's leaves still lay deep under the wild crab apple and dogwood trees and oak-leaved hydrangeas that Martha Clarke had years ago dug up and brought home from the woods, and that now seemed to thrive in a setting as undisturbed as their natural one. At the end of the curving walk (laid to miss a huge Spanish oak in the middle of the front yard) stood an old-fashioned clapboard house of the type New Orleans people call a "raised cottage." The central section, approached by a steep flight of steps, had a small, severely classical portico framing a heavy six-paneled door with leaded lights on either side and a fanlight above. At either side were wings, dropped back at right angles to the house.

From the front the house appeared to be one story, with a basement behind the steps, but the land on which it stood dropped steeply away to a bayou at the rear, and there was a spacious floor of bedrooms and storage areas built into the hill below the main floor and wings. When the family had been larger — when George and his brother Albert had been children — there had been a complex household living here: grandparents, parents, aunts, children, and servants; but now the lower floor was closed off and never used.

"Look at it, Daddy!" Newton said again. "Objectively. As if you were a stranger."

And indeed the house seemed to be dissolving into a shroud of Virginia creeper, ivy, and bignonia vines. Lattices on either side of the high front porch were rotting and breaking under tangled mounds of Confederate jasmine; laurel trees that had once been kept clipped like shrubs blocked the light from two of the front windows; a maze of fig vine, its tiny, dark green leaves pressed flat against brick and metal, had run up the drainpipes and chimneys at either end of the central section and cascaded down from the tops — had now even begun to grow out onto the roof, insinuating itself under the weathered cedar shakes.

"We *should* see about getting the vines cut back," George said. "Otherwise, we're going to have to buy a new roof. And with the expense of this illness, Aunt Elizabeth is in no position to pay for a roof." He stepped off the walk and made his way out into the yard for a better look at the house. A tall man, taller even than Newton and thin almost to emaciation, he picked his way through the tangle with delicate high steps, stretching his neck and cocking his head to one side like a long-legged, beaky water bird. He stopped beside a mound of honeysuckle and kicked the vines aside. "Look here, Louisa," he said. "The old sundial is under here. Pedestal is broken." He shook his head. "Too bad." Bending down, he pulled the vines away from the face and touched the raised figures on its surface.

"Couldn't tell time with it in this shade anyhow," Newton said.

"Son, it's been here a long time."

"Come out of the weeds, darling," Louisa said. "You may step on a snake"; and when he returned to the walk, she added, "If you want to save money, you men should *make* Mary Hartwell put her mother in the hospital. After all, in the long run we're the ones who pay through the nose for all this Medicare foolishness. Why should Aunt Elizabeth stay at home and consume every penny of that estate paying for nurses and medicine, when she could be getting some of our taxes back in free medical care?"

George looked pained. "Nobody can do anything with Mary Hartwell," he said. "She's always been hardheaded. And anyhow, it's not only a question of money, Louisa. Getting the vines off the roof is one thing, but turning the household arrangements upside-down is another. We've got everybody's feelings to consider."

"Besides," Newton said, "besides, you forget the hospital's been integrated. The place is swarming with nigras. They get pushed for space, she might even be put in a double with one."

"Elizabeth is too sick to know where she is or who else is there," Louisa said, "not to mention the fact that she's crazy about colored people. *She* might not mind. And she would be a great deal more comfortable in the hospital. Anyhow, you know very well that Dr. Gardner would see to it that she got a private room regardless of how crowded they are. It ought to be done." She took her husband's arm again and added with some urgency, "And there's this to consider, too, George. If you and Albert don't begin to take a firm stand — to get this situation under your control *now*, you're laying up trouble for yourselves in the future. You say yourself that Aunt Martha has always been eccentric. No telling what outlandish notions she may get."

"You just said that we should make allowances for eccentricity," George said.

"But not to the extent of getting into financial difficulties because . . ."

"That's what we're having this conference for," George said mildly. "To make some constructive decisions about the future. And you should try not to say too much, Louisa. After all, Aunt Elizabeth may have raised Albert and me, but Mary Hartwell and Francis are her own children."

"But all of you have the same responsibility to Martha," Louisa said. "And we *live* here. Francis is in New York and Mary Hartwell can go back to Memphis after her mother dies and leave the whole mess for us to struggle with."

"You'd think Mary Hartwell would take more interest in keeping the house up," Newton said. "She and Francis — they're going to inherit it. Gem of a place — could be turned into something impressive with a little outlay. How much? Twenty thousand — maybe thirty thousand dollars? I wouldn't mind owning it myself someday."

"She's been upset, son," George said. "And tired. It's not as simple as it looks."

"Yes," Louisa said. "It would be lovely for you, Newton. Someday."

The three of them climbed the stairs to the portico and Newton rang the doorbell. In a few minutes they heard slow footsteps in the hall and the sound of a key turning in the lock. An elderly man with a long intelligent face, dry yellowish skin, and a bald head opened the door and held it back for them to enter.

"Mrs. Clarke. Mr. Clarke. Newton." He spoke with a kind of exaggerated breathy formality and bowed slightly. "The family is in the study," he said. Then he smiled at Newton, the indulgent smile of an old man who has known a young one as a child and can scarcely believe he is grown. "Well," he said, "you haven't paid us a visit in a long time."

"Good morning, Harper," George said. "How's everybody doing today?"

"Mrs. Griswold had a bad night, I believe, but she's resting now."

"The front walk needs sweeping, Harper," Louisa said.

"Very well, Mrs. Clarke." He looked at Louisa and spoke in his breathy butler's voice, a slight smile of acquiescence on the wide firm lips, the eyes as neutral as if he were looking at a natural phenomenon — a stick to be moved out of the path or a vine to be tied up to the trellis.

The long wide hallway through which George and Louisa walked toward the small study at the back of the house was furnished with two or three cane-bottomed chairs and, beside the front door, an old plantation-made walnut table; its walls were hung with beautifully executed botanical prints and its floor covered with a worn Oriental runner. The dining room, too, had an air of austere simplicity — bare floors and long-used furniture.

Inside the dining room Louisa paused. "Harper is another complication we could get along without," she said. "He's too old to keep up with the yard; and he can begin drawing his social security next year. And, while we're on the subject, those grandchildren of his give me a very bad feeling. Since Lucy's gotten that fuzzy hairdo like the civil rights people wear, it's like having a stranger out here. A sitter with an Afro — really! And the fifteen-year-old boy . . . ! One look at him and you know he's headed for trouble."

"Now, Louisa. One thing at a time," George said. "Harper's as spry as he ever was. And besides, his competence and his grandchildren's behavior have nothing to do with each other. And you know how attached Aunt Martha is to him. Just let that subject alone — for the time being, anyhow."

Newton, who had stayed behind for a few moments' conversation with Harper, now joined his parents and together they went into the study whose windows opened on the back garden and the meandering bayou beyond. Here they found the rest of the family gathered: Albert Clarke, George's brother and a childless widower in his late fifties; Mary Hartwell Griswold Martin, their cousin; and Martha Clarke, the old lady who was a part of the reason for this conference. The only missing adult member of the family, aside from Elizabeth Griswold, who lay ill in her bedroom at the other end of the house, was Mary Hartwell's brother, Francis; he lived in New York and was seldom able to get away from his business long enough to come home.

The cousins were old friends who had grown up together (Mrs. Griswold had adopted George and Albert in their early teens after the death of their father in a hunting accident and of their mother from a heart attack); they took pleasure in each other's company and in the familiar surroundings of the home where they had been children together: the loud tick of the battered Willard clock on the mantel, the photographs of themselves and daguerreotypes of their forebears clustered around it, the worn but comfortable chairs, and the strong sharp smell of the chicory coffee that Harper brought in from the kitchen in old-fashioned blue willow cups. They were glad of a chance to visit together, even in these unhappy circumstances; and they fell into desultory cheerful conversation — talk of an impending local special election (the incumbent sheriff had died), news of the recent divorce of Homochitto's wealthiest doctor (whose wife, it was rumored, had run away with a hospital orderly fifteen years younger than she), and of the takeover of a large wholesale gasoline business through the surreptitious acquisition of proxies.

Their soft Southern voices rose and fell in a counterpoint of genteel gossip — George's plaintive and nasal as an oboe, Albert's deeper and with a vibrato in it that made him seem older than he was, Mary Hartwell's drawling and quiet. Louisa's voice alone seemed alien to the rest. She spoke rapidly like her son, and after thirty years of living in Homochitto still had the rhubarb-pie-and-clean-baseboards twang of Indiana.

Newton leaned back in the corner of the sofa, put his hands in his pockets, and listened, puckering his lips in a soundless whistle and looking around him with interest, as if he might be making an inventory of things that needed to be done. Twenty-seven years old, he had been in Homochitto a year since completing law school and serving his time in the army; he was beginning to take an interest in community and family affairs — in the inner workings of the Republican party and in these unhappy aunts who were the source of so much worry to his parents.

The room which Newton was examining opened to the south and east, and the green light of early summer poured in through tall windows onto an array of potted plants crowded together on two rickety tables: Joseph's coat, night-blooming cereus, Boston fern, green- and plum-colored wandering Jew, air plants cascading over the sides of the tables and drooping to the floor, and two spindly dieffenbachias that towered almost leafless to the ceiling. Tall, glass-fronted bookcases filled with leatherbound sets of the classics stood against one wall. On the others hung steel engravings of the Seven Ages of Man executed in a romantic mid-nineteenth-century style: a lady in a feathered hat and full, panniered skirt held a cherubic naked child while a maid knelt at her feet holding up a towel; a fresh-faced lad in a Byronic shirt charged the cannon's mouth; a toothless old man sat hunched in a chimney corner over the cane which he held before him, gripped in both hands. Everything in the room looked neglected — the leaves yellowing or drooping, the pots either too wet or too dry, the paint on the woodwork and heavy cypress doors yellow with age. The furniture had not been dusted for weeks, the floor needed waxing and the rug vacuuming, and the slipcovers were worn to threads on the arms of the sofa and wing chair.

Newton frowned and, taking one hand out of his pocket, ran his fingers lightly over the tabletop at his elbow and examined the trail they left in the dust. Then he began to watch his great-aunt who was sitting somewhat apart from the other members of the family and had not yet joined in the conversation.

She sat in a cane-bottomed rocker drawn close to the cold fireplace, an old woman, still vigorous, but poised at the brink of being very old. Her bright blue eyes, when she occasionally raised them to look from one to another of her family, were vague and unfocused. Most of the time this morning, she sat with her head bent and looked at her lap. Her skin was brown and leathery — the skin of one who has spent her life outdoors in the sun and wind — her strong brown hands mottled with "liver spots" like enormous brown freckles. Her hair was snow white — strikingly beautiful against the blue eyes and dark skin — and, even sitting still, she held her sturdy body tensely, as if nurturing a reserve of energy and passion that might yet be put to all kinds of uses. Her lips moved in a silent conversation with herself.

Newton, as if to draw her into the general talk, said, "Yes, Aunt Martha?"

But she did not reply.

At the opposite end of the house, lying shrunken and drugged in a rented hospital bed, her sister Elizabeth was dying of cancer. Elizabeth's suffering had dominated Martha's life now for more than a year. No matter what she happened to be thinking or doing, it came back to her at every moment and weighed on her so heavily that she sometimes felt she had scarcely the strength to pick up her fork at the table and eat. She had watched the disease run its course — slowly, as it does in old people — a third party in the house, endowed with the malignancy of moral evil. It seemed to her sometimes that, more than a physical disease, the cancer was a kind of hatred of joy and order and life that existed independently of her sister (for who could have loved joy and order and life more than Elizabeth?); that it had entered her body as the devils had entered the swine, measuring and opposing her strength with the cunning of consciousness; that if Elizabeth had been younger and stronger, the disease would have been swifter and more virulent, but, since she was tired and had no heart to oppose it, it moved with leisurely confidence, for a time almost unnoticed, insinuating itself with voluptuous pleasure into every cell, bringing in its wake the slow and then, suddenly, irretrievable erosion of their lives through confusion, grief, pain, interference, and finally, for Elizabeth, anguish, despair, and mindless sleep.

Martha could remember — as if it were years ago — a time when they had lived in a pristine order created by herself and her sister and Harper, an order (confirmed season by season like the order of a changing garden over the years since she had retired from teaching and since the children had been grown and gone) in which all three of them took the keenest pleasure. She heard the gentle slap of Elizabeth's house slippers on the hall floor and the stairs as she went down to breakfast. "It's eight o'clock," she whispered. The day lay before them. Breakfast, and then the house plants to be seen to. The back garden to be inspected. "The bank is washing behind the garage, Harper. What do you think we should put in to hold it? The shade is so deep here." "Well, Miss Martha" — she heard his voice, officious, yet full of his passion for growing things — "well, I'd like to see us move those slabs of moss from over yonder in that sunny spot. We could put some pieces of that little-leafed ivy where the moss is — scatter grass cuttings on the bank, so it won't wash till the ivy takes a hold. Just look at that moss — already got wood fern started in it. Wouldn't that be pretty? It would do better in the shade, and besides, you can hardly see it at all where it is, up behind that log . . ."

And Lucas . . . Where is he? He's feeling well again and he comes by . . . Too thin, far too thin. How am I going to get him to eat and get his strength back when I can't even . . . No! He comes by. He's well. Gaining weight. November, it might be — but a warm sunny spell after a rain. We'd try the cemetery. Yes, he can drive now. Leave the car by the gate and walk and *walk*. A wonderful flush of agarics, the smell of earth in them. We'd fill two baskets — the buttons shining like pearls in the yellow grass. *Can I still see them?* But Lucas tells me all he sees. The little fall warblers flickering in the cedar trees. The haws and swamp hollies, bare of leaves now but bent down with red berries. The first camellias and sasanquas blooming . . .

And then, home. Lunch. Lucas might stay. And then, in the afternoon, we'll go — where? Sister's working at the library today, and so . . . She saw Elizabeth, tiny and erect, her curly gray hair drawn into an untidy knot on top of her head, a child herself, encircled by children, reading aloud, tears shining in her eyes, as Robin Hood at the tower casement gathered his last strength, drew his longbow, and sped the arrow that would mark his grave. "Lay a green sod before my head, and another at my feet, and place my bent bow by my side . . ." How many times do you suppose she . . . ? And still cries! Her heart contracted with familiar pain.

And then, in the evening, supper and a game of pinochle or

Russian bank. I — we — both prefer pinochle, she said silently, as if to some friendly listener in her head. An occasional game of Russian bank, but it's slow . . .

No more pinochle.

Mary Hartwell is here, of course, and we can't play a two-handed game; but . . .

She felt sometimes that her whole body was vibrating with shock — even more shock than pain — as if someone had thrown a rock and struck her in the temple and she were now in the moment of falling. She found that she could think quite clearly about all the circumstances of her life up to the moment the rock was thrown, but that the "afterward," extending indefinitely into a confusing future, continued to elude her efforts to bring it to order.

Something like this has happened once before, she said to the companion in her head. Was it George? Or maybe the next generation. Newton? No, Newton never climbed a tree in his life. It was Francis. She saw him — the beloved little boy — a flashing vision: dirty face, scarred fat legs, dark-blond hair falling across the round high forehead, the gray bark against his grubby hand where he gripped at a branch too big for him to hold; the blue summer sky. *Aunt Martha! Help me!* Could it have been, not yesterday, but a whole lifetime ago?

Yes. And someone that year — one of the boys — had the finest rubber-gun I ever saw. Cut with ten notches and you could shoot off a succession of bands, just like a machine gun. The enemy is approaching! I reach up. Poor little fellow — lift him down quick. Nobody to see me do it. Would be humiliating because after all he's younger than the rest — they already think he's nothing but a baby. (Always my darling, gone now.) And then, without warning, a rock! Somebody had a slingshot

— must have. And I feel it. My whole body — my *bones* — vibrating. Not pain, a numb singing vibration. Even in my legs and arms, like the whole length of a plucked string. Everything up to the moment the rock is thrown — *clear*. I can think about. But then, confusion.

Mary Hartwell wants to tell Harper what to do and he doesn't want her to. Sometimes I think he's confused, too, but that's not it. He just doesn't want her to tell him what to do. Doesn't want the order of things to be lost. And all Sister's menus — what's happened to the things we used to eat? Mary Hartwell doesn't even shop for groceries on the same days, much less . . . Lucas — gone — sick. If Lucas came, we could talk about it and . . . Who would believe that our life could change so quickly — destroyed . . .

No more pinochle.

"That's not necessarily true," she said. "Sister . . ."

"What's that, Aunt Martha?" Newton was still watching her. "What's not necessarily true?"

"No, no," she said. "I wasn't talking to you," and lapsed into the inward clarity and confusion of her thoughts.

No more pinochle blazoned like the *Mene, mene, tekel, upharsin* of an angry god on the wall of her mind. She and Elizabeth would not sit opposite each other, not one more evening, cool and content on the back gallery, windows flung wide, the late sun going down.

I like daylight saving time, she thought. All this foolishness of Louisa's about not wanting Congress to change the clock — ridiculous! Sometimes I think if Louisa doesn't moderate her political prejudices, she's going to end up in — what do the children call it? — the loony bin. Because . . . what could be pleasanter? Nine o'clock and we're through with supper, but it's still light — that deep blue light of summer evenings; we're having a quiet game and the locusts are calling in the trees and you can hear the frogs beginning to sing to each other by the bayou . . .

"Dr. Alexander has been ill, I heard yesterday," Louisa was saying. "Pneumonia. I hadn't even realized he was in the hospital and he's already home. Did you know, Martha? Aunt Martha! Did you know Lucas Alexander had been in the hospital?"

Martha looked up. "Yes," she said. "Mary Hartwell took me to see him. He says he's much better now, but I'm concerned about him out there alone. He really hasn't been well for months. Flu and colds — first one thing and then another. I wish one of you boys would drive me out again one day soon. Do you think maybe . . . ?"

"Sunday afternoon, if you like," Louisa said. "George and I will take you."

"Newton says the doc's talking about selling his place and moving to town," George said.

"He is? That's a nice piece of land, you know it?" Albert said. He shook back his hair with a characteristic jerk of his head. Like his aunt, he had thick, snow white hair, brown skin, and blue eyes. Some people, looking at the striking contrasts in his coloring, considered him handsome, but in fact there was no particular distinction in his snub-nosed, thin-lipped face, and he sometimes looked out from beneath his white thatch with a kind of sly question in his eyes, as if he hoped to catch you in a lie, or at least an inadvertent gaucherie. His head was too large for his body ("I wear a size seven and three-fourths hat," he would say with the curious pride that self-absorbed people take in their own abnormalities) and his thick body, once erect and vigorous, was beginning to be slack and paunchy. "Part of the old Carlton place, it used to be, didn't it?" he continued. "Now that the Cole heirs have bought up the land around it, they'd probably pay through the nose to fill out their place with it. Do you handle his affairs, Newton?"

"Such as they are," Newton said. "He's a thorny old fellow to deal with and hardly worth the trouble in the long run."

"I reckon you'd better tell us what you've got on your mind this morning, Albert," George said. "Newton and I both have to get back downtown before lunch, much as I hate to cut this pleasant visit short."

"Well, I wouldn't have called you folks last night," Albert said, "if something hadn't come up that had to be decided right away. I know how busy everybody is — and also, of course, none of us wants to rock the boat now, while Aunt Elizabeth is so sick. But I ran into Howie Snyder yesterday and he had a suggestion to make that I think we should consider."

It would make such a difference if I could still drive. Damned cataracts! Awful, *awful* to be dependent on other people. I'm not like that, you know. I've always . . .

"Aunt Martha," Albert said, "what I'm going to say mainly concerns you, sweetheart, so listen to me." He rose from the sofa and, crossing the room, drew up a straight-backed chair beside her rocker, sat down, and took her hand in his. "I saw Cousin Howie Snyder yesterday," he repeated, emphasizing the "cousin." "He had a suggestion about our arrangements here — our difficulties — that I thought might work out for you — for all of us."

Albert . . . I believe he's beginning to think he's the town character. When did he start this "sweetheart" business? And just because his hair is as white as mine, he oughtn't to give up having it cut. Curling 'round his ears like a wig. "Albert," she said, "you ought to send those pants to the cleaners. In fact, if you want my opinion, you should get rid of them. You know a man shouldn't allow himself to go to pieces just because he hasn't a woman to look after him. And why don't you get your hair cut?"

Newton snickered.

"You can see anything you want to see, can't you, Aunt Martha?" Albert said. "Now listen to me, sweetheart. I want to talk to you about the future." He drew a deep breath. "You know how sick Aunt Elizabeth is," he said. "It's hard for us to admit, but . . ."

Mary Hartwell made a gesture of protest. "Really, Albert," she said. "Don't . . ."

"Mary Hartwell, we *must* face this situation. Aunt Martha, too." He broke off and, turning back to the old lady, continued. "Listen carefully now to what I have to say, so you can help us make a decision. We have to think about practical plans for the future. We want you to be comfortable and safe."

"You know I trust you and George, Albert," she said. "And Mary Hartwell. And of course Francis, if he were here. I'll go along with anything you think best." It's quite true, she thought, that I trust them to look out for me. They're good children, all of them. I know they're not going to stick me away in an old people's home or any dreadful thing like that. But there's no use in my trying to talk to them. No way to make them understand how seriously all this confusion and anguish is affecting me. Besides, it would only be painful for them if I told them.

"Aunt Elizabeth can't live very much longer," Albert said. "You know that." He hesitated and then added, "It's God's will, Aunt Martha; we have to accept it."

Again Mary Hartwell made a gesture of protest, but he continued. "Mary Hartwell will have to go back to her family, and you can't stay in this big old place alone."

Martha looked from one to another of them. Then, "Harper

and I can manage together well enough," she said. "I feel sure . . ."

"Not to mention the expense," he went on. "We have to take into consideration the way this neighborhood is changing. When I think of that colored slum backing right up to the bayou — not a stone's throw from the back door. Dangerous!" (Albert was too genteel to say "nigger" to his family or to black people. He used that word only to truck drivers and other such brutal folk, with whom, on the other hand, he was too polite to use a genteelism like "colored.")

" 'Colored slum'! Albert, that's a respectable neighborhood," Martha said. "It's no slum — it's *Harper's* neighborhood. And besides, even if it weren't, nobody's going to bother us. That's just foolishness. There's nothing here anybody wants — and goodness knows nobody could want *me*."

Albert rose and stood with his back to the cold fireplace and his hands under his coattails as if he were warming himself. "You know Howie retired about a year ago, and then Lydia died," he said, speaking a little too loudly, as if to a foreigner or a deaf person. "Do you remember that, Aunt Martha?"

She nodded. "Don't talk to me as if I were a simpleton, Albert," she said. "Of course I know Lydia Snyder is dead." Then, "Never mind, never mind," she said, half-reaching out to him with an apologetic gesture. "I don't mean to be cross."

"Well, Howie was telling me yesterday, he has a sale for his house. It's too big for him now. He's all alone. No responsibilities. No family. His son almost never gets back to Homochitto. Stationed in West Germany now and no telling where they'll send him next. I feel sorry for the poor fellow. Howie, I mean. He's lonely. Hasn't all that much money. You know he was edged out of Southern Hardboard when Consolidated Screw bought them out. Out on his ear after thirty years! And it hadn't been two years since he lost a bundle in the Caldwell Company failure. Tough!"

George started to speak. "As a matter of fact . . ."

"Yes, I know. It may have been his own fault. Probably shouldn't have risked that much money on anything as iffy as the Caldwell Company. But we all make mistakes. Anyhow, he's sold his house. Did I say that? And he doesn't want to move into a room. He wants a *home*. Of course he could get a little apartment, but he said he'd been thinking about us. About our dilemma out here. After all, he *is* a member of the family — it's not as if he were a stranger."

"Your fourth cousin," Martha said. "My third."

"He was wondering if we would be willing to rent him one of the downstairs bedrooms and the study. And meals, too. He could take his meals here. You don't want to eat alone day after day, Aunt Martha."

Martha felt such a pain and constriction of her heart that for a moment she thought she was going to faint. *My God!* she thought. And then, directing her thoughts through the ceiling and roof and toward the sky with all the force she could muster: *Someone! Please help me. Please don't let me feel how lonely I will be.* But the vaguely pantheistic deity who lived in the natural world she loved was silent. No comforting ghostly hand touched her shoulder.

Albert went on talking. "You'd have a man in the house to protect you. And a relatively young man. Five or six years older than I am, eh, George? Maybe sixty-three at the most."

"That's about right," George said.

"Times have changed, sweetheart," Albert said. "It's all very well to say that nobody will bother you, but none of the rest of us would rest easy at night with you out here alone. Oh, I know we could arrange to have Lucy continue to come at night, but

Lucy is scatterbrained. Hardly more than a child. And besides, that's an additional expense. As a matter of fact, I'd considered suggesting that *I* could move in, but that's got its drawbacks. I'm notionate and crotchety and so are you. If we got on each other's nerves, it would be a disaster, but with Howie everything could be on a more impersonal plane. Much easier. The other thing, of course, is that I'm on the road so much — out of town more than in. I wouldn't be any use to you as a protector."

"Don't you think we could wait a while before we settle all this, Albert?" Mary Hartwell said. "After all, I'm here and I will continue to be here. I can't go home and leave Mama as sick as she is."

"Of course it would be better if we could put it off," Albert said. "But you know it's only a matter of — maybe . . ." He hesitated, turned away from his aunt, and lowering his voice moved closer to Mary Hartwell as he spoke, ". . . weeks (maybe just *days*) before . . . Besides, Howie has already sold his house and given occupancy in thirty days. He has to decide what he's going to do. And this is a very lucky break for Aunt Martha. I'd hate to see us pass it up."

Mary Hartwell had been listening and frowning. She was a vigorous, motherly-looking woman of fifty, large bosomed and open faced with tired brown eyes; and there was a stubbornness not easily to be moved in the set of her jaw. She shook her head.

George cleared his throat. "Now we don't have to be in a hurry, Mary Hartwell," he said in a conciliatory voice. "We can do whatever we want to about Howie, you know that. And of course we're not going to upset you and Aunt Elizabeth. But let's not dismiss the subject without even thinking about it — the pros and cons, you know — and Aunt Martha's point of view. Albert's got a point, after all. What *are* we going to do?

We've all been worrying about it, and not talking about it isn't going to make it go away." Nervously he cleared his throat again. "Aunt Martha has her little social security," he said, "and we're all going to keep on helping. But this big place could get to be a terrible drain when your mother's income is — ah — cut off. It's going to be a problem."

"Besides," Albert said, "I've asked Howie to come out here and talk about it this morning. It's not going to hurt anybody to talk to him."

"You asked him out here without discussing it with us before-hand?" Mary Hartwell said. "Really, Albert!"

"I should keep my mouth shut, I suppose," Newton said, "but Albert hasn't done anything wrong, Mary Hartwell. Howie's a practical man — *practical*. Nothing sentimental about him. He won't get his feelings hurt — get sulky — if you don't take him in. Convenience. It's no more than a convenience for everybody."

Martha got up from her rocker and, after walking over to the long windows that opened on the back garden, stood gazing intently out. From this high vantage point she could look across the lawn and the circle of driveway behind the house and into the branches of trees rooted in the steep bank of the ravine that dropped down to the bayou. The light wavered in green and golden layers among the branches, almost as if the house were submerged in the clear water of a warm, sunny sea. The shapes of the trees, blurred, as by water, by the mist of cataracts across her eyes, were vague and indistinct, undulating in the light wind like huge masses of seaweed. She heard outside the familiar sounds of morning: the calls of blue jays announcing the arrival of Harper on the back steps and then the click of his hoe along the graveled edge of the driveway; the voices of children shouting to each other in yards that backed up to the bayou on the other side; the repeated *sweet, sweet* of a towhee. I wish I were outside, she thought. I would dig up and separate those jonquils by the scuppernong arbor.

". . . perhaps, once this crisis is over, is to get Aunt Martha an apartment in the Eastside Arms and you and Francis could get rid of the house."

"The house will be yours and George's, too," Mary Hartwell said. "Mama has left it to the four of us — and for Aunt Martha's use during her lifetime."

"Well . . ." Albert said.

"You know she thinks of you as her sons," Mary Hartwell said abruptly.

They fell silent, equally struck by a revulsion against talking of Elizabeth's will.

"The Eastside Arms is not a bad idea, Daddy," Newton said. "Close to all of us. No upkeep. Rent's reasonable. Doesn't make sense to maintain this place."

"I can't bear to think of uprooting her," Mary Hartwell said in a low voice which nevertheless came quite clearly to Martha's ears. "All these years. She has a right to spend the rest of her life here, if she wants to."

"But it does present problems," George said.

"I think it would be shocking to *sell* the house," Louisa said. "Couldn't you rent it out for a while, even if we have to move Martha? This neighborhood may be out of style now, but times change. Some of the old neighborhoods are getting to be quite popular in places like Memphis and Atlanta."

Isn't it strange that they're able to talk of disposing of me as if I were a child? Martha thought. I suppose I should resent it. But I'm too tired. Now, I'm going to think about something else. Birds. She began to listen intently for birdcalls and as she heard them — the towhee again, the clear whistle of a cardinal, the loud repetitive shout of a house wren, the raucous voices of the redheaded woodpeckers that lived by dozens all around the yard — she reconstructed in her mind the way the trees had once looked on days when she had stood here in the window with field glasses and followed the flashes of color among the thick leaves: the orange and rust and scarlet and blue of orioles and robins and tanagers and bluebirds weaving in and out of the branches like the most exotic of tropical fish. And concentrating carefully, she entered the geography of the sloping shadowy world along the bayou; followed the path as it took its crooked way downward from an almost invisible break in the cane thicket at the corner of the yard toward the footbridge that she and Harper had built so that he could get back and forth to work by the shortest route. Pushing aside a cascade of ferns at the dampest, shadiest point of the slope, she stood at the water's edge, shoulder-deep among green ranks of cattails, breathing in the damp earthy smell of the bayou and feeling the sharp drag of cattail blades against her arms. Is the wood duck nesting in her tree this year? I must remember to get Harper to take down the glasses and look for her . . .

Louisa's clipped twang cut through the soft voices of the others. "In my opinion, it's time for Harper to retire. We could clear the yard and have someone in to cut the grass once a week. If the cane were cut down (just leave enough to screen the house from the street) and three fourths of the shrubs and beds gotten rid of, the place would be easier to keep."

"Harper doesn't want to retire," Mary Hartwell said. "He needs the money."

"We're not running a charitable institution, after all, Mary Hartwell. As George said, this place is a drain on all of us, and it will be even more of one when your mother dies."

"Girls, we don't have to settle that today," George said.

Outside the jays began to scream.

A hawk maybe? Do you remember the year we nursed that hawk with the broken wing — red-tailed? Yes, he was. Flew into a wire and knocked himself out. What a racket the jays used to make whenever the children took him out in the yard. And he would come to George's fist for food like a trained falcon. Beautiful fierce creature! No, probably not a hawk. More likely another litter of cats turned loose and growing up wild down there. They'll be in the trees after the baby birds. If only people wouldn't . . . She turned away from the window. "Harper needs to do something about the cats," she said to no one in particular. "I'd be willing to bet from the fuss the jays are making that some miserable person has turned another litter loose along the bayou."

"But what can you do about them?" Louisa said. "Once they're loose down in there . . ."

"Sister used to put out milk — and then — I wonder how many dozen we've fattened up and given away?"

"Now you folks are bound to see that Howie's proposition is the solution to our difficulties," Albert said. "I don't want to uproot Aunt Martha any more than you do, Mary Hartwell. Neither do I want to spend a lot of money unnecessarily. With Howie's board money, we could run this place almost as cheaply as we could an apartment. Aunt Martha wouldn't be alone at night. And there isn't a reason in the world why his being here should upset her ordinary routine."

"I don't think he would interfere in your life," George said. "He would have his own quarters."

"I never cared for Howie Snyder," Martha said. "He shot the birds . . ." She laughed. "You boys used to shoot each other," she said. "That was all right. But Howie shot the birds."

"Martha!" (Unlike the men, Louisa had from the first days of her marriage called Martha and Elizabeth by their given names. "Neither one of them is my mother — or my aunt," she had said to George, "and this will make us more like *friends*.") "Martha! What do you mean, the boys used to shoot each other? Why, George and Albert never have a cross word."

"She's talking about wars," George said. "Rubber-guns and BB's. When we were children. But we didn't shoot each other, Aunt Martha — we were on the same side. We shot the Barbers — the kids on the other side of the bayou."

Martha looked up at him and an image flashed on her mind of the long-shanked, brown-haired lad aiming his weapon with deadly accuracy; his shoes scuffed and mud encrusted, his knickers unbuckled and flapping below his knees. *You?*

At this point the doorbell rang.

"Harper's out in the yard, Mary Hartwell," Martha said.

Mary Hartwell left the room and a few moments later returned, followed by a short, powerfully built but paunchy man in his early sixties.

Howie Snyder had been for many years a devoted parishioner in the Episcopal Church of the Redeemer, warden and senior warden, and yearly attendant at church retreats for men. There was a priestly quality about him as he went about his business, always dressed in an ill-fitting, dark suit and narrow dark tie. He came into a room officially, as if he might at any moment raise his hand and bless the congregation; whatever book he might be holding (and he was often making notes regarding his business affairs in a fat black notebook) would for some reason appear to be a prayerbook. Probably it was because he usually chose a notebook with a limp, grained cover such as one ordinarily sees on Bibles.

It was not that he was solemn. On the contrary, he was usually smiling — the queer kind of smile accompanied by a deeply penetrating look that one sees on the faces of certain people who seem to have a secret. Perhaps he did have a secret and perhaps it was of a religious nature; or perhaps his relationship with the Almighty kept him always smiling. On the other hand, some people said that his smile made you think he knew something about *you* — so it may be that it was the relationship of other people with the Almighty that made him smile.

There were, indeed, people in Homochitto who professed to feel uneasy in Howie's presence. He smiled too much, they said. But the Clarke and Griswold families thought of him simply as a cousin — a fixture in their lives — with the usual assortment of virtues and vices that cousins have, making himself sometimes pleasant company, sometimes useful, and sometimes a nuisance.

He was a rusty-looking man. Some people said he dyed his hair and small mustache to their peculiar shade of rust color; for surely at his age there should have been at least the beginning signs of gray. His complexion, too, was reddish, or, rather, his broad jowly face, his low brow and turned-up nose, and his hairy arms and hands were sprinkled with reddish brown freckles that gave an overall rusty look to his skin.

He came into the study briskly, nodding and speaking to everyone, went immediately up to Martha, and took her hand between two cold, damp palms. Hmm, Martha thought. Poor circulation? Nervous? "Well!" he said. "Well, Martha. I haven't seen you since . . ." He broke off. Then, "I did see you and Lucas Alexander wandering around the cemetery — when was it? Sometime last summer. Didn't I? With baskets? What were you doing? You're looking splendid. Young as ever. I know you're not a day over sixty." He paused, as if waiting for an acknowledgment of his little joke.

"I'm fifteen years older than you are, Howie." Martha withdrew her hand with a grudging smile. "You forget I taught you sixth grade in the old Homochitto academy. As for Lucas and me, we were probably out mushrooming. There are always meadow mushrooms in the cemetery in July after a good rain. But I don't remember seeing you."

"Be careful. The *lepiota molybdites* fruits at the same time. Deadly poison."

"To some people," Martha said. "Others it doesn't seem to bother. I didn't know you were interested in mushrooms, Howie."

"I used to gather them years ago — don't get out as much as I used to. But I could tell you places where you'd find some rarities for this part of the country. Morels, for example. I ran across some beautiful morels on a deer camp some years back, and I could take you right to the spot."

She looked at him without speaking. I suppose you're all right — you mean well. (Yes, he's bound to mean well.) But if you think Lucas and I would let you go mushrooming with us, you're mistaken. After a moment she said, "Yes, morels are a great delicacy. We used to find them occasionally when we were spryer."

Albert, hands clasped behind his back, looking a bit like an old-fashioned schoolmaster in his rumpled seersucker suit, leaned toward Howie encouragingly. "We've been talking about your suggestion," he said, "but we haven't reached a decision yet. Aunt Martha may need a few days to think things over. She . . . Well, as you know, things are in a state here and, the truth is, we're all so distressed over Aunt Elizabeth, it's hard for us to plan for the future."

"Of course it is," Howie said. "I thought about all that before I called you yesterday, and in fact I hesitated to call. But I had the opportunity for this sale and then, when I thought about Martha out here alone and all that unused space downstairs — another whole house really — I decided to go ahead and mention it. No hard feelings if it doesn't suit."

"I don't want to go anywhere," Martha said. "I . . . Of course, I *could* live in an apartment, if I had to, and I know we have to be realistic about money. But I would rather stay here." She spoke slowly in a low voice, as if the effort were almost too much for her. "It would be hard to leave the garden," she said. She was silent for a moment, then looked at Mary Hartwell and added, "We have Harper to think about, too."

"The garden," Howie said. "You do love your garden, don't you?"

"Yes," Martha said.

"It wouldn't be the first time you and I lived in the house together, after all," Howie said. "You ought to know pretty well what I'm like."

"What's that?"

"Remember the summer Lydia went home to nurse her mother? It was shortly after we were married — thirty years ago — more than that. And you and Elizabeth took me in for a couple of months."

"That's true. I had forgotten about it. Nineteen thirty-four? Thirty-five? Anyhow, it was during the Depression, wasn't it? The summer after James died. Sister was a new widow and I was working for the WPA for eleven dollars a week and we lived on salmon croquettes and grits and molasses."

"My Lord, yes," Howie said. "That was the same year Papa closed up the house and moved into the commissary to save on lights and gas. Pear summer and rabbit winter!"

This talk of the ordeal of the Great Depression seemed to generate a warmth and fellow feeling that for a moment drew the two older people together.

"You were a very accommodating boarder," Martha said. "We enjoyed your company. And I don't recall that you got tired of grits and molasses."

Mary Hartwell got up and, crossing the room, sat down in the straight chair that Albert had drawn up beside their aunt. "Perhaps it *is* the best thing, Aunt Martha," she said. "From your point of view. And there's nothing irrevocable about it. If Howie isn't comfortable or satisfied, he can leave. If we decide the expense of keeping the place is too great — or whatever — or if you're unhappy, we can always make a change."

"Exactly," Howie said. "We can give it a try. That is certainly the basis on which all of us should go into it, if we go into it at all."

CHAPTER 2

THE FOLLOWING WEEK, toward the end of a sultry June night, Elizabeth Griswold died, passing from deep coma to death without a sound: one breath, light as a sleeping child's, another, and then no more; her eighty years finished — with who knows what unmarked convulsion of pain, despair, or ecstasy deep inside the blind and silent carapace of flesh.

Martha and Mary Hartwell were in the room, Mary Hartwell bending over the bed, her fingers pressed lightly against the faint irregular pulse in her mother's shriveled yellow wrist. It stopped.

"Martha," she said quietly. Martha got up from the rocker by the window and crossed the room to the bed. Again and again Mary Hartwell laid her hand gently on the sunken, fleshless breast, as if it were possible that the breathing might catch and begin again.

"She's gone, darling," Martha said. "It's over." She pushed back a strand of crisply curling iron gray hair from her sister's still, yellow forehead. The heavy fragrance of the season's last gardenias, yellowing on bushes outside the bedroom windows, drifted through the room, mingled with the terrible smell of death: of feces and corruption.

The gardenias are still blooming — a late spring this year. This random thought ran through her head without warning while she was in the act of touching her dead sister's hair. And then

(It must be real! she thought. Something so solid couldn't be in my mind) she saw Elizabeth standing in the garden, bending over the birdbath, a smallish, leaden scallop shell borne up in the hands of a naked boy and set in a tangle of periwinkle. Her hair is caught up as she wore it when she was a young woman, twisted into a careless knot on top of her head, the curly brown strands escaping around her face, enhancing the pale Grecian profile. She has on a full skirt and a child, a baby no more than six months old, is riding on her hip. The moving air is sweet with flowers — gardenias, roses, and the last of the honeysuckle.

"Mary Hartwell," Martha murmured. And then, "Sister never really had a fine figure — her hips were too wide for her height."

In the shadowy room, lit only by a shaded lamp on the table beside the bed, Mary Hartwell continued to sit motionless beside her mother's body.

But there she is in the garden with the baby. The child, wearing a diaper and a thin voile shirt (Sister never believed in loading children down with clothes, even when it was the fashion) begins to crow and pound at her mother's bosom.

That was the day we baptized her twice, Martha thought. Of course. Right after we came home from church — a buzzing green summer noon.

Elizabeth swings the baby around and abruptly sets her down, screaming with delight, in the cool water of the scallop shell. "And I, too, baptize thee Mary Hartwell, in the name of sun and summer and of bitter wind and winter rain" — she heard the ironically chanted pronouncement, the drawn-out comical intonation of "bitter wind" — and of all creatures, creeping, running, flying, and swimming . . . To leaven Mama's Presbyterian passion," she said.

"Sister . . . Sister . . . Mary Hartwell, do you see . . . ?"

Mary Hartwell paid no attention.

These things do happen sometimes, Martha said to herself. Like dreams.

After another moment or two, she touched her niece gently on the shoulder. "Mary Hartwell," she said again, "it's over." And to herself numbly, Everything will be different now.

The two women looked at each other. There was nothing more to say.

Finally, "You'd better telephone Francis," Martha said. "And the other boys."

"Yes, I suppose I had," Mary Hartwell said.

Howie was waiting. He moved in almost immediately — as soon as the funeral was over and his rooms could be got ready for him. Since he was coming, Mary Hartwell said, it would be a good thing for all the arrangements to be made and the necessary work to be done before she had to go back to Memphis.

As it seemed to Martha, there was an undignified haste in the preparations. The day after the funeral Harper brought his grandsons Andrew and Matt to help him and together they cleared an accumulation of old furniture, junk, and the layered dust of years out of one of the downstairs bedrooms. Plumbers and painters followed and within three or four days everything was fresh and in working order. Mary Hartwell, sitting in the back study, which was to be Howie's sitting room and was located directly above his bedroom, wrote acknowledgments of flowers and messages of sympathy and occasionally gave directions to the workmen. Martha wandered through the house or sat staring out the study window and said very little.

Once or twice she protested: "Do we have to be in such a hurry, Mary Hartwell?"

"Aunt Martha, I want to get everything set up for you before I leave, so you won't have to worry about any of it."

It occurred to Martha that she had seen in herself at the time of her own mother's death the peculiarly obsessive energy with which Mary Hartwell had set to work — as if the settling of practical problems, the rearrangement of furniture, the consultations with lawyers, insurance men, painters, and plumbers would cover with a blanket of trivia the raw memory of death, the cold skeletal face and bloated belly, the stink of corruption that still permeated the very walls of Elizabeth's empty room. At the same time it was as if she herself were inextricably entangled in the details of Elizabeth's life, as if her own life were being hidden under the same blanket of senseless trivia. Don't read her letters, her lists! (The house was always littered with Elizabeth's lists of things to be done *today*.) They're hers, *hers!* The shame of their having a commonplace world in them! Will you throw them away — *all?* Even that last one, not an item of which she's yet marked off?

She felt the awful suffocation of being buried alive. But she said no more.

Within a week Mary Hartwell and Francis had done all that could be done until the probate period for their mother's will elapsed. Leaving untouched everything in the house except for Howie's rooms, their mother's papers, and her clothing (which Mary Hartwell gave away with frantic haste), they returned to their homes, one to New York, the other to Memphis.

Howie proved an ideal lodger. It was he, after all, and not Louisa who persuaded Harper to begin clearing out the front yard and garden. He put on a worn pair of army fatigues and worked alongside the old man to cut back the cane thicket and bring the wisteria vines under control, using a huge machete that he found in a room of the garage where George and Albert had once had a clubhouse. He honed the blade to a fine edge and swung into the thicket like a man half his age.

"I've always had an excess of energy," he said to Harper, "and that's a fact. It's still a problem to me to use it all up so I can sleep at night." He smiled his deep religious smile. "If you don't sleep at night," he said, "you liable to get into trouble, even at my age."

Harper laughed, a whinnying, slightly patronizing laugh that said without mistake, "I know I'm supposed to laugh at your little jokes, white man," and Howie said, "Come on now, Harper, don't give me any of your condescension, please. My jokes may be lousy, but you're not *that* much smarter than me."

Harper stared a moment, his yellow parchment face expressionless, and then smiled as cautiously as a sane man might smile at a lunatic. "You're pulling away too much of the mulch from around those wild hydrangeas, Mr. Snyder," he said. "Got to treat 'em like they're still in the woods or you won't keep 'em long."

"O.K. You're the expert around here."

Afterward, working together, they pulled down the rotting scuppernong arbor in the side yard and rooted out the gnarled old vines.

"They don't bear anymore in this shade. They *don't*," Harper kept muttering to himself. "No use to keep 'em." But he would glance guiltily toward the house from time to time. Martha, however, watched the destruction through the kitchen windows and said nothing.

Howie made friends, too, with Lucy, Harper's nineteen-year-old granddaughter, who cooked and halfheartedly cleaned the big, shabby old house.

It would have been clear enough to anyone who cared to observe her that Lucy was ready for something better in life than what she was doing and equally clear that she was not yet sure how she would go about getting it. She had made a beginning, evidently, by taking stock of and setting off to their greatest advantage her physical assets: a sexy, slightly steatopygic body and a head of classic dark African beauty with melting thyroidal eyes, a wide, sad, passionate mouth, and a nose flattened in the bridge but as delicately proportioned as an Egyptian queen's. She wore her hair cropped short in the African style and gold hoops in her ears. She had worn a uniform during the months that she nursed Mrs. Griswold; but now, in spite of Harper's disapproving frowns (Martha seemed not to notice or care what she had on), she was usually dressed in a gay cotton print, belted tightly around her slim waist. Shaking her head so that the gold hoops flashed and flicking a duster this way and that, she wandered through the house like a bird of paradise caught in a small-town zoo.

Things had been different here at the beginning, she was quick to tell Howie when he dropped into the kitchen in the mornings to pour himself a cup of coffee and sit idly stirring it, nodding sympathetically, while she talked. When she had come to work eighteen months earlier, at the beginning of the old lady's illness, the job had been ideal for her. She was the night sitter, coming in every evening at nine or ten o'clock. She helped Mrs. Griswold (who at that time, although weak and unsure of herself on her feet, was still up and about and would be for many months) get ready for bed, locked the house, and then lay down to sleep on a cot in the old lady's room. She had been in school at the time — a senior in high school — and her duties had been so light that she had been able to keep on going to school and to graduate the preceding spring.

"The pay wasn't all that good," she said. She had sat down at the kitchen table opposite him and was snapping a pile of beans and dropping them into a pan of water. "But after all, I was still a kid, and, besides, it was mostly nothing but sleeping. I was satisfied then. And I even saved some toward college. I *got* to go to college, don't you think?"

"Oh, I don't know," Howie said. "There are lots of ways to make a success besides going to college."

"Anyhow," Lucy said, "later it got harder — when she was so sick. But she never did make much fuss, even then. She was like a sick dog, you know — like all she wanted to do was crawl off and keep out of your way. And she quit eating and drinking at the last — hardly ever peed and *never* messed up the bed." She took her panful of beans to the stove and put them on to boil with a piece of ham hock. Howie continued to sip his coffee. "And besides," she went on, "they raised my pay. I was making a dollar an hour — just like the white day sitter. But now (now that she's dead), *uh-uh!* This ain't for me. I'm not spending my life in no white people's kitchen." She gazed at Howie questioningly and yet brazenly out of huge black eyes. "I want to get ahead in the world," she said. "I got my future to think about, Mr. Snyder. You see what I mean? I'm not staying in Homochitto, giving Grandpa half my money to take care them kids — and getting as old and stupid as him." (Lucy affected her own style of speech, as if in defiance of her grandfather's precise butlerisms.)

"What are you planning to do?" Howie asked. "You got enough money to go to school?"

"I could get one them grants and go someplace like Jackson State or maybe Alcorn," she said. "But I want something better than *that*, too. No-good schools turning out Baptist schoolteachers. But anyhow — regardless the future — I'm not staying here. I can go out to Madison Produce Company and make minimum wage — after a month or so even better — picking chickens. Save it all and then maybe in the fall — I don't know — I'd go to New York or Hollywood or someplace like that. There's lots of things girls like me can do *now*, they couldn't used to — I see 'em on the TV."

"Listen, Lucy," Howie said, "you wouldn't stick one day at picking chickens. Take it from me. That's too rough for a pretty girl like you."

She shook her head and made a little face. The earrings flashed. "You don't know me," she said. "I'm tough, too."

"You ever been out there?" Howie said. He looked at her with wet glistening eyes. "You got any idea what it's like? Well, I'm going to tell you. They've got a big old long narrow room, see, with a concrete floor and a long table down the middle of it with a pulley arrangement set up over it. And the pickers and gutters stand on each side of the table and the chickens come out of the steam room at one end on these hooks. They're live when they go in the steam room, see? The men in the starting room hang 'em on hooks by their feet and in they go, squawking and flapping, and the room is full of live steam. So when they come out, they're dead. (At least most of 'em are.) Scalding — steaming hot — stinking. And kind of sterilized, and also the feathers are loosened by the steam. And you got to grab 'em off the hooks — burn your hands doing it — and pull their feathers off, see, and then throw 'em down on this belt that runs down the middle of the table. And the next ones in line chop off their heads and feet and then the next ones gut 'em. You work out there all day and by night you're covered with these chicken-smelling wet feathers, and the floor under your feet and your shoes are all soaked and slick with blood and guts and chicken shit." He gave her a sidelong glance, as if to see if she would flinch at "shit," a word which a proper, elderly white man would never have used before her; but she did not appear to notice it. "And the stink!" he said. "If I was the devil, I'd transport that place straight to hell without a change." He smiled. "See what I mean?"

Lucy made a stubborn mouth. "I could stand it, if I made enough money," she said. And she did go one day to try it. But the next, she came back to the Griswold kitchen. "You know some them chickens even got tumors and all kinds of things," she told Howie, "but they don't care. They just chop 'em up and send 'em on down the table. I ain't never going to eat a piece of chicken again in my life, unless I see the whole bird first."

"Listen," Howie said, "I've got a good idea for you, Lucy. You've already got the beginnings of training to be a nurse. You know it? A year's course and you'd get a license to be an LPN. You know what that is? A licensed practical nurse. And in a city an LPN can make as much money as an RN makes down here. Did you ever think about that? I could look into some possibilities for you. I hear the government is getting ready to put in a training program at the hospital in Vicksburg. If we could set you up with that, you'd have it made. Stick around here for a while, if you're interested, at least until I can find out something about it."

"I don't know if I want to be a nurse," Lucy said doubtfully. "Like I said, I want to go to New York and maybe get on the TV."

"That's not as easy as you think — and, anyhow, all I'm saying is with a year's training you could make good money wherever you went," Howie said. "And who knows? You might meet a good-looking doctor who'd fall in love with you. Then you wouldn't have to worry about anything for the rest of your life. Doctors are *rich*. You ought to think it over."

Meanwhile, he began to pay her an extra ten dollars a week for cleaning his rooms and looking after his laundry. And he continued to come into the kitchen while she was preparing lunch, to sit at the kitchen table and fall into long, low-voiced conversations with her, punctuated now and then by her exclamations and giggles.

"I try to keep 'em satisfied," he said to Martha one morning after he had come into the house from working with Harper in the yard for a couple of hours and had stopped by the kitchen for a brief visit with Lucy. He spoke tentatively, as if to reassure her, or perhaps as if thinking that his friendship with the servants needed some explanation.

But: "I'm glad to see you getting to be friends," she said. "You know, Harper's been here a long time. I've worried a bit . . ." Her voice trailed off, not because she didn't know what she wished to say but because she seemed these days scarcely to have the energy to say anything.

In any case he understood her. "No, no," he said. "You won't have any trouble from me. I'm a reconciler. A *reconciler!* Always have been. A man who likes to see people get along with each other. An expediter of human relations." They were on the glassed-in porch overlooking the back garden and he sat down opposite her in an old creaking porch glider, pulled a cigar from his shirt pocket, and began to trim it with the small knife that always hung from his key chain. "I'm not good for a lot in this world," he said. "I know my shortcomings. Never was good-looking enough to turn the girls' heads. And no more than my share of brains. But I'm vigorous — and *persistent.* And there's one thing I *am* good for. My predestined role — to use a word you Presbyterians like — in church, in the family, in business, and so forth. Some reason or other, I can explain folks to each other so they can understand each other better.

That's the talent the good Lord gave me. I can make smooth the path, so to speak. Widen the gate. And I ain't like the bad steward in the Bible. I don't bury my talent in the earth. I use it — any way I can find to use it."

The glider creaked comfortably; a plume of smoke curled upward from Howie's cigar; his words buzzed at her ears. She seemed scarcely to pay more attention to them than to the smoke or to the creaking of the glider. He gazed at her with his deep sympathetic smile. "I know things are rough through here for you, Martha," he said. "I'd like to help you." He hesitated. "I'm no stranger to sorrow myself," he added. "We all have our crosses to bear. But it's the way we tackle 'em. Right?"

She looked at him and a flicker first of schoolteacherish amusement and then of curiosity penetrated her lethargy. She had never thought of him as a man who had had sorrow in his life, although . . .

"You know," he said, "we haven't seen much of each other the past few years. We need to renew our acquaintance — the old family ties."

With an effort she brought herself to nod.

"I've been so wrapped up in Lydia — so concerned about her — I haven't thought of much else," he said. "Her illness . . . And then, the past couple of years, business problems, too."

Lydia? she thought. Of course. She gazed fixedly at him, as one might at a stranger in a bus station who curiously resembles an old friend or relative. Strange how little one knows of the life even of someone who's lived almost next door for sixty years. We think of him as a cousin, somebody we know well, but we don't — not at all. And now he and I by this odd chance find ourselves living in the same house, as intimately as brother and sister — and probably for the rest of our lives. Is it possible? Yes, she thought with an inward shrug. Here we are whether I like it or not. Fortunate he's such a decent fellow. We'll get acquainted, maybe later.

And then: Lydia. I can remember when she used to go to school to me at the old Homochitto academy — thirty years ago? Pretty little thing she was then. All accommodation. No matter what you asked of her she was always willing. (Soft brown eyes and limber slim body. See her now, dancing. How all the boys loved to dance with her! Follow anyone.) But then . . . Disappeared completely over the years into that mountain of fat. From being so limber, so pliable, became immovable. When did it start? Soon after the birth of the son, wasn't it? I suppose that kind of difficulty is always sexual, she thought. Poor Howie! And after the boy was grown, he never spent any time here. As if he didn't care anything for either of them. Curious. A slight shudder ran over her body. The funeral! She recalled watching the pallbearers, ten of them (as many as could get a purchase on the oversized, specially built coffin), staggering from the hearse to the grave side with their burden. The son, slim and crisp in his uniform, gleaming birds on his shoulders, stood with head averted, face expressionless. But he must be a satisfaction to Howie. A general before he's through, no doubt.

As if he followed her thoughts, Howie spoke. "It was a cross the Lord put on her," he said. "Glandular. She couldn't help it. And I never blamed her, not for a minute. But William. I reckon he couldn't see it that way. I tried . . ." He gave a heavy sigh. "I just about had to raise him by myself, you know, Martha. Time he was ten or so she didn't get around much. *Couldn't.* I did the best I could with him. But he . . . Strange thing, and I wouldn't talk about it to just anybody, but he, he *blamed* it on her. He hated fat like you hate sin. He was *ashamed* of her from the time he was a little boy, even though I used to try to explain to him that you might hate the *sin* but if you're a good Christian, you got to love the sinner. Once he went off to school he never came home much — I reckon she was the reason. And I reckon, too, once you fall into a habit it's hard to change. And then, he's got his responsibilities."

Sin? More, Martha thought, as if some awful vision, some wholly irreconcilable circumstance of her life, had confronted her and she had begun frantically to shovel herself into an oozing grave of flesh. And who could know what it had been?

"Of course he has," she said. "It's the same thing with Francis. Except, I'm sure it must be even more difficult for William, being overseas so much of the time. But I know you're proud of him."

CHAPTER 3

OUTSIDE THE HOUSE, riding high and still above the roar of the freeway and the jumbled neighborhood of slums, genteel boarding houses, and low-cost government-financed apartment buildings, cut off from the rest of Homochitto by its wall of cane, time passed rapidly. The seasons changed. Summer came down like a steaming blanket on the old river town where everything was moving and shifting and growing and decaying at a dizzying pace.

Newton and his father joined forces with a group of local men and bought an interest in a projected new grain elevator and loading complex to be built near the waterfront docking area at the foot of the bluff on which the main part of Homochitto was built. Almost before the papers were signed, old buildings began to be torn down and ladies' clubs began to petition the city council to save this older section of the town from being sacrificed to the schemes of their husbands and brothers. The slum below the bluff and fronting on the river, they said, consisted mainly of pre-Civil War and, in some cases, eighteenth-century buildings. It would be a shame to tear them down, even though most of the houses were now tenements where the poorest of Homochitto's black people lived.

But the men maintained that, old or not, the slum must go

and the neighborhood be turned into an industrial park and expanded port facility. For Homochitto was now a potentially profitable river port, the river at the base of its bluffs carrying, as the years passed, a heavier and heavier traffic of barges loaded with oil and grain and soybeans and huge rocket components being floated down from factories in the North through the inland waterways system to Cape Kennedy.

In July, while this quarrel still raged in the local newspaper, Newton and Louisa went off to the Republican convention. They came home uneasy and dissatisfied at how things had gone there. They had wanted Reagan — a white-hatted cowboy to solve the problems of the Western world — and had gotten instead that jowly, Snopes-eyed Wall Street lawyer who, they feared, would compromise their deepest principles. Indeed, was there a politician left in the world who would not compromise the principles of a true conservative?

At home, while they were gone, Homochitto seethed like a pot of boiling jelly. Over the furious protests of the ladies the old jail had been torn down. How was it possible that no one could be convinced it was a quaint and historic building? Aaron Burr had been held there briefly after his capture down the river near Natchez. Murrel, the famous bandit of the Natchez Trace, had been a prisoner there; and one of the first lynchings in the Mississippi Territory had taken place in its basement, where a black man who murdered his master had been tied to a mattress-less iron cot, castrated, and brained.

Then, too, there was a rumor circulating that a certain local businessman who had contributed a thousand dollars to the campaign of Lyndon Johnson in 1964 had contracted syphilis on his vacation in the Virgin Islands and had given it to his wife, who in turn had infected her lover, another Johnson Democrat, and . . . and . . . and . . . Worst of all, a white girl had danced with a black boy when a group of white college students attended a James Brown concert at the local black VFW.

"What's happening in the world?" Louisa said to her husband after he had told her all the news. "What's going to become of us? Where are all the old integrities?" She and George were sitting out on their patio the afternoon of her return from the convention, Louisa neat and smiling as always, George stretched out in a lounge chair, his legs looking longer and more cadaverous than usual in a pair of plaid shorts she had brought back from Miami.

"Syphilis has been around for a long time," George said dryly. "And at least they're neither one Republicans. You have that to be thankful for." He had never been much interested in the processes of politics and did not consider himself a member of any party.

"It's no laughing matter, George," Louisa said, "and you know it."

"Another thing," he said. "The syphilis rumor has taken everybody's minds off the grain elevator. A month more and that will be a fait accompli — the elevator, I mean — and they'll all be better off for it whether they know it or not. Anything that brings money into this town is good for everybody in it. And nobody is going to remember a couple of old houses, a jail, and a colored church six months from now."

"That used to be a white church," Louisa said.

"*I* know that," George said. "I grew up here, after all, and you didn't. But what difference does that make?"

"George, I may be from the Middle West — and you know very well that a lot of people look down their noses at me for that very reason — but I do have a feeling for the history of Homochitto. That was the first Methodist church in the Mississippi Territory. Lorenzo Dow preached there."

"Lorenzo Dow! Who in the world is Lorenzo Dow?" George's plaintive voice was faintly amused.

"He was a famous Methodist circuit rider of the early eighteen hundreds," Louisa said.

"Well, please don't tell anybody about him, honey. That's one argument nobody has thought of yet. And Newton and I have got some money sunk in this elevator."

"That was a nice bell in that church," Louisa said thoughtfully. "I wonder what they're going to do with it? And the doors to the jail. Do you remember those old iron doors? Wouldn't they make lovely gates into a high-walled patio? Kind of quaint and primitive."

George looked at her for a moment before he spoke. Then, "Now, you don't need the jail doors. You hear me, Louisa? That's a little too much sugar for a dime. And I reckon Old Jerusalem will build a new church and put their bell in that. God knows, they held us up for enough money for that lot to build a cathedral."

"George," she said, "I wish you could have seen Newton at the convention. He was a real leader in the delegation. I was so proud of him — and I know he is going to be a force for good in the state."

"That's mighty fine, honey," George said.

~~~

If the outside world was changing (not only its shape and appearance, but perhaps its very nature) at an alarming rate, the reverse seemed to be true at the old Clarke house. There, events drifted by in a queer slow way that to the nieces and nephews probably seemed little different from the way the household had operated for years. No one except Howie even noticed that the Republican convention had taken place. Martha sat every day by the window and looked blindly out into the garden. Or she wandered out and absent-mindedly gathered flowers and stuck them into vases which she forgot to fill with water. On Tuesdays and Fridays Harper drove her to market and helped her to buy groceries. (This task had always been her sister's, and she did it badly.) Occasionally an old friend or the daughter of an old friend dropped in to call. George and Albert and Louisa came and went as they always had; and sometimes, on Sundays, one or another of them would drive her out to visit her old friend Lucas Alexander, who was still not entirely recovered from his springtime battle with pneumonia. But in August Dr. Alexander's niece invited him to visit her on the Gulf coast and Martha no longer had even that small diversion.

Newton, too, paid an occasional duty call; and one afternoon in late summer he spoke to his mother of his dissatisfaction at the way the household's business was being conducted. "Sometimes I think Aunt Martha is in a trance, Mama," he said. "A trance! I go out there in August and she's just swallowing the soup she was holding in her spoon in July. And the mail! Do you know she never opens the mail? Bills, letters, magazines — there's a stack of stuff on the desk in her room you should *see*. I wouldn't be surprised if she woke up one morning and the lights had been cut off."

"It's natural for her to be in a state," Louisa said. "After all, she's lived her whole life in the house with Elizabeth. Do you realize that? I suppose we're going to have to lend more of a hand to pull her out of it. I'll go out and go through the mail with her."

And in a way the effort to lend a hand brought about the beginning of a new kind of life that gradually took shape in the old house, unnoticed by anyone. Everything that contributed to it seemed ordinary, even inevitable.

First the family decided that for the time being, until Martha felt up to it, Newton should assume the responsibility of looking after his aunt's business, along with the probate of the will. Everyone, including Martha, agreed to this plan. He would make a quarterly accounting to Martha and to the family. At his own insistence (he was a man who liked things to be done in an orderly and legitimate way), they had him appointed conservator of the old lady's affairs.

"I should be held accountable, legally accountable," he told his father, "and that's the way to do it."

"I don't see any reason for us to appoint a *guardian* for Martha," his father said at first. "After all, she's in her right mind and she's as healthy as I am. The problem is, she's never had to run the house and pay the bills before. But once she begins to get over Aunt Elizabeth's death, it'll be better for her to take on those responsibilities — keep her alert."

"This is not a guardianship," Newton said. "It's a legal formality. But it should be done, if I am going to be in charge of the money even for a few months. It makes me accountable, and that's the way things ought to be."

Further discussion — of the problems of marketing and planning meals — ended when Howie volunteered for this task. He had followed the other members of the family down the walk after one of their visits, and when they were out of earshot of the house, complained, half-jokingly, that he and Martha were starving to death because she kept forgetting to tell Lucy what to fix for lunch. "I could do the shopping and plan the meals," he said. "You people say yourselves that it's never been Martha's job to market. Why should she take it on now when the fact is, I'd enjoy doing it?"

"But she needs *something* to do to pull her out of this lethargy," Louisa said. She turned earnestly to Albert. "What can you *do* to occupy yourself when you're seventy-five years old and half-blind? There's nothing left for her but the marketing."

"Maybe we can get her back to gardening," Albert said. "Let her putter around the yard and think she's doing something constructive. Harper can watch her. But if they're going to get a decent meal on the table, we'd better turn the shopping over to Howie."

"Albert, you sound like she's an inmate instead of your aunt," George said.

Albert shrugged. Then, "Why couldn't she take over Aunt Elizabeth's job at the library?" he suggested. "Being around children a couple of times a week might wake her up a bit."

"She doesn't see well enough to read aloud. And I don't know what else she could do down there," Louisa said.

"How about guild meetings?" Howie said. "Church work. That could be a great comfort to her."

George shook his head. "She's never been very churchy," he said. "I doubt if she's going to get that way now." He looked at his watch and opened the car door for his wife. "We have to be getting on, Louisa. I have a meeting tonight. We'll think of something," he added to Howie. "In the meantime you go ahead and get her to let you take over the shopping. She'll probably be delighted not to have to think about it."

"I'm going to mention church work to her, too," Howie said. "You can't tell — she might take to it."

But Martha paid no attention to any of their suggestions. In her own way and at her own speed, she began to emerge from the lethargy into which she had sunk. The weeks passed; summer was over and the wild September plums ripened. She and Lucy went out to the trees by the garage, Lucy shook the trees, and together they gathered buckets full of the fruit. The making of jelly — the sharp sweet smell of boiling juice in the steamy kitchen, the sight of row after row of filled glasses gleaming like jewels on the counter, filled her with familiar pleasure.

("Really!" Louisa said to George. "What's she going to do with all that jelly? It's absurd to make so much of it with nobody there but Howie to help her eat it." "She'll give it away," George said, "like she always does.")

When the sumac flamed scarlet against the somber green of the cedar trees along the eastern edge of the garden, she got out her binoculars, unused for a year or more, and tried to watch for migrating birds. Flocks of cedar waxwings appeared overnight in the yard and stripped the hollies of their berries before rising to some mysterious call and moving southward. She recognized them by their high, thin quavering voices, but could not see them. But that same day the myrtle warblers dropped out of the sky into the ligustrum bush not a foot from her bedroom window. She could see the flashing shuttle of their flight and sat entranced by their motion and their loud cries: *check, check.*

Early in November, after one of those warm, damp windy spells that brings up the meadow mushrooms on the pastures and lawns of the Deep South, Lucas Alexander got into his car and drove himself to town for the first time since spring. He and Martha went mushrooming together in the cemetery, as they had for years, and brought home baskets full of pearly, pink-gilled mushroom caps. She stood at the kitchen sink afterward, gently rinsing away the dirt and grass stems and laying the mushrooms on a towel to dry, and thought to herself: My heart has been broken more than once in my life, and I have thought each time it would never mend, but look, even now, this late, amazing! I feel it begin to beat again.

But there were indications during those months, after she began to come out of the absorption that followed Elizabeth's death, that other things were not yet as they should be with Martha. Once or twice she made a remark to George or Albert that they found puzzling or vaguely alarming: there was a bobcat prowling in the woods along the bayou, she said. She had heard his yowls. Or again, strange boys were shooting at the house with BB guns or perhaps even .410 shotguns. The shot had rained down on her head one morning while she and Harper were working in the yard. The cousins shrugged and dismissed these notions. There had not been a bobcat in the woods since the last time their father had trapped one back in 1923. And it was highly unlikely that anyone was shooting off a .410 within the city limits. The only boys around, Albert suggested playfully, were her own boys — himself and George — and they were certainly not shooting at anybody.

CHAPTER 4

IT WAS A DAY OR TWO after Martha and Lucas's mushroom hunt in the cemetery (when Newton came by the house with some papers for Martha to sign in connection with winding up the probate of Elizabeth's will), that Howie first mentioned his project — the plan which he may have had in mind from the day he first thought of moving into the Clarke household.

Newton had sat talking a little while with his aunt (as short a while as was consistent with courtesy — he was anxious to get back to his office). He turned the conversation toward the subject he thought she liked best — reminiscences of his own and his father's childhoods — and listened absently to a familiar tale or two. These always seemed to him to be unrelated to the world of reality. "She slicks up the past for me and for herself, too," he said to his mother afterward. For his own memories of childhood were not at all of ripe figs and cold creek water, but of marbles lost playing keepsies and of the Christmas when the jumping skates he had wanted carried him no more than a foot or two off the ground instead of letting him bound over hills and ditches like a kangaroo. And what she had to say of his father's and Albert's youth seemed to him equally lies. There had never been a time for them, or anyone, he would say, when poverty had been — he could not quite make out which — a challenge gallantly met or a condition of the good life. "All right for *her* to moon about the simple life, but *we* take care of her." He waited for a story to end and then got up and, leaning over her chair, brushed her forehead with a light kiss. He was hurrying out of the house when Howie waylayed him in the hall and asked him to come into his little sitting room for a few minutes.

"I need to talk to you, Newton," he said. "I'm afraid things are not going exactly as they should out here."

Newton looked at his watch.

"It'll only take us a few minutes," Howie said. "Come on back to my study," and he led the younger man toward the back of the house.

Howie had taken over for his own use the small back sitting room directly above his bedroom and opening downward into it by a steep enclosed stair like the companionway of a ship — the room where six months earlier the family had sat making plans for Martha's future. Like Martha's bedroom at the opposite end of the house, Howie's little study was the last room in the wing, jutting out toward the bayou, above the back garden, and its sunny windows had once been filled with growing things; but these had all been moved out, as had the other furnishings — the glass-fronted bookcases and secretary, the steel engravings of the Seven Ages of Man, and the shabby overstuffed furniture — to make room for Howie's possessions. On the floor was a green nylon carpet which looked very like funeral grass and snapped with static electricity. The walls were lined with framed battlefield maps: from Waterloo and Gettysburg to the Argonne Forest and the islands of the Pacific. Strategy and tactics had long been his hobby and he had drawn the maps himself and lettered in the names and arrows and legends in a small meticulous hand. The furniture, except for a roll-top desk from his father's commissary, was early twentieth century — a curious mixture of

Art Nouveau and Bauhaus. He and his wife had never cared for the Victorian and Empire pieces that most "old" Homochitto residents inherited from aunts and grandparents; and now the bentwood rockers and pieces of Tiffany glass, and the tubular steel Bauhaus armchairs gave the room a look of campy decorator chic that was strangely incongruous with the haphazard furnishings of the rest of the house. Newton sat down tensely in one of the steel and leather chairs, his eyes all the while moving restlessly about the room. He got out a cigarette. Howie took a cigar from his inside jacket pocket and lit it, using the high gas flame of a table lighter and sucking and puffing furiously, as cigar smokers do. Then he settled himself in his desk chair opposite Newton.

"I'll come right to the point, son," he said. "I'm concerned about your aunt. And about how this household is being run. I need a little more authority out here, if I'm going to keep things working for everybody."

"Authority!" Newton looked at him in some astonishment. "You're not supposed . . ." he began abruptly, but then he hesitated and corrected himself. "No need for you to worry yourself about Aunt Martha's eccentricities," he said. "I just hope she's not getting on your nerves. Only one thing to do about that. Keep out of the way. She's . . . Yeah, she's bound to be set in her ways and all that. But . . ."

"Wait a minute now, son," Howie said. "I'm not concerned about myself. Not at all. It's a good deal more complicated than that. You just hear me out, if you will, and then give me your opinion."

Newton suppressed another glance at his watch. "I'm listening," he said.

Earnestly Howie began to explain to him that Martha was not her old self. "I don't mean to imply that she's crazy," he said.

"But you know as people get up into their late seventies, naturally their judgment isn't going to work as well as it used to. And Martha's never been the most reasonable woman in the world — you may not be aware of that, but certainly your daddy would be. Now understand me, it isn't all that bad — yet. In fact, I haven't said a word about it to anyone. Your father or Albert or anybody else. But I'm no dummy. I'm here observing how the household operates — what goes on — and I tell you, Newton, some changes need to be made. In Martha's interest and in your family's interest."

"What are you talking about?" Newton said. "Go on and say what you mean."

"Now, for example, she has no regard for her own safety. Some days she gets it into her head to climb down that bank to the bayou and off she goes, as fast as she can scramble — maybe she's even carrying a shovel or a sack of fertilizer or dragging a hose. She's going to end up hurting herself. It's O.K. when Harper goes with her and watches her, but plenty of times he's busy — or else she don't even tell him she's going." He took a deep draw on his glowing cigar and let out a cloud of smoke, all the while looking closely at Newton, as if he had said something startling.

"Aunt Martha's always been like that," Newton said. "Active. Independent. She likes the outdoors."

"Yes," Howie said. "But now she's seventy — seventy what? Six or seven, I reckon. What kind of money you reckon it's going to run into when she breaks her hip and you folks have to pay for sitters around the clock?"

"Crissakes, Howie," Newton said. "You're a — a — regular bird of ill omen. We'll face that problem when we have to."

"If you make up your mind to face it *before* you have to — it and some others — you might end up by avoiding a helluva lot of trouble," Howie said. "Now look here. This is what I'm talking about — and I've had plenty of time to work it out in my mind the past few months. You've got (you and your family) three grown people out here looking after your aunt. Me, Harper, and Lucy (if you can call Lucy a grown person). She needs us all. But that don't make sense, does it — all that money and attention looking after one old lady? And believe me, this operation is costing money. You pay the bills, you're bound to see that yourself. And just wait 'til the first of the year when your taxes and insurance come due. It's gonna be a whack. And that's what led me to the project I want to discuss with you."

Newton stirred restlessly. "I got to get out of here, Howie," he said. "Got an appointment . . . Maybe next time I come back . . . ?"

"All right. Just one or two ideas for you to take with you. Now, look at this tremendous house. And look at that lonely old lady. And look at me — an able-bodied man, still young, with next to nothing to do. The idea hits you in the face. It's a natural. Why, the service we could do for this community! Immeasurable. And you're young and progressive, Newton. Interested in politics — in serving the community. You look at my proposition with an objective eye and think it over before you make up your mind."

Newton's impatience seemed to subside somewhat. "Proposition?" he said.

Howie leaned forward, drew a deep breath, and gently shook his cigar at Newton, scattering ashes on the grass-green rug. "Newton," he said, "I can name you, without even thinking twice, a dozen old folks in this town — I'm talking about people of means, people whose children wield *influence* — who live alone or with a servant or a son or daughter who maybe doesn't want 'em, and who would be a hell — just a *hell* — of a lot happier if they were independent and yet — not by themselves. Look what other towns have done with nice pleasant places for old folks. And there ain't a one in Homochitto. Not a one! Nothing but the county farm. You got to carry 'em all the way to Vicksburg or New Orleans. And some of 'em won't go. Think what we'd be doing for this town if we converted this house into — not an old folks' home, not at all — into a lovely, pleasant residence for old people — for *well-to-do* old people. He laid his cigar down on an ashtray and, pulling his black notebook out of his breast pocket, consulted it. "There's old Mrs. Wheeler," he said, "and the Strange brothers, and Mrs. Cathcart, just to name a few. Look at people like Miss Carrie Stock. Out there trying to make ends meet on maybe three-fifty, four hundred dollars a month. Doing her own cooking. Alone at night. All by herself! You mark my words, she's going to end up by setting fire to herself. For the money she's squeaking by on we could take care of her — why practically in luxury, and certainly in safety."

Newton was shaking his head in his jerky quick way. "Daddy wouldn't like it," he said. "He wouldn't hear of it — not if I know Daddy. You can bet your bottom dollar, none of 'em want to mess around with Aunt Martha's setup. Out of the frying pan into the fire. That's what he'd think."

"Now, *wait*. I told you to think about it before you made up your mind. Of course, there'd be some work setting it up. But that's where I come in. I'd be glad to take it on. I *need* something to do. And I want you to think about the good you'd be doing. For example. Look at somebody like old Mrs. Arthur Crane. You know she never got along with her daughter-in-law when she was young and active. Yet there she is, stuck in the house with her — having to take orders from her in her old age. I'll bet you Marian Crane leads that old lady a dog's life. Now, there's money there — plenty of it. Enough to pay, say, four hundred dollars a month, even four-fifty. Marian would jump at the chance to get rid of the old woman. And Arthur Junior would probably consent to it, if it didn't involve uprooting her and sending her off among strangers. And everybody would be happier.

"*Wait*. Let me finish before you say anything. This house has four bedrooms on this floor, not to mention the four besides mine downstairs. Suppose we just started with three or four old ladies. Just this floor. Nobody downstairs. No sick people. And on a very exclusive basis. People who would be congenial with your aunt. Suppose, my boy! You could pick up two thousand a month from the right four old ladies. Put a piece of it aside in case your aunt gets sick — or falls down and breaks a leg, which, believe me, the way she scrambles around, she's probably going to do. Pay me a reasonable salary to run the house. We'd need one more servant — somebody just to be available at night — but that wouldn't be much expense. Your family would end up paying all the expenses of this place, having money left over, and at the same time making four old people happier."

"But we don't know anything about running an establishment like that, Howie," Newton said. "No training for it — any of us."

"It don't take training, son. All it takes is a reasonably alert mind and a little common sense. What have you got to do? Buy groceries for a household of five or six people. Any fool can do that, and if he don't know how to begin with, he can learn pretty quick. Keep the servants on their toes. See that the old ladies get where they want to go — church and all. Set up a bingo game or a card game for 'em now and then. Take 'em for a drive. That's all there is to it." He got up and crossed the room to the small bar set up in a corner of the study. "Toddy?"

"No, thank you," Newton said.

"Are you sure? I'm not much of a drinker myself, but I like to see folks enjoy themselves."

Newton shook his head. "Seems to me," he said, "seems to me, Howie, you're asking for trouble. We got one old lady to look after, and you say yourself she's beginning to be a problem. We'd have four more old ladies. Four times as much of a problem."

Howie returned to his desk. "If I've got this one to worry with, I'd just as soon have four more," he said, "and I'd feel like I was doing something constructive. A real service to the community. And so would you and your family. You'd deserve as much credit as me."

But Newton, it appeared, was not interested in taking the risks and going to the trouble that such a service would require. He shook his head again.

"I want you to consider one more angle before you go, Newton," Howie said. "Just so you'll have all the facts. And that angle is *me*. I'm getting restless. I'm still young, this inactive life out here is beginning to get me down, and, naturally, I've been thinking about finding something to do that will interest me. The fact is, I wouldn't have retired last year, if I hadn't been forced to. I was up in Vicksburg for the day last week, just visiting friends, and I looked into an offer there to run the office for a construction firm. Starting in March and working over the next six months. Now, I'd hate to go off and leave you folks with this situation. I'd *hate* it. And, as I've said, I'd *prefer* to go into some kind of service. Something involving people. But that job in Vicksburg pays a terrific salary. And it ain't permanent. I could be looking around at the same time for something along this line. You know, old folks' homes are springing up all over the country, and people are needed to run 'em. There's a great future in it. And after all, I'm still young enough to have a future. You see?"

"Well . . ." Newton said. "Well . . ." Perhaps it had never occurred to him that Howie thought of himself as a man with a future. He hesitated and when he spoke again, his usual staccato style of speech was slower and more thoughtful. "I know Daddy and Albert would hate to see you go," he said.

"No more than I'd hate going."

"Aside . . . aside from the fact that it's been a pleasant relationship — satisfactory, you know, for all of us — it would — ah — mean figuring out something different for Aunt Martha."

"True."

"And, too, there's a lot in what you say. It would be a real service to the community, when you think about it from that angle."

Howie nodded and did not take his eyes from the young man.

"I for one would hate to sell the house," Newton said. "Sentimental attachment and so forth. I might want it myself someday."

"I hadn't thought of that," Howie said, "but it *is* the old family place, ain't it?"

"I'll think it over," Newton said, "and discuss it with . . . with Albert first. And then, if he thinks it might work, with my father. Albert is less set in his ways. Daddy would probably say no without giving it a thought. And then, we would have to consult Mary Hartwell. And Francis. They have an interest in the house, too."

Surprisingly enough, Newton and Albert had little difficulty convincing George that Howie's idea was a good one. For one thing, the financial burden of operating the place had turned out to be far greater than either of the nephews had realized it would be. Mrs. Griswold's considerable income (an annuity from her husband's insurance, along with a few stocks) was now cut off, and they realized for the first time that their aunt had in fact been practically supporting Martha. All she really had of her own were her small social security and teachers' retirement checks which, although they went into the household money, did not go far toward keeping the place operating. Now, of course, the expenses of the household were divided four ways, between the two men in Homochitto and Francis and Mary Hartwell. But even so, while all the cousins were reasonably well off, this outlay was beginning to be an inconvenience. And larger expenses faced the family in the future. The house would soon need a new roof and a coat of paint, the stove and refrigerator had both seen their best days, insurance and tax payments would be coming up in January. It might turn out that George would have to forgo buying Louisa the fur coat he had planned to give her for Christmas, and that Albert would not be able to make his annual hunting trip to Alberta for moose.

Another surprising development smoothed the way for Howie's project. Martha herself made no objection. She had a single stipulation which, once fulfilled, left her not only content, but happy with the arrangement.

Her stipulation concerned Lucas Alexander, who had told her a few days earlier, during their mushroom hunt in the cemetery, that he planned to move into town. True, he had said, he felt almost completely recovered from his springtime bout with pneumonia, but the time had come for a change. He felt it in the bone-deep cold of the country wintertime.

"I've always been a practical man," he had said, and Martha had laughed.

"Practical!"

"By my own lights," he had replied, "and sometimes by yours. Not necessarily by anyone else's. And what's practical now is for me not to farm anymore. I'm too old." He had been sitting beside her on a raised, boxlike granite vault in the cemetery. He knocked absently with his cane on the side of the vault, which gave out a sharp hollow sound.

"Lucas," she said, "you're looking better. Your color is much better." She anxiously examined the blur of his face, the vague contours of which she could make out through the veil of her cataracts, but every line of which she knew by heart — the heavy bush of unruly gray eyebrows above the deep-set slate blue eyes, the wide thin line of the ascetic mouth, the deep folds from the high-bridged nose disappearing into the firm jaw line; the whole face sharpened and eroded, first by weather and then by age and illness. "I'm better and so are you," she said, "and I hate to see you give up farming."

"I've made up my mind," he said. "I've been thinking about it, Martha. All the time I was with Howard and Leila this summer. And since I've gotten home. It doesn't work anymore."

"But to live in town? You don't realize how hard on you that would be. And all your projects. Have you thought about them?"

"Don't be alarmed," he said. "I have no intention of sitting down and taking root like a September lily." He spoke precisely enunciating every word clearly in a deep rough voice, in which she heard a hint of a quaver. Still not really strong, she thought.

He stretched out his long legs. "You know, Martha," he said, "I threw away a handful of those bulbs last fall when I was clearing out the back beds, and they put out roots and pulled themselves right under the ground. Amazing!" He continued to knock his stick against the granite box and gaze out across the bronze November landscape — oak trees and gums dropping their leaves on the mossy gravestones. A butterfly had lit on the stone at their feet. It feebly beat its faded black-ribbed and orange wings, but could not lift itself into the air. "Look," he said. "One last monarch from the fall migration." He pushed the tip of his cane under its body and when it crawled aboard, swung the cane and sent it sailing away on an updraft from the sun-warmed earth. Then he went on. "I'm going to rent the place — not sell it," he said. "I want to try town for a year and see how it goes. If it doesn't go, I can always move back to the country. And I'm going to find something interesting to do. Have you heard what Johns Hopkins is getting started with in the county? Something in the way of a genuine health department. It's one of those so-called pilot projects. You know, not a doctor in the county is going to give them the time of day. But I could help them. God knows, I am familiar enough with the shortcomings of the old system."

"Well," Martha had said, "it'll be nice to have you in town. I worry about you out there, especially in the winter. Where are you going to live?"

When Howie's plan was explained to Martha, therefore, her first thought was that it would give Lucas a place to live; and her stipulation was that she would go along happily if he could be persuaded to take one of the rooms. "Not upstairs," she said. "He wouldn't want to live in such an intimate arrangement with me, and certainly not if there were other women in the house. But all that space downstairs! We could turn Francis's old room directly under the north wing into a private retreat for him. He would even have his own entrance and, of course, a private bath."

Dr. Alexander was delighted with the plan. It seemed the perfect solution to his problems. Like Howie, but for other reasons, he had a limited income. A lifetime of hard work had left him with nothing to take care of him in his old age except his social security check and the income from his little farm. From 1925 until 1955 he had been the county health officer in Homochitto County — a position generally held in Mississippi in those days only by fools or cripples. During the years after the Second World War when all doctors could get rich unless they were alcoholic or incompetent (and some even under those circumstances), his monthly salary for looking after the purity of the public water supply and the health of food handlers, providing free treatment for syphilis, a clinic for poor babies, licensing service for midwives, periodic inspections of all public institutions, and free shots for typhoid, diphtheria, measles, and whooping cough in a county of 70,000 people had gradually been raised from $400 to $550 a month.

He had made a reputation for himself, not as a ne'er-do-well but as an eccentric, by his diatribes to the board of supervisors on the pollution of water by incoming industries and by his persistent and quixotic efforts (undertaken years before it became fashionable) to persuade people that the blacks in the county, through poverty, ignorance, and the indifference born of their own hopelessness, were slowly starving their children to death.

Forcibly retired from his job as an uncontrollable nuisance (after he wrote for the local paper a sweeping denunciation of the incumbent board of supervisors), he had continued to treat the black people who lived on or near his farm and to write letters to the Homochitto *Democrat* and the *Times-Picayune* in New Orleans on such subjects as the advantages of bio-degradable detergents and the threat of automobile exhaust fumes; but he had devoted most of his attention to farming.

He had not made a great deal of money at farming either, or, if he had, it was gone. Usually, when he finished meeting the obligations of his household, there was nothing left to save.

For his private life (and his professional life, too, in the sense that he was tied by circumstances to one place) had been controlled and limited by his wife's illness. He had watched her through thirty years of slowly advancing invalidism from Parkinson's disease, complicated in its later stages by multiple sclerosis; had lived all his life with death — even more intimately than other doctors. Unable to take any useful action, he had had to watch her day by day transformed by her suffering, physically and in the very center of her life.

What had been frivolity in the young girl became in the aging invalid vacancy; affection became the meek panic of a sick puppy; harmless vanity became a refusal to allow the world to see her, a horrible shame at her own sickness — as if the tremor were morally wrong, the dragging foot obscene. She shut herself into her room and, when he came in, concealed her shaking hand beneath her blouse, as if it were her naked sex.

He was a passionate monogamist; all the romance and commitment necessary to him (he had thought when he was a young man) would come within the bounds of a warm and orderly family life, children tumbling at his feet and growing strong and independent in the country air, wife competent and joyous, full of Tolstoyan virtue. But his life had not turned out so.

He could neither cure nor comfort his wife; and he bore the spectacle of her long agony, the ruin of all his hopes, as such men bear the obligations laid on them by their promises, stoically. In the early years of his trouble he admonished him-self with a certain priggish self-righteousness concerning his duties, read the *Meditations* of Marcus Aurelius, and even copied out and kept to hand as a bookmarker the admonition to "think steadily, as a Roman and a man, to do what thou hast in hand with perfect and simple dignity, and a feeling of affection, and freedom, and justice," taking care to put all the commas in the right places.

Later, he constructed his own private world, outside and around the chamber where his wife lived, requiring of himself only to be sure that she felt as safe and comfortable and un-threatened as he could make her.

They had been suddenly and mercifully freed — he from her and she from her hateful life — when she had died at fifty-seven of a coronary occlusion. He was in his early sixties then, just retired. Delivered from the necessity of making a minimum amount of money to pay for her nurses and medicines, he set-tled into his eccentricity.

He had always been indifferent to comfort. Now he could let the butane tank go unfilled and happily split fat pine knots and fallen oak logs in his woods. "I'd like to spend the rest of my life splitting logs," he had said to Martha. "That's a respect-able occupation. And productive. Warms you twice." He experimented with organic fertilizers and would not let an ounce of DDT on his place; raised vegetables with the notion that he might show his white neighbors an alternative to the cot-ton economy and his black ones an alternative to starvation. Most people thought he was "just plain crazy."

In any case, now, in his old age, unable any longer to split his own wood, beset with the difficulties of country life and with no one to help him, he agreed that the arrangement Martha of-fered him was exactly what he was looking for: space, privacy, and a place to eat decent home-cooked food. There was even a small coal grate in his room, and the prospect of having a scuttle of coal by his hearth and being able to sit and watch the fire in the winter evenings filled both him and Martha with pleasure.

At her insistence, he was offered a room for less than anyone else would pay — only three hundred dollars a month. He accepted immediately.

That was how Golden Age Acres got its start.

The changeover from a huge empty decaying house with one lonely old lady in it into a bona fide nursing home took place so rapidly that the family had scarcely consented to the first changes before it seemed the plans had been made and were in the process of being carried out. No one was quite sure how it happened so quickly.

George had, of course, written to Mary Hartwell and Francis before he and Albert gave their consent to the arrangements. Francis wrote back immediately to say that he was too far away and too unfamiliar with the circumstances to make a sensible decision and that consequently (and particularly since George and Albert had all the worry and nuisance of the daily business of looking after Aunt Martha) he felt the decision should be left to them. Mary Hartwell, on the other hand, telephoned to say that she had serious doubts about the advisability of taking on the responsibility of three or four more old ladies. (At first there was no question of renting the downstairs rooms except for the one that Lucas would use.) She would come down from Memphis and look into it before she could give her consent.

But a series of crises arose in her own family — one child had an emergency appendectomy, another almost immediately afterward broke his leg in a motorcycle accident; and she could not leave home or even give her serious attention to the old aunt whose life, after all, would not be much changed and whose financial situation would be improved by these arrangements.

She did discuss it with her husband before making up her mind — listing her doubts and observing that, among other things, she wouldn't be surprised if Howie were lying about his wonderful job in Vicksburg. "It's a very convenient lever," she said. But she added, too, that it would be grand after all these years for Martha and Lucas Alexander, whose friendship was so devoted, to share a home and each other's companionship in their old age. What a lovely time they would have puttering about the back garden and bayou together! It would fill a part of the gap left in Martha's life by her mother's death.

Her husband, Robert, relaxing with a drink and a crossword puzzle, grunted skeptically, however, and remarked that it would be unfortunate if propinquity proved too much for the friendship — "as has been known to happen," he added, "and with people a lot younger and more flexible than your aunt and that old doctor are likely to be." He looked at her over the top of his newspaper, a thin-faced man with graying reddish hair. "What's a nine-letter word for freckle?" he said.

"You should know," Mary Hartwell said. "You've got enough of them. And as for Martha and Lucas, you just don't realize how close they've been and what a genuine understanding they've always had."

Laying aside his newspaper, Robert Martin looked at his wife with interest. "You mean they were lovers?" he said. "Great! I didn't know your Aunt Martha had ever had a lover. Thought she was one of those frigid Southern schoolteacher types the woods used to be so full of. Why didn't they get married?" He got up, went over to the dictionary stand, and began to turn the pages of an unabridged dictionary.

"I didn't say they were lovers," Mary Hartwell replied. "Although I won't say I've never wondered about it. But the truth is, I don't know whether they were or not. No one ever discussed such a thing — Mama wouldn't have allowed it for a minute (speculation about other peoples' private lives, I mean). And then, too, I don't think you ever know the truth about your own family, do you? But I must have dismissed it sometime or other — probably because they *didn't* get married after his wife died. There was no reason not to, except that by then they were both in their sixties."

"*Lenticula*," Robert said. "I never saw that word."

"What?"

"*Lenticula* means freckle."

"Oh."

"In any case," he said, going back to the sofa, "Albert and George say that Martha herself wants to invite the old ladies in, and if *she's* happy about it, there's no reason for you to worry."

"I know, but I'd just like to get down there and see for myself before I decide. You know she's been almost as much a mother to me as Mama was, and I hate not to go and be sure."

"Well, go," Robert said. "I can manage with the kids for a few days."

"With *two* down? You couldn't possibly . . ."

That same night Albert called and told her again that if the plan were not carried out, Howie intended to leave. "Everything is going so well and Aunt Martha is chirping like a cricket," he said. "Let's take the bull by the horns and go ahead with it."

Reluctantly, Mary Hartwell gave her consent.

By the following week painters were everywhere in the old house, freshening up the interior; and Howie was bustling about with his notebook in his hand, reorganizing the kitchen and interviewing prospective residents and staff members. A local motel had recently refurnished its lobbies and he persuaded the family to let him buy the old lounge chairs and coffee tables and magazine racks "to jazz up the front hall and the sun parlor." (The back gallery had become a "sun parlor" now.) He ordered books on the operation of nursing homes and displayed them between onyx book ends on the desk in his study. Before long he was able to talk in a knowing way about geriatrics and related subjects.

No one, perhaps not even Howie, had realized how enthusiastic people would be at the prospect of an old peoples' home in Homochitto. Miss Carrie Stock had not been listed in Howie's notebook as "definitely committed" for more than a couple of days before word had spread through the town, and old people (or, rather, old peoples' children) were clamoring for the privilege of joining her. Before Lucas Alexander had finished settling his affairs and preparing for the move, three more families were "definitely committed." And when people learned that Lucas was to have a room, Howie immediately had a waiting list of men for the other downstairs rooms and had agreed to try to persuade the family to open the downstairs.

The first old lady moved in in mid-December — Miss Carrie Stock. She had no one with whom to share a family Christmas before she moved. Lucas went to the coast to his niece for the holidays, but he too was settled in his new quarters by New Year's. And others followed.

As for the Clarkes, it began to give all of them pleasure to hear from friends and acquaintances what a wonderful idea they had had and what a valuable service they were doing for the community. But they were quick to give Howie the credit. It was his idea, after all, and he was the one who would be mainly responsible for making it a success.

CHAPTER 5

"I LOOK AT THIS, Lucas" — Martha pushed up her sweater sleeve and held out a mottled and wrinkled brown arm — "or I take a cold look in the mirror in the morning, and I can't believe my eyes. Can this be mine?" She held the ancient clawlike hand close to her eyes, flexed it, and then took his wrist in a powerful grip. "Still strong, though. I haven't been wielding a shovel all these years for nothing." She laughed wryly. "Sometimes, lying in bed at night, waiting for the old bones to stop screaming, I say to myself, What in the world! How can it be? I'm seventy-six years old and I feel sixteen. Not the bones — I don't mean I'm that spry. But inside my head — curious about the future, full of commonplace expectations and frustrations. As if the world should be lying all before me. Isn't *something* supposed to happen — at least by the time you pass three score and ten — something that makes you get resigned to death — even welcome it? Aren't old people supposed to be — *different?* When Newton comes out here and pays me a visit, it's clear enough that *he* thinks I'm different — more in the line of a curious seashell than a human being. He listens — holds me to his ear and gets the sound of the sea — and then he carefully puts me down and goes away."

Lucas Alexander laughed and laid his hand for a moment on hers. They were sitting in a sunny sheltered spot south of the garage and above the bayou where they were out of the wind and out of sight of the house and could look down onto the bleak winter-stripped bayou bank. "Newton!" he said. "His attention's on himself — not on people or seashells; but after all, he's young. I have to say, though, Martha, he's one of the most self-absorbed young men I've ever had any dealings with. A glaze comes over his eyes when you try to communicate your intentions to him and, before you know what's happened, he's talking about politics or shooting turkeys."

"I know, I know. It's going to take a wife and children, and maybe even then . . ." She shook her head. "But what I was going to tell you . . . Is it possible we haven't been alone together since before you had pneumonia and my cataracts began to get bad? (No, we did have that one mushroom hunt in November, didn't we? I'm getting terrible about remembering things.) How have I borne it! I have so *much* to tell you. And . . . Anyhow, to begin with, about feeling sixteen again — of course, it's because you're here. The unbelievable luck of it. I was beginning to think we were going to have to get married to get out of the predicament we were in — just to see each other occasionally, *alone*."

"The same thought crossed my mind."

"That it had been an awful mistake, after all, not marrying ten years ago, that we had been crazy, superstitious or something, believing our life together was too set in its old mold to change. Did we think we would live forever? Never be sick or helpless? We were arrogant — as arrogant as if we were twenty."

"Yes," he said, "I suppose in a way it was arrogant."

Neither of them said anything for a moment — keeping to their silence about something both complex and important which after all these years perhaps neither really understood and which, in any case, they were loath to talk about; fearing to look into the grave where lay buried all the frustrations and failures, the doubts and disappointments of their life together. Was there, after all, anything to say now except *too late?*

Martha went on. "You know, Luke, in June, when Sister died and you were so sick — and everything was so terrible — and then later, when you were gone for so long, I thought something permanent had happened to me. Even if you'd been here, if we'd been alone together, I don't know whether I could have talked to you about it — I was in a kind of daze. And I thought, you know, that I would be like those African natives you read about who have the power of life and death over themselves. If you shut them up in a jail — if they're disgraced, whatever — they sit down on the floor with their legs crossed and their arms folded and die. That was what I thought I'd do, and I said to myself that you would approve. What could have made me think that? But anyhow, I hadn't the concentration for it.

"Even though I thought it was *necessary*. That I *had* to do it. Because I was no use to anybody and you know I can't bear that — it's intolerable.

"I suppose when I discovered that I couldn't order myself to die, I should have starved myself to death like Indian old people used to do in a bad winter — so as not to take food from the younger ones. But you know how I like to eat." She laughed the deep throaty laugh that had always stirred him. "I couldn't screw myself up to it," she said. "And then this happened. You, I mean. Who would believe I could be so lucky. And at my age! That *you* — after all these years . . ."

"And too late for us to take advantage of the opportunity," he said. He half suppressed a deep cough and she winced as if in pain for him, but all she said was, "We have to be careful with each other. We must pretend we're in separate houses — so as not to get in each other's way."

He touched her hand gently. "We've always managed," he said. "We're probably old enough to live together now."

"Too old. Not as bright as we once were. We have to . . . make an extra effort."

"You may not be bright," he said. "All I am is stiff — and annoyed at dragging this feeble casing around." He stirred and flexed his shoulders under the warmth of the noon sunshine. "Let's walk, Martha," he said. He stood up and drew her to her feet and they began to pace back and forth along the flagstone path paralleling the top of the embankment that sloped down to the bayou. "I don't know why that pneumonitis took such a toll," he said. "Exercise! Discipline! I'll be as fit as Picasso in a couple of months." He carried his long, emaciated body as erectly as a soldier and strode along, the eyebrows ruffled, the hawkish profile pushing fiercely into the wind. "And exercise will be good for you, too," he said. "You've been vegetating for six months."

"Slow down, Luke," she said. "Your legs are so much longer than mine. And besides, you forget I'm blind." She was almost running to keep up with him, white hair slipping from its confining pins. "You're right," she said. "We can do some walking. And, Luke! We can get out in the country now that you're here with a car and well enough to drive. Maybe in the spring we could even go fishing."

At the east end of the garden they turned and started back. He was walking more slowly now and had placed her arm inside his own.

"We'll have to be careful — about going to the country, I mean," she said. "We needn't tell anybody — needn't mention it. I wouldn't be surprised if the children made a lot of difficulties about my wandering around in the woods. Not to mention

Howie, who has developed a really annoying solicitude about my health."

"Howie?" he said. "It's none of Howie's business."

They paced along the walk in silence for a few minutes. Then, "Luke," she said, "there's something else I've been wanting to talk to you about. Wanting to and not wanting to. Thinking maybe if I ignored it, it would go away."

"Yes?" He looked down into her calm, blind-seeming blue eyes.

"I've had two or three strange experiences lately. It makes me uneasy. Things have . . . happened . . . that I can't explain."

"Like?"

"A couple of nights ago I dreamed . . ." She shuddered and then shrugged away her revulsion. "It was terrible, because it didn't seem then that it was a dream. Even now I'm half-convinced it wasn't a dream. But of course it had to be. So *real* — not divided off in my mind as a dream should be — much more like a waking memory. Anyhow, I dreamed that Mama was dead — except it was Sister, too — both of them rolled into one. They — *it* — was lying in Mama's big old four-poster in the nursery downstairs. You know, that was Mama and Papa's room years and years ago. And there was nobody to bury them. Everybody was gone. Strange — the boys and Mary Hartwell — in my dream I don't think they even existed. I don't remember once thinking of calling them — getting them to help. And I was paralyzed — lying in bed in my own room and couldn't move. But the smell — you know, of death — came drifting up. I knew it was coming, like fog, even before I smelled it — up the stairs and down the hall and into my room. And people came in — Lucy and someone else (Who is that other woman Howie had hired? Mrs. Crowder?) and a tall blond man —

a painter, he said he was (an artist, I mean, not a house painter). He looked so familiar to me, I kept thinking I knew him and then all at once I realized it was Newton. They took the furniture out of my room and began to paint furniture on the walls — chairs and tables and a bookcase with my books painted in it very convincingly, like a *trompe-l'oeil*. And I kept saying, Help me, help me, please. Somebody has to see about the body. It's downstairs in the nursery — can't you smell it? But they wouldn't look at me — just said I wouldn't need the furniture anymore, that the pictures would do as well. And I explained that they would have to help me get up so that I could bury Mama. I have a spade in the toolshed, I told them, a small-bladed one, easy for a woman to use. But all they said was that when it was time to take the body out, they would paint everything on the wall in there, too, so that no one would know the difference. After a while they went into the other room and began to carry things out of there. And Mrs Crowder said it would save trouble with dusting and keeping the place clean.

"Then I was down in the nursery and they weren't there at all anymore. And I saw her — it — whatever it was. The body. It was real, but on a painted bed. All bloated as if it had starved to death, you know, with the belly blown up and the flesh fallen away from the bones of the head, so there was only skin covering the skull, and teeth bucked out like the teeth of a skeleton. Do you remember the pictures of the people in Buchenwald when it was first liberated? Dreadful!

"That's all," she said. "It stopped and I was up, standing in the nursery, looking at the bed. I had walked all the way downstairs in my sleep. Lucy must have heard me, because . . ."

"Is Lucy here at night?"

Martha nodded. "She's on call all night. I suppose it's a good thing, especially with Mrs. Wheeler here. And she works a day shift, too, but after this week the new nurse — the one in my dream — will take the morning shift, and Lucy will just be on from eleven until seven. Anyhow, she came in, and I must finally have gone back to bed — that part of it is all mixed up in my mind. But the dream! It's not mixed up a bit — but as real as us out here walking right now. It won't let me alone. I keep thinking and thinking of it and seeing it. And the most disturbing part is that I couldn't — almost still can't — convince myself it was a dream. Ask Lucy. She thought I was crazy, I suppose. The next night when she came on (last night, I mean), I made her go down to the nursery with me to look at the bed again. I hadn't told anybody else about it — just couldn't. But I couldn't *believe* the body wasn't there." She shrugged. "Lucy finally convinced me it was all in my head." She was silent a moment. Then, "That's the kind of thing I'm talking about, Lucas. This last time was the worst, but it's happened before." They continued to pace slowly through the garden, and she said no more, turning the horror around in her mind and waiting for him to speak.

He bent to the ground at his feet, picked up a couple of pecans fallen from the huge tree above their heads, crushed the shells between his hands and, taking out the meats, ate one and handed one to her. She looked at it and put it in the pocket of the shabby old blue sweater she wore.

"Dreams," he said at last, reluctantly. "You're bound to have some bad dreams along through here. I know how difficult Elizabeth's illness was."

"Arteriosclerosis," she said. "You don't want to tell me, but that's what it is."

"No! Not necessarily. Not at all. You can have that kind of experience at any age."

"I remember very well how Mama used to confuse dreams

with reality," Martha said, "but not until she was old."

Again he was silent.

"We may as well be realistic," she said. "My memory isn't as good as it once was, either."

"Well, go ahead and have a checkup, if it'll make you feel better. Tell Carr about it and let him look you over. He might put you on a little nicotinic acid. Or maybe there's something new that's better."

"That's *bad*, Luke," she said. "Not being able to separate dreams from reality. Senile psychosis is what you call it."

"You've always had too much imagination for your own good," he said. "What did Lucy say?"

"Oh, Lucy! She took it in and knew well enough what was going on. It's all very well for Louisa to say she's simpleminded, but she knows what she wants to know. Too much. If it weren't for Harper . . ."

"If it weren't for Harper, what?"

"I'd fire her — protect myself against her."

"Protect yourself!" He stopped short for a moment and looked searchingly at her again. "What could she do to hurt you?"

"I know, I know. It sounds paranoid, doesn't it? But I was afraid for *anyone* to know — that it might make them want to shut me up. Especially Lucy. Just in the past few months, since Sister died — since Howie came — she's changed. It's as if she's — waiting for something."

"You don't have to keep her on, if you don't like her," he said.

"It's more that she doesn't like *me* than that I don't like her. I'm too old to bother with disliking people. And besides, she interests me. I mean — just because I'm not used to the way these young Negroes behave, does that mean they're bad? I

mean, you know, a threat to *me?* I can't start dismissing everything out of hand that isn't exactly like it was five years ago, or
twenty-five years ago." She shook her head. "No," she said,
"because, besides that, I don't want to rock the boat. She needs
the job. Harper needs her to be working — she does help him
with the younger ones, you know. And there probably isn't a
soul in Homochitto outside of Howie and me who would put up
with her. She doesn't care *what* she says, you know, to old people or white people — or anybody. But Howie takes it in his
stride — he's very easy and good with her."

"What do you think she's waiting for?" Lucas said.

"Oh, Lucas." (She called his name almost every time she
spoke, as if the sound gave her pleasure or reassured her.) "You
make it sound so silly — so unreasonable. But what I really think
she's waiting for is to take some advantage of me — to — somehow — get, use *power*."

"That *is* a little bit out of line, Martha," he said. "But if that's
how you feel, maybe you *should* let her go."

She shook her head. "Even if it weren't for Harper," she
said, "and for realizing myself how silly it is, I couldn't let her
go. When you get right down to it — I *can't*. I'm not in charge
anymore. Things are — different — now that Howie has this
complex household to run and all of us to look after. You've
just gotten here and you don't realize it yet."

"Well, if you can't, or don't want to do anything about it,
then put it out of your mind," he said. "Forget it. If anything
happens that you don't like, if she continues to make you uneasy,
you can always make an issue of it when you have to. But for
now, forget it. You're probably wrong, anyhow, you know."

"There," she said. "I really just needed to tell you about it. It
makes all the difference."

"Are you getting tired?"

"No, no. The walk is doing me good. Blowing out the cob-webs. We'll have to make it a little longer every day."

Inside the house the drapes at the study window moved and Howie stood looking out at them, his round face close to the pane, his eyes following as they continued to walk up and down the garden. Then, after a little while, the door of his bedroom opened and he came down the walk to join them, stepping along with his swinging priestly walk, as if he might be leading a pro-cession. He stopped in front of them and folded his arms, wear-ing, as always, a dark suit that was slightly too small for him, the fabric stretched taut across his shoulders and solid paunch. "Well!" he said. "Beautiful day for January. Feels like April."

"Yes, we're enjoying the sun," Lucas said courteously.

"You folks aren't overdoing the exercise, are you? You know, Doc, you've been a pretty sick man."

A peculiarly opaque look came into the doctor's eyes, but he only said, "I'm feeling fine, Howie. I need the exercise."

"Another thing, Doc. I want you to talk a little reason to this lady," Howie said. "She scrambles around out here like a gazelle. You convince her for me she's got to be careful. She might fall."

"Don't worry about Martha," Lucas said. "She's an excellent judge of what she can do."

"I'm careful, Howie," Martha said. "I really am."

"I'll tell you the truth, though," Howie said. "Some of these other old ladies gonna look out the window and see you and get notions they can do the same thing. And they can't. We liable to end up with a house full of broken hips. See what I mean?

It'd be a big help if you'd kind of slow down. I'm just trying to keep everybody happy."

"It wouldn't be good for me to slow down," Martha said calmly but stubbornly. "I've got to go on living like I've always lived."

"O.K. O.K. But kind of take it easy when you see 'em watching."

"I think you'll find your ladies will all be better off if they get some exercise," Lucas said. "If I were you, I'd encourage them to walk every day — good for the circulation."

"Well, that's a thought, Doc. But it might take more supervision than we can manage. By the way," he added, turning to Martha, "how do you like Crawley?"

"Crawley?"

"You know, our new nurse. Not here yet — Lucy's doing a double shift until she gets her business straightened out. But you met her the other day, remember? When I took her around and showed her the place."

"Crawley?" Lucas said abruptly. "A nurse? From around here?"

"That's right. Mrs. Thelma Crawley. She's gonna be a crackerjack. Real experienced."

"I believe I know her," Lucas said. "But she's not a nurse. She used to be a midwife twenty years ago when I was working for the county. And not a very good one, either. Did you know . . . ?" But he hesitated and then did not finish his sentence.

"Well, she won't have to worry about delivering any babies here," Howie said. "Will she, Martha?" Martha smiled politely and he went on. "I was lucky to get her. She's been working at Charity in New Orleans — just moved back here a couple of weeks ago. Experienced. Likes old people."

"Howie," Lucas said, "I've been meaning to offer to help you work with your sitters. I can teach Lucy — and Mrs. Crawley, too, if she's the one I remember — a few fundamentals about taking care of old people — sterile techniques, how to give shots, and so forth."

"Well . . ." Howie said. "I wouldn't want to put it on you, Doc. You being retired and all. And not too well. And living here. It might not look right."

"Somebody ought to give them a little instruction and supervision," Lucas said. "If not me, how about the county health nurse? I could get in touch with her and ask her to come out."

"No, no," Howie said. "I don't think that's necessary."

"Have you thought about what a mess you'd be in if you got a staph infection in here? You might end up having to close the place. And, incidentally, do you expect to get licensed? What class? You have to have an LPN on duty to get a fourth-class license, you know."

Howie shook his head. "You got the wrong idea, Doc. This ain't a commercial venture. This is a *home*. We don't need to fool around with county nurses and licenses and such as that. Change the atmosphere altogether. But say, now that I think about it, I expect you're right about teaching Lucy to give shots and all, if you don't mind doing it. And Crawley too, if she needs it. Mighty nice of you to offer. Just so long as it ain't an imposition." He glanced at his watch. "Now, you folks have walked long enough today, you hear me? That's really what I came out here to tell you. You got to worry about taking care of yourselves as well as other people. Lunch'll be ready in ten minutes or so. O.K.? See you then?"

He continued on his way, following the flagstone walk toward the garage. At this point Lucy Harper came out from the service area beyond the garage with an empty trash basket in each hand,

and he paused to wait for her to catch up with him. Her black hair was combed high and she wore a fillet of brass to hold it in place. She had a fringed shawl with yellow and green and blue stripes thrown over her shoulders.

"You got to start wearing a uniform, Lucy," he said. "We're in business now."

"I reckon," she said.

"We're on our way. Crawley's gonna wear a uniform and cap and everything. Like a real nurse. And Dr. Alexander says he's gonna teach you to give shots and all."

She flashed him a sullen look.

"Besides, you distract me."

"Watch out, white man," she said. But she let him take one of the two baskets from her and walked beside him toward the house.

"I ain't a white man, Lucy," he said. "I'm what you might call, like it says in the old riddle, black and white and red all over."

"Yeah?"

They were at the back steps now, and Howie paused to let her precede him. He jerked his head toward Martha and Lucas, who were still marching up and down the walk. "What do you think of that pair, honey?" he said. "You've seen more of her than anybody else."

"Crazy old woman," Lucy said. "But she tries to do right. She never has given me any trouble."

"And him? Seems to me he could make a nuisance of himself."

"I don't never think about him," Lucy said. "Or any of them others, either, if I can help it."

CHAPTER 6

WITHIN ANOTHER MONTH Howie had completed the transformation of the Clarke house into Golden Age Acres. The old spare and airy look of the wide halls and gallery was gone. Motel lobby furniture lined the walls in stiff groups; and several large artificial philodendrons and rubber plants — gifts of old Mrs. Cathcart's son, who was the owner of a wholesale florists' supply shop — filled in the empty corners. Some of the new residents had wished to bring in pieces of their own furniture and, to make room for them, Albert and George had taken away for their own use various family pieces: the plantation-built four-posters in two of the bedrooms, a couple of cane-bottomed rockers, and the Empire chest and armoire in their Aunt Elizabeth's old room. When Howie had suggested that the botanical prints on the hall walls might not appeal to everyone, Martha had taken them down and hung them in her room. Howie had replaced them with a hodgepodge of reproductions picked up for a dollar apiece at a local garage sale: green willow trees drooping over a blue lake, steamboats and cotton bales, and such famous masterpieces as *Dignity and Impudence* and *The Gleaners*. He had set up tables in the sun parlor — one for checkers and one for cards — and installed in the living room for the use of residents who had not brought their own, a television set that chattered all day long of lives in perpetual crisis.

Other changes and improvements were in the works for the future. Howie spoke of new kitchen equipment and even of adding a wing to the house; or, rather, a separate two-story building out where the scuppernong arbor had stood. There, he said, all rooms would be double or even triple and could be rented for less money. But these projects were for the future — perhaps in a year or two. Thus far, he had mentioned them only to Lucy. For the present, as he told the cousins, the main thing was to concentrate on learning to operate the home as efficiently as possible. More was involved, he had discovered, than an occasional bingo game.

Now there were ten residents (four old men downstairs and five old ladies besides Martha on the main floor) settled in their separate rooms, the wrench and excitement of moving over, filling their days with idle conversation, television, and bickering; waiting, always waiting, for the visits of friends and relatives.

Lucas alone among them had specific hours when he left the house to work with the new Johns Hopkins health project; and he and Martha spent their evenings together in his room. He would read aloud to her, or they would sit, idly watching the fire leap and collapse inward, and talk of his day's work or be companionably silent. He wrote to the Library of Congress and had Martha's name put on their list to receive a record player and books for the blind, so that she would have something to occupy her days, and they regularly took their walks and drove out into the country, even in the coldest weather.

But the others in the house were not so resourceful. At first, when they began to show their restlessness, Howie tried to enlist the services of church circles and guilds and the local Kings' Daughters chapter to pay calls and take them out driving. But curiously, the local ladies, so diligent in their support of selfless organizations like the Junior League, Legion Auxiliary, Gray

Ladies, missionary aid societies, and Jaycettes, did not respond to the boredom of old people any more enthusiastically than they responded to the poverty of black people. It was as if, now, the old people were as invisible as blacks had been in the days before they began to wear outlandish clothes and march and protest and demand the vote. Howie did not press the ladies. As he told Newton, he saw no point in monkeying around with community good will.

But then the old people began to get sick. It had been possible, of course, to stipulate that no invalids would be taken; but it was not possible to keep them all healthy after they arrived. The first disaster happened almost immediately after the home opened. Miss Carrie Stock, small and erect as a wren in her stripy shirtwaist dresses and smooth gray hair, was a woman in her seventies, used all her life to cooking and cleaning and gardening and teaching. She looked about her, for a month, spoke happily of leisure and companionship, mended all her clothes, arranged and rearranged her room, tried to persuade the cook to let her pick greens or wash dishes, fell increasingly silent, and on the thirtieth day had a stroke. Now she lay motionless in a hospital bed in the small back bedroom next to the kitchen which had once been the cook's room.

In some ways it turned out to be easier to take care of her than of the well inmates. ("Every cloud has a silver lining," Howie observed to Lucy.) She had a tube down her nose for feeding and all you had to do was keep her clean and turn her over every now and then. Other people, sometimes ailing or addled or spiteful or willful or angry, wandered in and out of the house, stumbled over unfamiliar thresholds, slipped and fell in the bathroom, left the faucets running, soiled their beds, and in general made nuisances of themselves.

Within a few months others of the feebler and less responsible patients became chair- or bed-ridden. Two of the old men, twin brothers and widowers, suffered almost simultaneously a mysterious impairment of balance which led Howie to keep them confined mostly to wheelchairs. Mrs. Wheeler, who from the beginning had walked with some difficulty and who usually had no idea where she was going, now walked not at all.

In April Howie moved the invalids to the lower floor of the house — the Strange brothers sharing one room and Mrs. Wheeler and Miss Carrie Stock (now generally referred to by the staff as "the Vegetable") sharing another. Lucas at his end of the basement, stubbornly refusing to give up his fireplace and outside entrance, and Howie at his were the only two well people downstairs.

How much pleasanter and more attractive this arrangement was! Now when visitors came in, they were in a far more cheerful and inviting environment. All the depressing scenes of the sickroom were tucked out of sight. On the long, glassed-in porch that Howie called the sun parlor, Mrs. Cathcart, Miss Rebecca Steinman, and a new arrival, Mrs. Aldridge, played gin rummy or watched television or read. Mr. Howard, a spry old bachelor and retired accountant, took over the cook's bedroom which had been vacated by Miss Carrie. He was a maker of model cars and his toys filled a display case at one end of the sun parlor. On their good days the Strange brothers were allowed to sit for a while in the back garden. They were country men, had farmed all their lives, and did not like either cards or television, so the upstairs sun parlor was no loss to them. They talked interminably to each other of breeds of cattle and strains of cotton, of ancient deer hunts, of bream and crappie and bass fishing, of the best time to gather poke salad, and of the hidden places where muscadines were still to be found. But at least they weren't crazy.

"You've got to hide the sick ones and the crazy ones, if you want the relatives to stay happy," Howie had said to Lucas on the day when all the room changes were made. "That's a fact of life that I've just had to face up to. Listen to Wheeler, for example. We can't have that kind of thing going on where everybody in the house can hear it. It's too depressing." He jerked his head toward the front bedroom where Mrs. Wheeler lay in a hospital bed. At regular intervals, as if it were a part of the process of metabolism, she gave out a kind of moaning sigh. And, when she heard footsteps or voices in the hall, she spoke in a quiet, persuasive, reasonable voice.

"Just come in to see me, dear," she said. "Please come into my room for a moment. Just for a moment. I won't keep you long." Or, "Would you mind calling James for me, dear? I'm sure he's at his office. He'll come right out, if you tell him where I am."

"Mrs. Crawley could pay some attention to her *right now*," Lucas said. "She's in the kitchen gossiping with the cook instead of up here where she belongs. Trash," he muttered, his deep rough voice quavering slightly. "Crawley and the other one, too."

"You mean Ruby?" Howie said. "She puts a pretty good meal on the table."

"Mainly Mrs. Crawley," Lucas said. "I know her, Howie. I had an experience with her some years ago." He hesitated. Then, "It's a matter of record," he said. "If you had asked for a recommendation on her from the health department, they would have told you. She was a midwife. She performed an illegal abortion, probably dozens of them, as a matter of fact; but in this case the girl was brought in to the hospital with septicemia. Mrs. Crawley was arrested, indicted, but then the girl got cold feet and refused to testify. Nothing ever came of it except that we took her license, of course. That's when she left Homochitto."

He grimaced. "I don't like to bear tales. I would never have mentioned any of this — she's entitled to forget the mistakes in her past, after all. But she's not performing up to standards here. I come upstairs to get Martha, and I invariably find her in the kitchen instead of seeing about the patients. And that septicemia keeps nagging at me. You and I know that this is a situation where the nurses' aides have got to keep people scrupulously clean and where . . . Well, you ought to keep a sharp eye on her."

"Like you say, nobody ought to have to keep dragging his past after him," Howie said. "But thank you, Doc. I'll . . . Well, now, speak of the devil. Here she is," he said, looking past Lucas down the hall. "We were getting ready to call you, Mrs. Crawley. What you got there, anyhow?"

"Orange juice for Wheeler." The woman approaching them in a starched and shining uniform (Howie demanded a neat appearance from the help and, although neatness was next to impossible for Mrs. Crawley, she did appear to be clean) was fat in the blowzy way that women go in late middle age when they've always run to fat — with a heavy sagging bosom and shaking hips and thighs. Tousled red hair, a gold tooth in a wide ingratiating smile and a black patch over one eye gave her a rakish look, as if she might be the happy wife of a successful retired pirate. She continued on her way down the hall, opened the door into Mrs. Wheeler's room, and went in. Lucas and Howie followed.

"You can't expect to get college graduates for a dollar and a quarter an hour, Doc," Howie said in a low voice. "These folks do their best. But I *will* say I wish Crawley'd get herself a plain tooth. And I'm going to make her start wearing her glass eye.

That's the main trouble with her. You get a feeling from it
— you know you do — that some way you can't trust her.
But you can. She's got a heart of gold."

Lucas shook his head. "I'm not talking about teeth," he said.
"I don't give a damn about her teeth." He paused in the doorway to Mrs. Wheeler's room and looked in. Spread over the bed
and tied down to convert it into a low cage in which the old
lady could not sit up was a kind of cargo net. She grasped the
meshes and looked through, a shriveled and mad old monkey.
"Come in, dears; I need you," she said.

Mrs. Crawley set the glass on the bedside table and began to
untie a corner of the net. "Look here, now, Maggie," she said.
"Look what a treat we got for Maggie this morning."

Lucas walked over to the bed, thrust his hand through the
mesh, and gently touched her hair. "What is it you need, Mrs.
Wheeler?"

"Just visit with me for a little while, dear. Just a few minutes. *Please?* I won't keep you long."

Mrs. Crawley threw the net back. "Sit up, Maggie," she said.
"Open wide for Crawley."

"James will be here shortly," the old lady said. "We can
explain our difficulties to him and I'm sure he'll be able to help."

"Who's James?" Lucas said.

Howie shrugged. "Son. Lives in New Orleans and don't get
up here very often."

Mrs. Crawley pulled the old lady to a sitting position and
thrust the glass against her teeth.

Lucas touched the net. "This won't do, you know, Howie,"
he said. "It really won't."

"Keeps her from trying to climb over the side rails," Howie
said. "She might break her neck. But it's just temporary, Doc.
That's what I was telling you. Once we get 'em all downstairs,

close together where one person can look after all four of 'em, we can get rid of this net thing and make her happy. And the Strange twins, too. Keep each other company. Makes an extra room if we need it. The right tranquilizers for everybody," he added. "That's what we've got to concentrate on. I can see the place just as quiet and orderly — peaceful. Why you ought to see what they've done up at Whitfield with drugs! Everybody in the place is as happy as a kid with a sugar tit. Some of 'em sleep practically all day. Tranquilizers! We just hadn't found the right combination for Wheeler yet."

Lucas shook his head impatiently. "You could probably get the Stranges back on their feet, if you worked at it," he said. "I'd be glad to help Mrs. Crawley set up some simple exercises for them — to build muscle tone and so forth."

"Well, now, ain't that sweet?" Mrs. Crawley said. And then, "Finish your juice, Maggie. Hurry up now. Drink up for Crawley. Drink up!"

"Do you think it would be safe?" Howie said. "I mean, if they were up, shaky as they are, somebody would have to be watching 'em all the time."

"That's the truth, too," Mrs. Crawley said.

"You wouldn't let a child or a young adult lie in bed like a sack until he lost the use of his legs," Lucas said. "What's the difference here? These folks don't want to be helpless, any more than you or I do."

Mrs. Wheeler sat on the edge of the bed and flexed her feet. "I'm glad to have you with me," she said. "I lead a somewhat isolated life, you know — even though James is a faithful visitor."

Mrs. Crawley put the glass to her lips again, but she turned her head jerkily away and the juice dribbled down her cheek and chin. "No," she said. "I don't want any more." "Now, look what a mess you've made," Mrs. Crawley said. "Shame on you, Maggie!"

"Mrs. Wheeler," Lucas said, "Mr. Snyder is going to move you to another room where you'll have more company. Would you like that?"

The old lady frowned. Then, "So long as you're sure James will be able to find me," she said.

"I've got to admit I've made mistakes on some of these folks," Howie said. "That won't happen again now that I'm learning the ropes. You got to weed out the healthy nuts to start with. And the moaners and shouters. Bedridden nuts — *quiet* bedridden nuts — I can manage. But not the well ones. And the noisy ones depress the visitors too much."

Lucas gazed at him, trembling, his lips pinched tight and the big vein in his temple throbbing. He mastered himself, jerked his head toward the door and managed to say, "Shall we . . . ? Outside . . . ?" In the hall, brows drawn together in a ferocious scowl, he continued: "You ought to be a doctor, Howie. You never allow yourself to be affected by the emotions — the anguish — of other people, do you?"

"Well now, I wouldn't say that," Howie said. "The truth is, I love 'em all, every one of 'em." He hesitated. "But I try to be objective," he said.

"You ought to be careful," Lucas said. "Some people might mistake your objectivity for callousness."

"Now, Doc, I thought I could be frank with you. You're supposed to be a realistic man. It ain't that I'm callous. Not at all. Don't you see that if we run the visitors off it's bad for the patients' morale? I maybe put it too bluntly, but Wheeler wasn't paying any attention to me. And as for the healthy nuts, it's the simple truth. We can't handle 'em. Look at Crane, for example, and what a headache she is. I can't even get her to move downstairs. But now that we've got her, it wouldn't look good to people if we tried to get rid of her."

"Let me know if you want me to work out some exercises for the Stranges," Lucas said. He turned and strode down the hall and out the front door.

What Howie had said about Mrs. Arthur Crane, Sr., was certainly true. She had been a problem from the day she arrived at Golden Age. As Howie had surmised when he was making up his first list of prospective clients, her son Arthur was one of the people in Homochitto most pleased to hear the news that there was to be a local — truly first-class and exclusive — home for old people in town. His mother, a tall, raw-boned old woman of great strength of character and vitality, had become an almost intolerable burden to him and his wife. Until recently she had been able to live in an apartment in the same building with them, but she had become more and more senile over the past year. Nothing they did seemed to please her, and she made their lives miserable with paranoid suspicions and fantasies of theft and loss.

She had begun getting out of bed at night, roaming through her apartment, taking every dish and pot and pan and piece of silver out of the cupboards in the kitchen and every stitch of clothing out of the closets, piling things on the floor and on chairs and counters and pawing through them in a frenzy of anxiety, looking for something lost or stolen, and then, not finding it, falling asleep exhausted on the sofa in the living room; to awaken the next morning and stare about her, bewildered and terrified at the wreckage that surrounded her. Then she would call her son to come over and, waving her long arms, would shout at him, "Look! Look! Arthur! They've been here again. Who are they? What are they after? Can't the police stop them? Can't anybody stop them? What's the matter with you — a great strapping man like you — to let them do this to me?"

And Arthur, a slender gentle man with soft brown eyes and his mother's long limbs, would go patiently over the apartment with her, finding whatever she said was lost, explaining again and again that nothing had been stolen, no one had been there, until at last, exasperated, he would say, "Listen, Mother! Listen. *Look at me.* Are you listening? You did it yourself and now you can't remember. Do you hear me?"

She would seize his arm with a grip as strong as a man's and gaze into his eyes. "You're *in* with them," she would say. "I know. You and Marian are in with them. It's her fault. She's turned you against me."

Tranquilizers had had only the effect of driving her into depressions, more manageable but no less distressing than her frenzies. One night she had wandered out of her apartment dressed in nothing but her long flannel nightgown and had been picked up by the police in the little Confederate Memorial Park nearby sitting like a homeless ghost on the brick coping of the goldfish pond. Shortly thereafter her son had moved her into the apartment with himself and his wife. There had been no other choice except to send her to a home in Vicksburg or Natchez, and Arthur had not been able to bring himself to do that.

Soon, when her anxieties would respond to no other therapy, the Cranes' family doctor had started the old lady on elixir of Demerol reinforced with Librium. This measure had, in fact, been Arthur's idea. He had a hazy notion that she might live thereafter in a kind of happy drug-induced dream; but the effect had been less dramatic than he had hoped. She was quieter, it was true, and sometimes even content, but anguish and bewilderment still haunted her waking and sleeping dreams.

Howie Snyder was not aware of this background or of the degree of Mrs. Crane's disturbance when he admitted her to Golden Age. "Mother's getting senile," Arthur told him. "You'll have to keep an eye on her. We have her on a couple of tranquilizers," he added, "and that keeps things under control." He turned over to Howie her bottles of medicine, wrote out the dosage schedule, said good-bye to her, and departed. Perhaps he was afraid that if the truth were known Howie would refuse to take her; or it may have been that after the goldfish pond episode, he assumed that everyone in Homochitto knew she was crazy.

The first few weeks after she came were hectic. She wept a great deal — quietly during the hours immediately after a dose of medicine, more frantically when it was almost time for another. Again and again she turned out the contents of her drawers. Her underwear had been stolen, or the brass tray that her uncle had brought her from India, or a quilt that had belonged to her grandmother. Twice, when someone inadvertently left the front door open, she slipped out of the house and wandered away. The first time, Lucy found her at the corner by the freeway standing quietly under the streetlight looking around with wondering eyes, as if she were in a foreign land; but the second time, the staff spent a frantic hour looking for her before it occurred to Howie to go back to her old apartment building. There he found her, sitting on a bench in the foyer muttering to herself, her shoulders slumped and her strong skinny hands gripping each other convulsively in her lap.

"Marian and Arthur are not at home," she said to Howie, "and I'm locked out. Locked out of my own house."

"You live with us now, Mrs. Crane," Howie said. "Come along, let's go home."

She opened her purse. "I wrote this down for everybody to see when I'm dead," she said, taking out a small notebook. "It's about my life." She began to read. "*One*: three years, seven months nursing Mama with broken hip. Died of pneumonia, November fourteenth, nineteen thirty-nine. *Two*: Old Auntie. No children. Cancer. Six months, mostly in severe pain. Died June, nineteen forty-two. *Three*: Daddy. Heart attack, spring, nineteen forty-four. Invalid seven years. Died Christmas Day, nineteen fifty-one." She looked up. "He was up and down," she said, "not bedridden the whole time. And he was *cheerful*. Jack helped me, but it was *my* responsibility. Everybody knows . . ."

"Come along, Mrs. Crane," Howie said again. "Your things are all in your own room and everyone is waiting for you to come home."

"Three years, seven months," she said, "plus six months, plus seven years. That's a total of eleven years and a month. And now they throw me on the city dump."

"They want you to be happy with us, dear lady," Howie said. "And you can be, if only you'll relax."

She turned on him a look of fierce enmity. "You're in with them, too," she said.

But then, without reason, as it seemed, she allowed herself to be led out to the car and taken back to Golden Age.

For some weeks she was docile, but in April she began, in another paroxysm of suspicion, to look for lost and stolen possessions, and almost daily stirred the contents of her room into chaos. One morning at breakfast, shortly after the general shift in patients' room assignments, she got up from the table, picked up a glass of water, and threw it at Howie, who was sitting across the table from her. "I'm *here!*" she shouted. "You can take my things, but you can't erase *me.*"

Howie, always an agile man, dodged, and the glass shattered on the floor. "Dear lady . . . !" he said.

"I'll kill you! If you keep on taking my things, I'll kill you!"

The old people, eating their breakfasts at two round chromium-plated and plastic-topped tables in the spacious high-ceilinged dining room, fell for a moment into astonished silence. Mrs. Cathcart, as soft and plump and wrinkled as a stuffed pussy cat, looked at her plate and mechanically lifted her fork, as if she could not bear to be a witness to this painful crisis in Mrs. Crane's life. Miss Rebecca Steinman, a Jewish spinster with sharp old eyes as merry and curious and malicious as a child's, chuckled. "Look out, there, Howie," she muttered. "It's a dangerous world." The Strange twins in their wheelchairs nodded knowingly at each other and pushed themselves back from their table to get a better view of the scene. "Well, well," said one. And the other, "Here, here." Mrs. Aldridge, a tall, wispy old lady, slender and shy as a night heron, got up and with the help of a cane made her way out of the dining room.

Martha rose and dropped her napkin on her plate. "Ethel," she said, "let me . . ." Lucas too got up.

But before either of them could cross the room Mrs. Crawley, who was sitting at the table with Howie and Mrs. Crane and the Stranges, got up from her place and took Mrs. Crane by the arm.

"Now, honey," she said. "Now, Ethel, we ain't going to act like that, hmmm? Are we? Why, old Crawley thought it was a baby in here having a temper tantrum. But Ethel is a *big* girl."

Mrs. Crane shook her arm loose and looked all around the room. She gazed at the Willard clock sitting silent on the mantelpiece and at the wall above it where two calendar landscapes, two pictures, of huge-eyed children and one of a family of dogs such as usually hangs on the wall of a veterinarian's office, had replaced the portrait of an early Griswold that had once hung there; at the chrome and plastic tables; at the metal food cart which stood where the walnut sideboard had once been. Then she looked at Martha. "You've lost your things, too, haven't you?" she said. "Don't you know there's a *meaning* in it?"

But, as abruptly as the rage had shaken her, it subsided. She crossed the room, followed by Mrs. Crawley and stopped in the doorway. "You can go on telling people I'm crazy if you like," she said to Howie. "It seems to make Arthur and Marian feel better." She looked at Mrs. Crawley. "Don't say another word to me and don't touch me," she said. "I'm going to my room now. I won't inconvenience you people any further."

She sat quietly all morning in her room, came out without protest for lunch, and afterward sat by the window in the sun parlor and gazed out into the back garden, pale green now and blue and golden with the wild phlox and daffodils of early spring. She was alone there. Lucas, wearing a light windbreaker against the damp, was striding up and down the garden walk. The other old people had gone to their rooms for after-lunch naps or were watching "As the World Turns" on their own TV sets. Howie had gone off to do the week's grocery shopping; and Harper was helping Ruby clear up the dishes in the kitchen.

It happened only by chance that Lucas, at the far end of the walk, as he turned to tramp back toward the garage, glanced up and saw her standing, her long gaunt body clearly visible through the glass, an expression of serious resolution on her face, her cane raised above her head in both hands and swung back above her shoulder very much as a baseball player holds a bat. He had time only to think: What in the world is she doing?

Is she going to knock the glass out? and to take one long stride before she brought the cane forward and, awkwardly but with considerable force, swung it around and struck herself in the head, just above the ear. The first blow staggered her, but she struck again, and then a third time before the long skinny legs buckled and she fell to the brick floor of the gallery. By that time Lucas was running toward the house.

She lay crumpled on the floor like a bundle of sticks haphazardly covered with a piece of faded cotton print. Lucas felt her pulse, gently palpated the lumps already beginning to rise on her head, opened her eyes one after the other, and looked into them, and then called Harper. Together the two men carried her to her room and laid her on the bed; then Lucas covered her with a wool throw which lay at the foot of the bed. He stood looking at her for a few minutes.

"She had pneumonia five years ago," he said in a low voice. "I remember when she was in the hospital. If it had been nineteen forty she would have died of it." He glanced at Harper. "To watch someone suffer and almost die, so as to be able to watch him suffer more and die more slowly a few years later — that's what makes a man prefer wood-chopping to medicine."

Mrs. Crane moaned, stirred, and raised her hand to her head without opening her eyes. Harper's thin yellow face had on it an expression of impersonal compassion. He said nothing.

"Did you see what happened?" Lucas asked.

Harper shook his head.

"Well, now what?" Lucas said. "First, I'd better call Arthur Crane."

"You better . . ." Harper hesitated. Then almost in spite of himself, as it seemed, he said. "Mr. Snyder ought to be here in a little, Dr. Alexander. We could wait a few minutes and . . ."

Lucas looked curiously at him and started to speak, but at that moment they heard the sound of Howie's car slewing the gravel on the driveway. Lucas called Mrs. Crawley to stay in the room and the two men set off together toward the back of the house, Harper to unload and put away the groceries and Lucas to tell Howie what had happened.

"I don't believe she's done any more than give herself a slight concussion," he said. "But after you call Arthur you'd better take her to the hospital, if you want to play it safe, and get an X ray." They were standing in the kitchen talking while Harper moved about putting away cans and packages.

"Bad business, bad business," Howie muttered. "Imagine doing a damn fool thing like that. She's plumb nutty." He drummed impatiently on the tabletop with strong blunt fingers. "Very depressing effect on the others, if it gets out. Can't . . ." He broke off and gave Lucas a queer look. "Where did you say you were when it happened?"

"I was walking — out in the back. Just happened to look up and see her standing there swinging that cane like she was getting ready to drive one over the fence."

"And Harper?"

Harper crumpled a brown paper bag and dropped it in the trash. "I didn't hear a thing," he said. "Back here with the water running."

"She probably lost her balance," Howie said. "Hit her head on the floor."

"What?"

"I expect she lost her balance," Howie said again firmly.

"I *saw* her hit herself in the head with the cane," Lucas said. "Not once but three times. But you're right about one thing, Howie. There's no reason for any of the others to know anything about it — it's none of their business. And Arthur and his wife already know what condition she's in. It can't come as any shock to them."

Howie continued to frown.

"You should probably get her out of here," Lucas said. "You aren't equipped . . ."

"Who is?" Howie abruptly asked. "And besides, you could have made a mistake, Doc. Your eyes probably ain't as good as they once were. Truth is, I hate to distress her folks with a miserable tale like that. What's the point in it? And I don't want it to get out in town. I'll just tell Marian Crane that . . ."

"Take it from me," Lucas said, "you'd better get Mrs. Crane down to the hospital and get her checked over — to protect yourself and the home, if nothing else. And you'd better tell Arthur about it, not Marian. And tell him exactly what happened. You don't tell folks the truth and you're going to end up with trouble."

Howie did not seem to be listening. "Maybe her doctor would step up the amount of Demerol she gets," he said, "and try something with it besides Librium. That might settle her hash."

"Howie," Lucas said, "I'd be cautious about getting doctors to prescribe addictive drugs for these people, even when they're willing. It sounds like a good way to keep an unruly patient quiet and happy, and there are a few men in town who'll prescribe them pretty indiscriminately, but sometimes it backfires. You end up with more trouble than you had to begin with. Besides," he added, "they have a right to stay in charge of their own brains."

"Doc, you're so *conservative*," Howie said. "But I just can't stand to see these folks suffer. Why they're like my own children to me."

When Arthur Crane and his wife came to Golden Age later

that afternoon, at Howie's call, the old lady was conscious. A doctor had seen her, found evidence of a slight concussion, and told Howie to keep her in bed for a day or two.

"She fell," Howie told them. "Out in the sun parlor back there, overlooking the garden. We're not sure exactly how it happened. Harper had left her there after lunch, just enjoying the afternoon sun, and Dr. Alexander was in the garden." He shook his head sadly.

They were in the dining room just outside Howie's study door during this conversation. Harper and Mrs. Crawley moved in and out of the room, laying the tables for supper. Lucas was standing on the other side of the room in front of the mantel-piece, gently shifting the old pendulum clock from one spot to another — he had been tinkering with it for days, putting new cords on the weights, oiling and adjusting its works, and now he was attempting to level it; but the house had settled and the mantel had buckled over the years, so that he was having considerable difficulty.

Howie called to him. "Hey, Doc, the Cranes are here. The doc kinda thought he saw her waving her cane around her head like she'd lost her balance," he said, "like she might be trying to catch herself, you know, and . . . Well, that floor out there is brick, of course, and she had a nasty fall."

Lucas slipped a dime under one foot of the clock, gave the pendulum a push, and then turned to join the group. "Arthur," he said, "Howie is trying to soften it for you a bit, make it easier on you, because he's . . . kindhearted. But I did see it all quite clearly. Your mother struck herself on the head with her cane — deliberately. Not once, but three times."

Harper put the last knife and fork in place and left the room. Mrs. Crawley, idly rearranging the silver, watched Lucas's and Howie's faces, watched Harper go, and after a moment followed him into the pantry. "What do you think about all that?" she said in a low voice.

Harper shrugged. "Like I told Mr. Snyder, I didn't see it happen." He hesitated and then, as if he felt he should add something, "Poor old lady."

"Ain't you the cautious one!"

"I'll go bring in the paper, ma'am, if you want me to. I just remembered I left some of my tools out."

Crawley laughed. "O.K. O.K."

In the dining room Marian Crane had taken her husband's arm and moved forward a step, as if to protect him. A tightly corseted, rumpy little woman with stubby hands and feet like small hoofs, she looked as skittish and ready to kick out as an ill-tempered Shetland pony. "Really, Dr. Alexander!" she said. "Really, that's fantastic."

"Deliberately?" Arthur Crane said. He gazed at Lucas out of soft brown eyes and cleared his throat nervously. "You mean she was trying to kill herself or something?"

"You know, she's been pretty disturbed ever since she got here," Lucas said.

"Dr. Alexander, my mother is disturbed, no matter where she is."

"The doc may be mistaken," Howie said. "It all happened so quick. Or maybe I misunderstood what he said earlier."

Mrs. Crane seemed to relax. "Golden Age is so lovely," she said to Howie. "I *know* it's the right place for Mother Crane. After all, she has friends here. Marie Aldridge — and of course Martha, too. Old friends. And the garden is so lovely. Once she makes the adjustment . . ."

"She's doing great," Howie said. "We get her on the right combination of tranquilizers, everything's going to be fine."

As the Cranes closed the front door behind them, Howie

smiled his whiskery smile at Lucas and clapped him on the shoulder. The rusty freckles stood out like scars on his face and arms. "You let me down, Doc," he said genially. "I mean, when I was just trying to avoid unpleasantness. What good does it do to tell a man such an unpleasant thing about his poor old mother, huh? Now it ain't right for you to let me down like that, is it? I need your *help*."

"A grown man deserves the truth," Lucas said stiffly. He turned back toward the mantel where the pendulum of the old clock was no longer moving. "In any case, I'm too old to start lying," he said. "So don't depend on me."

Outside, the Cranes started in silence down the long front walk. Then Arthur paused and stood looking back at the old house that seemed now to be melting into the twilight grove of moss-hung trees and dark vines. Marian took his arm and turned him back toward the street.

Halfway down the walk they passed Harper, who was coming toward them with the evening paper in his hand. He nodded and spoke their names courteously, but they passed him by as if he were invisible.

"Lucas Alexander has always been a little bit queer," Marian said, "and now he's getting old on top of it. Hit herself on the head, indeed! That's ridiculous, Arthur. Why, it's probably even *impossible*. And obviously Howie Snyder doesn't believe it happened that way."

"No, he didn't seem to agree with Lucas, did he?" Arthur said.

They passed under the arching cane and down the brick steps. Arthur opened the car door for his wife and stood absently watching her get in, groping at the same time for the car keys in his trousers pocket. Then he sighed. "Poor old miserable Mother," he said. He got into the car on his side and sat for a few minutes with his hands on the steering wheel. Then he sighed again. At last he turned the ignition switch and started the car. "Where to?" he said.

"We might stop by to see the Carters, if you like," his wife said. "They'd probably give us a drink and cheer us up."

They drove away toward the noise and flash of traffic at the end of Clarke Street, where the street intersected with the four-lane by-pass inside which the town of Homochitto nestled like the eye inside a hurricane. Behind them the street was quiet and empty of traffic. The old houses, gray with age and dust, sank back into their straggly yards and drew about them the obliterating night.

In the garden at Golden Age Matthew Harper gathered his tools and, loading them into his wheelbarrow, trundled them back to the toolshed behind the house, where he put everything methodically away. Then he went into the kitchen and handed the paper to Mrs. Crawley, who stood leaning against the counter whistling softly and watching him as he put on his starched white waiter's jacket and began to help Ruby serve the supper. He filled the plates and carried them in to the round tables in the dining room, his face, out of the habit and discipline of years, quiet and expressionless. But he felt Mrs. Crawley's unfocused stare as keenly as if she had dragged across his shoulders the jagged edge of a broken knife blade.

CHAPTER 7

MATTHEW HARPER'S VIEW of himself and his role in the complex world he lived in was modest; but it was as self-confident as the view of an old bass that flicks its tail and looks out upon its own deep pool, the wily survivor of a dozen years of outwitting gar and snakes and cats and coons and fishermen. "I'm *lucky*," he had said again and again in his life, not only to himself, but aloud to his four grandchildren. "I know how to be lucky, and I intend to teach you, the way it was taught me. I can always turn my hand to something I care about doing, and that makes work play even when it wears you to the bone. That's the biggest part of luck. Sometimes," he would say, "a man is not resourceful enough or lucky enough to make even a dime with what he cares about doing; and sometimes he doesn't learn how to care about doing things. But my mama knew that secret — how to care about doing things — and my luck probably begins in having that particular mama.

"I favor her," he would say to the children. "I have the Mandingo features like she had." Harper would be sitting during these conversations by the fire in the small house across the bayou from the Clarke house where he lived with his four grandchildren; and he might be caning a chair — a job that he took great pleasure in, because, as he put it, it takes some skill and it turns out to be pretty as well as useful, but at the same time it leaves room in your mind for thinking or for talking. He would be leaning over the chair seat, weaving the withes of wet cane in and out of the design, watching his work with a skilled and alert and critical eye, the firelight and lamplight giving his skin a golden cast and throwing shifting shadows on his long attentive face, whose features (flat nose, firm wide mouth, and large brown eyes) were composed in the absorbed expression of the working craftsman.

"Now, listen," he would say. "Some people might think I'm making that up about Mandingo, because it's rare that one of our people knows the tribe his ancestors came from. But the fact is, my mother's grandfather *knew* he was Mandingo. He came from Africa and he was as light as I am. He lived to be ninety-seven years old and I myself saw him when I was a child. That's where our skin comes from, see? Not from white. We have no blood from white men. But the Mandingo are a light-skinned people. I got it, and you, Andrew, and you, Matt; Lucy and Gertrude favor their daddy's family more. Now these are things you children ought to remember," he would say. "It's a good thing to remember where you came from and who your people were. It's just one more aid in this torn-up world to keeping your head screwed on.

"If you don't know where you came from, you won't know where your caves are," he would say, "and if people are going to survive, they've got to keep track of their hiding places." He would look from one to another of the children's solemn listening faces. "That's another thing," he would add. "Hiding places. We all need to have hiding places and we all need to learn how to disappear in this world. That's part of learning how to be lucky." Thus he talked to them winter evenings before his fire and summer evenings sitting on his little front porch, hidden by a screen of morning glory and queen's wreath vines from the westering sun and the busy street.

Sometimes they listened and sometimes, impatient to be off, they stood on one foot and then on the other, and at the first pause dashed down the steps and away. "O.K., Grandpa. O.K."

"Wait now," he would say. "I'm not through." Or, "You better *listen* to me, now. I *know* . . ."

Harper was a self-educated man — a passionate reader who had learned to read before he went to school, from the newspapers that papered the walls and served as insulation in his first home. He had not gone much to school until he had moved into Homochitto from the country when he was ten, but his mother was a house servant; she could read and figure, and she helped him with his lessons and, looking to his future, taught him the manners and customs and speech of white people.

He had cultivated from the time he was fifteen (big for his age and with his voice already deep in his chest) the formality of manner and precision of pronunciation that made white people have an unusual confidence in him. It was as if they felt he was born to be a butler. That year (when he was fifteen) he got his first job, chasing a pair of four-year-old twin boys and waiting on table in the house where his mother cooked. He never afterward had trouble keeping a job, even during the Depression, although it is true that from 1932 until 1937 he earned only seven dollars a week — plus meals, uniforms, and take-homes. But he never went hungry, any more than his mother or his father had before him. His job was a front, insurance against notice — one of his "caves." If anyone wanted to know what Matt Harper did, he was the Calhouns' houseboy and his mother (or, later, his wife) was the Calhouns' cook. Or the Aldridges' or the Griswolds' or whomever he happened to have chosen as protector for the moment. His other activities were screened by the conventionality of his daytime life and he was free to use his off hours unremarked. No threat, Harper. No one would dream that he might step out of line. But in truth he had cultivated a couple of questionable skills with which he turned a penny here and there. Sometimes he boot-legged, making corn whiskey in an old still that his mother and father had brought in from the country when they moved. If the sheriff was friendly and relaxed and protection not too ex-pensive, there would be four prosperous years for the family. In a reform term he would turn to other things. He was an astute and cautious gambler and could always earn a few dol-lars in an evening's game of blackjack or bourrée. He caned chairs for a select white clientele. He sold surplus produce from his garden. Before the neighborhood he lived in was taken into the city, he sometimes raised a few pigs and chickens and sold the eggs and the piglets.

He never advertised his skill at caning, relying instead on his connections in the white community to bring him a little bus-iness now and then. He even thought sometimes as he grew older that caning was becoming such a rare skill it was perhaps a mistake to keep on with it. It made him too outstanding.

For Harper was a man to whom obscurity was vital — he did not wish to be remarked upon. And to a degree, he would tell the children, it was a flaw in him that he could not resist ac-quiring a skill. (It might be better for all of them, for example, if his homebrew were only barely drinkable instead of the best in south Mississippi.) It was for the sake of their future ob-scurity that he taught none of the grandchildren how to cane, although he did teach them, for other reasons, such old-fashioned crafts as whiskey- and wine-making, gardening, and meat-curing, among other things.

It is not surprising when a black man recognizes and acts upon the principle that obscurity is valuable — Harper had certainly learned it from his mother and father. But it was his own thoughtfulness that led him to codify his convictions, so to speak, and to be obsessed with passing them on to his child and his grandchildren.

His reading had brought him to the hobby from which came his convictions about obscurity and the history — not to mention the *future* — of the human race. He had happened one day when he was a man in his thirties on an article in one of the discarded magazines that he regularly took home from his job (at the Griswolds' now) — an article on Charles Leonard Woolley's excavation of the royal tombs at Ur of the Chaldees. There, he learned, an inconceivably long time ago, not a hundred or a thousand years, but two thousand years before the birth of Christ, a millennium before Abraham wandered in the desert and journeyed down from Ur into Egypt; there, in the very cradle of the human world, men had raised their first city heavenward out of the plains and forests of earth. The evidence of its existence still lay under the desert sun, under mounds of earth that the years had laid down above it; and the evidence was not only in stone and brick walls, in broken pots and clay tablets, but in the bodies of the people who had lived there.

Fascinated, he read how at that place on some immeasurably distant day in the past, a king had died — had died or had been ceremonially murdered according to the ritual practice of the religion he and his people lived by. How he had gone or been carried down into a huge, vaulted, brick-lined tomb, followed by all his court: his queen, wearing her crown of gold and

carnelian and lapis lazuli and her great lunate golden earrings;
the ladies in waiting dressed in scarlet robes with gold and silver
ribbons in their hair; the courtiers with their bronze swords at
their sides; the servants and chariot drivers. How they had all
lain quietly down to die, side by side in crowded but orderly
rows, their jewels and badges of office in place, had lain down in
the very spot where they still lay — the driver in the chariot; the
groom at the oxen's heads, his finger bones among the crumbling
bits of reins; the court musician, the bones of his arms crossed
protectively over the remains of his golden bull-headed harp.

Harper was thunderstruck. It had never before crossed his
mind that men were willing — eager, as it appeared — to be
victims, to die without reason at the hands of other men who
were equally eager to kill them; to abandon, not the miserable,
tormented life of a slave, a near beast, but the rich and joyous,
ceremonious and powerful world of king and courtier, warrior
and priest.

But there it was, the very earliest record of a true civilization, a great city, left not in terms of exhilaration at having come
out of the forest, off the harsh plains, but in murder, the murder
of the very flower of a kingdom.

Until he read this article, Harper had thought of his own
life and of the lives and misfortunes of his people, as the result
of more immediate and alterable causes than human nature; of,
that is, the industrial revolution and the need for cheap labor;
of the insanity of frightened, greedy, and evil men under the
pressure of outlandish circumstances — all causes that the passage of time and a new economic and political climate were
changing, so that eventually black people would be able to take
their chances in the world under the same conditions as white
people. He never thought that way again.

He began, shortly after he read the article on Ur, to study

murder, to collect atrocities. He totted up the score of bodies, read of the variety of means men used to kill each other. And, as the years passed, he became more and more firmly convinced that the time might — *would* — come when he or his child, and later, after his daughter's death, the grandchildren for whom he was responsible, would need all their brains and skills and instincts and knowledge of the past to act sensibly — to survive.

He read how the soldiers of Genghis Khan had in a week murdered one million six hundred thousand inhabitants of the city of Herat in Afghanistan. He mulled over that figure for days; and years later, when he read of the extermination of the Jews in Europe, he thought of it again. It had taken Hitler four years to murder six million Jews. The great Khan had killed more than a million and a half people in a few days. Even if one halved the number or quartered it, to make allowances for the exaggerations of ancient chroniclers, it was staggering. He could scarcely take it in. *How?* How was it even physically possible? It seemed to him that the soldiers, no matter how dedicated, would have grown too weary for the work, their sword hands blistered, their blades dulled. No blood frenzy this (for frenzy, he thought, could last at most only a few hours — hardly longer than sexual passion), but the routine job of a soldier, taken up every morning after reveille, as routine as the scalding deaths of chickens in the local poultry plant.

And how many soldiers had it taken to kill that many men? Even if they had gone at their work with a will?

Harper had already, in his younger days, acquainted himself with the history of his own people. He knew before he began his study of murder that forty million men had died on their way to the slave-operated plantations of the new world. He had studied the diagrams of ships showing how many living bodies could be stuffed into a hold of such and such proportions, and how many would survive the trip across the ocean. (Less than half under poor circumstances: if the ship were becalmed and the water ran low, or if the captain were unusually cruel, or if smallpox broke out. None perhaps, if the slaver were caught by patrol boats and had to throw his chain-weighted cargo overboard to avoid detection.) He had mulled over the interesting notion that, given half as many bodies with the same amount of space and food, the slaver would have had as much or more and healthier livestock to deliver to the market. Here, too, the killing must have been in part gratuitous, even inconvenient and unpleasant, and the profits reduced by the policies of the slaver.

He had read, too, of lynching. He did not rely for his knowledge of this subject on the lynchings in his lifetime in Homochitto County, although like any good black parents, his mother and father had told him of these, and, like most black men his age, he numbered at least one victim among his own acquaintances. But he pursued the subject in his precise pedantic way, and he knew that 2954 black men had — as a matter of record — been lynched in the United States between 1889 and 1932, some mercifully hanged or shot, some mutilated and tortured and beaten or burned to death. God alone knew how many unrecorded there were.

But these studies Harper had undertaken before he read of Ur of the Chaldees. Afterward he fitted them into a larger framework.

As the years passed, story followed story into the series of notebooks that he began to keep: the extermination of the kulaks by the Bolsheviks in the execution of the first five-year plan; the massacre of the Armenians by the Turks after the First World War; and then, rising like an uncontrollable flood, the savage slaughter of the late thirties and the forties — the "final solution" of the Jewish question, the massacres of Babi Yar and the Katyn Forest, the fire-bombing of Dresden, and at last Hiroshima. A high watermark in the bloody course of human history? He doubted it. But still, in the years that followed 1945, the slaughter was less spectacular. Mau Mau killed Englishmen and Englishmen killed Mau Mau, drill sergeants killed Marine recruits, white Southerners killed black Southerners, Americans killed Koreans and Vietnamese, and Koreans and Vietnamese killed each other. Ordinary men killed their wives and children, or, like the fellow on the clock tower at the University of Texas, they killed random and anonymous strangers.

He had thought, when he read of the liberation of the concentration camps at the end of the Second World War that, for the obscurity of its causes, for sheer numbers, and for the incredible docility of the victims (numbered and turned in by their rabbis, standing in line for their turn in the gas chamber; even, obedient to the last, digging their own graves), the slaughter of the Jews must be the greatest and most interesting of all the murders in modern times; but then, a few years later, he came upon the history of the Belgian colonization of the Congo — less complex, perhaps, in terms of causes, but more staggering in numbers.

Like any complacent white man, Harper had, until he read this dark tale, thought of Africa as an almost empty continent, peopled by wandering tribes of primitive people. He read with astonishment that there had been nearly 40 million people in the Congo basin when the Belgians had "colonized" it. Twenty years later, all but 11 million were dead — starved to death, worked to death, beaten to death, *murdered* by their colonizers.

Harper puzzled long and strenuously over these horrible events. Had the killers been no more than hired hands, like the hit men of the modern Mafia, who, he read, looked upon their work as a business like any other business? And, if this were true, how was it possible that human business could include as one of its commonplaces the perpetration of mass murder? Had the businessmen taken from their work the kind of satisfaction that he felt in a good batch of homebrew or a chair well caned? And the victims: would he be so gullible as they?

Harper was careful to explain to his grandchildren when he talked to them about these serious matters that one should not make the mistake of believing, because one reads the paper and hears the daily news on the TV, that men are readier in modern times to murder one another than they have always been. He opened his Bible and, turning the pages, pointed out the words that caught his eye:

"And they slew of Moab at that time about ten thousand men . . . and there escaped not a man."

". . . and the Lord delivered the Canaanites and the Perizzites into their hand . . ."

". . . Shamgar, son of Anath, which slew of the Philistines six hundred men with an oxgoad . . ."

And he read and explained to them as they grew older the theories of anthropologists regarding the connection between human sacrifice and human and vegetable fertility. How men had once believed that the blood of sacrificial victims fell upon the soil and made it fruitful, while the victims returned to their ancestors — to some form of immortality.

He recognized, of course, that there were supposed to be categories of murder — that the ceremonial burials of a king and his court or the willingness of Abraham to plunge a knife into his son's breast, were classified by men as different phenomena from the annihilation for practical reasons of the population of a rebellious city, of the Jews of Europe, or from the lynching of black men like himself. But in his own mind he found the distinction not only unclear but, from the point of view of the victims, irrelevant. He reasoned, for example, that the priestly caste of an early civilization profited as much and as little from the system it supported as Hitler's lieutenants profited from the "final solution"; and, on the other hand, that the lynch mobs of the South might have considered, probably did consider, themselves participants in a sacred ceremony that safeguarded the purity of their blood lines and the chastity of their women and perhaps even contributed to the fertility of the soil.

It might seem from the attention Harper lavished on these abysses of human nature that he was himself about to become the kind of victim or killer that he kept obsessively reading about. But his interest was as objective as the interest of a mathematician in the process of constructing and solving a problem. He knew himself to be on the brink of drawing from all these scattered facts an insight valid not only for him but for all men.

He sat on the porch of his little house during the long summer evenings when, until seven or eight o'clock, it would still be possible to read by the waning summer twilight, and held his books and magazines close to his nose and his nearsighted eyes, sniffing out like a hound after a fox gone to ground the trail of his quarry. The four-o'clocks growing by his stoop breathed out their heady perfume; the last bees tumbled drunkenly in the cups of the althea blossoms that gleamed pale lavender in the tree at the corner of the yard; in the spider web that stretched between the spindles of his porch railing a captured fly wearily buzzed and beat its wings; his grandchildren and the neighbor children scrambled up and down the steep steps that led up the banked hillside to his house, counting and dashing in the frenzied haste of a game of red light; and he read on, the books sometimes dropping to his lap as he fell into thought or copied into his notebook some sentence that he wanted to remember, or imagined himself into the circumstances of the people he read about.

The practice of imagining himself into the shoes of a victim might someday be useful to him, he thought, just as the practice of imagining himself into the circumstances of a wreck (rehearsing the turning off of the ignition and throwing oneself onto the floor of the car) might one day be useful to the driver of an automobile.

He went back often in his mind during these ruminations to the royal tomb at Ur of the Chaldees, to the ladies in waiting and warriors lying down in orderly rows, to the court musician and groom and charioteer. He saw himself on the day of the funeral rites, standing under the shimmering white light of a summer sky among the train of courtiers and servants, waiting his turn to go down into the vaulted tomb. He held the bridle of the ox as it moved its head to look inquiringly around at him; and the gold bells on the bridle flashed in the sun and tinkled softly, a thin random song. The cold breath of the open grave touched his face. He saw himself young, not more than twenty, dressed in the harness and badges of his rank, waiting for death.

How had it happened? Had he been seduced by priests and even by his parents into the belief that a short and glittering life and an eternity in some equally glittering court of the underworld was better than siring children, better than planting and gathering good harvests and bad for the full span of a lifetime and sleeping at last in the anonymous shallow grave of a slave or a peasant? Did he have children already, and, if so, how did they manage to survive the loss of their father? Perhaps, he allowed himself to think, a crafty old grandfather had raised them.

And at the last, once the young groom found himself trapped, the mouth of the dark vaulted chamber yawning before him; once the full understanding of his fate dawned on him, would there still have been some way to escape? There was one detail that Harper had read in his article, of a lady in waiting whose silver badge of rank, instead of being bound about the crumbling skull as it was with the other ladies, was rolled up in its silver ribbon and still clutched by the finger bones in the pocket of her robe. Her body, too, was not disposed serenely in its place like the others, but lay crouched near the sealed-up entrance to the tomb. She, perhaps, among all those buried there, had not consented to her fate, had hidden the talisman of rank, and, slipping back into the crowd, had not drunk her drugged death cup with the others. She had meant to escape. Perhaps she *had* escaped, and then at the last moment had been caught and thrust down among the rest — awake for how many days among all those sleepers? Harper was sure that he would never *never* have ended up in that brick-lined trench, stretching his neck and opening his silly lips to the poison like a baby bird for a worm, and as if he had no more brains than the ox. He would have tried like the girl and he would have succeeded.

For the insight that he groped toward, the synthesis into one coherent whole of all these disparate facts about how people die and why they die, did come to him in the course of time; and he built it into his life and began to try to build it into the life of his child and later into the lives of his grandchildren.

First, he said to himself, at some time in the past, maybe even before he learned how to make a fire to warm himself, a man looked at the body of his mate or his child torn by the claws of a tiger or trampled by a mammoth or starved to death in the winter of an approaching glacial age, and he said, *I, too, must die. I will not be anymore. The world will go on without me.* He became a man that day — not with the knowledge of the use of tools, not with the discovery of fire, not with the acquisition of language, but *that* day, when he learned that he would die.

Harper came to believe with all his heart that it was the knowledge of death that led men to kill each other. Of course, he said to himself, I know men die every day for love or vengeance or power; but *this*, this gratuitous killing and dying comes out of illusion: the illusion that by choosing death for himself or for someone else, a man can transcend his fate, can give the lie to his own helplessness when Death chooses him.

The priest who fertilized the earth with the blood of his victim, the killers of Jews and black men, the destroyers of cities, all, had been moved at some deep place in their souls by the illusion that they could control the Killer by standing in his place. Even the great conquerors, the Genghis Khans and Alexanders, he was convinced, had acted, not, as they themselves may have believed, out of necessity or love of power or intoxication with their own strength, but out of their fury and outrage, greater than the fury and outrage of ordinary men, at their helplessness before the One finally greater and more terrible than they.

Harper was carried away by the profundity of his insight. It lifted him out of the blind alley of race and into a larger humanity, because with it he stopped thinking of the black man as victim and began to think instead of the fate of all men. His insight, curious and tragic though it was, filled him with greater joy than he had ever felt before — at his marriage or the birth of his child or at any of those natural events that had given him most joy: the blooming of his roses or the perfection of the very best homebrew he ever made. And he pursued his insight and began to classify men and experiences in its light.

He divided men into categories according to how they lived

with the knowledge of death, and he decided that there had always been four kinds of people. The first were those — murderer and murdered — who had organized and over thousands of years had continued to perpetuate this game — the believers: conquerors and heroes, martyrs and saints and inquisitors, high-minded and imaginative men, who gave their own deaths (or their victims'), as they believed, in the name of life. Then there was that crawling tangle of vermin who profited by murder and always expected to stay clear of it — the ticket venders at public hangings, the makers and sellers of better poisons, the despoilers of corpses. There were the muddleheaded, the stupid, those who blundered from one side to the other without ever having a notion of what they were doing, always hoping vaguely to be safe, expecting something other than what they got, filled with outrage and self-pity when they were finally and irretrievably cast in the role either of killer or of victim; those who died saying, I don't understand what's going on. Or, Why me?

Finally, Harper thought, there were the celebrators of life, men like himself, who by wit and wile and strength and caution and silence and cowardice and industry and luck and love lived out their lives, begat their children, held in their arms their grandchildren and great-grandchildren, and over these same millennia kept the human race from wiping itself out. Those who had looked into the face of death, had seen the vision of their own bodies lying swollen and rotting in the grave, and had chosen to live without illusion, to cane chairs and raise children, to be fully human, joyful, to subsume their anguish under their humanity. This, he thought, is the peculiarly human nobility, the courage of every man who day by day lives in joy and anguish with his death.

I'm not going to find those people in the history books and

the magazine articles, Harper thought. Any more than I could expect to open *Time* magazine and find a picture of myself. Not likely. But they've always been around, just as sure as I'm sitting here on my front porch tonight smelling these four-o'clocks and hearing those children yell *Red light*. It amused him, in fact, to think to himself exactly where people like him might have been and how they might have acted under particular sets of circumstances. He thought of the lives of peaceful families lived out in the waning days of the Roman Empire, when emperors were murdered every year, when armies slaughtered each other and savage Goths and Vandals roamed the countryside as freely as the sheriff's deputies now roamed Homochitto County. Certainly those Roman farmers, a great many of them, had managed to survive and to insure the survival of their children in spite of armies and emperors. Because, he thought, that's who all these Italians are descended from.

Now then, he would say to himself, absently watching the last convulsive flicker of the fly's wing against the confining web, How did they manage? Some of them would have had protectors — local big shots (like the Aldridges or Newton Clarke in Homochitto) who looked after their own people. But big shots don't always make it either; bigger shots come along and, *blam*, there's your protection lying in a ditch with his brains blown out. So they would have had a second and even a third line of defense. They would have had places to hide — places with supplies for a few days maybe, water and food and all, maybe even seeds and so forth for the next spring's planting, so they could keep out of the way. Let 'em burn your house, if it had to be, and then come out afterward and start over again. He thought of caves in the hillsides close by the farmhouses, like the storm cellars to which farmers in the tornado belt fled when they saw a twister coming.

But they'd have to do better than that, he thought, if they really wanted to make it.

And then one day he read with delight of the Etruscan tombs under the fields of Italy — how for thousands of years they had lain there, low mounds in the fields of grain and the kitchen gardens of peasant homesteads, plowed over season after season, as invisible as if they did not exist, but concealing snug stone chambers beneath the earth. *That's where they hid!* He was delighted with the notion. He imagined his peasant family hearing the approach of the soldiers and looters, saw them slip silently down under the mound and roll a stone or pull sod over the entrance and sit there, hands on the mouths of crying babies, while cavalry and foot soldiers clashed in battle above their heads and fires licked at the sides of their home; saw them as they waited in the cool earth-smelling darkness, hold up a flickering candle to look at the painted figures dancing in procession around the tomb walls, the flute players, their fingers delicately poised on the stops of a double flute, the graceful women, their faces framed in dark ringlets, arms raised heavenward and bodies draped in transparent chitons and robes of blue and gold; the bearded men reclining at the feast with kraters of wine at their sides. The candles flared and guttered and his frightened peasants gazed about them, scarcely even wondering who these mysterious dancers were, or perhaps thinking that they were images of the very gods who had built these hidden vaults for the protection of peasants and had kept the knowledge of them from bloodthirsty Huns. Yes, he thought, even tombs can have their uses for a resourceful man.

But it seems, he thought then, as if *we*, if we're that resourceful and cautious and brave and all, as if we would be on the increase and *they*, running around above our heads all these years crazily killing each other by the millions, would be on the decrease. Natural selection ought to be working for us. But such doesn't appear to be the case. On the contrary, it looks like they're on the increase instead of us. That the chances of everybody getting wiped altogether *out* are better all the time.

But it's not a question of genes and chromosomes, he said to himself, and that's where the difficulty lies. If you could breed the knowledge of death and the hatred of death out of a man, you'd have to be breeding him into unconsciousness (unless you could breed him into reproducing by dividing, like an amoeba) and, if he was unconscious, that would mean he wasn't a man anymore. Every one of us have got to be capable of that knowledge and that dread, and then we've got to act on it according to our own lights. Every gene that makes a piece of a human being is bound to have death and the knowledge of death sitting right in the middle of it. And I could just as easily have a child or a grandchild that would need to drown the knowledge in blood as the next man.

But Harper made himself profoundly uneasy with such arid fatalism and, in his life, he paid no attention to his own conclusions. Instead, he tried to teach his daughter and later, his grandchildren to live like the heroes he admired: like the Italian peasants who survived the marauding armies of the Huns, like the Jews in the sewers of Warsaw, like Ulysses clinging to the wool under the belly of Polyphemus's sheep, like Brer Rabbit, crying, "Fo' God, Brer Fox, *please* don't th'ow me in the briar patch."

And he explained to them that he and they lived in a time of testing for mankind.

"Not just for us," he would say. "Don't get mixed up because we live *where* we live and *how* we live and think the testing is for black people alone. Black people have an advantage in it, like the Jews ought to have had an advantage against Hitler (although as it turned out they didn't) because survival had always been their business. But this time it's different. Everybody in the world that cares about being human has got to start thinking about surviving — got to get their minds right about death."

It gave Harper the greatest satisfaction to talk of these matters to his grandchildren. "It's coming," he would say, almost joyfully. "Maybe not in my time but in yours." And then he would go on to explain to them all the fascinating things they would need to know: how to make bread and cure meat, how to catch fish and find salt, how to treat boils and midwife babies; how to make a cave and how to live in one; how to be invisible in a town full of people; and how, if it proved necessary, to keep a government, a whole society, from even knowing you were alive.

When they were young, the grandchildren listened, absorbed. They, too, would have liked to have hid in a tomb while Huns galloped hallooing over their heads. Later, Harper's obsession began to bore them and they paid less attention to him. But to him the subject never became boring. He grew into it and it into him until they were one; and he did not care that the children thought him dull and maybe even crazy. When the time came, he believed, all that he had said would come back to them and they would use it.

One other flaw in his theory of history continued to make Harper uneasy; and this was his feeling that there were times among men for other sorts of heroes, heroes who were both glamorous and self-sacrificing, whose deaths served the future of mankind in ways that his modest tricksters were too craven to imitate. Would such a time not come to him or his and would they not, on his account, be unprepared for it?

All very well to feel a kinship with old Galileo, who had recanted to save his skin. But would it not have been better (certainly nobler) to have died for his beliefs? Was survival worthwhile if it meant trembling like a cornered rat in the darkness beneath one's fields?

Sternly Harper told himself that nobility was a temptation to be resisted like the temptation to cruelty, not so unattractive, but for him equally immoral and maybe even more destructive. Not, he said to himself, that you're likely to have many opportunities to be noble. You ought to be satisfied with killing a rattlesnake in the garden every now and then. Mrs. Griswold thinks that's noble enough for anybody.

On the other hand (Harper pulled his withe of cane patiently in and out of the pattern, tied it neatly off, and picked up another from the bucket), on the other hand, a trickier part of the same problem had to do with the point at which meekness itself became destructive. If the Jews had turned on their destroyers early in the game, surely their fate would have been different. Should they not have risen up everywhere and stood fast? Not to be acting out some silly dream of glory or immortality, but in defense of the very core of their humanity?

Well, yes, he would say to himself. And my people, too. There are times . . . Everybody knows there are times. But where? At what point? And then he would shrug the problem off with the thought that the point most probably would not come for him and, if it did, he would *know* it.

Given this view of the world and a man's role in it, and his own ideal of himself as acting consciously in his role, Harper found himself bewildered and chagrined at the age of sixty-two (not so sharp as I used to be!) to find himself working as a kind of combination orderly and handyman in an old people's home.

The transformation of his first line of defense, his first "cave" — the Griswold-Clarke household — into Golden Age Acres took him by surprise. He scarcely knew it was happening until it was done; and even then he could not make up his mind about its significance to him and his family. His first impulse when he began to be aware of the depth of the change had been to quit, to retreat to the next cave; but here was Lucy — uncontrollable, as she had been for several years, and not, he feared, as bright as she needed to be (She doesn't have the Mandingo mind. No getting around it) — making good money and at the same time needing more than ever his watchful supervision. And, less important, but at the same time a part of his world that habit and age made it painful for him to abandon, here was his garden, his fern-dripping bayou bank, his fruit trees and his roses (mine and hers, he would say to himself, thinking of Martha, but mostly mine); and here *she* was — Martha. For reasons that he did not wish to analyze, he felt faintly uncomfortable at the prospect of leaving her.

Instead of acting in this complex situation, he told himself that he must not be hasty. He would watch and wait. And he began to watch with even more than ordinary attention. What were Howie Snyder and Mrs. Crawley — muddle-heads, martyrs, or ghouls? And what was this curious business of taking care of other peoples' old people? How was Snyder's part in it to be explained, and, more immediately important, what was its significance and what its dangers to him and his: to Lucy, all too ready to snap like a just-fledged bass at the first glittering silver spoon dangled in front of its nose; and to his continuing capacity to function as a protector to the younger ones?

Of course there's a profit in it, he said to himself. It's a new business waiting for the enterprising man to exploit it. It may, after all, be as simple as that — may not involve anything else. But as time passed, he began to know in his bones and in the raised hairs on his arms that there was danger in the air.

"The world is a complicated place to live in and to make up your mind about," he said to the grandchildren, "and it's no use saying it's simple. Don't make the mistake of thinking that, like in books, you can choose a way to be, once and for all, and the rest will follow and fall into place. You got to choose every day of your life. Now, remember this: Your Mandingo great-great-grandpa, he was a merchant once. He had his own slaves. But he ended up a slave." He sighed. "Sometimes," he said, "it seems like a man has to rise right up out of his coffin saying, 'Hey, wait a minute, I changed my mind. I want to do different.' "

And the children said, "Yes, Grandpa, O.K., Grandpa," and went their ways. Only Andrew, the younger boy, by now a lad of twelve, light-skinned, long-headed, and flat-nosed like him, with firm lips, alert eyes, and, already, a faintly ironic smile, seemed sometimes to be listening.

CHAPTER 8

WHEN GEORGE CLARKE heard from Lucas of Mrs. Crane's "fall," he stopped by Newton's office to discuss it with him. "I don't like it," he said. He stretched his long neck nervously. "Sometimes I wish we hadn't gotten mixed up in this, son. It's too depressing."

Newton got up and closed the door into his outer office so that his secretary would not hear the conversation. Then he returned to his desk and sat down across from his father, the picture of a successful young lawyer in his tan cord suit and gleaming cordovan shoes. The bookshelves lining the wall behind his desk were close-packed with buckram-bound volumes of *American Jurisprudence*, the *Mississippi Code*, and the *Southern Reporter*, with his great-grandfather's leather-bound *American Law Reviews* occupying the place of honor. The polished surface of his desk was bare except for a beautifully carved jade elephant given him quite recently by his mother, in celebration of his election as president of the Mississippi *Young Republicans*.

"It's a service, Daddy," he said now. "Any time you're doing a community service, you're going to have some depressing times — some bad times. You know that."

"I reckon so," George said. "But, son, it seems to me we could have just stuck with Aunt Martha. She's the only one *we* care about. How'd we get into all this other business, anyhow?"

"Now, Daddy," Newton said, "you know how we got into it."

"Waiting to die," George said. "That's what they're all doing. And Mrs. Crane couldn't wait. I hate to think about your Aunt Martha out there with . . ."

"Aunt Martha is *happy*," Newton said. "And most of the rest of 'em wouldn't be happy any place they were. Especially somebody like old Mrs. Crane."

George shook his head. "I think about how the place used to be," he said. "Always a house full of children. And that summer we had the hawk . . . Yes, I know; I've told you too many times already about my hawk. But it sticks to my mind. Who else but Aunt Elizabeth and Aunt Martha would let a boy keep a hurt hawk in his room? And then — he looked guiltily at his son and away — "I think about *myself*, too," he said, the plaintive voice low and uncertain. "Will it be like that for me when I'm old? When other people will be making decisions for me? I tell you the truth, son, it'd be better for us all if we'd done this the old way — like families used to do, when everybody lived together and made the best of it and you paid a little nigger fifty cents a day to run after the old folks."

"Well, we can't do that, Daddy," Newton said impatiently. "There aren't any little niggers for fifty cents a day anymore. Got to live with things the way they are. You *know* that, don't you? Don't you? You're just tormenting yourself. Punishing yourself."

"She put up a rope swing for us in the elm tree in the side yard one year," George said. "Even then, the lowest branches were thirty feet off the ground. She got a spool of thread, unwound it, and tied one end to an arrow; and then she tied fishing line to the thread and rope to the fishing line. I reckon she spent an hour trying to shoot the arrow over the right branch; but she did it finally. She made it work. Do you remember that part in *Swiss Family Robinson* where . . . ?"

"Daddy! I know how crazy you were about Aunt Martha when you were little. But you can't — you can*not* — let it get in the way of your judgment. You've got to be practical. *Practical.* Sentimentality's not a bit of help to her."

"I reckon you're right, son, but I don't exactly call it sentimental to look after your own."

"You've got a knack — a *knack* — for putting things in a way that'll make you miserable and conscience-stricken," Newton said. "But she *is* happy. That's a fact. Leave her out of it. Think of the rest of 'em as part of a business deal (that's what it is, after all) and you won't get depressed about it. I told you last month, and it's true, this is a good investment for everybody. Including the patients — or whatever they are. They're getting their money's worth and so are we. And you know Howie. He's a *good* person. Doing everything he can to keep 'em happy."

"Yes," George said. "I know Howie is good. But sometimes I think he may be a little bit — stupid. Obtuse. And in the long run, stupidity can be as — as . . . You'll think I'm foolish, son, but it can be as destructive as badness. For example, if you're stupid and self-confident both, you can do a disastrous lot of damage."

"Now, what does *that* mean, Daddy? Really! Of course Howie's no brain. He wouldn't be out there running the place if he were. But he has a way about him . . . He's clever. And what he's always saying — that he's a reconciler and so forth — that's the truth. He gets around the families and keeps 'em satisfied. Keeps the old folks quiet. (This thing with Mrs. Crane is an exception, you know.) He's clever enough for the job and that's all that's needed."

George shook his head. "Some things maybe people shouldn't get reconciled to," he said.

"Like old age?"

"No, no," George said. "That's not what I mean. I know you *have* to reconcile yourself to that. And I suppose you're right. We have to reconcile ourselves to this." He drew his long legs under him, preparing to rise. "I know you're busy," he said.

"No. While you're here there are a couple of other things we need to talk about."

The long and complex conversation which followed concerned investments: the grain elevator business, the state of the rice crop and of futures in cotton and soybeans, the degree to which he and Newton had extended themselves and the resources that were available to them to cover certain necessary but unforeseen expenses.

"Don't get cold feet, now, son," George said reassuringly. "It's all going to pay off in the long run. All we have to do is keep these balls in the air a little longer — until the elevator gets in the black."

Newton nodded. "I've been looking into some possibilities for tax write-offs that we've overlooked," he said. "And . . ." He gave his father a sidelong glance as if he had not quite made up his mind to say what he was thinking, but then went on: "I think we've got another opportunity here in connection with Golden Age that we ought not to pass up," he said. "Listen, now, and try to be objective."

George craned his neck and his expression changed from one of absorbed and alert interest to one of anxiety.

The account that followed was one of the need for nursing homes in Vicksburg and Port Gibson. "This is a wide-open field," Newton said. "Medicaid homes, I mean, where the federal government and the Welfare Department guarantee three hundred dollars a month for every patient. It's just waiting for the man who has a few dollars to invest in it. If it weren't for Howie, I doubt if I'd ever have thought about it, Daddy, but there Howie is, and he's been looking into it and has all the facts at his finger tips. As he put it to me, it's just like these catfish farms."

"Catfish farms?" George said.

"You know what I'm talking about. This business of raising catfish for sale that's gotten so profitable in the last couple of years. Why, that business is growing so fast, the fellows with the ponds can sell all their fingerlings to people stocking new farms. They don't even need to raise 'em to eating size. You get in on the ground floor with something new like that and you've got it made.

"Here's the deal," he went on. "Howie's got his eye on lots in Vicksburg and Port Gibson, and he's got a couple of local investors in each place. You know, he hasn't a dime of his own — he's just expediting, in return for a small share if we get it set up — and of course a managing job — general manager for all three. What he needs from us is money. And I think . . ." He checked himself. "I'd like to know what you think about this proposition. Can we keep one more ball in the air?"

"I don't know, son," George began doubtfully. "I don't know . . ."

But for all his plaintive manner and his scruples, George Clarke was a man who found the business of keeping balls in the air a fascinating pursuit, and before he left the book-lined law office that morning, Newton had persuaded him to borrow money from the bank, putting up for collateral various securities that he had been holding in reserve; and they had made plans to draw Albert into the venture.

"Another thing," Newton said, after they had completed their plans. "I know you're not interested in politics, but . . ."

"I'm interested in you, son, and that means I'm going to be interested in politics, from now on, I reckon."

"Well, this business of doing something for the old folks (black as well as white, you know, in these Medicaid outfits) is not going to hurt me politically. Our homes could be models for the whole state, you know it? And when the time comes — when I need it — I can get the media coverage. Gravy — pure gravy." Newton glanced at his watch. "I reckon that about covers everything," he said. "And I do have an eleven o'clock appointment."

George got up and Newton rose, too. He was always polite to his elders and often said that one of the basic problems in the modern world was the collapse of good manners. "One more thing," he said. "This is something that struck me awhile back when you were talking about Mrs. Crane. We've got to incorporate. Right away."

"You mean for the Medicaid project?"

"That, too. But right now, for Golden Age. I don't know how I ever let that get by me. Too busy with politics, I reckon." He stroked the smooth back of his jade elephant. "Essential," he said. "We're vulnerable out there, all of us. Once we incorporate, though, nobody will be responsible for anything that happens. Individually, I mean. The *corporation* will be responsible. And that's the way we ought to set it up. O.K.?"

CHAPTER 9

MARTHA HEARD a light step in the hall outside her bedroom door, the whispering rustle of silk (taffeta?), and opened her eyes, instantly awake. She lay on her back in a narrow scroll-backed day bed set against the wall under windows that opened to the south and east. The high moon filled her room with clear light, pale as a lemon lily in early morning. She lifted her eyes and gazed out the window at the moon, hazed and rainbowed by her blindness, caught in a black filigree of leaves and branches. All about her she heard movement — the breathing of sleepers, footsteps of the wakeful. Mary Hartwell? Home from a dance? She lifted her arm, held out her hand, and turned it slowly in the moonlight, all the while gazing curiously at it. What time is it? She sat up in bed, heard a whisper, a man's rough voice, and afterward a smothered giggle. The boys are with her — no need to worry. She heard George's plaintive drawl and a moment later the opening of the bedroom door.

Mary Hartwell stood in the moonlit room, smiling. "We're home." Reddish brown hair hung to her shoulders in loose waves. Gold taffeta stiff about her feet.

Silly child thinks she looks like Rita Hayworth.

The taffeta moved, strands of hair drifted across her face, as if a breeze were blowing.

This room has always gotten the Gulf breeze, Martha thought. "Leave the door open when you go," she said, feeling all at once a vague uneasy conviction that it might not be a good thing to close the door. Why? If there is something threatening outside, wouldn't it be better to shut it out? "It's all a matter of air pressure," she said. "There is still some air outside, but I don't think there is much left in here. I don't want to create a vacuum."

Mary Hartwell nodded.

"What time is it? Have you told your mother you're home? No, wait! Are you going? Stay!"

Mary Hartwell slowly shook her head. She was gone.

Martha felt the threat of a vast emptiness, as if the house were sealed and airless. "Don't close the door," she said again, but the door sucked shut. The walls of her room swelled inward, buckling under pressure of the outside air.

Where did everybody go?

The house was silent. She saw around her as through glass panes the arrangement of empty cubes, walls creaking, leaning inward.

Mary Hartwell was here, she thought. Was that a long time ago? Then: Somebody is in trouble. Francis?

Again she raised her hand in the moonlight. It moved in an animated way as if flexing to run a scale on the piano; and she examined it with detached interest, as if it might be a landscape: the brown blotches, muddy lakes, and the network of veins, a system of blue mountain ridges with dry stretches of wrinkled sand at their bases.

Mary Hartwell was here, was here, was here; and George and George and George and Albert. Francis is in bed, in bed; whispering, still gazing at her ancient hand.

But then, wide awake, aware of the lucid working of her conscious mind: I was dreaming! One of those queer waking dreams: Howie's voice, not George's. Lucy.

The house is full of people, but not of us. In every room; in the bed where Sister and Johnny slept, a stranger sleeps; in the nursery; in the boys' rooms stripped of their trophies: of birds' nests and snakeskins and Latin grammars. Old men, old women, breathing out dead breath into the stale air. She shuddered. My plants are dead. Plastic plants in the front hall neither grow nor die. Plastic flowers dusty and unwilting in the parlor. Has Lucas fixed the clock?

She was aware of a tingling ache in her arm and let her hand drop to her lap. I am still sitting up in bed. I was holding out my hand and looking at it. Mary Hartwell . . . I dreamed . . . She lay back calmly. I'm going to think . . . to think of something until I fall asleep again, something without . . . anxiety . . . attached, out of the past, happy. Going to think — of what?

Do you remember . . . first time Lucas and I took the children out on the *Delta Queen?* August afternoon. July? It was the middle of July. Was it nineteen thirty-three? The peak of summer, sky piled to the meridian with white thunderheads, silver light at the edges, wind blowing. The children wild with joy. We were up high, on the top deck, and then in the wheelhouse, because Lucas knew the captain. Old Captain Sharp from Port Gibson? Funny little bandy-legged man, no taller than I, in his captain's hat and grand uniform with gold-braid stripes and frogs, fancy as an admiral, and the children awe-struck, gazing at him all popeyed and silent. And he let them hold the wheel. See Mary Hartwell now, standing on tiptoe looking through the spokes. She had on white shorts and those red barefoot sandals she was so crazy about that summer. Thin legs, like little limber willow branches. Band playing. What an uproar! Could it have been Bud Scott's? Nobody else plays that loud. No. Bud died in '31, didn't he? Was it Little Winn? And later, at the stern, the paddle wheel turning up mountains of white water. The wind blew harder. Water sparkling under the sun like cut steel. The willow trees streaming with wind on the towhead there by Old River Chute, bending and streaming. Down we went with the current, rushing along, and then below town — we must have been off Lamb's Landing, yes, I remember that's where we were, because we were in close to the bank where the current isn't so strong; and I saw the Lamb children on the landing waiting to watch us go by. And Captain Sharp in the wheelhouse. Turned us away from the bank, out into the channel, so that he could swing us around and head back upstream. And the wind, the wind, and the sky darker now and he would bring us up into the wind and then the bed . . . the boat . . . high old stern-wheeler sitting like an empty tub right on top of the water . . . would fall off before the wind and swing 'round again, and there we were, in the middle of the river, in a storm, swinging 'round like a yo-yo at the end of a string; and every time we swung by the landing, there would be the Lamb children, waving and screaming and running up and down the wharf. Black sky rushing by overhead and the clumsy old boat swinging in the wind. Do you remember how Lucas shouted? Hey, children! We're in a storm! Hey, Lucky! Hanging on to Francis's shirttail (and he wanted to climb up on the railing on the top deck) and Mary Hartwell's hand. Lovely! How sad that some people are afraid of wind and weather . . . But *we* . . . Lucas . . . Eyebrows black then, and already a farmer's brown leathery skin, and his eyes — blue, almost to

black, so piercing and hawkish. And I loved him. Lucas . . .
And he . . . And he . . . I've been lucky all my life, Martha
thought drowsily.

She dozed off.

Other people in the house were still wakeful. Lucy, starched
skirt rustling, nurse's cap set back on her hair, moved quietly
about, opening doors and checking the old people. She had
given out pills and filled water glasses an hour and a half earlier.
Everyone seemed to be alseep. Howie came in, locked the front
door, spoke to her, and went down to his bedroom. Lucy stared
after him, her face expressionless. After she finished her
rounds upstairs, she went down to the lower floor; here, tip-
toeing down the dim hall, she glanced into every room except
Lucas Alexander's. (He kept his door locked and except in the
worst weather would go out his outside door and walk around
the house to go upstairs. It kept the smell of sickness out of his
room, he said. He'd had enough of that in his life) and at last
sat down at the makeshift nurse's station in the downstairs hall
—a desk set into a jog in the wall that had once been a closet.
She was drowsy. The house was quiet. With any luck there
would be nothing to do for two or three hours, maybe longer.
She might slip into the supply closet and nap on the cot set up
there. She waited.

In a few minutes Howie, in a robe and slippers, came out of
his room and joined her. "How's it going? Everything shut
down for the night?"

She shrugged. "Everybody's 'sleep — right now."

He laid a freckled reddish hand on her smooth arm, a dark
polished brown under the light from the desk lamp. She

shivered and moved away, folding her arms across her bosom and looking up at him inquiringly.

"I'm wide awake," he said in a low voice. "Not ready to go to bed yet. Have a drink with me?"

"I've decided I don't think it's a good idea for me to take a drink with you, Mr. Snyder."

Howie opened his eyes wide. "We've done it before, ain't we, Lucy?"

"Yeah, but it's going to get me in trouble one way or another. The last time I took a drink with you — remember? Coupla weeks ago? Well, someway or other Mrs. Crawley found out about it. Did you know that? She told Grandpa she heard I was drinking with you."

Howie frowned. "How could she have? It was in the middle of the night. She wasn't even here."

"I've got my ideas about it," Lucy said. "One them bald-headed old twins musta poked his head out the door and seen us. Grandpa says she's in there jawing with them all the time. But she thinks she's got a right to talk about me!"

"Listen," Howie said, "Crawley ain't like that. If she mentioned us to your granddad, she didn't mean any harm. She's a good woman, Lucy. Got her faults, sure, and I make allowances for them, but a *good* heart — and she'll do anything I tell her to do — understand? You might say I have a strong influence over her."

"What do you mean by that?" Lucy said.

"Never mind, never mind. I don't mean anything. Just don't worry your head about old Crawley. I'll straighten her out." Howie pulled out the straight-backed chair next to the desk and, sitting down diagonally across from Lucy, began to speak earnestly, his broad face full of a kind of serious piety, as if he might be addressing a Sunday-school class. "The way I look at

it is this, Lucy," he said. "We're doing the Lord's work, helping
these old folk. And it's *tough* — a real tough job. We got to
support each other — I mean give each other *moral* support.
Find ways to work with each other — to get along together
and save our strength for the hard times. Nobody's business but
ours how we do it. And nobody in the world can *really* say
what we do down here in the middle of the night — not so anybody would believe 'em."

Lucy, gazing off down the dim silent hallway, said nothing.

"Look at it this way," he said. "The Lord ain't going to be-
grudge us any little lift that helps us on our way. Did you know
it says in the Bible that wine maketh glad the heart of man? And,
hey, listen, remember how those old monks in Switzerland used
to tie little barrels of whiskey onto the dogs' collars when they
sent 'em out to rescue the freezing travelers?"

"I ain't thinking about the Lord, or about any old monks,
either," Lucy said. "I'm thinking about Grandpa getting mad
at me. And also about my boy friend. He'd cut both our th'oats,
he knew I was in here socializing with a white man." She gave
him a sidelong look, both sullen and lascivious.

"You know Harper wouldn't tell your boy friend," Howie
said. "He don't want that kind of trouble."

But Lucy kept her shoulders straight and made a stern face
like a child who has rehearsed her lesson and is ready to recite.
"And that ain't all, Mr. Snyder," she said. "I'm going to tell
you the truth: I ain't happy. I put off talking about it and *put*
off, because the money's good and all, for *this* town, that is, and
Grandpa needs me, but . . ." She looked at him out of huge,
thyroidal dark eyes and shook her head so that the gold hoops
in her ears, incongruous under the severe nurse's cap, glimmered
in the lamplight. "You told me you was going to work on getting me into that nurses' program at Vicksburg. And then when

we talked about it in March, you said you'd written off and all. That's why I stayed on. But here, another three months gone by and you hadn't done nothin' yet. When I'm going to go?"

"You know how long it takes the government to get one of those programs going, Lucy. All the red tape and paperwork. We'll hear from 'em pretty soon."

"Soon! Umph."

"Anyhow, you're making good money working for us. You just said so yourself. I bet you make more right now than most nurses. Counting tips from relatives and all."

"I'm trying to talk straight, Mr. Snyder. You know none these folks don't tip."

"Besides," Howie said, "I'm beginning to think you don't need to go to that nurses' school. You've already learned as much here, probably more, than you'd learn up there."

"But I hadn't got no certificate saying so," Lucy said. She continued to look at him sternly with her arms folded.

Howie reached across the desk, laid his hand on her forearm again, and stroked the smooth skin gently. When she pulled away, he closed his hand on her wrist and held it for a moment. "You're beautiful, Lucy. You know it? You don't need a certificate to prove that."

"I ain't going to sleep with you," she said. "We might as well get that straight once and for all without no delay. My boy friend . . ."

"I know your boy friend," Howie said. "He drives a tractor for Alton Calvitt, doesn't he? Making what? Eight dollars a day? Not as much as you do. First step up for you, Lucy, is to get rid of him. You're going to have better than him in this world."

"You're an old man, Mr. Snyder — excuse my saying so — and a white man."

"Listen, I'm not talking about *that*. I'm talking about your future."

"Yeah, that's what I'm talking about, too."

"You're young, child." Howie said, "and if you want to get ahead in the world, if you want to have a good life, you ought to listen to a man with experience. Somebody who can tell you how things really are. Somebody who has your welfare at heart." He reached across the desk, took her by the shoulder, and, looking deep into her eyes, gave her a gentle shake. "This is how things are, Lucy. You've got three alternatives. You can scrape together a little bit of money and go to New York or Hollywood to try to break into television. You're good-looking enough, but you haven't got the talent or the training it takes. You're not going to make it. That's a jungle out there, Lucy. If you don't get raped or murdered or both, you gonna end up drudging — riding the subway to some fancy apartment and washing some rich white woman's dishes and looking after her kids. It's a fact, Lucy. Same as you might be doing down here — only no fresh air and lousy food. And *cold* — Jesus! All right, alternative number two: Go on up to Vicksburg and get in that nurses' training program; or get you a scholarship to Jackson College or Alcorn or some other two-bit nigger school. That's right. Nigger school. That's what they are and you might as well face it. You end up with a nigger education doing a nigger job.

"Now, three: Stick with me. You're not a nigger to me, Lucy. You're a human soul. You know that. I want to see every person I come in contact with fulfill his potential. I'm a serious man, Lucy, and, believe me, I'm doing the Lord's work in this world. Look-a-here! The future, the *world*, is before us. We got a mission, see? We doing something *has* to be done. And there just ain't any limit to the number of people, black and white, it has to be done for. More old people every day. I mean, you know, on account of the wonders of medicine and all. When I say I'm thinking about the future, I mean I'm thinking about expansion. We're going to have a *chain* of nursing homes. For black and white. Separate and together — let 'em take their choice. Now, if you got the patience (and, being young, that's the hardest part of it), if you got the patience to stick with me, I'm going to gradually teach you all about it. Buying food and all. Keeping records. Et cetera. And when we begin to expand, you're going to move up. Not all at once. I'm not trying to fool you, see? But gradually you're going to move up."

Lucy had been listening intently. This time, when he absently began to stroke her wrist again, she did not move. "What do you mean, I'm going to move up?" she said. "And when is it going to start?"

"I mean, like eventually, I would expect you to be the superintendent of one of the homes, see? In *charge*. Making five, six hundred a month. I'm negotiating now with a group in Port Gibson that wants me to start a home there. Also, I'm looking into another type setup. Medicaid. Where you've got an integrated home, see? And the government pays everything for some patients and up to three hundred dollars a month for others. What I got in mind is to begin by teaching you about buying food and counting calories and planning meals and all that. (Did you know these old people ain't supposed to have nearly as much to eat as you and me, for example? It ain't good for 'em. You manage that calorie business and menu planning *right*, and you can really save money.) Anyhow, that's what I've been intending to talk to you about. Then, when we get the first Medicare home going, you could start off as dietician. But you got to be patient, Lucy. All that don't come about in a day. It takes planning and work." He gripped her wrist and smiled at her.

"Lucy," he said, "I'm telling you, you got the world before you. You gonna end up in an executive position — maybe before you're twenty-five." Abruptly he let go of her and stood up. "I'm tired," he said. "I've had a rough day and I need a drink. Come on down to my room. I got some books there I can give you to read — on diets and all."

Lucy gave him a long, popeyed look. "It's true you're different," she said.

"What?"

"You're telling the truth when you say you're not like other white people. You know what I told my boy friend the other night? I said, I wonder what he (meaning you) ever did to a nigger that he's got to be paying for it all the time, acting like he likes us so much. Not just me — I could understand that, if you want to sleep with me — but Grandpa and Ruby, too."

"That ain't the way it is," Howie said. "I told you I was color-blind. I got convictions, deep convictions. I want everybody to be alike, see? And that's the plain truth."

"Well," she said, "I'm going to tell you the plain truth about me. I don't mind all that much sleeping with you. (I just *said* that about being afraid of my boy friend.) I been sleeping around since I was fourteen and I've put up with all kinds — for money and for pleasure. I like men and that's a fact — although I will say I hadn't had anybody as old as you. But I don't trust you to . . ."

Howie smiled at her lovingly. "Lots of things an old man knows about women that a young one hasn't had time to find out," he said. "And a young man pleases himself, while an old one knows he has to please the woman."

". . . to do what you *say* you're going to do."

"Well, I can understand that," Howie said. "But you might try this, Lucy. Make up your mind to gamble on it. Wait and

see. Give me six months and see if my plans don't begin to work
out, and that means including you. If they don't — why, you
can be saving your money while you're waiting and getting
yourself in a better position to go. What difference does six
months make? Am I right?"

Lucas, too, was restless. The brilliance of the moonlight pouring in his open window gave the world outside the deep blue and
golden aspect of twilight and he rose to it as eagerly as a boy,
full of a kind of childish joy at being awake when everyone else
was sleeping. He had always been a night prowler — getting up
(in the years when his wife had been an invalid) after the house
was quiet, and wandering outdoors to look at the wheeling night
sky or taking a flashlight and walking a hundred yards to the
bank of the creek that ran behind his house to stand and listen to
the quiet lapping of water, constant under the deafening chorus
of frogs and Katydids and night birds. Sometimes, in his pajamas,
shabby old cotton robe, and a pair of worn tennis shoes, with
strings dragging, he would go out into his vegetable garden at
two or three on just such a moonlit night as this and chop weeds
for an hour or more.

"Good way to get rid of your frustrations," he would say
afterward to Martha — stopping by the house to bring her a
basket of tomatoes and okra and summer squash. "Chop! That's
Fred Nielson, cut off at the root — *e-radicated*. He's blocked
me every damn time I've tried to get through a county bond issue to clean up the sewage around Old River Chute. Crawling
with typhoid out there. *Crawling* with it! And whack! That's
Parsons out at the paper mill — the filth he's pouring into the
river is staggering. And here's Poison Ivy McCay. Uproot him

before he kills everybody in his end of the county with DDT."

"People have to poison boll weevils," Martha would say mildly.

"Listen to me," Lucas said. "Do you know what the effective life of DDT is? A lot longer than yours — in fact, just about infinite. And it builds up in the tissues. It's *people* that are going to end up dead, not just boll weevils."

Tonight he got up, smiling to himself and thinking of those days and battles. Sometimes I won. Often enough to make it worth the battles? *All dead now* crossed his mind. I outlived them all. Niggardly satisfaction.

He put on his robe and walked out his bedroom door directly into the garden. Early in April, as soon as the ground was warm, he had planted mint and basil and thyme and dill in a sunny spot beside his door; and now the sharp fragrance of the leaves drifted upward into the still night air. Bending stiffly, he broke off a sprig of mint and breathed its green sweetness. He crossed the moonlit lawn and began to pace up and down the flagstone walk at the edge of the ravine. The night was cool — chilly for June. The dew-drenched grass dragged coldly across his ankles and soaked through the canvas of his shoes. He knew he should not be outdoors; but he drew the old robe about him and continued to walk rapidly up and down, looking now at his feet to check his footing on the slippery flagstones, now at the deep sky. Two very brilliant stars hung undimmed quite near the moon. Jupiter? And the other? He paced in and out of the shadows of the great trees that began now to move and sigh in a light wind. The beauty of the world — the pale light behind the black fretwork of night leaves; the passionate rise and fall of locusts' voices; the smell of mint on his hands — was almost more than he could bear. He quickened his pace, walking furiously up and down and gazing all around him. That one's moving. Must be Jupiter. But too fast — look at it now in relation to the other one. Must be one of those damned satellites. Is there one left in orbit big enough to shine like that? He thought with a twinge of fury of the astronauts and their exploits and silly talk. Out there polluting the universe. Used to be we thought we had only to wrestle with the pollution of the world — and my corner of it was Homochitto County. But now — the universe! Filth and detritus in that pure black vacuum. Enough to drive a sane man to . . . ! What's that thing? "When a man sees . . . ?" No, slipped my mind. And they! In their white jumpsuits and their flattop haircuts. Like damned Boy Scouts at the Grand Canyon, dropping their gum wrappers and sending post cards home to Mom. "Boy, I'll tell you, this is somep'n." "Makes a fella realize they's reely a God." While the past, thank God, is silent. Leave it to the poets: Stout Cortes, silent on a peak in Darien.

Lucas ground his teeth and endured the loud grating rasp in his head until the hair rose on his arms.

Deep in the ravine that dropped away at his feet a whippoorwill called, was silent, repeated its call, claiming for its own the night's humming beauty. Cats moaned, snarled, fell to quarreling over by the plum thicket. A caught mouse shrieked. Lucas shivered. Damned cats. Bayou's full of them. And then: Martha — funny how she's gotten that thing about cats and you can't shake her out of it. Harper: She's been that way a good while, Doc. You just hadn't noticed it. Gradually got to worrying herself more and more about the cats eating the birds — specially the towhees and water thrushes, because she says they nest on the ground. Lucas smiled. Not true — nothing new about it. She always cared about every wild creature. She stood above him, balancing on a fallen log in the green woods, peering into a low-hung oriole's nest, while he lay on pine needles and breathed their fragrance. Green needles etched in fans across the bright summer sky, the green, intoxicating, resinous heat throbbing all around them. Come down to me for a little while — almost time to start back. He closed his hand on her smooth brown ankle. When was that? What year? What wood? How many summer afternoons in how many parts of the deep woods have we lain together in the humming heat? Lucky, I reckon, in that way, that we could never live together, weren't we? Thrived on concealment and difficulty and separation all those years — never got stale. Yes, every man to his own life, think-ing with scorn of married men in their stale beds every night, with their stale wives turning away in boredom and hatred. But children. We should have had children.

The wind blew up suddenly and high clouds obscured the moon. Getting darker. And I'm hungry.

In the kitchen he snapped on a light and tiptoed guiltily about, looking for a box of crackers he had bought and hidden a few days earlier. ("The inmates will kindly refrain from keep-ing food or using unauthorized electrical appliances in their rooms.") And why shouldn't I be in here? Ridiculous to feel like a child raiding the pantry at boarding school. He found the crackers and a chunk of cheese that he had concealed in the broom closet to keep Ruby from turning it into macaroni and cheese, and got out a half-empty bottle of chianti, also con-cealed at the back of a high shelf in the broom closet. Won't let them get to me. Damn it, I live here. I bought the damned wine. He put his bottle on a tray with the cheese and crackers and a glass and, tennis shoes softly slapping the worn floorboards, walked back through the dining room and hall and onto the gallery that looked out across the garden. The clouds were blowing away to the west and the moonlight poured in; he did not bother to turn on a light, but set his feast on a little wicker table and sat down in the chair beside it, beginning to feel again the excitement of being up and alone in the middle of the night. He poured out a glass of wine and, leaning back with a sigh of pleasure, took a sip. He was aware of the creaking settling sounds of the old house and then for a moment, before he dismissed it as imagined, of a low moan from the room behind him. Old houses make almost human noises . . . Whose room? Mrs. Cathcart's: the most peaceable and probably the sanest of the lot of us. Wonder why her kids shoved her off here? He glanced over his shoulder at the window opening from Mrs. Cathcart's room onto the gallery, but it was dark. "When a man comes to feel . . ." Let's see, that's . . . He shivered and put down his glass. Keeps coming to me, tail end of some quotation, and I can't . . . Whose room did it use to be anyhow? Wasn't it, yes, the nursery, and, in her last illness, Martha's mother's room? Remember the dream she was telling me? No. She said the nursery was downstairs. Couldn't put it out of her mind for weeks — of the bloated body on the bed and the starved face. And nobody would bury . . . I had not intended to think of that — of Martha and her dreams and fancies and her — future, such as it is.

Drives me crazy repeating herself! Over and over, the same story, too. Curious business, the human brain — no blood to those threads and the effect — so exceedingly specific. The hallucinations of a particular type — the loss of memory selective in time and content. And then, suddenly, everything clear.

But it's worse. Worse every week. Get them to send her out to DeBakey or — what's his name? — the other fellow in Houston. Consider the possibility of scraping the big artery back there. I should have talked to Carr about it after I sent her to him in February. Nicotinic acid — hardly more than a placebo . . . Snatching at straws. *She's seventy-seven years old.*

They're not going to put her through any radical circulatory surgery. Ridiculous idea. Wouldn't do any good anyhow — and I know well enough it's in all the small vessels, too, dozens of little blockages. She knows it herself. I see it in her face.

The fierce eyebrows and thin wide mouth were drawn into a grimace of anguish and frustration. Yes, she knows it, grits her teeth and keeps her mouth shut, except for that one time, while I . . . I've just refused (or haven't bothered) to think about it. Playing games with wine and cheese in the middle of the night like a schoolboy, taking my walks and tinkering with clocks, and she's losing her mind right before my eyes. Why? Simple enough, that. Nothing I can do. Why think about it? Maybe it won't progress — have to hope to God a stroke carries her off in a hurry — this damned long-lived family! The old lady lived to be nearly ninety, didn't she? And what about me? That's another reason I've been playing games — to keep from thinking of myself. No way for either of us to go but down. Pain and debility — ugh! But I *won't* shove it out. I've always looked at things and I will look at our old age. "When a man . . ." That's what kept coming into my head earlier. "When a man comes to feel that it is rational, he goes and hangs himself at once." Epictetus? And Martha? Would she . . . ? No. Not time. Not desperate enough for us to think of that solution — not yet, anyhow. Besides, we're not — never have been — stoics, after all. Joyless kind of life, to be always persuading yourself that the pains of living are not painful, that you're free from human attachments, don't object to dying — in short, that all that's good — precious — is a matter of indifference. And, yes, I want to *live*, to work, to watch the night sky — a little longer. He drank off his glass of wine with conscious relish, and began to nibble at a piece of cheese, heard again, this time more clearly distinct from the house sounds, the moaning noise that he had thought earlier came from the bedroom behind him. *Am I getting nutty, too?*

He got up and, going into the hall, gently opened the door to Mrs. Cathcart's room a crack and listened. The old lady moved, the bedsprings creaked and, yes, she *was* moaning quietly to herself, a soft animal noise that seemed more meant to bring its own comfort in pain and tension than to bring help. He sat down in a chair against the wall outside her door, carefully tied his shoes, stood up, tightened the belt to his robe, and ran his fingers through his hair and eyebrows so that he looked slightly less disheveled. Then he opened the door a bit wider, knocked, and looked in.

"Mrs. Cathcart? Don't be alarmed, it's just me — Lucas — *Doctor* Alexander. I was sitting out on the gallery and I heard your voice and wondered — thought maybe you might need some help. Are you ill? Can't sleep?"

"I . . . I think I had a nightmare," she said, the soft voice rising like a ghost's voice out of the darkness. "I'll be all right."

He heard the springs creak again and a sharp intake of breath. "Does something hurt you? May I come in?"

"Pain in my back," she said. "I thought maybe . . . maybe it was part of the dream . . . somebody stuck a . . . yes . . . a long hatpin with a — it was quite lovely — a gold bowknot set with turquoise." She laughed softly. "I believe Mama had a hatpin like that years ago. Stuck it in my back, all the way through me. But it . . . it still seems to hurt. Yes, please come in, Dr. Alexander. I . . . hate to admit it, but I was a little bit frightened. Waked up from that dream and then I thought I heard something — footsteps? — and someone moaning. Maybe I was just hearing you out on the porch — or myself. And then this pain — it didn't go away — a kind of burning pain in my back, as if it might be raw. But . . ."

Lucas groped for the switch by the door, turned on the over-head light, and walked over to the bed. She lay on her back, her plump, short arms on top of the covers like dolls' arms. She looked up at him with blinking, light-blinded eyes, brushing back strands of grayish yellow hair from a softly wrinkled pussycat face. "But it's still there," she went on. "Something's wrong. I've been in bed the past few days with a touch of flu, really just a cold, and I thought this afternoon there was some-thing wrong with my back."

"Let's see." With the absent-minded skill of long practice, Lucas helped her to turn on her side and, using the bed sheet, draped her body as if in examination room. Then he eased the crumpled nightgown up over her withered buttocks, drew a chair up to the side of the bed and, sitting down, began to exam-ine the soft, frail old skin.

Nothing quite so horrifying, very harbinger of death, with-ered buttocks and white bush of an old woman. (Still con-scious of bodies, my age and condition of impotence!) Never could help admiring a young woman's body, even on the table; lacked that essential detachment, always did. Her brown skin and smooth belly. A little bit convex. I liked a woman with some flesh on her. And her shoulders then. Then. Still see the structure. Articulation of the clavicle and shoulder girdle, and the shadow there at the base of sterno-mastoid, lovely. She should have had a child. Gave that up for me. Lucky. I was al-ways lucky. To have had a woman like that and work I loved. More than a man has any right to expect of the world. But now! Now we have to die, we have to find a way to die.

"What do you think it is, Dr. Alexander?"

"You've got some abrasions here, Mrs. Cathcart. That's what's bothering you. Happens if you're not careful when you stay in bed a few days — especially after you get to be our age.

I'll get Lucy and show her what to do for you, and then tomorrow we can get a sheepskin for you to sleep on for a few days. That ought to fix you up. And get up tomorrow, if you possibly can, at least for part of the day."

"Mr. Snyder said I should stay in bed until this flu clears up."

"No, no. Get up! Not good to stay in bed. I'll call Lucy," he repeated. "I expect she's at the desk downstairs."

"I'm better already," she said. "Sometimes a little . . . human company . . . in the night . . ."

"Yes," he said.

"Can't understand . . . She gave me a shot and usually that makes me sleep. No pain at all. I . . ." She hesitated, then continued. "I hate to sound like a complaining old woman," she said. "So boring. But I've had a good deal of difficulty sleeping for some weeks. Sciatica. And the shots . . . But lately, they haven't worked so well."

"I see," he said. A disposable syringe lay in an ashtray beside her bed. He picked it up and looked at it, pulled back the plunger, and forced out a drop or two of clear liquid left in the cylinder. He touched it with his finger and tasted it. "What do you take to help you sleep — for pain, Mrs. Cathcart?"

"I don't know what that is," she said. "I used to take aspirin. But, recently . . . Demerol, maybe? Codeine? All I know is it usually makes my leg stop hurting."

He put his hand on her mattress and pressed it down. "You need a board under your mattress for one thing," he said. "It's too soft. And you should sleep on your side with your legs drawn up — like this." He got up. "I'll find Lucy and give her something for that place on your back."

The hall downstairs was empty, and he sat down at Lucy's desk to consider exactly what it was that he had discovered. Damn it, none of my business. Get Lucy in trouble, she gets fired, Harper takes her side, he quits — what a mess! Hold on a minute, now. Going too fast. Let's see, let's see. How do I know . . . ? First place, I haven't kept up with new drugs for ten years. Could there be something new for pain that looks and tastes like water? Not likely, is it? Just hope the water's sterile, if that's what it is. Would she have enough gumption to use sterile water? He made a grimace of frustration and disgust and combed his fingers roughly though his wild gray hair and eyebrows. Another thing, why jump at the conclusion that it's Lucy? Could easily be the other one — that miserable slattern, Crawley. Wasn't she mixed up years ago in some mess about drugs? Yes. More likely Crawley. But now, what to do about it? He shrugged impatiently, as if he might be trying to shake off the limitations of his life: his age, his reputation as an eccentric, the strange collection of people (well-meaning?) by whom he was surrounded. Do nothing tonight, he thought. Am I going to rush around the house like a loony yelling about drugs? No. Find Lucy and get the old lady comfortably settled. Where is she, anyhow?

He glanced up and down the silent shadowy hall, stood up, walked over to the window, and looked out into the darkness for a few moments, hands in his bathrobe pockets, shoulders hunched. Out there with her boy friend, I'd be willing to bet, and that's not good either. Little featherbrain. He saw the arrogant head on its long graceful neck, the sidelong glance out of huge dark eyes, tranquil and knowing, the long body, draped with careful exaggeration for the effect of breast and thigh and round belly on . . . who? Whatever man happened to pass by, he supposed, ruefully recognizing in himself the faint stirring of tumescence. Just as well Howie finally got her into a uniform. Damned seething cauldron down here of impotent, frustrated old men. Yeah — me and the Strange brothers. And Howie? *Where the hell is she?*

He turned away from the window and went to his room, fumbling briefly at the locked door, rooting in his bathrobe pocket for the key, and at last letting himself in. Inside, he went over to his chest of drawers and selected from an array on top a couple of cans and bottles from which he mixed a simple concoction of cornstarch and boric acid. I'll take it upstairs myself. Then: But she oughtn't to be allowed to get away with it. It's not safe with all these ailing old people. He made up his mind and, instead of going upstairs, walked to Howie's end of the house and, pausing outside his bedroom door, raised his hand to the miniature knocker with *Snyder* engraved on it. It seemed fleetingly to him, as he put his hand on the knocker, that he heard the murmur of a voice inside? Talking to himself? To God, maybe, the pious old son of a bitch. He knocked. Silence inside. He knocked again, coughing his dry habitual cough, and this time a sleepy mumble answered him.

"It's me, Howie," he said. "Lucas. Could I speak to you for a minute? One of the ladies upstairs is sick."

After a brief interval Howie came to the door, resplendent in a black silk bathrobe with golden scrollwork curling around his shoulders and down his flanks, his bare skinny legs sticking out below the hem like the fleshless legs of a marionette.

"Sorry to bother you," Lucas said, and he explained what had happened. "Can't find Lucy," he concluded, "or I wouldn't have waked you up."

"Can't find her?" Howie blinked stupidly, as if he were still half-asleep.

"She must have left the house. Meeting somebody, maybe? That won't do, you know. She's got to stay on the job. Especially since there's no one else awake in the house on this shift. Nothing serious this time, of course, but another time there might be."

"Yes," Howie said. "Hmmm. Well." Then, in a low voice, "I think I've got a pretty good idea where she is. Put my finger on her, all right. Ha, ha. She and that boy friend of hers . . ."

"Well, find her and send her upstairs," Lucas said. "I'm going to take this boric acid and cornstarch to Mrs. Cathcart. That's a bedsore she's got and this is as good a way to treat it as you can find. *Bedsore*, Howie! Probably caused in part by neglect on the part of the sitters and certainly by staying in bed when she ought to be up. Send Lucy to me when you find her and I'll show her how to treat it. Tomorrow I can talk to both of 'em — Harper, too — about how to prevent them in the future." He turned and went down the hall and up the stairs at his own end of the house.

"The old man is a goddamned nuisance," Howie muttered to Lucy when he had closed the door. "We don't watch out, he's going to cause us some trouble. Get up now, honey, and get on up there. Let's see. Where were you anyway? You just stepped outside to speak a word or two with your boy friend. Y'all don't get to see much of each other a-tall now that you're on the night shift, do you? I reckon I'll be able to overlook it this time, but let's don't let it happen again, y'understand?"

Then: "I wonder what in the world he was doing wandering around the house this time of night, anyhow."

Lucy, pulling on her stockings and slipping her feet into white nurses' shoes, shrugged indifferently.

"He was in the old lady's bedroom in the middle of the night. Looking at her nekkid body without another soul present. Doctors just don't do that, you know it? And it don't look right, does it? You reckon she's really got a bedsore? I doubt it. And if she does, you get it cleared up on the double. Y'hear me?"

Back in his room half an hour later, Lucas was still sleepless. Moonlight flooded the garden outside his windows and, gazing out, he saw the moon, still caught, as it seemed to him, in the same branches where it had hung when he had first gone out an hour or more earlier. He stood in his open doorway and the odor of mint and basil rose and swirled around him. Had he been dreaming? He saw again in the half-light and the alcohol stink of her room the withered body of the old woman on the bed upstairs, Lucy bending down to it, and felt again the stirring of his own sex. He had stood by the bed with his arms folded and directed Lucy as she handled the soft old pussycat body, bathed and dried the sore and sprinkled the sheet with cornstarch; he had rubbed his thumb and forefinger over the sheet, testing its silky smoothness. Suddenly he saw Lucy's long and graceful neck encased in a tier of golden rings, her shoulders bare. (*What's happening to me?*) He shook his head sternly and turned his thoughts toward the needle and empty syringe on the table. He had asked Lucy what was in it, what the old lady was getting for her pain, and she had shrugged and said she didn't know — Crawley left it out every night and she (Lucy) gave the shot, that was all she knew. But she had looked at him curiously. "What do you care, anyhow?" she had said. No dream that. The sullen brazen voice rang in his old man's ears. Impudent, she'd been, insulting, even. No, it's not Lucy, he thought. If it were, she'd be more cautious. Or is she capable of caution?

But who? What's going on here and what does it mean to me

— and to Martha? That's what I need to know. He could not bear to close his door and shut out the garden smells and, leaving it swung wide, went back to his bed and lay there stiff as a soldier on his thin pillow and hard mattress, mustache bristling above stern lips and slate blue eyes thoughtful, staring out into the brilliant night. He had the dread of drugs, the knowledge of their treachery, native to a good doctor. A terrible sense of danger and confusion passed over him like a wave of nausea. I have to think clearly from now on, he said to himself. Let's see, now. Water. I *know* it was water. Who did it and why? And who prescribed a narcotic by injection for Mrs. Cathcart? Isn't that in itself a little bit out of line — for sciatica? Something else involved? He snatched at this notion as if it might simplify his problem. Cancer, maybe? Then: Hell no, she hasn't got cancer. I'm clutching at straws. They're giving her that stuff, whatever it is, for sciatica.

Let's see, let's see. He remembered Howie's repeated observations on how to keep everybody happy. "The right tranquilizer, that's all we need." He had said it about Mrs. Wheeler and about Mrs. Crane and about the Strange brothers. His notion of a happy home for old people would be one where everybody was drugged into docility. Nothing startling in that, Lucas thought grimly. Standard with plenty of people. So he would have encouraged the use of drugs. Exaggerated the need in this case and that, maybe? The stronger and longer-lasting, the better. Lucas saw them all — himself, Martha, and the rest — lying helpless, drugged and docile, in their beds, like so many breathing corpses, staring sheep-eyed and incurious at their keepers. Panic swept over him. *I've got to get out of this place.*

Wait now, he thought. Wait. That's not what I started thinking about. Somebody is stealing the stuff, whatever it is. Bound to be Crawley, if it's not Lucy. Easy enough for her to do it. And if she's got a problem — if she's ever been on the stuff, the temptation . . . And no medical control. Not even an LPN to keep track of it. What was it that she was involved in years ago — a drug scandal? No, it had been an illegal abortion.

But suppose she *is* stealing it. Does Howie know? Because . . . If he does . . . Abyss there! Why wouldn't he have fired her? Involved himself? Or is *he* *t*aking the stuff? No. I know the man. True he's obtuse, a bit insensitive. Follows the line of least resistance when he can get away with it. But he's doing the best he can. It's obvious on the face of it he doesn't know what's going on. He wouldn't play with that kind of dynamite. A drug scandal and his "home" (He does take some pride in it. And besides it's a living — not to be sneezed at at his age) would be wrecked. All I need to do is alert him. We can keep our eyes open for a few days. Make absolutely *sure*. And then, too, if I could get him to talk to a reliable man about this drug business, about being *cautious* — acquire a little more sophistication. But he'll have to find a replacement for Crawley — miserable woman. *If* it's true. No jumping to conclusions. Got to be sure. Sleep, he thought. I ought to . . . He began to breathe deeply and, regularly, one by one, to name and then to tense and relax his muscles, an old trick for inviting sleep. First the toes, left foot, right foot (*extensor longus digitorum*), the calf (*gastrocnemius* and *peroneus longus*), thigh (*biceps femoris*); now, *gluteus maximus* . . . *Why do I feel so helpless?* As if I were a prisoner here. I know what Martha meant when she said she felt sometimes as if Lucy were a threat. He clenched and relaxed his fists and then flexed one finger at a time. Sleep . . . Ridiculous, he thought. Ridiculous! One of those panic exaggerations that I'm prone to at night. Put it out of my mind. We are, after all, among decent people. And who has the last say? Martha's relatives, of course. George Clarke has nothing but her best interests (and that means my best interests) at heart. He turned abruptly on his side, pounded his thin pillow into shape, and closed his eyes.

He lay thus, eyes closed, until almost day. As the sky lightened, he heard the mourning doves begin to call and, feeling somewhat comforted by their cool voices, fell asleep.

Upstairs Martha roused again from an anxious doze. Lucas . . . She remembered then that he was sleeping in the room beneath her and sighed contentedly. She, too, looked out at the moonlit garden and wondered what time it was.

We never hear the town clock strike anymore. Why? We used to . . . Is it not working, maybe? Too far away? We used to hear it, yes, but the world used to be quieter. She saw the cross-hatchings of mullions engraved by the moonlight on her bedroom floor and remembered drowsily that the windows were closed. Air conditioning. We don't even hear the crickets — don't hear the geese flying over in the spring and fall. But . . . The cats moaned and yowled to each other briefly in the ravine. Miserable creatures! We can't help hearing *them*, she thought. Lucas . . . She drew the knowledge of his presence about her like a soft blanket and she, too, drifted into sleep.

CHAPTER 10

His attempt the next day to communicate his troubled state of mind to Howie was unsuccessful. It was as if what he had to say came out with some significance other than he had intended; or as if his plain words bounded off Howie's ears without penetrating to the brain and came back, echoing and resounding as from an opposing mountain, to confuse the sense of those that followed. Lucas's ears rang.

I may be getting deaf, too, along with everything else, he thought.

But he could hear quite clearly, through the closed windows of Howie's study and above the hum of the air-conditioning unit, the liquid whistle of the cardinal that he saw swinging, scarlet against the stiff dark leaves of a loquat tree at the corner of the yard.

Not deaf. Confusion!

Howie's voice grumbled, gruff but whining, "Now, Doc. Now, Doc," and the cardinal's whistle pierced through like an arrow of music, the note of an avian flute. The lawn sprinkler spun under the loquat tree, beating the dark shining leaves with a tattoo (Do I hear even that?) of dissolving crystals. In their wheelchairs in the shade of the elm at the corner of the yard, the Strange brothers sat and talked of turkey hunts and coon dogs. He saw their moving lips and gesticulating arms that with imaginary guns led the flight of imaginary birds.

He turned away from the window and confronted Howie's broad, anxiously questioning face and alert powerful figure. Seated at the roll-top desk that Lucas remembered having seen years earlier in the Snyder commissary, Howie extended a spatulate hand, palm down, as if commanding the waters to be still. "Lucas," he said, "I don't get what you're driving at." He picked up a handful of round brass tokens from the black glass ashtray at his elbow and clinked them repeatedly through his fingers. "Seems to me like everything's going along pretty good," he said.

Lucas did not answer. What *did* he mean, after all, that was too difficult for Howie to take in or in some way inacceptable to him? Mrs. Cathcart was up this morning in her wheelchair, cheerful and comfortable. And Lucy? Was it so monstrous that she had stepped outdoors to speak to her boy friend? The drugs? Howie had dismissed his suspicions about the drugs as too preposterous to consider even for an instant. Perhaps his accusations had been the result of one of those middle-of-the night attacks of anxiety to which he knew he had always been susceptible. Or might it not be even worse than a simple attack of anxiety? Weren't his suspicions slightly paranoid? Another throbbing vision of Lucy's beauty, the long dark legs and high buttocks, the sullen Egyptian face, not simply seen, but felt with swelling specificity in his groin.

I never slept with a black woman, he thought. And now I'm too old even to want to. Too bad. His heart was wrung with a sudden irrational anguish. No! That's not what I want to think or talk about.

He drew a deep breath, seeming to feel in all the labyrinthine reaches of his lungs the weight and location of every minute

branching capillary, of every alveolus past which was
borne the oxygen that never reached his blood. He held his
face sternly expressionless and looked directly at Howie. "Mrs.
Crawley *is* stealing drugs," he said, and felt himself falter before Howie's confidence, felt the force of his opposing per-
sonality, as if it emanated like waves of electrons from those
rusty living freckles.

"Crawley? Drugs? *Crawley?*" Here Howie, clinking his
stack of brass tokens from hand to hand, introduced into the
conversation an implication that at first Lucas missed because he
had begun to concentrate on the tokens, one of which, escaping the stack, staggered across the desk and clunked down
directly in front of him.

While Howie talked (". . . your prejudices . . . let bygones be bygones . . ."), Lucas picked it up and turned it over
in his hand. *Old River Commissary*, he read on one side, and
on the other: 50¢. He knew well enough what the token
signified. Like most farmers in the area, Howie's father had
paid off his hands at least in part with this play money exchange-
able only at his own commissary. Just another indication!
Lucas thought in a sudden access of rage. And then: If we
could sweep it all away! Start over! Everything we've
touched is contaminated, diseased, drowning in moral confusion!
But start over where? With what?

Howie stopped speaking and looked at him curiously. Lucas
held out the token without comment.

"I keep 'em for sentimental reasons," Howie said. "Reminds
me of my boyhood." He went on. "Were you listening to me,
Doc?" He put the pile of tokens back in the ashtray and
turned it slowly between his hairy hands, looking sadly at Lucas
from beneath the heavy rufous brows. "I'm saying you don't
know Crawley, if you think that," he said. "You've got some

kinda fixed idea about her that just ain't *right*. And besides, I watch that drug cabinet like a hawk. Nobody has a key but me and I check the stuff with Crawley every day. We're not getting into that kind of trouble at Golden Age. Not while I'm in charge."

Lucas ignored those words, "fixed idea," and went on, as he thought, methodically and unemotionally: first, the possibility that Mrs. Crawley might be making substitutions after the drugs left Howie's supervision; then, her background, the loss of her license, and her callous and patronizing behavior toward people like Mrs. Wheeler.

"You know how important it is not to strip these people of their dignity — even somebody like Mrs. Wheeler, who's crazy," he said. "Mrs. Crawley doesn't mean to do it, maybe. She doesn't realize . . . But perhaps in the long run that part of it is more important than the drugs."

Howie's expression of puzzled anxiety had not changed. "Crawley's sweet to Wheeler, Doc," he said. "Why, she treats her like a baby. You know, she said to me just the other day, 'I never let myself forget,' she said, 'that ever one of these old folks is somebody's mother — or daddy.'"

Curious, Lucas thought, curious thing with these people: some flaw in the expression of feeling. Question: Is the feeling real and only the expression of it flawed, or . . . ? He began again, stubbornly. "Never mind that for the time being," he said. "Let's go back to the drugs." He told Howie again what he had observed the night before. "Water," he said. "That was water in that syringe. And I don't think it's Lucy who's doing it. Lucy has other preoccupations. But *somebody* put water in that syringe. There are symptoms you could be on the lookout for," he went on. "Contraction of the pupils, of course, and then any unusual euphoria or excited irritability . . .

Now wait a minute, Howie. Don't say anything yet. I'm not —" (He felt a twinge of revulsion at his own pompousness even while he was still speaking the words.) "I'm not without human sympathy. Maybe she doesn't have a drug problem herself. Hell, for all I know she may be taking it to her suffering old mother. And besides, I see her limitations and I know she's bound to have her difficulties, financial and otherwise. I also know you have a hard time getting a competent person for this kind of job. I've been running up against the same thing all my life. But *drugs*, Howie! Stop and think! This is a legal situation as well as a medical one. You're vulnerable here. I'm telling you, I've learned, and you're going to have to learn, to be ruthless where the drug laws are involved. And not only the law. The comfort, even the safety (if I may put it so strongly) of your . . ." He hesitated over the words "patients" and "inmates" and finished, "your — these people are concerned."

But Howie repeated himself. "That's a *fixation* of yours, Doc," he said. "That business about Crawley. She's good — the salt of the earth. Sure, you're right. I ought not to (and I *don't*) put anything ahead of taking care of my people. And that includes your — er — prejudices. So . . ." He smiled significantly and, raking his fingernails through the forest on the backs of his hands, fell silent.

Lucas stiffened. "What do you mean, my prejudices?"

"Well, now, Doc, you know what I mean. You *know*. After all these years, to still be talking about that little episode with her — like it was *yesterday*. I mean, excuse me, but you have something of a tendency to be self-righteous, you know it? Here, you already destroyed this poor lady's means of making a living once. Ain't once enough? And since you last mentioned it to me, I've been into the background of it, too. Crawley's got her side. It ain't as if she was running

some kind of abortion racket, after all. *One* time. *One time.*
One little mistake. And the girl wouldn't testify."

"She died," Lucas said shortly. "She might have changed her
mind, if she'd had time. And who knows how many
others there were before her."

"Died *later*. Nothing to do with the abortion."

"She undoubtedly had an abscessed liver," Lucas said.
"From the same septicemia that put her in the hospital in the
first place. If we'd been able to do an autopsy — but her
father . . ."

"Ne'mind, ne'mind," Howie said. "We're just spinning our
wheels talking about all this ancient history. You can take it
from me, Doc, I'm gonna go over the whole situation. I
won't miss a trick. I run a taut ship and don't you doubt that
for a minute. But what I'm trying to put across to you for
your own good is, Relax. Ain't we been instructed in plain
words 'Judge not that ye be not judged?' Now, you ought to
think about that some, Doc. I know you don't go to church and
all — you're fallen away. But think about it."

"Fallen away!" Lucas glared, then laughed helplessly.

"There's advice for everybody in the Good Book," Howie
said. "Even the infidel. Stop and think about it and you'll see
that's simple good advice. Like casting your bread on the
waters and all. I mean if you trust people, even when you know
they're not trustworthy (I'm not implying for a minute, you
understand, that Crawley isn't trustworthy. I'm taking a hypo-
thetical case), well if you trust 'em, why, it puts them off their
guard and you can keep up with what they're doing. See?
Enough rope . . ."

Lucas stood up, favoring his left leg in which he felt these
days an incipient numbness and an occasional twinge of pain.
Disk about gone, he thought, and then, *Helpless!*

Howie picked up his brass tokens and clinked them from hand to hand. "One thing that interests me about that old case, though," he said. "How'd you manage to take her license when you couldn't get the girl to testify?"

"She never *had* a license," Lucas said. "Some piece of paper hanging on her wall that didn't mean a thing. God knows where she got it."

Howie raised an eyebrow. "Well, now, that was convenient for you, wasn't it? I mean, like you were the one put 'em out and you were the one said if they were the real thing."

Lucas laughed again. "Howie," he said, "you and I have a communication problem."

"No, no. I'm right with you, Doc. And like I said, I'm going to look into all you're talking about. I appreciate your interest."

Lucas left the office and started out of the house, shaking his head and muttering. "Like arguing with a feather pillow," he said to himself. "Every place you punch it, your fist sinks in." And then, "Lunatics. That's what I'm contending with around here. Bunch of damn lunatics." But the judgment did nothing to dispel his anxiety. His own and Martha's situation seemed as dangerous as he had thought it to be. He rehearsed to himself all that had happened the night before, and his doubts returned. Forgetting Lucy and Mrs. Cathcart's bedsore, there was still the syringe with water in it. There it is, he thought. No way to conjure it away. And now, on top of that, I've got to worry about what he thinks of me and what he intends to do about it.

For what Howie had said, plainly enough, was that it had been his vindictiveness that had cost Mrs. Crawley her license and that now, with the same vindictiveness, he was pursuing her again.

And maybe it's true, he thought. I always *was* one to bull

my way ahead regardless of consequences, wasn't I? Isn't that why they wanted to get rid of me at the health department in the first place? I did set myself up in judgment plenty of times. I *had* to. And now every rag, tag, and bobtail in the county has the power to set himself up in judgment on me. A wave of panic swept over him. *I've got to get out of here*, he thought. And then, *But Martha! What about Martha? I've brought her to this — I. And now . . .*

He was striding down the front walk as he went over all these things in his mind (In good weather he always walked the ten blocks downtown to his morning stint at the new public health project) and he pulled up and stood stock-still, looking about him. On the front porch Mr. Howard sat bent over a lapboard with the plastic bits of a model car spread out before him. On either side, bounding the yard, dense green walls of cane leaned inward. The house sank into its shadows. A tall figure with bent shoulders, balancing herself with a metal walker — Mrs. Aldridge? — passed slowly down the hallway and disappeared into the back regions of the house. He heard the click of Harper's hoe and saw him in a corner of the yard chopping at the encroaching cane. He stood a few minutes looking at the composed and intelligent face, the strong hands handling the hoe with the competence of a lifetime. Harper glanced up at him with a nod and then looked back at his work. Lucas crossed the yard, stood beside him, responded to his courteous good morning, and watched him work. "Harper?" he said.

The other man stopped. "Yes, Dr. Alexander?"

"I call the black people I work with downtown 'Mister' and 'Miss,'" Lucas said. "It comes as easy as if I'd always done it. Would you like me to say 'Mister' to you?"

A flicker of alarm crossed Harper's face, and he shook his head. "I don't think that would be advisable here, Dr. Alexan-

APOSTLES OF LIGHT 169

der," he said. "And besides, that kind of thing doesn't bother me. I forgot all that long ago — before some of these folks even began thinking about it."

"The reason I ask," Lucas said, "is I need your advice. I wanted you to know how I'm asking for it."

Harper nodded cautiously.

"You've worked for the Clarkes and Griswolds a long time. What do you think is going on here?"

"What do you mean, what's going on?" Harper asked.

"I mean *this*." Lucas waved his hand at the house. "This Golden Age thing. Do you think it's — O.K.? I mean, some days I feel it closing in on us. We're old, Harper — Martha and I. Neither of us has children. I could leave, of course. But Martha is more or less helpless here. Every now and then I get — panicky." He grimaced contemptuously at his own weakness. "I get the feeling that I should be looking out for our future — if we've got one — and that this is not the place to be doing it. And, being old, you know, I wonder if it isn't all in my imagination."

Harper leaned on his hoe and seemed to be searching his mind for a suitable answer. At last he said, "I don't know that I would want to be living in an old folks' home, Dr. Alexander. I mean, I like to feel independent. I wouldn't want all these folks looking out after me and checking up on me — even if they got the the best of intentions." This answer seemed to satisfy him and he began to chip absent-mindedly at a cane root.

"I even worry about Lucy," Lucas said. "Do you?"

"Lucy!" Harper looked startled. "Lucy's hardheaded. Got to have her own way. And she's flighty — young. Sometimes I could wish she'd do different. But she's making good money."

"That's not what I mean," Lucas said. "I don't think this is a good place for Lucy to be getting a start. They . . ." He started to say that the stink of corruption was in the air, but hesitated and said instead, "Things may not be *right* here. That's the feeling I have. And I want to know if you have it, too."

Harper shook his head slowly, the yellow face expressionless, the old eyes veiled.

"I don't *trust* myself anymore," Lucas said.

He left Harper gazing after him, looking as puzzled as Howie had looked. At the freeway crossing he stood and waited for the traffic signal to tell him to cross and watched the streams of cars rushing past him in both directions. Ants, he thought. So many ants in a kicked-open anthill. Except that instead of every one of us having his own job and his own ant destiny, it's as if we've got our signals mixed and somehow got at cross-purposes with each other. Then: I shouldn't have done that — talked to Harper like that. What's getting into me? Weak! Trying to draw him into it. And Lucy! What do I mean by making that remark about Lucy? That's not like me. If you can't be direct, then keep your mouth shut. And stay out of other people's business.

The light changed, but he did not notice it.

All of them, he thought — Harper, Lucy, Mrs. Crawley, probably even Howie — all of them may simply be trying to survive. I reckon that's what I forget. I fancy up their motives.

And Crawley! He thought of her life, of the years of emptying bedpans and bathing sick bodies in a huge city hospital, of the glass eye and the gold tooth worn like medals won in some brutal battle with the world, of the insouciance, the gaiety of her smile, even though it must seem to her most of the time that the world was bent in some mindless way on her destruction.

Howie's right, he thought. I could be at least as charitable to-ward her as I expect her to be toward — us.

A hand touched his sleeve and a voice broke into his reverie. It was a child from one of the neighboring houses, a boy of twelve or so with all the solicitude of an Eagle Scout. "You having trouble getting across the street, sir? Can I help you?"

Lucas smiled ruefully. "Thank you, son. I must have fallen to thinking. I reckon I can make it on my own," he said.

CHAPTER 11

THE IMMEDIATE RESULT of Lucas's conversation with Howie was a consultation next morning between Howie and Mrs. Crawley and, afterward, a trip by Mrs. Crawley to the attic of Golden Age. She took Harper with her and on the way explained to him the problem that was troubling her.

"Ruby and me been putting the dirty laundry and all up here, see?" she said. "You got to put it somewhere while you waiting for 'em to pick it up. The laundry service don't come around but twice a week and the garbage truck once. If we had a incinerator like a regular-type home or a hospital — but we don't; and not likely to get one, much as they cost. It struck me all of a sudden while me and Mr. Snyder was talking over some management problems this morning — suppose Ruby might be coming down the stairs with a load for the laundry truck and she might open the door" — they had started up the steep enclosed stairs to the attic — "and that very minute some visitor would be walking down the hall — or, even more likely, the old doc — and get a whiff of it! A wonder it hasn't already happened. I told Mr. Snyder we'd better get things in shape up here and, well, he said he didn't even know what we was doing with it all. Shows you how much he knows about anything — *I* run this place. He thought we flushed it down the john or something. But a lot more is involved than a few disposable pads,

even if you could flush them down the john, which you can't —
don't do that, for God's sake! And what are you going to do
with it — drawsheets and mattress pads and so forth? Obviously the attic is the best place to keep things out of sight between laundry and garbage runs. But, if I know Ruby . . ."

She opened the door at the top of the stairs and stepped into
the attic. Harper followed her. A cloud of iridescent green
flies rose from a pile of excrement-smeared, urine-soaked
linens in one corner of the room, stirred the stifling ammoniac
air, buzzed, circled, and settled again.

"You see?" she said. "I was right."

Harper stood behind her at the top of the stairs, a pail of hot
water and disinfectant in his left hand, a mop and broom
over his right shoulder, his eyes flickering over the room.

Roughly finished, its walls plastered and whitewashed, the
wide, pegged cypress floor boards stained and aged almost
black, it had been once, long before his time, a bedroom. Brass
hooks for hanging clothing were mounted in a polished walnut
board under the eaves; built-in corner cupboards at one end
stood open and empty. There was a fireplace against the inside
wall with a plain pine mantel over it and beside it an open door
to a waist-high, tin-lined cabinet. Almost empty of furniture,
the room seemed to Harper to be filled with a curious hollow
sound compounded of the buzzing of the flies, the echo of
Mrs. Crawley's footsteps, and a faint murmur, emanating from
walls and floor, of random thin voices.

He held his breath, scarcely feeling the weight of the pail
handle or the pressure of mop and broom on his shoulder.
Voices? *Voices?* Ridiculous. He drew a breath, felt the invol-
untary contraction of his stomach muscles, and then, mas-
tering his nausea, breathed again and looked about him.

Years ago, he knew, the children, George's and Albert's

generation, had used the attic as a clubhouse. A card table still stood in one corner with four stools around it and a pack of old Bicycle cards scattered across its surface; a tin tray and some chipped doll dishes were stacked on one of the shelves in the wall cabinet next to the mantel and a tattered notice tacked on the wall above read, *Beware all Strangers! Trespassers will be Killed! (signed) Bloddy Four.*

A tiny smile touched Harper's alert and cautious face. Francis? Yes — he had lettered the sign. And Martha and Mrs. Griswold had left it all these years because it amused them, when they occasionally came to the attic, to see it hanging there.

And if Martha were to see the attic now?

Three twenty-gallon garbage cans stood against the wall and around them, too, the flies buzzed. Two of the cans had tight-fitting lids, but the third lid was bent, and the flies crawled slowly in and out. At the far end of the room under a pair of arched dormers through which filtered the green light of a shady June morning stood several trunks and wooden boxes filled with old letters, papers, and magazines which had evidently once been tied in neat piles and bundles. Rats had gnawed through the side of one of the boxes, the lid of one trunk was broken in, and the contents, a dusty shambles of chewed paper and droppings, had spilled out on the floor. Except for the cans of refuse and the pile of sheets, everything in the room — floor, walls, boxes, and papers — was covered with a fine sifting of dust criss-crossed with tiny paw prints.

"Rats bound to get in those cans when the lids are left off," Mrs. Crawley said. "And if I know Ruby, they're left off more than they're put on. Do rats eat shit?"

"I don't think so."

When was the last time anybody had been up here — anybody but these people? Before Mrs. Griswold got sick?

A tremor went through Harper, as if the ground had moved slightly under his feet, and he felt as if at any moment a crack might open into which all their lives would be precipitated. I got to keep my mouth shut, he thought. He set down his pail and leaned the mop and broom against the wall. The broom fell over with a thump and the green flies rose, buzzed, and settled to their feast.

"Clean," Mrs. Crawley said. "I want things to be clean. Everything dirty out of sight."

Harper walked to the end of the room and began struggling to raise one of the windows.

"That's right." She joined him. "And the ones over there too. We need a draft through here. I wonder how long since these was open? Jesus! If the board of health ever got up here . . . ! And if the old doc gets a whiff of it, it won't be fifteen minutes before they're here. Come on, gimme a hand. This one is stuck." With considerable difficulty they raised the windows and braced them with pieces of sawed-off broomstick that lay on the sills. Fresh air began to move through the room and carry off the stench.

"Not that stink bothers me," Mrs. Crawley said. "True, I'm clean, like I said. My uniform is always starched, shoes polished, and so forth." She touched her crackling skirt as if to check the quality of its starchiness and then ran her hand over her flaming hair. "But stink never has bothered me and never will. O.K. I'm going to clean up this mess of paper over here." She was carrying a roll of plastic trash bags and she tore several off and handed them to Harper. "You get the sheets and rags into a couple of these and the disposable pads into another. Be sure you tie 'em up good. And then I'll sweep and you can come behind me with the mop. O.K.?"

"No," she went on, "stink don't bother me. The things I

saw and smelled when I was working at Charity in New Orleans would make your hair stand on end, and that's the truth. But not mine. I was broke young to the stink of the world." She paused as if waiting for Harper to speak, but he had picked up a broomstick and was using it to push filthy sheets into a bag, and he neither looked up nor said anything.

"Dead fish," she said. "That's what I started out with. And the stink of dead fish is the worst there is." She shook out a bag and began to stuff into it the letters and papers that were piled in the trunks under the window and scattered on the floor around them. "This is a fire hazard," she said. "The way these people musta lived! Tsk, tsk."

It doesn't make the least difference what happens to all those papers, Harper said to himself. Miss Martha will never know anything about it and nobody else cares. My fault, he added severely. What have I been thinking about not to notice what's going on up here? Dr. Alexander is right. Something . . .

"Hey, Jesus, some of these letters are *old*," Mrs. Crawley said. "This one says — uh — April twenty-seventh, eighteen twenty-three." She crumpled it and jammed it into the bag. "Now, what was I telling you? Fish! Yeah. My old man was a commercial fisherman. The stink of fish is right down in my bones." Stretching out her hands, she flexed and examined them as if in admiration. "In my bones! But I can't smell it. I trained my nose along with the rest of me to be indifferent." She sniffed at her hands, grinned her wide gleaming grin, and went on. "I can see him now — my old man — like he used to come in at night: reeking, blood and guts on his hands, pants legs soggy — and my mother looking at him like she's actually glad to see him. 'Simon Peter and Andrew,' she'd say (she knew her Bible), 'and James and John, the sons of Zebedee, was all fishermen.' Like he gave a damn. She was dumb, Harper, dumber than most niggers. She married below her and she was so dumb, I don't believe she ever had sense enough to know what happened to her."

Harper put down the plastic bag he was filling and stood for a moment staring at her. Finish with this mess and get out of here, he was thinking.

"Yes, I know you're a nigger and all," she said, "but if you listen to *me*, you can act on the principles I learned from my youth. Here's something I know, for example. A nigger, no matter how ignorant and stupid, has got to be a realist. Like me when I was a child — he can't afford no silly dreams, if he wants to survive. *You* know that, too, don't you? You've got the power to rise above your circumstances, same as I had; so I feel like it ain't a waste of time to give you the benefit of my experience." She paused. Then, "I wouldn't tell a white person all this, you understand. I've got my reputation to think about. But I was born and grew up down on the edge of Bookertown — niggers across the street and all around. I know niggers, and I know when I see one that's different." She had finished stuffing the old papers into her plastic bag, and now she closed the last trunk and taking up the broom began to sweep.

"Maybe if you dipped that broom in my bucket, it wouldn't raise so much dust," Harper said.

"We just got to put up with it. I'll be through here in a minute and you can lay it with the mop. My mother," she went on, "I'll say this about her. She tried. She come from high-class people — her daddy was a preacher and his before him, or so she said — and she tried to keep up the family name. But all she had in her head was scraps of how things used to be, and they was never any good to us. Like this is the kind of thing she would do. If a tramp come along (this was the Depression and the Southern Railroad tracks run right behind our house), she'd ask him in. 'Never turn a stranger from your door,' she'd say, and she'd sit him down and feed him something, if it was only cold greens and fatback. I can see her now, preening herself like some kind of nutty, long-necked, droopy-tailed chicken, saying, 'Don't worry about supper, children; the Lord will provide.' Or, 'Lay not up for yourselves treasure on earth where rust doth corrupt,' et cetera. While we watched him eat the last of whatever it was we had in the house. When she would do something like that, that was when I first begun to know she was crazy as well as dumb. You could hardly blame my daddy for hitting her. I felt like hitting her myself.

"But *he* — that's another matter. *His* craziness . . ." She shook her head. "He was a terrible man. To give you an example — first thing comes to mind — living in Bookertown and all, naturally he hated you people. He'd just as soon kill you or any other nigger as stomp a catfish. And not even trouble to conceal it — no, he'd brag about it. Fortunately, in those days nobody paid much attention to what you did to niggers, so he never tangled with the law . . ."

Harper knew he could not let this pass. "Mrs. Crawley . . ." His voice was balanced judiciously between warning and pleading.

"Now, Harper, don't get your back up. I told you I was just giving you an example. See, there's a purpose in all I say, and I'm going to eventually get to it." She sat down on one of the wooden boxes. "Here," she said, "sit down on that trunk and let the dust settle before you start mopping. Sit down! It'll hold you up."

Harper sat sideways on the trunk lid, leaned across the window sill, and, gazing out into the fresh summer morning, breathed deeply to clear his lungs of the dusty air. She was silent for a few minutes and he waited, he did not know for what. The flies were drifting by ones and twos toward the light of the open windows and out into the sunshine. The dust began to settle. The attic, although still hot, was becoming almost tolerable. But it seemed again to Harper that he could hear the faint sound of voices, and from the chimney a distant breathy roar. The hair rose along his forearms. He looked up and out and saw a plane moving across the cloudless sky — the morning flight coming in from New Orleans.

"What's that noise?" Mrs. Crawley said abruptly.

"Airplane." As if to convince himself, he crossed the room and bending down by the empty fireplace, listened. "The chimney catches the sound," he said, returning to his seat by the window. "Makes it louder."

"Oh," she said, and then, thoughtfully, as it seemed, "When I said, 'Fortunately nobody cared what you did to niggers,' I meant fortunately for *him*. As a matter of fact, it wasn't even fortunate for me that he never got in trouble with the law. I would have been better off if he had — if he'd ended up in Parchman. I'd a been *glad* to see him in Parchman. At least we coulda got on welfare. And it was no privilege, Jesus knows, to live in the house with him. Because he wasn't just mean to niggers. He hated all people. He lived like he saw us all through a curtain of blood. Keep out of his way. That's all you could do.

"And my poor mama. I musta asked myself fifty times a day why she didn't leave him. Nothing could've been worse than living with him. But I really knew, even then — it was all part of the Bible business. That was her craziness. She didn't have no sense of proportion. She thought sane people — like the ones who went to church and all, and had money — actually believed that stuff . . . Now I want you to listen to all I'm saying, Harper. I didn't get you up in this attic just to put sheets in a bag. Ruby could've done every bit of it. I wanted you and me to have a chance to *talk*."

Harper turned back from the window and faced her. "Yes, ma'am," he said. "I'm listening."

"What I want to tell you first is that their being crazy drove me in a different direction. I said to myself that I would live in a different way — I wouldn't destroy myself — with mean craziness or good craziness. I'd think about the future and provide for it. The future! That's what counts with me and that's what should count with you."

"My mother was a Bible reader," Harper said. "A great believer in charity."

"But *mine!* If my old man threw the meat cleaver at her, that was the hand of God. I can see her now, pregnant. (I was the oldest and she had four after me — four that lived, I mean; two, three others that didn't. And would've had more, I reckon, if *she* had lived.) I can see her, six or seven months gone, after he beat her. One eye purple, lip cut, laying on an old piece of sofa with the stuffing coming out of it. I musta seen her like that more than once, it's so clear . . . Propped up on one elbow, looking at you out of one good eye, holding a piece of pig's liver over the other one (if she had a dime to send to the store to get the liver with). 'A woman is like a fig tree,' she'd say. 'God means her to be fruitful and bear.'

"And one of those times I said to myself: You maybe, but not me! I was ten or eleven at the time and I never faltered after that. I begun to plan. I cut myself off from them, never paid any attention to them anymore except to dodge *him*. I kept my wits about me. You might find it hard to believe, Harper, that a child eleven years old would be able to make a plan and carry it through, if it took two or three years. But like they teach you in church, twelve years old, you're morally responsible for all you do. And I was old for my age. Had to be from my circumstances.

"First thing I did, I looked at the girls and women I knew, raised in circumstances like mine, and I saw that some of 'em was working in the ten-cent stores, some of 'em was doing a little hustling, some of 'em already raising a string of kids. The chances any of 'em would ever be rich and happy was slight. Well, I said to myself, 'Where are the people who are rich and happy and what are they doing?' I begun to study the newspapers. My old man would always have stacks of papers — and it didn't matter to me what day or even what year they was for. It was the message I was studying. I looked at the pictures — and there they were! The ladies in their big hats and the men who run the Coca-Cola company and the laundries and all and the thousand-acre farms. And right away I seen the pictures nearly always had something to do with church. Ladies' Auxiliaries, Harvest Bazaars, Community Fund, and so forth. Now, I will say that it might not be the case someplace else (like you hear people talk a lot these days about those rich atheist communists like the Rockefellers and all in New York, but in Mississippi — then or now — you're not going to find many rich atheists. The only ones didn't seem to have to bother with the church was the bootleggers. Well, clearly you got a wider choice of fields, if you stick with the churchgoers. Everybody can't be a bootlegger. And looka here, that didn't last anyhow, because prohibition went out. I'm going to tell you something else I thought about at the time, Harper, reading the papers and all. What about a life of crime? But those bank robbers and their girl friends that you would see their pictures so often in those days, they didn't look rich and they didn't look happy. And the men, some of 'em, looked as crazy as my old man."

After all, she's harmless. I *think*. Not a ghoul. A blunderer. All I have to do is be patient a little while and then go on about my business. Harper gazed over Mrs. Crawley's shoulder at the sign above the mantel and smiled again, while the sound of her voice droned on and on.

". . . started going up town to a rich church — First Baptist . . . dressed up like I was somebody, if I had to steal to do it. You'll never see a run in *my* stockings. My eyes . . . And my hair dyed a nice dark red to show off my pale skin . . ." Suddenly she was silent. Then, "Shh," she said. "Listen."

Again the sound of faraway voices. Again the hair rose on Harper's arms.

She got up and crossed the room to the cabinet beside the mantel, picked up a dusty dish from the tea set, turned it over, put it down, and, to Harper's astonishment, stuck her head inside the cabinet. He rose and crossed the room to join her. Out of the wall, as it seemed, he heard a woman's soft voice speaking. ". . . better, Duane. And Dr. Alexander says . . ." The voice subsided to a murmur. Then he heard a man: ". . . getting any younger. I reckon you have to expect . . ." The woman interrupted. "How are the children?" "Ursula . . ." Strangest of all, below their conversation another voice could be heard: "Come . . . cooommme . . . cooomme . . ." like the humming drone of a top.

Mrs. Crawley stared at Harper. "Wheeler!" she said. "How . . . ?"

Harper straightened up, stared into the cabinet, and at last laughed grimly. "Ghosts," he said. "My mama would've said it was ghosts and for a minute that's what *I* thought." Again he laughed. "I reckon that's what it is." He gave the cabinet in its recess in the wall a gentle push and it moved creakily. "It's a dumbwaiter," he said. "I had forgotten. The shaft goes all the way to the basement. Used to be in the kitchen, when that was in the basement years ago. I can remember when the children . . ." He broke off. "Closets now," he said. "One in Mrs. Cathcart's room and one right under it in Mrs. Wheeler's room. That's all."

"Shh," Mrs. Crawley said. "What'd he say?"

". . . got to go, Mama." Another unintelligible murmur and then, ". . . out of town all next week."

Mrs. Crawley shrugged and gave the tin wall of the cabinet a resounding thump. The sound echoed and reechoed through the attic. "That'll give 'em something to think about," she said. "Maybe shut old Wheeler up for a few minutes." She crossed the room and returned to her seat on the box.

Harper picked up his mop and dipped it in the bucket.

Mrs. Crawley laughed. "I could make their hair stand on end, if I come up here in the middle of the night and give that thing a few thumps," she said. "But to go back to what we was talking about, that was one thing in my favor — looks. And like I said, we come from good people."

Harper looked up from his mopping and took in the wildly angled glass eye and the flashing good one, the flaming hair, the wide smile with its glints of gold, the pendulous breasts and sagging belly. She raised her hand and touched her hair as if his glance were a tribute to her beauty. Then she went on.

"So, pretty soon I was up on how they acted and talked and what they wore and all. I was *ready*. I got married. Not but fourteen, but everybody thought I was seventeen. My mother had died by then. In fact, I married just a few weeks after she died. Already had a man picked out and was working on him *before* she died — a man that seemed to me to fill the bill. I knew I couldn't aim too high. I wasn't going to land the Ford dealer's eighteen-year-old son. The way I figured it, I would cast

around for a fellow in his thirties who was still a bachelor —
somebody who'd always been too timid to go out with the girls.
I didn't want him to be smart. He might look too hard at what
I was and back off, scared. So I was willing to settle for some-
thing like maybe a clerk at the post office — I wasn't particular
— I knew it was just the first step up. And you know yourself,
Harper, there are plenty of men like that around. I lied about
my age and we got married. It was as simple as that.

"My clerk and me was divorced in thirty-six. He didn't do
me as much good as I expected. A man needs more brains
than he had to make it — even in the post office. But I had put
those years to a good use, always planning for the future. What
money he gave me, I saved it. I picked up a little, hustling in the
daytime (*Quietly*. Not a soul knew it), and I saved every cent
of it. Also, I'd got aholt of a midwife's license, just by accident,
through some connections I made at the time, and I kept it by
me. Who knows what you may need sometime or other? That
was my philosophy and still is. So I left him, feeling like I could
make it on my own. Then a terrible thing happened to me during that period of my life, Harper. It was the late thirties and
I was on the loose. I felt *free* — still young and full of life and
power. I forgot all about the way people are supposed to act
and I paid for it. The Baptists had read me out when I got
divorced, and I thought to myself: I got a profession, got my
looks, got a little money; I don't need to worry with these folks.
Well, I was wrong. When they realized I was free they bided
their time and then they come down on me like a band of wild
Indians. And it was the old doc here they used to do it with.
Yes, he's one of 'em. Always has been and always will be.

"You see, this is another principle you got to grasp. Sane
people — successful people — want you to be like them, *and
they're right!* They know anybody commences to act like they

don't care who's in charge, it's a threat. So they don't want you to go straying off on sprees of love or good living or even just saying what you think. They know it's dangerous and they take action."

"I don't think I understand exactly what you're talking about, Mrs. Crawley," Harper said. He swung his mop methodically back and forth on the floor, stopping occasionally to disentangle it from the splintery boards. "I just go my way and do my job," he went on. "It won't be but three years until I begin drawing my social security — if I wait until I'm sixty-five."

"Of course you don't know what I'm talking about," she said. "That's what I've got you up here for — to explain these things. And you may decide it's worth a lot more than social security to . . ." She broke off. "I'll come to that. First, I want to tell you how come I got tangled up with the old doc. Sit back down here now and listen to me."

"Yes, ma'am," Harper said.

"What happened was kinda peculiar. There was this kid I got acquainted with and in a way she reminded me of myself when I'd been that age. Her circumstances was *savage.* She come in to me out of the cold rain one February night in the rooming house where I was staying and I took one look at her and after that she was all I thought about for two years or longer. She had a thin little body with bones like willow sticks (couldn't have been more than fifteen at the time I took up with her) and eyes as pale green as cottonwood leaves in April; and she had a look about her that I'd seen on my own brothers and sisters, and on my own self, for that matter, when somebody's hit you one time too many and you don't even believe in pain no more. Don't feel nothing. Yeah, she was like another self to me. Blank and waiting — waiting for the bastard who sees the world through a curtain of blood to tear her apart.

"It had never crossed my mind before to think of sleeping with a woman — you know, that I was queer or anything like that. There certainly wouldn't have been no profit in it . . ."

Harper watched her with alert attention, holding himself so still that his very breath did not move his chest. He might have been a polished yellow stone resting on the trunk lid instead of a man. At this point, however, he decided to interrupt, the pompous butler's voice coming as if disembodied from the motionless mask of his face. "I'm what you might call a student of human character, Mrs. Crawley," he said. "I mean," he added cautiously, "people's life stories interest me and I think it's a . . ." He hesitated. ". . . a privilege to hear them. But also something you said awhile ago struck me. That about . . . a nigger having to be a realist. I certainly — ah — tend to agree with that. And, you know, my sense of — reality — tells me you might be sorry later you've been so — so frank with me. If . . ."

"You hadn't gotten through the tenderfoot course, Harper," she said. "If you had, you'd know that I can say anything I please to you. I could sit up here and tell you I'm the one killed Emmett Till and it could be true and it wouldn't hurt me, because all I got to do is tell anybody else asks me about it that you're lying. You know no nigger man better start telling lies on a white woman. Civil rights hadn't changed that.

"But in another way, that makes an advantage for us — we can be friends, because the same thing works the other way around. You can tell me what *you* think and how *you* feel. The reason is because *not* talking to me is useless — I could always make something up against you and people would believe it."

"Maybe not everybody," Harper said.

She shrugged. "The ones who count," she said. "But I'm not going to say anything against you. What I'm trying to show you is that we can be *friends*. It's a lonesome world, Harper. A person needs somebody he can talk to, even a strong person like me." She drew a deep breath, Harper nodded his head with a slight smile that might be taken for agreement and sympathy, and she began to speak again about her youth. "I never thought of a thing but that girl for two years," she said. "She reminded me of my mother, too, you know — I mean in her gentle ways and how she would give away whatever she had to anybody wanted it. But of course she was mostly giving herself to me and so I wasn't warned like I should've been by the way she was like Mama. Yeah, those are the most dangerous people in the world. You'll get into trouble any time you tangle with 'em.

"Well, it's not a long story and I won't drag it out. She gave herself away once too often — to some sad traveling sales-man used to come around and stay at the rooming house where we lived. She was sorry for him, she said. She got pregnant — not seventeen yet. See, if I'd had my wits about me, it'd have been different. I'd have studied her assets and begun to teach her how to use them . . .

"I aborted her. I had learned how to do everything right, even if my license was a phony. It's easy enough to catch onto, if you watch a few. I made sure everything I used was *clean*. I've always been a clean person — more so than most. So it couldn't have been my fault — not any of it.

"But she got sick and died all the same. And of course they *said* it was me. I had stepped out of line and they used the first thing come to hand. Oh, it drives a successful person crazy to see anybody step out of line — even if it's some harmless nothing like the kids now letting their hair grow and all. When I got myself back together, I realized that. I don't even hold it against the old doc. He was doing his part like the rest of 'em." She shrugged and was silent.

Harper looked doubtful. "I wouldn't call Dr. Alexander successful," he said.

"He may not've made it to the top, but he was trying. He knew all right that you've got to keep everybody in line. Why else would he have come down on me like he did? For *nothing?*" The sun flashed on her glass eye and it seemed to flicker and move in its socket. "However that was," she said, "it was a long time ago. *We're* in charge now — and he's the one stepping out of line. A long time," she said thoughtfully. "Thirty years. But I never forgot it.

"The second time I got put down was nothing but bad luck. I had moved upward. My second husband was a hospital orderly. My third was a lab technician. My fourth was a drug salesman and he owned a laundromat besides. He woulda left me well-fixed, if it hadn't been for the bad luck. We had a house in Gentilly, all French provincial furniture, freezer full of TV dinners, and a girl to come in and do the heavy cleaning and ironing. Wouldn't you like that kind of life, Harper? You know you would. We was *solid.* We gave to all the good causes like Community Fund and Citizens' Council and all. And in fact we was on our way back from a district meeting of the Council when we had the wreck. Killed him and made a mess of my life. Not just my eye, which was bad enough, but come to find out he didn't own much of an interest in the laundromat at all. He was just *beginning* to buy on it. So there I was, flat broke, a glass eye to buy, a stack of doctor's and hospital bills to pay, not to mention funeral expenses (I'll say this for myself. I didn't give him no two-bit social security funeral), starting all over again at the bottom. And I wasn't young either — past fifty.

"Again, I had some assets. It doesn't hurt nobody who needs to make a living to have been married to a lab technician and a hospital orderly and a drug salesman. And I had worked awhile at Charity during the time I was married to the orderly. Soon as I was able I went back to Charity and got into the drug business. The channels was available to me — people around Charity knew me and trusted me. And, being a nurse and all, I was doing good and helping the suffering. It was a satisfying life to me, and, as for the pay, that didn't matter — my profits come from elsewhere. It lasted five years and then the supervisor begun to get greedy. I was fortunate enough to see the end coming in time to get out before the crackdown — the supervisor and one of the pharmacists, they ended up on the short end of the stick." Mrs. Crawley smiled pleasantly. "I believe they went to the federal pen," she said, "but I was gone by then. I'd been looking around for months for a new career, and from all I could see, nursing homes, for somebody with my background, were the coming thing. So here I am. Brought my little nest egg with me. I haven't invested it yet — I want to be sure I'm satisfied with Snyder's plans and my part in them. But as far as the field is concerned, I know I'm right. More people getting old and helpless all the time — the wonders of medical science, you know — and somebody's got to take care of 'em.

"Now, you might ask yourself why I told you all this, Harper, but I been observing and listening and it's plain to me you could be the key to the future of our plans. I mean, these people seem to trust you. Now that we (and by "we" I mean me, if I go in on it, and Snyder; but I could mean you), now that we're getting ready to expand, we got to have their confidence — Clarke's nieces and nephews and all. If they know we're doing a good job, if this place always looks sharp and nobody don't give nobody no trouble, and if they're making money, they're going to stay happy.

"This could mean a lot to you and Lucy." She leaned forward and looked intently at him, the good eye narrowed and alert, the glass one seeming to stare at the wall behind his right shoulder. "You may not think I know who and what you spend your time thinking about but I do. It's them children, ain't it? I see it. But take a friendly word of advice and don't go off the deep end over them like I did over that girl I loved — it won't do them or you no good. Keep your eyes open for the main chance, observe appearances and teach them to do the same — that's how to look out for them. And I'm here to tell you that right now we could be the main chance."

A flicker of alarm crossed Harper's face. He hunched one shoulder forward and crossed his arms as if he might be concealing something within them, but then, recovering himself, "Yes, ma'am," he said. "I'm gonna do right by my grandchildren."

"Sure you are. All I'm saying is I could help you do better." She had observed the alarm and added, "You don't need to worry about the law. I'm not at all planning to stay in the drug business. I hadn't sold *no* drugs in this town. Does it make sense to take that kind of risk when you can invest your time and money legally? Of course not. All I want with you is to lay my cards on the table as to how I operate and my philosophy and all, so you'll feel confidence in me and know what's going on. You'll know what to expect, you'll feel safe, knowing I'm an honest, dependable person. Then you'll be able to help us and help yourself."

She looked steadily at him. "You're a cautious one, Harper," she said, "and that's good. But I want to be sure we understand each other. When I was thinking about talking all this over with you, see, I said to myself, I never seen a nigger yet didn't hate white people, especially a yellow one. So don't waste my time telling me you don't hate these people you been working for for nickels and take-homes the last thirty years. I *know*.

And I reckon for good measure you hate me and Snyder, too. But what I'm telling you is, you don't have to hate me. That's where I and the Citizens' Council part company. I believe two people like us can work together as individuals. We can be *true* to each other. See?"

"Yes, ma'am. I think I see what you're getting at."

"All right, then. To go on: Like I was saying, this setup could mean a lot to you and your family. I reckon Lucy's already told you how much it could mean to her." She paused as if wondering how far it might be possible to explore Lucy's involvement.

"Lucy told me she's thinking about taking that nurses' course in Vicksburg. I don't know whether I think it's a good idea."

"We can probably work things so she don't have to take it. Anyhow, you all don't need to make up your minds about that right off. Our problem now is something else. We done run into a hitch here that you could help us untangle. The old doc is getting to be a menace. Every place you turn he's got his nose into our business. Drugs, for instance. He's worrying about where Snyder keeps 'em and who gives the shots. It's none of his business. Sanitation. *Sanitation!* With the standards I maintain, he's got the nerve to complain to Howie about sanitation. That's why we're up here this morning. It struck me like a bolt of lightning while I was talking to Snyder that the old doc might sic the health department on us. And that's just the start of it. He's already been griping about the net we use to keep Wheeler out of trouble. And we *got* to use it. Otherwise you couldn't leave her alone for ten minutes. Lucy gets pretty busy at night, you know." She gave Harper one of her gold-glinting grins. "I mean, being here by herself and all. Well, that's one thing. Another: yesterday night he creeps into Cathcart's room in the middle of the night and accuses us of letting her get a bedsore. No!" She raised her hand as if Harper had spoken. "Of course she hadn't got no bedsore. He dreamed it up out of his head. You see? He's going to be nothing but trouble to us. And you're the one person could back him up in his nutty stories — the one person Clarke's relatives might believe, that is. Because it'll be easy enough to keep them from believing the old people, if any of them get involved. They're all off their rockers — more or less, depending on the case. It's only the doc we need to plan for. Well, what do you say, Harper? Are you with us?"

Harper stood up and looked out the window. From where he stood he could see the lush green of the cane thicket and of the trees he had tended for thirty years — tulip poplars, blooming now, their green blossoms as exotic as orchids; the elm in the corner of the yard, its massive trunk gray with lichen; the fruit trees: pears and figs and peaches that he had pruned and sprayed year after year with loving care and that now Howie Snyder wished to clear away; and along the property line two bare spaces — one where the scuppernong arbor had stood, the other where every year until this one he had had a vegetable garden. Just now, he thought, it would be coming to its peak. He could not see the sloping mossy bank of the bayou but he heard a water thrush call from the cattail bed along its edge. He looked back at Mrs. Crawley, his face expressionless. "My main interest is my grandchildren," he said. "They have nobody to look after their future but me." He raised the sash of the open window an inch, took out the piece of broomstick with which it had been propped, and let it carefully down. "But I'm not sure I know exactly what you want with me," he added.

"It's simple enough," she said. "The chief thing is to keep this place operating smoothly, to keep everybody *clean* and quiet — the cages hosed down and the animals fed, you might say. That's the key to a profitable home — and a *good* home. And to look out for the doc. Keep him satisfied if we can. And if we can't — well, we'll face that when we come to it. There are ways . . . But all you got to do is be on the lookout to keep him satisfied and be ready to back us up, if we need you."

Harper closed the other window and began to gather up his cleaning equipment. "As you said already, I'm a cautious man, Mrs. Crawley," he said. "You can be sure I'm not going to do anything that'll hurt my children's future. I got three more to raise, after all, and Gertrude's not ten yet. And you can be sure I like things to operate — smoothly." His nostrils flared. He walked to the other end of the room and, taking a piece of newspaper from the top of a box there, whacked a huge green fly that buzzed around the closed mouth of the garbage can.

"I'm gonna watch out after you," she said. "You wait and see. You and Lucy are gonna have your place in this organization. And we're all gonna make money. Rich and respectable, that's what we're gonna be. Y'all'll be able to thumb your noses at the richest niggers in the state."

CHAPTER 12

Two images more — of sexual license and of cruelty — set
Lucas on a course of action. Walking the corridors and gardens of Golden Age in his accustomed sleeplessness, he came,
one rainy August night, as he returned down the stairs on noiseless slippers, carrying his glass of wine and plate of cheese and
crackers from the pantry, upon Lucy sitting at her desk in the
dim midnight hall. Howie stood behind her; his freckled hands,
the skin glowing green under the lamp on the desk, squeezed
her young breasts (claws! green powerful claws of a dinosaur),
while she sat passive and expressionless, the glistening dark eyes
staring at the wall in front of her, her own hands folded and
resting on the desk as neatly as the hands of a child at prayer.

The light was blinking over the Strange brothers' bedroom
door. On and off, on and off, on and off — a distress signal in the
dim silence.

Without a word Lucas turned, went up the stairs he had just
come down, and made his way around the house to his own outside door.

In his dreams that night Lucy came and stood naked beside
his bed. She reached out her hand to him and he tried to rise
but, looking down, saw that his legs (skinny and old, the muscle
gone to nothing, the shin fuzzed with sparse white hair) were
fastened to the foot of his bed with a chain and padlock. A

green lizard came crawling out of his pocket, ran down his thigh, and began to tear with green claws at his bare ankle.

The next morning, before he had succeeded in ordering his thoughts (before he had even gone upstairs for breakfast), he heard Mrs. Crawley's penetrating voice from Mrs. Wheeler's room. On impulse he walked (noiseless again, but this time deliberately noiseless) down the hall and looked in through the half-open door.

There were two hospital beds in the room, two slat-backed oak chairs of the sort that go with old-fashioned office furniture, and a painted chest. In the bed farthest from the door lay Miss Carrie Stock, her face turned toward the door, her eyes half-open. She lay still, unable to move any part of her body except her eyelids. A tube protruded from her nose and was taped to her cheek. Mrs. Wheeler crouched in the nearer bed watching Mrs. Crawley, back to the door, smoke from the cigarette in her mouth curling around her head, tie the cargo net to the bed's raised side.

"Yeah, honey." She spoke indistinctly around the cigarette. "We got to put it back on."

Mrs. Wheeler reached out and grasped the meshes of the net with a skinny arthritis-twisted hand, and gave it a shake.

"Can't leave you down here, *loose*, because you won't mind Crawley. You got to learn to *mind*, you know it? You see how our little cabbage over there minds, don't you?" She jerked her head at the other bed with its leaden, motionless freight. "I don't have to put no net over her."

At the word "cabbage" Miss Carrie raised her lids. A muscle below her right eye twitched. She looked at Mrs. Crawley and then her eyes shifted to Lucas. She opened her eyes wide and gazed at him for a long moment, and then closed them. She made a low croaking sound. Then she opened her eyes, looked at Lucas, and blinked. Once. Twice.

"Come," Mrs. Wheeler said.

"Now, if you don't behave, Mr. Snyder's gonna *git* you. You hear? You keep trying to pull this net loose and he's liable to lose his temper and come down here with his gre't big ol' red-hot pliers and pinch your fingers off."

"Come," Mrs. Wheeler said. "Come."

Mrs. Crawley took the cigarette from her mouth and held it close to the ancient claw that still clutched the net. Mrs. Wheeler snatched back her hand and thrust it into her mouth.

"You see?" Mrs. Crawley laughed.

Mrs. Wheeler took her hand from her mouth. "Come," she said. "Come, come, come." She did not speak aloud but in a breathy passionate whisper, as if her voice were not meant to be heard in the confines of her room, but someplace beyond, far away, where it would be blown by the wind of her need. She shook the net tentatively. "James?" she said. "Come. Come."

Mrs. Crawley laughed. "If you don't look like a little ol' monkey, I never saw it," she said. "I'm gonna bring you some peanuts." She moved to the other end of the bed and retied a loose knot. "Yeah," she said. "Peanuts for breakfast. You'd like that, wouldn't you?"

She turned to leave the room and saw Lucas standing in the hall. "Good morning, Doc," she said gaily. "Like I was telling my little monkey here, breakfast is about ready." Her gold teeth flashed in a wide smile. "You coming up?"

Lucas turned away and went up the stairs at his own end of the hall.

Later that morning from his office at the new health center he made two telephone calls, one to George and one to Albert, asking them to meet with him that afternoon either in his room or in Howie's office on matters vital to Martha's health and to the operation of the home. He asked George to telephone Howie and arrange the meeting with him. They agreed upon three o'clock in Howie's office.

Lucas had no wish to talk with Howie before the meeting. When he had finished his work at the health center, he walked three blocks to the hotel coffee shop and, to avoid going back to Golden Age, ordered his lunch there and afterward sat for an hour over coffee, turning the pages of a magazine and trying to read. He had scarcely touched his lunch. He was filled with a hollow unattached dread, unable to think of the consequences of his intended acts.

At twenty minutes to three he set out briskly for Golden Age, alert to the world about him. He observed that the trees and grass were getting a drab August look and that the cotton-woods, harbingers of winter, had already begun to shed their leaves. Waiting for the light to change where his street crossed the freeway, he heard a familiar *skree-ree* high in the air and, looking upward, saw two kites wheeling above the city, their heads flashing white in the light-filled sky. Thunderheads were piling up along the southern horizon. He was conscious that he had been walking too fast. He was having some difficulty breathing and felt a light scratching and itching in his throat. Allergy? This late in life! To compound the emphysema? Yes, it's ragweed season. The constriction of those terminal bronchi-oles can be exacerbated by tension, you know, he said to himself with detachment. He crossed the street when the light changed, gently shaking his wrists, flexing and relaxing set after set of muscles and allowing himself only one thought about the im-pending meeting: I mustn't be out of breath when I begin to talk. As he stepped up on the curb, his stomach lurched and contracted with nausea and he felt the flow of saliva under his tongue. He proceeded more and more slowly along the last block, breathing lightly and carefully, climbed the steps, and stood resting at the top. Harper was on the front porch, the mail in his hand.

Erect and soldierly as always, a slight frown on his long ascetic face, Lucas strode down the walk, nodded to Harper, and went into the house. In the hall he paused, running his fingers through his mustache and hair, looking about him, and thinking briefly of how it had once looked here: Martha's beautiful botanical prints on the walls, the worn Oriental rugs punctuating the bare length of floor. He gazed at Howie's giant plastic rubber plants and artificial mother-in-law's tongue, squared his shoulders, and continued on his way.

In Howie's study he found them waiting for him; Howie, seated at the roll-top commissary desk, was speaking earnestly to the other three men (Newton had come, too). He broke off and rose when Lucas entered. "Well, Doc. Well, here we are, just wondering what's up."

The other three men rose, too, and Newton deferentially pulled an easy chair forward for Lucas.

"No, no. Sit down, George, Albert. Sit down." Lucas sat down himself, brushing away their solicitude as if it were cobwebs, and began immediately to tell them what was on his mind. First, Mrs. Crawley. Her background. His anxiety because she was in charge of the drugs in the house. Her manner with the patients. And finally the scene with Mrs. Wheeler that he had witnessed that morning.

"And not only Mrs. Wheeler," he said. "Miss Carrie. She — she *looked* at me — *blinked*. And her eyes . . . She may be aware of everything that's going on around her. And if she is, how could Mrs. Crawley not know it? Has anyone troubled . . . ?"

"Blinked?" Howie gave a short laugh. "Yes, she can blink, Doc. No denying that."

Lucas hurried on, as if afraid he might change his mind. Lucy. His having several times found her gone from her place in the hall and having assumed she was outside meeting her "boy friend." He pronounced the word with distaste.

They sat in silence as he talked; and he felt his nausea returning — as if they might be meeting in the captain's quarters on a disabled ship staggering through a storm. The military accessories, the maps on the wall with pins marking the already forgotten campaigns of World War II and the more ancient ones of World War I and of Gettysburg and Shiloh, intensified the illusion. The floor (deck?), it seemed, slanted under his feet, tilting first one way and then another, and the men themselves seemed to be leaning toward him as if to counteract the slant of the floor.

But he knew well enough the reason for his nausea. He no longer blocked it out. He was going to have to speak of the tableau he had seen in the dark hall the night before — of Howie bending over Lucy, his hands on her breasts, while the light over the Stranges' bedroom door blinked on and off. As he continued to speak of Lucy's boy friend, he was saying to himself, *No.* I won't say anything about *that.* I *can't.* Too . . . Too . . . And answering himself, I *have* to. Howie is the one who has to go. Just forcing him to fire Crawley is not going to solve anything.

The Clarkes listened, nodding, and, when Lucas paused, George cleared his throat and said, "Hmmm."

"Times have changed, you know, Lucas," Albert said. "Young folks now . . ."

"Wait a minute please, Albert. I'd better finish before you say anything." He raked at his mustache and looked fiercely

from one to the other. "I want *all* of you to know that it is difficult for me to tell you these things," he said. "If it weren't necessary, if I didn't know that you need to hear them, that you
wouldn't want me to be silent, I would — *leave.* Go away, before I opened my mouth. But I *have* to go on." He drew a deep
and painful breath. "How shall I say it? No way except to blurt
it out. Damn it, I can't help how it sounds. I *have* to . . ."

While he described the scene, he saw their three faces (he did
not look at Howie) hanging (bewildered? unhappy? skeptical?)
in the smoky, dizzying stateroom air, fogged now by the cigar
that Howie had picked up and painstakingly brought to life during the time Lucas had been talking. When he had finished his
account, Lucas looked directly at Howie. (My eyeballs feel
tight. Scotoma in left visual field. Glaucoma? Hypochon-
dria!) He went on in a low monotone. "Damn it," he said, "I
don't care who you sleep with — any woman in Homochitto,
black, white, blue, or green. God knows you're welcome to
your sex life. I congratulate you. But *here? Here?* Do you
really have so little regard for your own professionalism — for
the necessary, *minimal* standards . . . ?"

As he spoke, he saw a look come over Howie's face, a look,
unmistakably, of pity and tolerant understanding, and, when he
saw it, the word he had sought earlier exploded in his mind: Dangerous! Too dangerous! But still, obsessed with projecting to
the three Clarke men his outrage and concern, he did not say to
himself who it was the danger threatened. Not until he saw
them (or saw Albert and Newton — George was studying his
feet with passionate intensity) looking back at Howie, Newton
with raised eyebrows, Albert shaking his beautiful snowy mane
sadly. Then he knew that the danger was to him — and even
more than to him, to Martha. *I* can leave, he thought. But
Martha? Abruptly he was silent.

Howie and Newton continued to look at each other. George raised his head and made a tiny gesture toward Newton, as if inviting him to speak, raising his hand from his lap and turning it palm up as if in supplication. But Newton said nothing.

Albert shrugged. "Well, now," he said. "Well, now." But he did not go on.

Howie sat solidly at his desk, his arms folded as they had been through all this part of Lucas's recital. His cigar smoldered in the ashtray. His face still had on it the expression of interested compassion that Lucas had recognized. His ginger mustache drooped sadly.

Newton got up and, moving around behind Howie, stood next to the desk and rested one hand on it. Behind him Lucas could see the expanse of the South Pacific, dotted with pins at tiny islands like Iwo and Eniwetok and Wake. In front of him Howie rocked slightly in the desk chair and its springs groaned. Newton, hovering behind Howie as if he might be protecting him, spoke: "Serious charges. *Serious*, Dr. Alexander! *Sure* you want to . . . ?" gulping down whole clauses, as if his headlong speed might deflect Lucas from his course.

Lucas went on doggedly. "You people are not living here," he said. "I am. I see it, every day." I'm tired, he thought. Tired. "It's not *abuse*," he said. "It would be easier to convince you if people were suffering physical abuse. But they will — in time. She will twist an arm, tie a restrainer too tight, shove that cigarette against live flesh. Give her time and freedom and it will happen." Still speaking into their silence, he said, "I thought about it a long time. I mean, I had seen, as I say, evidence of this kind of thing over a period of weeks — months. God knows, I don't want to make trouble. I didn't want to see it, to believe it. I tried to put it out of my mind — to hope it would go away. But it wouldn't. It didn't. And then last night, when I saw *him* down there, I made up my mind we would *have* to face up to it. For Martha's sake. For everybody. I suppose I hold it in check to a degree, just by being here. But what if I had a stroke and died tonight? I could, you know. Martha — all of them — would be out here, *trapped*. With this woman whom I saw threaten poor old Mrs. Wheeler with a lighted cigarette, and with — with Howie, here, whose behavior . . . And Lucy, miserable child . . ." He looked directly at George and called his name and at last George looked at him. "Do you believe anything Martha says?" he asked. "Would you believe her if she told you things were bad out here, and she had no one to back her up?"

George shuddered, leaning sideways in his chair almost as if his thin, insubstantial body were blown out of plumb by the force of Lucas's words.

Then, "Of course I would," he said. "I mean, she has an occasional lapse, but . . . in general . . ."

Newton, his long-chinned, whiskey-ad face composed in a thoughtful lawyer's frown, picked up a pencil from the desk top and lightly beat a tattoo on the desk. "Beside the point, Daddy," he said. "Excuse me. Question is . . . Yes, the question: Dr. Alexander's charges against Howie and Mrs. Crawley and — Lucy, I suppose. That's the question."

Albert smiled, his geniality matching Howie's tolerance. He looked at Lucas, the bright blue eyes alert behind startlingly white brows.

He always gives the appearance of looking out and up from behind the screen of his eyebrows, Lucas thought, and the eyes have a tendency to jump, almost as if he has a nystagmus. Could that be? "Do you have any trouble with your eyes, Albert?" he said abruptly.

"Newton's right," Albert said. "And if *you'll* excuse *me*,

Lucas, my putting it so bluntly, I mean; but with the best will in the world, it's not whether we would believe anything Martha had to say, but whether we believe what you're saying."

George flinched.

"I mean," Albert went on, "you might be mistaken, you know. All of us are getting older and, as you say, our eyes ain't exactly what they used to be. And aside from that, Howie here ain't exactly a stranger, you know. We're all of us cousins. Cousins and friends. We *trust* him. We can't just take you on your word."

"I know," Lucas said. "That's the problem, all right."

"And Christians, too," Albert said. "Howie, here, is a *lay* reader. He used to be senior warden. Now you might think about that and wonder if maybe you ain't just plain wrong."

Affects the eighteenth-century gentleman's "ain't," Lucas thought. Last shred of a genteel Southern background. *Am* I crazy? Green lizard on my leg.

"Wait a minute now, friends," George said. The plaintive voice was full of emotion. "Wait a *minute*. Let's stop and think who we *all* are here. Lucas as well as Howie. We've got a *lifetime* behind us. Lifetime of trust in each other's good will and — honor. Yes, honor. That's not too strong a word here. Now, I'm sure nobody is in any doubt about those things. Right? This is a terrible misunderstanding. We can talk it out among ourselves and make an adjustment here and there and — and — iron out the wrinkles and — and so forth . . ."

"Daddy!"

"I am in doubt about Howie's *honor* and Mrs. Crawley's good will and Lucy's judgment," Lucas said. "And Albert is in doubt about my truthfulness. Newton," he added, with an ironic bow in the young man's direction, "seems to be presiding." I should have resisted that, he thought.

The springs of the desk chair creaked as Howie leaned back, took two puffs on his cigar, and laid it down in the square black ashtray on his desk. "Right," he said. "George and Albert are right. We got too much behind us to get mad at each other. Newton, I reckon you and the doc here may not realize it, but you folks are real family to me. I *lived* here with Martha and Elizabeth during the early part of the Depression. Ain't that right, George? I'd just as soon cut my arm off as . . ." He broke off. Then, "Now, let me make myself clear. I ain't *thinking* about justifying myself to the doc. What kind of a reaction would that be — with my own family? With fifty years of friendship behind us? What could I say about myself that you don't already know? I wouldn't — *couldn't* — dignify such an accusation with . . ." He looked significantly up over his shoulder at Newton. "No, let me put it another way," he said. "It would be doing the doc himself an injustice for me to argue with him. Let me just say that I'm sure he believes that every word he's saying is the truth. Why, I'll go even farther than that. I'm close enough to getting old to understand all those feelings of helplessness and — er — persecution, et cetera, that old age is bound to bring. I have nothing but sympathy with those feelings. I may be in the same boat myself one of these days. And I can see that when you begin to feel helpless, the next step might be to imagine that the people who are trying to look after you are really out to get you. That's all, now. That's enough. I'll say no more about that. No hard feelings, Doc. Hear? You got everybody's best interests at heart, and I'm the one who knows it."

"Now," Newton said.

"Wait, wait! That ain't all. I take it back." He opened both arms in an expansive gesture. "I want to say this, too. Our life at Golden Age is an open book. You gentlemen know that. Feel free to talk to my people. Right? Right now, if you want to. See if everything is operating to your satisfaction. Come any hour of the day — or *night* — and see what we're up to out here." He gave a little ironic chuckle. "Any time," he said. "And not only that, I want you to know that I welcome suggestions. I'm anxious to improve things. I want my folks to be *happy*."

"I would like to know if you have any doubts about Mrs. Crawley as a — sitter. A *keeper*. And if you are accusing me of lying about last night," Lucas said.

"*Doc*." A tinge of irritability crept into Howie's voice. "I've already told these folks I ain't going to be put in the position of defending myself and my people against . . ." His voice trailed off.

"Now," Newton said again. "Here's what we need to do. Daddy? Albert? If you agree. We're the board here, right? No use — no point — too painful to everybody. Spare everybody's feelings if Lucas and Howie — if you two let us talk this over, among ourselves. O.K.? O.K."

Lucas got up, already thinking, *What next? What next? Nothing is going to happen here*, already turning over in his mind alternative plans. The thought of Mrs. Wheeler in her cage (Come. Come), of Mrs. Crane at bay in the dining room doorway (I won't inconvenience you people any further), of Miss Carrie alone, abandoned in her narrow bed, of the Stranges and their dreams of woodland life, of poke salad, chinquapins, and wild mustard greens, passed through his mind. I can't help them. If I can do anything to extricate Martha, that's the best I can manage.

Howie rose, too, and bowed to Lucas with that curious smile

of his, a smile of complicity that seemed to say, I know *you* —
and you know me. At the door he paused to let Lucas precede
him.

In the dining room, with the door closed behind them, Lucas
stopped and for a moment they looked at each other. Then,
"There's one thing that puzzles me," Lucas said. "I don't see
why you're not willing to throw Mrs. Crawley to the wolves.
Not only is she replaceable, but she's going to continue to be a
source of trouble to you. It would be to your advantage to get
rid of her."

"Would that pacify you, Doc?" Howie shook his head. "Besides," he said patiently, "I *like* Crawley. She's good at her job.
The children can see how good she is with their old folks — always joshing 'em and so forth. Also, if I got rid of her now,
I'd be admitting you were right, wouldn't I? From my point
of view, if we're going to talk about it, it's hard for me to see
what you've got against her — or me," he added. "Why you've
got it in for us. I really am running an ideal place out here.
Now, ain't I? Admit it."

"Howie," Lucas said, "nobody can hear us talking now. You
don't need to put up a front."

"I'm not putting up a front," Howie said. "I'm sincere." He
looked kindly at the old man. "Doc," he said, "you remember
what it says in the Bible about pride goeth before destruction
and all? You think you too good for the rest of us. Too *righteous*. Just remember what happened to Job, righteous as he
was."

Lucas could feel the blood throbbing in his carotid arteries.
He was dizzy again. He tried to draw a deep breath and
wheezed like an old engine.

"Don't you think you ought to have a physical examination,
Doc? I mean, I been reading up on this problem of the blood

supply to the brain and all — what do they call it? cerebral ischemia? Leads to sexual phantasies, among other things. It's nothing to be ashamed of. You know, Lucy says she . . ." He reached out as he was speaking as if to place a comforting hand on Lucas's shoulder and Lucas recoiled.

"Lucy says what?" he said.

But Howie shrugged. "Oh, nothing," he said. "Never mind." He turned away and strolled out into the sun parlor, where he paused and entered into a conversation with Mrs. Cathcart and Miss Rebecca Steinman, who were playing gin rummy at the table next to the windows.

Lucas stood outside the doorway to the study. There was a murmur of voices from within, but he paid no attention to it. His gaze was fixed on the mantel clock that he had spent so many hours puttering with. Its hands still stood at a quarter past three, where they had stood when he had last tried to balance it. He walked with stiff puppetlike motions across the room to the mantel, opened the clock door, and stood staring into its interior. He reached up, gave the pendulum a light shove, and watched it begin its majestic slow swing. He tried to breathe deeply, to relax the constriction in his lungs. At the same time, he seemed to himself to hear, to feel, the pounding of the blood in the carotid and basal arteries, a thunder of blood in his ears, and a kind of minute crepitation in the capillaries, as if the thrombocytes might be breaking loose and crackling down the corridors of his body. I am seventy-six years old. Cerebral ischemia! Maybe I didn't even see what I think I saw. He thought of Mrs. Crane and of Martha. Curious, the functioning of a man's brain in senility that makes it possible for him to be speaking, thinking sensibly at one moment, and at the next to be off on the wildest of fantasies. I dreamed of Lucy last night. Naked.

Tick, tock, tick, tock, the clock said. You, can, leave, *tock,* leave, *tock,* leave, *tock.* Slowly and more slowly. One last *tock.* Silence.

Lucas looked at the motionless pendulum, then he closed the clock door, went out into the sun parlor, and walked slowly along toward Martha's room, passing the card game where Howie was chuckling at some joke of his own making, while the two old ladies gazed at him with polite smiles and waited to resume their game. At the threshold of the doorway to the hall, he stumbled.

"Look out there, Doc! Watch your step." It was Howie. He had turned away from the card game and now he headed in the direction of the kitchen.

Martha! Lucas hurried toward her room as if toward refuge from his treachery. Empty. She had turned off the air conditioning and opened her windows, but in spite of the August weather, the room seemed pleasant and airy after the damp chill of the rest of the house, pulsing with live air and real heat, curtains (loosely woven white linen, worn threadbare by years of washing) blowing in the Gulf breeze. An ironstone washstand pitcher on the mantel held peppergrass and sunflowers that they had gathered on a ditchbank earlier in the week. There were her prints, hanging on the wall opposite her bed. He walked over to her desk, cluttered, now that she was too blind to use it, with snapshots of the children, one stack weighted with the magnifying glass she used to examine them. George at fourteen in his Sunday suit — Norfolk jacket, and knickers neatly buckled about skinny legs in knee socks. Francis and Mary Hartwell just back from a morning of crawfishing, standing side by side and wearing those funny old straw hats with balled fringe around the wide brims like the ones children and black people used to wear. They were smiling in triumph, each holding up a giant crawdad. Albert with a shotgun and a couple of mallards looking as sly as if he had shot them out of season. Francis's and Mary Hartwell's children in various poses. Newton? He turned the pictures over and found one of Newton in the cap and gown of college graduation. *What happened to them? Have they all, for some mysterious reason (a new virus first identified in the last third of the twentieth century), become less than human?*

He strode to the open window and looked out, but he could see no one in the garden. Hurrying again, half-stumbling on the stairs, forgetting that at his age he must move cautiously, above all things must not fall and break a bone, he dashed out into the yard and stopped to listen. Yes. He heard her voice and then Harper's from behind the garage. Even in his own distress it crossed his mind that he must not alarm her, and he stood still for a few moments controlling his breathing. Then he went slowly around the corner of the garage.

She was sitting on the ground with a dandelion digger in her strong brown hand. The sun made of her hair an aureole of silver around the leathery skin of her face. She looked up at him smiling, the bright blue eyes as young and merry as a girl's. "Look what we're doing, Luke — Harper and I. We've kept it a secret from Howie, haven't we, Harper? (He can't see us back here.) So he won't bother us while we're getting it ready. And then in the fall when he has greens and cabbage and beets and onions for the table — a real fall garden — look, the cushaws and honeydews are beginning to get ripe, even though we were so late getting them in — he'll be so pleased, he'll let us go on with it. And next spring . . ."

His heart, the muscle in his upper arm, the very spot behind the sternum where he knew he would feel the pain of a thrombosis, contracted with the pain of his love for her. He dropped to his knees on the ground beside her and took her hand in his, paying no attention to Harper, who was raking lumps from the dirt at the other end of the cleared space. He took the dandelion digger from her and laid it on the ground. "Martha," he said. "Martha!"

She looked at him, waiting, alert, expectant.

"Martha," he said, "why don't we get married and get out of here? O.K.? I don't think we'd better stay here any longer. All right?"

"All right, Luke," she said. "Of course. If that's what you think we should do."

Newton tapped nervously on Howie's desk with his pencil and the three men looked at each other, each one waiting for the others to begin. At last, deferentially, "Well, Daddy? What do you think?"

But Albert spoke. "Lucas has always been a nut," he said. "You know that's the truth, George. Look at the position he put the health department — the whole medical profession — in, not five years ago when those Yankee doctors came in here and started talking about starving niggers." (Under the pressure of the afternoon's events he had forgotten, it appeared, that such a word as "nigger" was for use on the road — with truck drivers, service station operators, and such; and that to his family and his "own" black people he said "colored folks.")

"A nut, maybe," Newton said. "Or maybe it was self-interest. He's got a job with 'em now."

"No, no," George said. "It's not self-interest, son. Lucas is sincere. He's always been sincere — misguided, maybe; but he never got anything out of it for himself."

"Not sharp enough," Albert muttered. "But he's been sharp enough and selfish enough to keep Aunt Martha dangling all these years — never . . ."

"Albert! Are we going into Aunt Martha's private life at *this* stage? My God!"

"Well," Newton said, "let's put the best name to it we can — he's eccentric. O.K.? We're all agreed on that? Well, then, are we going to believe *any* of this rigamarole he brought in here this afternoon?"

"We have to do him the courtesy of looking into it," George said. "At least. Out of respect for his age and being a doctor and so forth. We could talk to Mrs. Crawley and Lucy and — maybe Harper. We *know* Lucas *means* well. Don't we?"

"*Harper?*" Albert said. "It would be a very delicate matter to involve Harper in the question of Lucy's relations with Howie Snyder."

"I didn't mean . . ." George's voice trailed off and the two older men looked at each other mutely, appalled at the tangle they were planning to cut into.

"I doubt if he'd care," Newton said. "After all, they . . ."

"Oppressive in here," George said. "Smoky." He reached across the desk and put out Howie's still-smoking cigar and then got up and opened a window. The distant thunder of freeway traffic grew louder.

"There *are* some problems here, all right," Newton said slowly. "Now, let's see what they are. Let's look at 'em. When you stop to think about it, we could have a mess on our hands before we knew what was happening. Suppose some of the families got wind of this? Scandal! Wouldn't make any difference whether it was true or not. Would it? I can see the local Democrats making use of it, too. I mean my connection with it. Unscrupulous bastards. Don't care if they're playing around with

the lives of these poor old folks out here. See? Just suppose
Lucas went to his cronies down at this so-called health center.
All Democrats. Makes my skin crawl just to think about it.
And suppose we decide to stand behind Howie and face the
possibility of political flak. Aunt Martha's going to be in an uproar. Probably get Mary Hartwell down here. Everybody's going to have some second thoughts. No way we can come out of
it without the boat getting rocked — *hard*. Now, I'm just talking about possibilities, but it's possibilities we've got to consider
— contingencies. After all, my position in the state is *important*
and I'm not speaking selfishly. It's important to a lot more people than me."

"Newton, it doesn't sound to me like you're even thinking
about the possibility that it might be true — some of it, anyhow," George said. "Wouldn't it be better, considering that
possibility, just to close the place up and look after Aunt Martha
the way we should have in the first place? That's what Daddy
would have done," he added wistfully.

"You mean we should give in to this crazy old man who you
say yourselves should have married Aunt Martha and assumed
responsibility for her fifteen years ago?"

"Crackers," Albert said. "That's what he is. Crackers."

"We've got to look into it," George said stubbornly. "Some
way."

"Daddy, you're not being reasonable. I don't believe you've
thought it through carefully enough. You heard what Howie
was saying before Lucas got here — his plans for the future.
Good plans. And plans that we are already deeply involved in.
We're going to be furnishing a service to old people — you
know how desperately needed it is — statewide. Especially if we
get accredited for Medicare and Medicaid. Look how fine it will
be for black people." "They *need* these homes. And (not, of

course, that it should be a deciding factor) it is not going to hurt the Republican image for me to be involved in a worthwhile project like this. As for Lucy — you *know* — common sense is bound to tell you all Howie's thinking about is training her for a job."

"Yeah," Albert said. "And that's another plus. It's the kind of work *everybody* approves of for nigras. Not much different from what they've always done, but at the same time there's some money and status in it for 'em."

"I don't *care* about the Republicans," George said. "I just don't. I don't mean I don't care about you, son, of course," he added hastily. "But I don't see what any of this has to do with politics."

"Must be some way we can satisfy everybody — let's see, let's see." Newton sat down in Howie's desk chair and, cocking a shining tan shoe on his knee, nodded reassuringly at his father. "I know we've got to do the right thing, Daddy," he said. "I *want* to do the right thing. The question is: What?" Then, "Approach it from both directions. Withhold judgment on Lucas for the time being. Nose around a bit to make sure everything is O.K. *Cautiously*. Reassure Lucas. Tell him we're looking into it. But we've got to keep the patients out of it. Got to avoid scandal. And if we find that Lucas is imagining things, then we're going to have to work out some way to . . ." He glanced at his father. "Convince him he's wrong and do it some way so it won't upset Aunt Martha."

"Umph," Albert said. "That's a tall order — next to impossible. Ain't it?"

George remarked plaintively that it was going to be hard to investigate the charges, if they couldn't talk to anybody about them.

"Tempest in a teapot," Newton said. "That's what it is. The

idea of our having to take up our time with all this nonsense! Let's see, now. We'll make it a point, Daddy, a *point* to come out here a little more often. Come unexpectedly. Keep our eyes open. Look in on some of the other old folks. Et cetera. You can do that without anybody noticing. Martha's always here as an excuse for a visit. Meanwhile, damn, what are we going to say to Howie? Got to save his face, after all, while we're checking things out. And what are we going to say to Lucas?"

"I'm telling you, if you want to keep Howie," Albert said, "you'd better drop this business about Lucy *right now*. Disgusting idea! Out of the question to even think about such a thing happening out here. When I think what Brent Cathcart would say, if he thought he had exposed his mother to such a situation . . . Ugh!"

"But . . ." George had begun, when there was a knock at the study door.

"Yes?" Newton said. "Come in."

The door opened inward and Mrs. Crawley appeared, crackling with starch and competence in her incandescent uniform, her smile wide and confident and her good eye full of purpose. "I don't like to interrupt you folks's business," she said, "but the truth is I saw you was in here, and I thought to myself there probably wouldn't be another chance for me to see all three of you at onct, and so I just made myself bold enough to take this one." She closed the door behind her and continued. "I had to come to one of y'all," she said. "I just thought I'd better. I couldn't see my way clear to taking it to Mr. Snyder even though . . ."

"What's on your mind, Mrs. Crawley?" Albert said kindly.

The smile vanished and she sighed, her face now composed and serious. "No way around it. I got to out with it. But in confidence, you understand."

"Mrs. Crawley, we can't keep anything from Mr. Snyder. After all, he's in charge out here. It isn't proper for you to come to us over his head," Albert said.

"You'll see what I mean when I explain it to you," she said. "I'll put it to you and you'll see what I mean. We had a little incident out here a couple of days ago. Not important — *really*. *I'm* not upset by it. Not me. I seen *every*thing in my time — being a nurse and all. But somebody needs to know about it besides me. And this is what it is. The old doc — Dr. Alexander (He's a old man, now. I know that. *Weak*) — he done a bad thing. Like, I mean, you know, they all get notions sometimes and you got to jolly 'em along and all. That's what we're here for. But he's a pretty active old fellow and . . . Now, mind you, he may not even know he done it. That happens, too, sometimes."

"What *is* it, Mrs. Crawley. What did he do?"

"He — uh — he was — uh . . ." She appeared to be overcome by embarrassment, one eye cast modestly down, the other rolled out. "He was laying down in his room, you know, and Lucy, she knocked and went in (He had rung his bell, you understand. This was at night) and . . . and . . . Well, he made a *suggestion* to her, pore old gent. He asked her to take off her clothes and let him look at her. Can you believe it? Him with emphysema and all. Well, it didn't upset Lucy too bad. She's a levelheaded girl. She knew she could handle him, anyhow, so she played like she thought he was joking; didn't move out of his way or nothing, just says, you know, 'Can I do anything for you, Dr. Alexander? You need a sleeping pill or what?' And he grabs her by the hand and wants her to — to . . ."

"Never *mind*, Mrs. Crawley." This was a croak from George. "Don't — *please* don't tell us any more unless it is absolutely necessary."

"Daddy! Daddy, it *is* necessary — for the good of the home. We have to hear this story out."

"Well, there ain't much more to it. He wanted her to — you know, feel him — like bragging he could still get a . . ."

"All *right*," George groaned.

"And she just pulled away from him and, well, if she'd been white, you know, she could've made trouble for him and all; but being a nigger, she just kinda shushed him a little bit like he was a baby, which of course he is — they all are. And went on off, and next day she told me about it because, you know, she was scared a little bit. Like if it kept on happening it might get blamed on her some way, and she wanted somebody to know about it and all. But she didn't want to make nothing of it — didn't want to take it to Mr. Snyder because, him being in charge and so proper, you know, being, like he is, so active in the church and all — she was afraid the pore old doc would get it from him. He might make something big of it. And nothing needs to be made of it. But it looked like to me somebody ought to know about it besides me. Just in case . . . I don't mean that *Lucy* would make any trouble. She understands. In fact, if you want to talk to her about it, she . . ."

"No!" George said. "I don't think that will be necessary."

When she had finally gone, hurried out of the room by Newton's staccato reassurances, the three men sat silent. Albert studied Howie's map of the Battle of the Bulge. George shook his head and craned his long neck and swallowed as if he might have a stone lodged in his gullet. Newton appeared to be thinking.

"There's your explanation," Albert grumbled at last. "He's senile."

No one replied.

Albert (looking slyly from under his heavy white brows):

"Do you remember when old Aunt Amy Griswold used to think she was being held prisoner in a whorehouse, George? Remember that? Curious how an old lady like that — somebody you wouldn't even have thought knew the word . . ."

"The question still," Newton said, "is what are we going to do?"

"Well, it's clear to me that Howie is the man we'd better discuss it with," Albert said. "All of it. He has to deal with it."

"I don't know what we would have done in a messy situation like that if it hadn't been for Howie," Newton told his mother afterward. "Sensible! He's always sensible. If he hadn't been . . . Dr. Alexander's condition — pitiful! And . . . well, you can see the implications — all the ramifications . . . But he'll go out on a limb to make things work for everybody."

"Yes," said George, "poor Lucas. Let's hope Howie can get things back on an even keel. I was ready to throw in the towel — I really was. God knows I wish we'd never gotten into this. But Newton convinced me that it would be — well, bordering on irresponsible. We can't just think about Aunt Martha and disregard everybody else."

They had walked into the house after their conference with Howie to find drinks and supper waiting for them, and now they were sitting on the patio together talking over the day's events. The cool sound of a splashing fountain seemed to take the edge from the August heat. The two men held martinis in their hands and Louisa was slicing ham for sandwiches at the glass-topped patio table.

"Lucas is a sick man," Newton said. "But Howie has hit on the way to deal with him. If things go as we hope, he won't make any more difficulty. Dr. Blanks — you know, Mama, that new young internist from Meridian — has been treating a couple of the old folks out there and Howie says he will prescribe this new drug for Lucas — something especially designed for the unruly patient, for the borderline case — can't be committed, won't take his medicine, et cetera. Once Lucas has had that stuff slipped into his orange juice for a week or so, he'll be biddable — meek as a kitten — and then we can get him onto one of the more conventional tranquilizers." He got up and, crossing to the table, picked up a sliver of ham from the platter. "Mmmm, this is good, Mama. Your ham! Always the best."

Louisa laid down the knife and fork and tenderly patted his arm. "Darling, your father and I — we can't *tell* you what it means to have you help us with family problems."

"God willing, he won't have to help us with many more like this," George said.

CHAPTER 13

IT SEEMED NOW to Lucas that he was functioning at the top of his capacity. He felt like a young man on a tiger hunt, adrenalin pumping through his body, every nerve alert for danger. He explained to Martha all that had happened and the hazards that he believed to be facing them. "If we can manage without consulting anybody," he said, "even about finding a place to live, they will have to accept the fact that we are going our own way. I don't mean," he added, "that George and Albert don't want everything for you that you might want for yourself. I'm simply in doubt . . ." He broke off and began again carefully. "I don't need to explain what I mean to you," he said. "You saw it before I did. It's true, as you said, that we are old and that younger people have a tendency to treat older people like children — that all people will be tempted to use whatever power they have over other people. But Albert and George are decent men and they love you. Even though they may have the power to enforce their will on you, I think we can show them that we are reasonable and determined and content with our own decisions; and then they will go along with us. But we have to show them. As for Howie, he'll be so glad to get rid of me, he'll cheer us on our way."

All this he said while they were still sitting on the ground in Harper and Martha's garden behind the garage.

"I don't want to hurt the children's feelings," Martha said doubtfully. "Mary Hartwell and Francis, too. Shouldn't we phone them? And besides, Lucas, you know they're going to think we're crazy."

He was still holding her strong mottled brown hand in both of his. The dandelion digger lay on the ground beside them. The sun beat down with all its August strength and sweat rolled down their seamed and anxious faces. "Trust me, Martha," he said. "I *know* we'd better do it this way."

That same afternoon he took her to the Johns Hopkins health project and in the lab there had a young intern run the Wassermans that were a legal requirement for buying a marriage license. In this way he avoided seeing any of the local doctors and nurses who might relay the news to the family. He ate supper at the home, drank his nightly glass of wine at bedtime, and slept soundly that night — more soundly, he noticed the next morning, than he ordinarily slept. He awoke with a headache and a feeling of dull lethargy; but he had never been a man to give in to illness and he was still wholly intent upon his project. He took a shower, dressed, hurried upstairs to the kitchen, poured himself a cup of coffee from the pot on the kitchen stove, and set out for town, as he sometimes did, without waiting for breakfast. He drove, for he had errands to run.

At his office he went carefully over the FOR RENT section of the morning paper, made several phone calls for appointments, and completed some odds and ends of paperwork on his desk. Then he went to the bank, opened his safe-deposit box, and got out the gold wedding band that had belonged to his mother. As the morning passed, he felt better. It crossed his mind that if he had had more than two glasses of wine the night before, he would think he had a hangover. Getting more susceptible to alcohol? Just at noon, before going home for lunch, he went by the courthouse to apply for a marriage license. He was aware that his and Martha's marriage after all these years would be interesting to every old-timer at the courthouse and that the news of it would spread quickly, and he timed his visit carefully, waiting until the circuit clerk and the middle-aged deputy, whom he had known for years, were both out to lunch. He was waited on by a young woman who did not know him.

He ate lunch at Golden Age and immediately afterward he and Martha set out to look at the apartments and small houses he had seen advertised in the morning's paper.

He began during this outing to feel a peculiarly leaden and unnatural drowsiness; not illness, but a detachment from himself such as he had never felt before. As the afternoon advanced, it became so marked that during their inspection of the third house he dropped behind Martha and leaning against a wall in an empty corridor surreptitiously counted his pulse. A trifle fast, he noted, but does it matter? He roused himself enough to go on to one more house, still feeling in his bones, in spite of this curious detachment, the urgency of making and implementing decisions. They settled on a furnished apartment. Martha had wanted a house with room enough for a small garden, but the apartment they found was the lower floor of an old house, and the owner gave them permission to do as they liked with the back yard.

That night he went to bed immediately after supper and for the first time in — How long? For as long as he could remember, he thought next morning when he woke to find the sun streaming in his south window — he slept through the night without awakening once. Heavy-footed, he stumbled to the bathroom, wondering at the retentive power of his old man's bladder that had so often played him false, and at this sudden cessation of his lifelong insomnia. Strange, he said to himself, following his doctor's habit of keeping track of the functioning of his body as a watch repairman might check the ticking of his watch. Emotional? Relief at having made the decision? But I don't feel like myself. And what happened to last night? He had begun to dress when there was a tap at the door. He was about to say, "Come in," when he realized that he had on only his shorts. What's the matter with me? He pulled on his robe, drew a deep breath, crossed the room with determined briskness, and opened the door. Mrs. Crawley stood in the hall, gleaming.

"Hi, Doc," she said. "Didn't hear no noise in here and I just wondered if you was awake."

"Yes, I am," he said.

"Coming up to breakfast?"

"Yes," he said. "I overslept a bit. I'll be up shortly." His tongue felt thick and numb against the roof of his mouth.

"Well, everbody was about through, and I was going to offer to bring it down to you, if you wanted me to," she said.

He frowned in puzzlement. "I never have breakfast in my room," he said slowly.

"First time for everything," she said. "Sleep good?"

"Yes," he said. "I did. I slept — better than I have in years." He closed the door and stood leaning against it for — how long? He was not sure. Then with all the power of concentrating himself that he could muster he raised his left hand, laid it in his right palm, and counted his pulse. Fast. It had been fast yesterday afternoon. He went into the bathroom and gazed at his face in the mirror. He turned on the faucet and, bending down, splashed his face with cold water. Then he dried it and looked into the mirror again. Some dilatation of the pupils? What's the matter with me?

He finished dressing and started up the stairs, watching his feet with interest as they lifted themselves from step to step. In the dining room, empty now except for Howie and the cook, Ruby, who was clearing away the dishes, he started across the room to his place, the only one still laid. A glass of orange juice stood beside the knife. Ruby brought in a cup of coffee from the kitchen. Leaning against the mantelpiece and surveying his domain with a proprietary air, Howie gave him that deeply intimate, smilingly knowing look that he had learned to detest.

Howie is a good man, he thought with a surge of happiness. A *good* man. He understands us all. He sat down at his place and stared at his orange juice glass. *Howie?* Slowly he turned his head and looked again into that loving smile. A sign appeared in the air between him and Howie, a word printed in orange capitals and enclosed in a little balloon: BROMIDE. Then beneath BROMIDE a set of words in small letters: *Symptoms: dilatation of pupils, pulse rapid, skin dry.* He looked down at the fragile puckered skin of his hand and shrugged. *I have been tranquilized.* Carefully he lifted his glass and held it in front of him. Another balloon appeared. *How?* He felt no sense of danger — only balloons of fact floating like the dialogue in a comic strip with strings hanging down toward his mouth. He put the glass to his lips and took one sip. Another balloon: *Martha would like to hear about this.* Another: *My judgment may be impaired.* At this thought, he felt a kind of benign contentment that he wished to share. He drank half of his orange juice, set his glass down, and stood up. Ruby came in through the door from the kitchen.

"I'll be back in a minute," Lucas said. "If you don't mind, just leave my breakfast on the table for me."

He paused near the head of the stairs. Probably I should just go downstairs and go to sleep, he said to himself. But *Martha* in orange letters floated off down the hall toward her room and he followed it as slowly as if he might be walking through arctic wastes in thick-soled boots and fur-lined clothing. He knocked at her door and heard her deep, soft, beloved voice. "Come in."

Inside, he sat down in a straight chair by the door. She was across the room from him sitting near the window in her low rocker. On the table next to her a record turned slowly on the talking-book machine and a disembodied voice read: "Down through the treacherous passes between the islands of the Aleutian chain and southward into the open Pacific, the herds of fur seals are moving. Left behind are two small islands, treeless bits of volcanic soil thrust up . . ."

"I'm getting ready to go to sleep, Martha," he said. He laughed. "I need to take a little nap and I thought . . . What did I think?" He laughed. "Something I wanted to tell you before I lay down, but I have to wait for it to float by."

"Sleep?" she said. "You're not going to work?"

"Now once more the seals turn south, to roam down along the sheer underwater cliffs of the continent's edge, where the rocky foundations fall away steeply into the deep sea," the machine said.

"There was something," Lucas said again, "something I should say, but I've forgotten what it is. Sleepy."

She reached across the table and cut off the machine. "Lucas, you just got up," she said. "Are you ill?"

"Yes," he said. A balloon floated past his eyes and he read the words inside it aloud to her: "*In a way I am ill. Tranquil. Could Howie have given me a tranquilizer? How?*" He closed his eyes. Then he began to read a new balloon. "*We are in danger, Martha,*" he read, "*but it doesn't seem to worry me.*" His lids were heavy, heavy, but he forced his eyes open, not yet relinquishing the habit of sixty years of self-discipline and self-observation. "Pupils dilated," he said. "Somebody gave me a bromide last night, I believe. Must have. And something else, maybe. New drug? Stronger than necessary. Old age? Besides, always been susceptible to drugs. But it doesn't matter." He closed his eyes again. "It doesn't matter," he said drowsily. "We — could — listen — to that book — together. Seals?"

Martha got up and walked over to him. She took him by the shoulder and gave him a gentle shake. He opened his eyes.

"Are you sure it's not something else?" she said. "Your heart or something?"

He shook his head. "Not a chance."

"They — without your knowing it?"

He nodded. "Bound to be. Turn the machine on. What was that about seals?"

"Lucas!" She shook him harder. "Is it possible? What shall we do?"

He sat perfectly still, erect, his eyes closed, and did not answer for a moment. Then, "I'm not worried," he said, ". . . I don't think."

"Is there an antidote to it?" she said. "Try to think. What could I give you to help you wake up?"

He shook his head slowly. "I wanted to come in here — to you," he said, and opened his eyes and smiled at her.

She stepped to the door of her room and turned the key to lock it; then she pulled up another straight chair close to his and sat down. "Coffee?" she said. "Maybe one of my caffeine pills?"

"I think I'll go downstairs and take a short nap," he said.

She crossed the room to her bedside table, got a small piece of ice from the thermos pitcher there, and, wrapping it in a handkerchief, rubbed it over his face and neck. He shivered.

"Lucas, when do you think you took this — whatever it is?"

"Maybe . . . Last night at supper? Yesterday at noon, too? I remember . . . Began feeling strange yesterday afternoon when we were . . . house hunting."

"But, how?" she said. "And why?"

"Must have been in — my food." He shrugged. "Why? I reckon the reason you do things to people is because you can. Hard — *hard* — to abstain from — use of power." Then, "It doesn't matter," he said. "I feel fine."

"What shall we do?" she said. She stood up again, walked all around her room, looked in her closet as if an answer might be hidden there, looked out the window, came back, and sat down. Again she ran the ice over his face. "Are you awake?" she said.

"Chloral hydrate," he said. "I just thought of that."

"The first thing we'd better do is call George."

"No," he said slowly. "Would be — inadvisable to — consult — your family. Reason you — do things — to people . . ."

"Not George," she said. "He wouldn't be a party to . . . to . . ."

"Putting me away?" Lucas laughed happily. "Should we risk finding out?"

"But . . ."

"Not until I'm at myself. All right?"

She dropped the wet handkerchief in her lap and took both his hands in hers. "Lucas," she said. "Lucas! I'm *afraid*. Suppose . . . Suppose I forget what I'm doing and . . . You know, like I do sometimes, and . . ."

Lucas closed his eyes.

She stared at him sitting there, the long face slack and peaceful, the fierce mustache drooping. "I can't do that," she said. "I'll *have* to keep my brains working. All right. This part is simple. All we have to do is keep you out of sight until this wears off. That's *all*. Then, after that, you — maybe we — mustn't eat here anymore. Have you had your breakfast?"

He shook his head. "Half a glass of orange juice."

"There may have been something in that. Can you stand up?"

He nodded.

"This is what we're going to do. We'll fix you a blanket pallet on the bathroom floor and you can go in there and sleep it off. Even until tomorrow, if you have to. Ruby only goes in my bath to clean it on Tuesday and Friday. If Howie or anyone comes in, I'll tell them you've left, that you decided you didn't want any breakfast and left to walk downtown. Is that all right?" she said anxiously. "Do you think that's the best thing to do?"

"You're in charge," he said.

She laughed at his beatific smile. "They've made a damn fool of you, haven't they?" she said, and going to her closet, gathered up a comforter, a sheet, and a pillow and made a pallet in the bathroom. "Come on," she said. "I can keep them out of here, if I have to lock myself in with you."

There on the floor, scarcely harder than his own thin mattress, he slept for three hours. Martha had no difficulty concealing his presence. Howie, after one inquiry, seemed satisfied that he had gone on to the health department, as Martha said he had.

"He seemed drowsy and vague," she said. "I was a bit worried about him. But he was in a good humor. Do you think he's all right?" Over the thundering of her heart she was sure she heard a faint snore from the bathroom. But Howie heard nothing and went away content.

At noon Lucas roused, this time more alert. Martha gave him a cup of coffee that she had brought in from the kitchen in her thermos pitcher and together they put the easy chair in the bathroom for him to sit on. She locked the door, turned on the talking-book machine, and under cover of its sound talked with him in a low voice.

"Lucas, are you better? We've got to get you some food."

"I'm fine," he said. "Nothing to worry about."

"You're not fine yet," she said, "or you wouldn't say there's nothing to worry about. You stay right here, will you? *Will* you? I'm going to lunch and somehow I'll bring you something to eat."

"I'll do whatever you say, Martha," he said docilely.

In the back garden she picked a tomato. She brought it back to the room and left it with him. "Sit still," she said. "You might fall down. I'll be back." She put on a housedress with capacious pockets. "This is a kind of adventure, isn't it?" she said. "More excitement than we've had in years. Are we up to it? Yes," she answered herself. At the table she managed to slip a couple of pieces of bread into one pocket. In the other, wrapped in a paper napkin, she concealed a meatball. She picked at her lunch, too excited to eat. Afterward she went to the kitchen. "Too hot for hot food, Ruby," she said. "I would like to take a piece of fruit to my room." She got a small bunch of grapes from the refrigerator. In her room, she made him a meatball and tomato sandwich. "No mayonnaise," she said. "Just eat it and don't think about it." For dessert she gave him the grapes and another cup of coffee.

"I'm better," he said. "One more little nap." He dropped off in an instant, sitting up in the chair in the bathroom.

"Dear God," she said aloud, "let him be all right by tonight. They'll begin looking for him tonight."

At four-thirty he was still sleeping.

I'm afraid, she said to herself. He may die. What shall I do? She stood with hands knotted together and gazed blindly out the window, her seamed brown face drawn and anxious, the old housedress buttoned awry, so that the hem on one side was two inches longer than on the other. The tension of her effort was so great that she seemed to herself to hear the creaking of strained cables inside her brain and to sense a kind of slipping, slipping, as if worn gears were ready to give way. But she held fast to her resolve. Methodically she considered alternatives (Keep him in my room all night? Tell Howie his niece and nephew are in town and he has called to say he is having dinner with them? Mary Hartwell? Francis? Wouldn't they help us? Let's see, let's see. The simplest, least noticeable thing. Improvise. Maybe when he wakes up it will have worn off completely). She made up her mind to rouse him. She turned on the talking machine, wet a cloth with cold water, and bathed his face and throat, at the same time speaking softly to him. "Lucas? Lucas? Wake up."

He opened his eyes and looked at her dazedly, then looked all around him, squeezed his eyes shut, sneezed, and cleared his throat.

"Shh," she said. "How are you?"

"What time is it?"

"Nearly five o'clock. Are you better?"

"I don't know yet," he said. "Where am I?"

"Dear God," she said. "You're in my room. You've got to wake up. You've been sleeping all day."

Again she locked him in the bathroom in case anyone came into her room while she was gone and went to the kitchen where she refilled her thermos pitcher with hot coffee ("You be 'wake all night, you keep on drinking coffee," Ruby said to her), got a glass of ice, and returned to her room. He drank the coffee and she rubbed his face and throat with ice.

"I'm hungry," he said. Then, "Cold. Good." He took a towel from her and dried his face. "Martha," he said, "they're going to trap me."

She shook her head. "I believe you're all right, darling," she said. "Aren't you? I was so *afraid*. I kept seeing Howie, like a . . . like . . . That cat smile, you know, and . . . But I kept my wits about me."

He stood up and took a couple of turns around her room. "I feel normal," he said. "Legs not shaky. No balloons. Did you see all those balloons? I'm awake." They stared at each other. "Normal," he said, "if normal is terrified."

"What now?" she said. "Mary Hartwell . . ."

"Do they know I'm in here?"

"No."

"All right. Let's see. I've been downtown all day. I just got back. I'm in a very good humor. And . . . and . . . They've got to think I'm still getting my sugar tit. How can we manage that? Nothing to rock the boat, not one little ripple, until we're out. Here, Martha, help me with this chair." Together they dragged the easy chair back into the bedroom and he sat down. "Now," he said. "I am drowsy but happy. I ate lunch downtown. I'm not very hungry and don't plan to eat supper, but I would like — what? Another glass of orange juice and some cheese and crackers here in your room. Maybe a glass of sherry. How's that? Gives 'em something to put the knockout drops in. Then I think I'll go downstairs to bed early. Get out of here, both of us, first thing in the morning. Got to have some food, though, Martha. I'm *starving*."

"We have another day's wait before we can get married,

Lucas. What are we going to do about that?" she said. "Harper! Can't we trust Harper to bring us something to eat?" And then, "Oh, Lucas, *please*, let me call George."

He shook his head.

"Mary Hartwell, then. I know she can't have anything to do with this."

"Maybe I can get by on crackers," he said.

CHAPTER 14

IT WAS already too late. The young deputy circuit clerk had commented to her fellow workers on the appearance of the distinguished-looking elderly gentleman who had applied for a marriage license; the clerk had glanced at the application; Newton, as he often did, had dropped into the office on business and heard the news. By five o'clock on the day of Lucas's long sleep the family had gathered at Golden Age — the seriousness of the occasion such that George had brought Louisa along. "If the going gets rough," he said to her, "Aunt Martha is going to need a woman with her." What for, he wasn't sure; but he *was* sure that neither he nor Albert nor Newton had any relish for this murky and wholly unfortunate business. I just wish Mary Hartwell were here, he said to himself. But on second thought he decided that she might only add to everyone's confusion and distress.

Again they were crowded into the little room where they had first consulted together about Martha's future. Somehow it seemed as if, in the fifteen months that had passed, the room had got smaller — the walls had drawn closer to each other — so that there was scarcely space for them to sit comfortably in Howie's chrome and leather chairs; and the ceiling pressed down as if it were lower, or as if the bright green funeral-grass rug were growing thicker and pushing the furniture upward.

When they first came in and were waiting for Howie to come up from his bedroom, Louisa looked uneasily about her and remarked to Albert in a whisper that she had never before realized what abominable taste Howie had. "It manages to seem hot and cold in here at the same time," she said. "Or maybe it was Lydia."

"Lydia never took an interest in the house . . ." Albert began, but he went no further, for at that moment Howie entered, alert and smiling, and the conference began with anxious questions from Newton: Where was Lucas? Did Howie know that he had gone downtown the preceding day and taken out, or rather applied for, a marriage license? Had he gotten the tranquilizer and started Lucas on it? In short, what was going on?

Howie answered calmly enough that Lucas had been started on the tranquilizer, that he had slept heavily the night before, had seemed perfectly quiet — even drowsy — at breakfast, and had gone downtown as usual. As for the marriage license . . . He shrugged. A new development, he said, but hardly out of line with the rest of his erratic behavior.

"He's not driving his car in the condition he's in?"

Howie shook his head. "He got away from me yesterday afternoon, but I took the precaution last night of disconnecting the ignition wires," he said. "He hasn't tried to use it today — walked downtown like he always does in good weather."

"Howie, you don't seem to be as alarmed as we are about this marriage license development," Albert said. "We've got to do something quick. We can't let Lucas and Aunt Martha get married."

George, leaning awkwardly back in a very low armchair,

his long legs drawn up so that his knees were almost as high as his shoulders, looked unhappily from one to another of his family and said nothing.

Howie, it appeared, was not worried. By now, he said, Lucas was probably so docile that it would be easy to dissuade him from his venture. In fact, he might already have forgotten it.

George cleared his throat. "What about Aunt Martha?" he said. "She's not going to have forgotten it. And she's going to think it's mighty peculiar if *he* has."

"I'm thinking about Martha, George," Howie said. "More than about anybody else, myself included. But she may not even know he's been down there. Had you thought about that? She's so vague sometimes . . . And the doc's behavior lately has been so erratic . . . The point is, we ought not to stir either one of 'em up, unless we have to. Give the dust a chance to settle."

". . . all very well for you to be making educated guesses about how things *might* be," Newton said. "But how do you know — how do you *know?* — they're not going to the first J.P. they can get hold of and get married? *Married!*" He gave a short laugh. "And then we'd be in a mess. They might not even come back here. Go wandering off in the county somewhere. With his mental condition what it is, no telling what direction he'd go galloping off in. We've got responsibilities, Howie. Responsibilities."

"If we really want things to settle down," George said, "we can let them go on and get married and get out of here."

Albert shook his white mane. "Impossible, George. You know they're not capable of looking after each other. Just goes to show you he's even more out of it than we thought. We can't turn Aunt Martha over to him. Nothing but trouble."

"Daddy," Newton said, "do you realize that you're talking

about a senile — or disturbed — seventy-five-year-old man who has been making advances to a teen-age Negro girl and then projecting his fantasies onto Howie?"

"Not to mention other considerations." The light from the window glanced off the diamond pin on Louisa's shoulder and gleamed in blue highlights from her neatly waved gray hair. "We'd be the laughingstock of Homochitto," she said. "And Newton has his duty. His *image*. He's a public man."

George got abruptly up from his chair, crossed the room in three steps, stumbling over Howie's legs on the way, and, thrusting his hands into his pockets, stood, shoulders hunched as if against the wind, with his back to them all.

His wife and son and brother looked at each other. Louisa made a palms-up gesture of bewilderment. No one spoke for a moment. Then George turned around, his frail emaciated silhouette exaggerated by the light behind him, his face in shadow. "Now, listen," he said. "Nobody — not one of the four of us — has asked himself or the others (not once since this business of Lucas's making advances to Lucy came up): What is *really* happening? Lucas was right yesterday. Either he is crazy or Howie and Mrs. Crawley are lying." He turned to Newton. "I can't help it, son," he said. "I can't put that out of my mind. We don't *know*."

"George!" Louisa said.

Howie put his hands on his desk, as if about to rise from his chair. "I can understand your distress, George, old friend," he said. "These poor old folks are your own. Both of 'em. I see it." He paused significantly. "Maybe I ought to get out of here and let you folks discuss your problems without me."

"Wait, now," Newton said. "Wait a minute." And then to his father in a voice consciously slowed to its most patient and reasonable pace: "We *did* discuss it, Daddy. Right here in this room. We *agreed* on a sensible course and we're following it. Now this business of the marriage license is just one more item that does nothing but bear out our original decision — conviction — about what's going on."

"One thing we have to consider here," Albert said, "is that we're a *corporation* now. All of us, Howie included, have got to vote our shares in the best interests of the corporation, you know. We've got a considerable stake here. And we've got our corporate image to think of, as well as Newton's."

At this point Howie subsided quietly in his place and began to turn his black glass ashtray noiselessly around and around.

"Image!" George said. "*Image?*"

Louisa's eyes had filled with tears. "George Clarke," she said, "if you let your imagination get worked up to the point where you endanger your son's political and professional future, I will never forgive you. *Never.*"

"Now, Mama," Newton said. "Hold on." He shook his head at her ever so slightly with a warning frown. "We've got to satisfy Daddy's scruples. He wants to be sure we're doing the right thing. He *has* to be." He crossed the room to his father's side. "Come on," he said. "Sit down, Daddy. We're going to work this thing out. No political career is worth sacrificing family harmony for."

When they were all seated again, Albert leaned forward in his chair and began to speak earnestly to his brother. "As I see it, George," he said, "you may not be looking at this thing straight. You've let your emotions — your love for Aunt Martha — run away with you. Hold on, now. Hear me out. Here's what you haven't thought about. If every single thing Lucas said was true, you still wouldn't want to see him and Aunt Martha get married, now would you? All else aside, that's the nuttiest damned idea I ever heard of in all my life. Here she is, already beginning to get senile and all, and you'd turn her over to a man who wouldn't marry her in the days when she was bound to be crying her heart out over him every night. A man who dragged her good name and ours through all the mud in Homochitto County. No! You're bound to have felt about that just as strongly as I have all these years. Admit it."

"I suppose I may have thought about it," George said in a low voice. "But it was none of our business. Other people have to live their lives. Besides, that has nothing to do with this."

". . . a man who, whether he's telling the truth or not, is sick and old and eccentric. He might take her back out in the country to that farm of his where half the time they don't even have the butane to heat the house." He hunched his shoulders and, gripping his knees with white-knuckled hands, leaned toward George and spoke in a low, quavering, sibilant voice. "A selfish, self-centered, nigger-loving, bastard *nut* who ran around on his invalid wife and has made Aunt Martha's life a scandal and a laughingstock for thirty-five years."

"Do you know what Ernie Butler said when I saw him in his office? He said, 'Well, it took them quite a while to make up their minds, didn't it?'" Newton shrugged and gave an embarrassed laugh. "What could I say?"

George looked at Albert in some wonder. "I didn't know you hated Lucas Alexander," he said.

"I don't hate him," Albert said shortly. "I'm talking about facts. And, as I said yesterday, to take his word against Howie's — knowing all that we know . . . To even *think* of taking his word against Howie's . . . !" He shook his head, sat back in his chair, and folded his arms. "Never!"

"Albert is right, George. Getting married now will be an open admission of the truth about their affair," Louisa said. "And besides, that doesn't even take into consideration some other important things. Lucas's connection with that communist health project, for example. Do you want to bring *that* into the family?"

"Affair! Communist!" George brushed at his ears as if at a swarm of bees. "That's all ridiculous, Louisa. Ridiculous."

"Lucas is the very type of individual who is gnawing at the roots of our society," Louisa said. "I mean it. He represents everything Newton is fighting against."

George sighed. "Do you mean he's a Democrat?" he plaintively asked.

Again Louisa's eyes filled with tears. She dabbed at them with a crumpled handkerchief. "You'd think we were your enemies," she said, "instead of your own wife and son just trying, like you are, to do the right thing."

"Daddy, we can't joke about this." Newton was still speaking in his most reasonable and objective manner. "It's a fact that Lucas is not responsible. It's a fact that if we get into some kind of scandal out here, it will jeopardize the whole Golden Age project. And it's a fact that Lucas is trying to get us into a scandal. And incidentally," he added, turning abruptly to Howie, "where is he? Shouldn't he be here? And where is Aunt Martha?"

"He should be getting home any time now," Howie said calmly. "And when he gets here we'll be able to assess his condition and make some sensible decisions." He paused. Then, "May I say something, folks, to ease your minds? You're all unduly upset here. The doc is gonna come home and he's gonna be quiet and sleepy. He's gonna eat his supper and go to bed. Martha is not gonna notice a thing. That's the way these old folks are. I *know* 'em. Lucas'll probably sleep all day tomorrow. All we have to do is adjust his dose upward a little bit. (And incidentally, that relaxation is gonna be good for his emphysema, too.) You all, if you'll excuse my saying so, have got yourselves worked up over nothing, just because you've got too many strong feelings about things that have happened in the past. Now my advice for us is to sleep on it. We've got another whole day to make decisions, if they have to be made, you know. There's the three-day waiting period before they can get married — *if*, that is, *if* this marriage is a serious project and not some fool notion that Lucas has dreamed up like he's dreamed up the rest of what he's said and done lately.

"As for me," he went on, "once we've got all this ironed out, I'm willing to get entirely *out*, if that's what you want. I care a lot more about the best thing for my people than I care about this job, and that's the truth."

"No," Albert said. "You *stay*. Lucas is not going to bully me. I'm with you all the way, Howie."

Howie turned to George. "I give you my word, friend," he said solemnly, "my word before God that I want only the best for you and yours."

Louisa stared at George, her round pleasant face drawn into an expression of intense anxiety. "Darling?" she said. "All right, darling?"

"Daddy, what Howie is advising is right," Newton said. "He's *right*. We can afford to wait another day. Let the dust settle, as he says. Go along with us that far."

George looked from one to another of his family and he saw in their faces nothing but love and deep concern. "All right," he said. "I can't go against you all. I'll wait and see what happens tomorrow."

No one of them looked at any other or said any more as they filed out of the study into the dining room, where they came face to face with Lucas and Martha, who were on their way to the kitchen to give orders for Lucas's ice cream and orange juice. They had still not decided whether to trust Harper to bring Lucas some food before he went home at seven o'clock. Martha had her hand in Lucas's arm. She could feel in it the faintest tremor of weakness and could sense in his stride an uncertainty wholly foreign to him. In the wide doorway she confronted her family and looked from one to another of their faces. Impulsively George held out his arms to her.

Tears sprang to her eyes. "George!" she said. "*You* will help us. I know you will."

Lucas stiffened. "Martha," he said in a low calm voice, "let it be."

George put his arms around his aunt and began unhappily to pat her shoulder. "Louisa?" he said, as if by calling on his wife's name he might conjure up some happy banishment of their difficulties.

Miss Rebecca Steinman, playing solitaire at the card table in the sun parlor, paused in her game at Martha's cry of anguish and watched the little drama with sharp and intelligent black eyes.

Howie glanced first at Lucas and then at Miss Steinman. He touched Newton's arm and spoke in a whisper, scarcely moving his lips. "Not out here. Get 'em outa sight."

"All right, Howie. Better let us handle this," Newton said.

They had, in fact, all had the same thought. Without a word they gathered around Martha and Lucas and, before Miss Steinman was sure anything had happened, everyone had vanished into Howie's office except Howie, who retreated in the direction of the kitchen.

There was no way Martha could have allowed herself to believe of her nephews — her *children*, as she had always thought of them — that they were parties to a bizarre plot against Lucas to "put him away." Howie: yes. Mrs. Crawley: without a doubt. But George and Albert? She had humored Lucas in his inclusion of them, thinking that time would straighten out his misconception. Now, having called on George for help, she felt strength and confidence flow all through her tired body; and she began immediately, words tumbling over each other, to explain what had been done to Lucas and why.

"But we're willing to let you deal with . . . with all that — with what Lucas told you about day before yesterday. We — we haven't the strength, much as I hate to admit it. Right, Lucas?" They were standing close together in the crowded little study, and she still had her hand in his arm. She went on without waiting for a reply. "We know you'll do what's best for everybody. All we want is to get married and get a place of our own." Here she began to sense in their silence reservations with which she was confident she could deal. "Maybe it seems foolish to you for us to get married," she said. "I can understand that." When no one answered, she continued strongly. "Nevertheless, it's what we want. We're both in good health. There's no reason in the world why we shouldn't spend our last years together."

"Together — but *here*," Louisa said, "where we can be sure that you . . ." She glanced briefly at Lucas. ". . . both of you are well taken care of."

"Don't you think we've known each other long enough to get married and set up housekeeping?" Martha's little joke fell into silence. After a moment she went on: "Don't you see, children," she said, "that we can't possibly stay here after what Lucas has said to and about Howie, and what Howie has done to him? It would be out of the question. Luke, tell them. Lucas!"

Lucas, white and trembling, sat down in the chair closest to the door. "Martha," he said, "I am . . . I have . . ." He paused, then resolutely drew himself up. "It's true, George," he said. "We *can't* stay here. You can see that."

"Aunt Martha," Albert said heavily. "I don't think you are aware of all that has happened. We would like to save you . . . To protect you from . . ."

"From myself? It's not necessary, Albert. I'm sorry if you children don't approve, but we *are* going to get married. And we *can't* stay here. In fact, we may leave tonight."

"Tonight!" George said. *"Tonight?* Come on, now, Aunt Martha. Let's think about it a few days. What's the hurry — after all these years?"

"George, we're going to do it. Lucas has already applied for the license."

"Well, now, sweetheart," Albert said, "you're going to force us to talk about some unpleasant things. The fact is, you can't go anywhere with Lucas tonight — or any other night, and that's all there is to it."

"Look at him, Aunt Martha! It's plain he's not a well man," George said.

At this point, feeling a weakness in her knees and the thunder of blood in her ears, Martha carefully sat down in a straight-backed chair against the wall and gazing across the room at Lucas tried hard to see the expression on his face. Is that stuff getting to him again? she thought. God help us. Then: I'll be quiet a minute and see what they are going to say.

Five minutes later she and Lucas had both heard what they had to say — Albert was the spokesman — and she sat with her head bent, staring, in a daze, as it seemed, at the floor.

Louisa pulled a chair close to hers and sitting down took her hand. This was evidently the point that George had anticipated, when Aunt Martha would "need a woman."

Across the room Lucas, too, was silent. Martha no longer tried to look at him.

". . . so you can see, darling, how out of the question . . ." Louisa was saying.

And George: "He . . . I feel sure he didn't . . . He *couldn't* have realized what he was doing. We all know that. But that's all the more reason . . ."

"Albert," Lucas said slowly, the deep precise voice quavering, "I can't stay here and listen to this." He got up. "I — leave — this — house — now!" He crossed the room to Martha, laid his hand lightly on her shoulder, and looked down at her. "It's all right," he said. "I'll come to get you in the morning."

"Luke," she said, "don't go. We can — "

"No. I'd better get out. In the morning."

Behind him Newton and Albert exchanged a glance, Newton signaled Albert to follow Lucas, and they both drew aside to let him leave the room.

Martha crossed her ankles neatly and continued to look at the floor. Her face was expressionless. Sweat had burst out on her forehead and upper lip, and a drop trickled down toward her eye. She suppressed the impulse to clench her fists, and allowed her hand to lie limply in Louisa's. She appeared to them all to be in deep distress.

"George," Albert said, "I'm going to get Aunt Martha a glass of sherry. And I'll make sure Dr. Alexander is all right." To Martha he added, "We didn't *want* to offend him — or to distress you, sweetheart. That's the God's truth. It couldn't be helped."

Not for a moment did it occur to Martha to believe her

family's story about Lucy. As soon as she had understood through Albert's circumlocutions what he was saying, she had had to suppress, first the impulse to laugh aloud; then, in an instant, when it had sunk in on her with all its implications, a rage so murderous that she could scarcely believe it of herself; and finally, when Lucas left the room, flashes of sickening and desperate terror. What would happen to them?

Everything depends on my staying calm, she thought. *Calm.* I have to stay calm. Have to . . .

She raised her head and shook off Louisa's hand. "This house is mine," she said, "for my lifetime." She had not known she would say it. "It is in Sister's will. You will get all these people out of my house — all of them. As I said, Lucas and I will leave. I understand that it will take some weeks for the families to make arrangements for the — *prisoners.* When the house is empty, you will turn it over to me."

"My God," George said, "listen to reason, Aunt Martha. All we're trying to do is to keep you comfortable . . . and *safe.*"

Newton drew up a chair and sat down on her other side. "Aunt Martha," he said, "I'm your lawyer. Your conservator. I'm bound by law and by my own scruples to look after your interests — your best interests." He paused, and it seemed to her to his credit that he found it difficult to get the next sentence said. ". . . Besides, I . . . love you. We all . . ."

It was that curious word, "conservator," that drew her up short, filled her with cold caution. Deliberately relaxing again, looking again at the floor in front of Howie's desk chair (where she saw a spot of darkness throbbing as if it were alive), she pretended to hear him out. Our lives may depend on what I do now, she thought. Who knows what's happened to poor Luke? Words penetrated her intense effort at concentration: ". . . your age and health . . . And in all of our best judg-

ment . . ." "An old family friend like Judge Carey . . ." "Lucas . . . Everybody, *everybody* knows . . ."

"Darling," Louisa said. "Martha . . . *sweetheart.*"

At this point Albert came back into the room with the glass
of sherry and handed it to her. She looked at it without expression (*hemlock?*), took two cautious sips, and set it down. She
had decided on a course of action. "All right, children," she
said evenly. "You're right. I'm upset. And I'm too old to
allow myself to get so upset. It's bad for my blood pressure.
I'm going to my room now. I want to lie down for a little while.
To think and to rest. I promise you I won't take this outside the
family until we have all thought it over and talked it over
again. Give me a day or two." With an effort she added,
"George is right. There is no point in being hasty. All right?"

"Would you like me to go with you and keep you company
for a little while?" Louisa said.

"No. I need to be quiet. To lie down." *Lucas?* she said to
herself. *Lucy?* Again amusement and fury swept alternately
over her. She stood up.

"Fair enough," George said. "You know we . . ."

"Yes." She looked at him. "I know." She allowed him to
kiss her, felt his dry lips against her damp forehead.

In her room she sat down on the bed and opening the drawer
of her bedside table took out an old address book. She crossed
the room to her desk, picked up her magnifying glass, and, turning the pages of the little book, found what she was looking
for. She returned to the bed, sat down again, and dialed O
on her telephone. "Operator," she said, "I wish to make a
person-to-person call. The number is . . . I wish to speak
to Mrs. Robert Martin. Yes." And then, after a brief interval,
"Mary Hartwell?"

She saw, framed in the window of her room, the head and

shoulders of a huge cat. Paws resting on the sill, it was looking intently in at her. She closed her eyes. Not there. I know it isn't there.

CHAPTER 15

HOWIE AND MRS. CRAWLEY had been standing in low-voiced conversation in the doorway between the pantry and the dining room, keeping all the while an eye on the closed door of Howie's study. When Lucas came out, they crossed the room and, one on each side, maneuvered him toward the hall and the stairway that led down to his room. At the head of the stairs, Howie paused long enough to exchange a glance with Mrs. Crawley.

"Weak as a kitten," he said. "I'll get Harper to undress him."

There was no visible reaction from Lucas to this remark.

Downstairs, he went directly to his bed, stumbling against a chair and leaning heavily on Mrs. Crawley. "Sleepy," he mumbled. ". . . lie down a little while. Call me when supper . . ." He broke off.

Mrs. Crawley sat down in the easy chair by his fireplace and paid no further attention to him.

Through half-closed eyes Lucas could see the square of late afternoon light that marked the outside entrance to his room. His door was open; the odor of mint drifted in.

Mint and dill and the brilliance of moonlight in his doorway. When had that been?

He was wide awake, alert, feeling, except for an uncontrollable tremor in his hands and knees, strong and collected. Upstairs, he had seen Howie and Mrs. Crawley approaching him across the dining room and had made an immediate decision. He would risk nothing tonight. They were too strong for him. Now, he could still feel in the muscles of his upper arm a dull ache at the point where Howie had seized him with the powerful cold grip of a man half his age. He crossed his arms on his chest and surreptitiously massaged the muscle. He was thinking calmly of Martha, of the steps they should take to-morrow, of the future, when without warning he saw his old vision of Lucy: the long neck, the sullen mouth, the sidelong glance of huge dark eyes. Rings of gold about her neck and on her arms, like the accouterments of an African queen. The fragrance of mint drifted through the room.

His belly contracted in a convulsion of nausea. Could it be true? Did I? Did I ask her to touch me? Could I have done it in a dream, in what seemed a dream to me at the time — like Martha's dream of her mother's body in the nursery bed? Yes. Of course I could. My age — anything is possible.

He imagined with the specificity of a long-ago memorized anatomical drawing the structure of the inside of his head, the location of all the snakelike veins and arteries that curled around his brain, saw the swelling of a weakened wall here, a fatty dam choking off the flow of blood there. *Rotting.* Alive but already rotting.

"When a man comes to feel that it is rational, he goes and hangs himself at once . . ." But — Martha?

She's upstairs with *them.* Alone. Afraid.

He drew a rasping asthmatic breath. Mrs. Crawley picked up yesterday's paper from the table and turned to the comics.

Can't afford an emphysema attack now. I have to think clearly. *Relax!* he said to his lungs. Let go. He began care-fully, without a sound, to flex and relax his muscles: *extensor longus digitorum, gastrocnemius* . . . He breathed more easily.

Harper. Hadn't he and Martha been going to find Harper when the family had stopped them? What had they planned to say to him? Had they even made up their minds?

No time for weakness. *Biceps femoris, gluteus maximus.* Curious. Our lives — our fate — still matter to me. As if I were still a man.

There was a knock at the door and Mrs. Crawley rose and let Harper in. Lucas did not move except to begin again to flex his toes inside his shoes. *Extensor longus digitorum.*

"Mr. Snyder says I'm to stay with Dr. Alexander," Harper said. "You can tell Ruby to bring his supper down."

"He's all tuckered out, pore old fella," Mrs. Crawley said in a whisper. "May be asleep. But wake him up to feed him. Call me if you have any trouble. And be *sure* he drinks his hot chocolate. O.K.?"

Harper nodded. When she had gone, he closed the door and continued to stand against the wall just inside the room, looking alertly about him.

Lucas could hear Mrs. Crawley's steps retreating down the hall and then thudding on the stairs. He sat up. He had made up his mind. "Harper," he said in a low shaky voice, "come over here, please, and sit down where we can talk." He moved carefully to the easy chair next to the fireplace and indicated to Harper the chair across from it where Martha usually sat. "Hurry," he said. "Sit. We haven't much time."

Harper sat down gingerly on the front edge of the chair, feet planted side by side in front of him, back straight, stared at Lucas as at a ghost, and said nothing.

"I have some things to tell you," Lucas said. "I don't know

. . . You may already know all about them." He looked sternly into Harper's expressionless eyes. "But you may not," he said. "I'm taking the chance that you don't know, because I . . . I *think* you care about Martha; and I know you are bound to care about your grandchildren — about Lucy." For the second time that day he told his story, this time with the additions he had heard in Howie's office.

". . . and that's what they're saying." He leaned forward, rested his head on the heels of his hands, and looked at Harper from beneath wild gray brows. "I'm tired," he said. "And Martha — God knows what they're saying and doing to her. Can you help us?"

Matthew Harper, scrambling for his caves, said nothing.

Lucas sat up straight and continued to look directly at Harper. "Maybe I did that," he said. "Not likely, but possible. But suppose I didn't, Harper. *Suppose!* Then Lucy has agreed to go along with these people — do you see? — in a lie. Because . . . Because I'm a threat to them."

Slowly Harper shook his head. "Probably you didn't do that, Dr. Alexander," he said. "Lucy — she's so scatterbrained . . ."

"No. Not the question. What I'm trying to get you to see is *Lucy's* situation. Not just us, but what's best for her. This affair with Snyder? This *corruption?*" He shook his head. "She's young." He started to say, "beautiful," but hesitated and said instead, "You don't want her tied up with — tainted by — these people. You can't want that. Jesus Christ!"

The expression of bewilderment (studied? faked?) on Harper's long yellow face made him break off. "Melodramatic," he said. "I know it sounds melodramatic." He shrugged his shoulders angrily, as if to shed a weight from them. "But it's all true. Our *lives* are at stake — Martha's and mine. Do you see that? And she's their — instrument."

"I don't know what to think, Dr. Alexander," Harper said.

"If you can get her to tell the truth," Lucas said, ". . . get her to see what she will do to herself — how destructive this lie is — not only to us, but to her — to her life . . . People can't live by lies, Harper, by using other people. *Can't*. And Snyder . . ."

Harper looked at him curiously, on his face the same look of impersonal compassion that Lucas had seen on it when they had picked Mrs. Crane up from the sun parlor floor and carried her to her room that day so many months before. What he said, almost against his will, as it seemed, was, "Lies are not always destructive to people like us, Dr. Alexander. Sometimes useful. Sometimes necessary."

But Lucas was far away. "That would do it," he said. "If she refused to go along, I think we could extricate ourselves. Lawyer. Get her to a lawyer, that's what we need to do. Get a statement from her. Go to court, if we have to. Don't hesitate, Harper," he said. "Before God, I promise there won't be any — repercussions for her. Why should there be?"

"We would both lose our jobs," Harper said. "Taking for granted, of course, that you're telling the truth, Dr. Alexander. I mean, I know you *think* you are, but . . ."

"No. Don't worry about that. Don't! You know you can get a job, Harper. A dozen families in Homochitto would jump at the chance to get you to work for them. And Lucy? I'll — I'll help her. The people at the health project. We can . . ."

"After we went to court against Newton Clarke?" Harper shook his head. "No, sir." He stirred restlessly in his place. Then he stood up. "Ruby'll be coming down with your supper in a minute, sir," he said.

"What can I eat?" Lucas looked at him desperately. "I'm afraid to eat their food. I told you they've been giving me some kind of drug." He passed a trembling hand over his drawn and weary face.

"I'll try to come down before I leave and bring you something," Harper said. Then, again unwillingly, he burst out, "We don't want to get mixed up in this white people's mess, Dr. Alexander. Can't afford to. Never could, never can afford to. Neither me nor Lucy. All we want is to work and be let alone."

"And Martha? Not me — why should I be anything to you? But *Martha?* If the thing were the other way around? What do you think she would do for you?"

"I don't know," Harper said calmly. "Depends on what was at stake, I reckon. For her, I mean. She's always seemed to me to be a realist. Never a victim. It's hard to say."

"Victim?" Lucas had no idea what Harper was talking about. They gazed at each other across a chasm of misunderstanding. "She's going to be a victim, all right."

"I'll try to bring you down something to eat," Harper said. "*Please.* For Martha's sake. For Lucy."

"I'll talk to Lucy," Harper said at last, "and see what she says."

"Sure they asked me if I would say that," Lucy said. "Why not? It's nothing to me. The old doc *is* crazy. Running around the woods collecting up toadstools and eating 'em. He might just as easy have done that to me as not. Fact is, I ain't saying he didn't. I been in his room and seen him looking at me sometimes like . . . Besides, Grandpa, it ain't gonna make any change in his life. He's *old* — be dead in a couple of years. But this job and all is gonna make a big difference to me." She gave Harper a sidelong glance. "And you're as crazy as he is, far as that goes, to be worrying about it. What do we care about them?"

"That was my first thought, Lucy," Harper said calmly. "The important thing here is to decide what's best for us. We got the kids to think about. And I got you to think about, if you won't think about yourself. We got to sit down here quietly and figure what's going on and how you ought to act. Do you see that?"

"No, I don't. All I got to do is say he got after me to feel him up. That's all. Ain't nothing gonna come of any of it except a better job for me."

"He and Miss Martha aren't dead yet," Harper said, "and they're not crazy either. They can make trouble for these people — and for us."

"*Miss Martha!*" Lucy mimicked his inflection. "I don't give a hoot about *Miss* Martha. I want that job Howie promised me."

"You're a fool," Harper said.

They stood facing each other in the sitting room of Harper's little house. Lucy tapped her foot as if poised for flight, jingled the gold bangle bracelets on her left arm, and gazed at Harper defiantly.

"Lucy," he said, "try to forget I'm your grandpa. You're a grown woman. Try to sit down here with me like we were both just people and let's figure out what's going on. It's important for us to do that. Just for a minute, grant that it's important."

She stared at the stern old face, the sharp brown eyes, so often veiled and expressionless, now full of anxiety and love. Then: "Yeah, I know it's important," she said. "I know that."

Then, "O.K. If it'll make you feel better, I'll talk about it. What
you want to know?"

There were a great many things Harper did not need to ask
Lucy, things that he already knew. He had been watching, as
was his lifelong habit, ever since the day he first realized that the
Clarke household was becoming a new and unknown factor in
their lives. And after Lucas had said to him, standing by the
broken sundial in the front garden that day, "I worry about
Lucy, too . . . Things may not be *right* here," he had been as
alert as a vixen with a new litter of pups to care for. He had
sniffed out and listened for and watched with those always expressionless eyes every shifting inflection, every tiny exchange
of words and glances in the old house, looking for — what? For
the data that might lead him to a decision about what was going
on and what to do about it. He had heard Mrs. Crawley out
that day in the attic and afterward had been meticulously careful to tread the line he established in his mind to keep her sure
of him. He had come down into the lower floor of Golden Age
more than once and seen the signal light blinking, blinking over
the Strange brothers' door while Lucy's desk stood deserted
and the hall empty; had glanced into the room where "the
Vegetable" lay with wide-open eyes and trembling lips, where
Mrs. Wheeler continued to say in a reasonable voice, "Would
you come in, please — just for a moment? I won't keep you";
had found her one day lying in her own urine and feces, tangled
like a trembling trapped rabbit in the confining net.

He had struggled to feed this data into his "system," had puzzled over his "categories." Was there something he had not
taken into account? How could it be that these people, instead
of being engaged in their proper work of profiting from death,

were (if one could trust one's senses) keeping people alive? Was there something wrong with his categories? And Howie? They said he had kept his wife alive all those years, too, had indulged her in her gluttony and nursed her in her illness, and grieved at her death.

He had seen Howie one day looking speculatively at Miss Rebecca Steinman and had asked Lucy afterward if he ever spoke of her. "Sure he does," she had said. "He says she's liable to end up like the old doc — a troublemaker. He says she's too unpredictable. He's gonna get her on tranquilizers soon as he can."

"These people don't fit into the system," he muttered. "Something wrong somewhere."

"You so busy worrying about your old system all these years," Lucy said, "you done forgot we're real. But I don't give a shit for your old system. I got to think about my future."

He shook his head. "That's what the system's for," he said. "Survival."

"Survival! Who wants to be picking dewberries and caning chairs all their lives just to survive? Who wants to survive in one them tombs you always talking about? I'm going to be rich and live in a city — and not no Harlem ghetto, either."

Harper shook his head. "We got to stay away from cities, Lucy," he said. "Do you know in the bottom of the Dark Ages not but twenty-five thousand people lived in Rome? The rest of 'em dead — of the plague and the Huns and starvation. And it had been the greatest city in the world. It was the *country* people who managed to . . ."

"Huns! Dark Ages! Jesus Christ, Grandpa! You're the living proof your theory don't work. Yours or no other theory. You so busy worrying about fitting everybody into it, you've forgot the first thing you need to know about scrambling."

"No," he said. "I've always taught you all to scramble."

"According to theories. Not according to anything going on in *my* life. All I got to know about Howie is he's a bastard and he's a sucker."

"No," Harper said. "You may be right about me spending too much time worrying about my theories, but don't you make the mistake of thinking Howie Snyder is a sucker."

"*Stupid*. He's stupid."

"Stupid is dangerous. He could be stupid and you the sucker."

"He's mean," she said. "I'll grant you he's got a streak of meanness in him. But where does that fit into your system?"

It was after this conversation that he began to watch Howie and Lucy together, and drew the conclusion that she was sleeping with him. It came as no shock to him, then, one day in the kitchen, when Snyder deliberately laid a rusty hand on her shoulder and let it slide gently down her slender arm, at the same time giving him (Harper) a sidelong knowing glance.

Testing him? He felt the prick of panic in his heart. But still, surveying all their circumstances, he had taken no action. He too was old, after all, and he had three young children to care for.

Now, in answer to Lucy's question, "What do you want to know?" he answered, "I don't know, Lucy. I don't know. I just want you and the children to get along, and my mind tells me" — he used here an old expression of his mother's, with the notion that it might evoke in Lucy the affection, the resonances that it evoked in him — "my mind tells me we've got trouble here." He sat down on the worn and sagging sofa that had been given to them when the Griswold house became Golden Age and looked miserably up at her.

Lucy threw herself down beside him. "Oh, Grandpa," she said, "I care about you and the kids and all. I do. And as for

Snyder . . ." She shuddered. "But I got to make some kind of a life. I *got* to. You can't help me anymore. I got to do it my way."

"I know you do," he said. "But I'm trying to make you see what you're getting into. Listen a minute. There's drug trouble here, for one thing. The doctor mentioned it and Mrs. Crawley mentioned it. Both of 'em. Somebody's taking drugs. And if the doctor gets into some kind of court case, if he and Miss Martha get their backs up and fight these people, who do you think is going to end up getting blamed for the drug stealing? Howie? Crawley? No, Lucy. None of them. You. *You!* Don't you see that?"

"You all stirred up over nothing," she said. "Sure, Crawley's taken some them drugs a few times. You can do it easy with the old people. How they gonna know what you giving them? Or how much? But she ain't selling it or anything, Grandpa. She takes it herself — tranquilizers and Demerol and all — when she gets to feeling low. She says Demerol makes you feel great — *happy.* That's all there is to it. Not enough that anybody's ever gonna know the difference. And no way to prove it. How's a couple of crazy old people gonna prove anything like that?"

Harper shook his head. "Dangerous," he said stubbornly. "Dangerous."

"Look here, for instance. They didn't even have to get a doctor to give 'em a prescription for this stuff they been giving the doctor to quiet him down. Plenty of things out there that nobody keeps track of. Like, you know, this stuff they use on television to knock you out that they call a Mickey Finn. They got that. And Nervine and stuff like that. You don't even need a prescription to get that, and it'll make you goofy as old Wheeler."

"He's got friends," Harper said. "The doctor — people down at the new health department."

"I don't see 'em coming out to see him," Lucy said. "They don't know nothing. And don't care either."

"Here's another thing, Lucy," Harper said. "I've been work-ing for Miss Martha thirty years. She's . . . She's . . . I know what you're going to say, but she's always been decent to me — and to you, too. She's like — almost like a friend. I can't help caring what happens to her."

"Friend! And you calling *me* a fool? You with your proper talk and your butler's coat and your *Miss* Martha! I call her a friend when she invites me and you to sit down with her in the parlor. And 'til then, I'm going to tell you, Grandpa, I don't feel nothing but good, if I got the power to make her hop. And the old doc, too."

"*Lucy*. All your life I've told you not to waste yourself on that kind of foolishness. It'll eat you up like acid."

"Grandpa, you're crazy. That's all. Crazy."

"I'm asking you, *please* — don't tell that lie for them. Don't get yourself tangled up with them any more than you already are. Get out. Quit. We'll find something else. I'll help you go to school or whatever you want to do. You know I got some money put back, Lucy. I'll help you."

Lucy shrugged and shook her head, but then, as if to soften what she had to say, she laid her hand gently on his arm. The gold bangles clinked against each other. "I already decided," she said. "I'm sorry, Grandpa, but I got to go forward. It's too late for me to back out. One of these days you'll see I was right." It was time now for her to begin the night shift and she got up to leave the house. At the door she stopped. "You *got* to back me up," she said. "You really be getting us into it, if you try to go against me." She shook the bangles and smiled. "These real eighteen-karat gold," she said. "You know where they come from? They belonged to Howie's dead wife. And now they *mine*. Hang on, Grandpa. We going to be rich and happy. What difference it makes about them?"

After she had gone, Harper sat for a long time in the little parlor. The house was silent, the children asleep. Once he muttered aloud: "Lucy's no Mandingo and that's a fact."

After a while he got up and going to the chest in the bedroom he shared with Matt and Andrew he got out his stack of notebooks and clippings and took them back to the living room, where he thumbed idly through them, stopping here and there at an entry that had given him particular satisfaction: Genghis Khan's slaughter at Herat; the colonization of the Congo; the Etruscan tombs. He sat a long time motionless with the notebooks in his lap and thought of his children. Saw Howie's hand on Lucy's arm and, it seemed to him now, saw the downy hair rise and the flesh shrink at his touch. *And I stood by and did nothing.* A cold stone lodged itself under his heart.

"Evil," he muttered. "Evil," and his own flesh puckered and grew cold.

But *they*, he thought, lying in their beds, waiting for their shots, lying in their own piss and vomit, blind and paralyzed and crazy, they *are* the dead — the breathing dead. And Snyder and Crawley, walking all through the house in the day and in the night, dispensing pain and relief, they don't *have* to kill anybody. They are already the keepers of the dead.

Lucy, he thought, *come away!*

He closed his notebook. It doesn't matter how much I worked on it or thought about it or whether it's right or wrong. None of it is any use to us now. No place to hide. No place to hide.

When the cathedral clock struck twelve, even though he knew he had to get up and get the children off to school in the morning before he went to work, he was still sitting there, thinking.

CHAPTER 16

EARLY THE NEXT MORNING Mary Hartwell boarded the daily
Southern Airways flight from Memphis to New Orleans. At
eight forty-five it would bring her, unannounced (as she had
promised Martha), into the Homochitto airport. Capable and
motherly in her sensible, low-heeled walking shoes and dark
cotton print dress, her gray-streaked brown hair (hair that
Martha remembered hanging loose and shining to her shoulders)
drawn into a knot low on her neck, she stepped briskly down
the aisle and settled herself next to an earnest bearded lad who
was going, he told her, to find a place to live in New Orleans
before the beginning of the fall semester at Tulane.

"And you're from Memphis?" she said. "My son Bob has
been thinking of Tulane. Tell me . . ."

And so they fell into conversation, talking first of colleges
and common acquaintances, then, as they began to relax with
each other, of politics, racism, Vietnam, drugs, and even (each
one with studied objectivity: "I know a couple who . . .")
sexual freedom.

The plane droned steadily on and they looked down through
wisps of cloud at ox-bow lakes, willow-bordered creeks, green
cane thickets, and the broad ancient twisting river, a landscape
that still seemed prehistoric, Mary Hartwell observed, as if a
brontosaurus might any moment raise its long neck and look

dully up at them, or a tyrannosaurus rex reach up and snatch
them from the sky. "Does it look like that to you?"

But the boy wanted to talk about himself, and she listened and
replied, accepting without visible shock his talk of mescaline
and pot, of communes and Castro and the pill, interrupting now
and then with, "Bob says . . ." or "My daughter Elizabeth . . ."

The seatbelt sign blinked on, the plane banked and turned,
dropped rapidly down and screeched along the runway at
Homochitto.

"If only more parents were like you," he said, as she un-
fastened her seat belt and gathered her belongings. "What a difference it would make!"

She smiled and nodded and said good-bye, but, "What difference?" she muttered to herself, as she got off the plane, and
then, as she claimed her bag, "They probably are."

In the airport limousine she put aside her habitual preoccu-
pation with her children's lives, with the subjects she and her
husband talked of when they lay sleepless at three in the morning (Had Bob not better take the college boards at least once
for practice? Would Elizabeth decide to marry the young man
with whom, although everyone was careful not to speak of it,
they knew she was living? And *was* that boy who always hung
around the house smelling like marijuana going to drag Francis
into some dreadful trouble? No! Francis is too level-headed
for . . .) and concerned herself with her responsibilities at
Golden Age.

At ten-thirty she was climbing the concrete steps and passing
under the arching cane that opened on the old beloved house,
still, in spite of change — of vanished arbors and trellises and
years — full of her life: her childhood and youth and her
mother's death. She had spent the preceding hour and a half in

conversation with her cousin — her foster brother — George. Familiar with his morning habits, she had gone directly to his house; had pushed open the ancient iron doors from the jail (Louisa had won that argument) hung now in a wall made of bricks reclaimed from Old Jerusalem Church; had drunk coffee from the blue willow-patterned cups which she had used through the years of her girlhood; had sat surrounded by the pale rose and white-veined green of caladium leaves and the deep blue of nut orchids blooming in every pot and bed around the edges of the square brick court — witness to the careful thought Louisa had given to relieving the monotony of a dry August garden.

Shut away in this shady oasis, in a quiet interrupted only by the splash of a fountain (George pointed out to her how they had rigged the leaden boy from the old Clarke garden with a tiny pump, so that water bubbled continually in his scallop shell), they talked of many things. Of Robert Martin's business, of the traps to be encountered in the stock market, of discussable adolescent crises (broken legs, college boards), of Newton Clarke's meteoric rise in state Republican circles, of Mary Hartwell's feeling of guilt because she had been unable to share more fully the burden of looking after their aunt. There was an elegiac quality to their conversation. They talked of old days, of George's hawk, of Elizabeth Griswold's remembered beauty, even of the sound of her soft querying voice, reading aloud on a winter evening; of bows and arrows and rubber-gun wars; of excursions with Martha and Lucas on the *Delta Queen* and all-day picnics on Cole's Creek. Times gone, their very quality irretrievable in this strange, cold, threatening world they and their children lived in.

They talked of old age and death and of harsh choices to be made. Of what they each one meant to do when they grew old.

"I'll never be a burden . . ." "Nursing home for me . . ." Joked even of the hoarded bottle of sleeping pills, saved against doctors who would not let you die. "If you've still got sense enough left to take them . . ."

George spoke then of all that had happened in the past few days. "I knew we had to tell you about it," he said. "We would have gotten in touch with you today anyhow . . ."

Presumably he believed that he spoke the truth. As even Lucas would be the first to admit, *had* admitted on several occasions, George was a *good* man.

The conversation, of course, was in the context of Mary Hartwell's telling him that Aunt Martha had called her the night before, half-hysterical, with wild talk of being a prisoner in her own house, of Lucas's being a prisoner, and, at the end, a last enigmatic remark about cats prowling the house and yard. "Like Mother's body," Martha had said, "and like the furniture painted on the walls. I *know* it's like that." None of it had made any sense.

George explained everything to his anxious cousin. Dr. Blanks, he ended by saying, had put Lucas on a mild tranquilizer. "He has emphysema, too, you know, and any kind of nervous tension can bring on an attack — no joke at his age and with his history of respiratory trouble. Or so Dr. Blanks told Howie. Damn it, it's a mess, a *mess*," he finished. "You don't know how I've hated it — hated to see Aunt Martha getting into this shape. Hated the conflict. If only . . . But there it is. They're old. Helpless. Unreasonable. And Albert . . . I don't share his resentment of Lucas, but, whatever his reasons, he's right. You can see . . ." His voice trailed off. Then, more strongly, "No *right* thing to do here," he said. "All we can manage is what's least bad. But go on out and see for yourself. Give us your slant on it."

She sat staring at him. Then: "Lucas Alexander! At his age? *Lucy?* Really, George!"

He looked at her with some embarrassment. "After all, Mary Hartwell," he said, "young people don't necessarily have a monopoly on sexual difficulties. As Albert said the other day, Great-aunt Amy Griswold used to think she was a prisoner in a whorehouse. Do you remember that?"

And so when Mary Hartwell appeared, framed by the over-arching cane, on the brick walk leading to Golden Age, Martha was sitting on the high front porch in one of the lightweight vinyl and aluminum chairs with which Howie had replaced the old-fashioned captain's chairs that had once stood in a neat row, two on either side of the front door. She stared, made out the identity of the blurred figure of her niece by the slightly slew-footed walk and erect carriage, and hurried down the front steps to meet her. She had not seen Mary Hartwell since the week after Elizabeth's death, and memories of that difficult anguished time came rushing back. She stumbled once, where the roots of an ancient crape myrtle tree had heaved the bricks out of their bed (I *know* to avoid that spot. Keep calm), and half fell into her niece's arms.

"I was thinking about Sister," she blurted out. "How *hard* for you it is to come home — not like living here all the time, so that one gets accustomed *gradually* . . ." She interrupted herself. "I'm sorry I've had to put our troubles on you, Mary Hartwell, but . . ."

"Aunt Martha! It's all right. I've put mine on you more than once."

Across Martha's mind flashed the same vision she had had the morning of Elizabeth's death: the summer garden, odor of gardenias heavy in the air, the leaden scallop shell in its tangle of periwinkle, and Elizabeth holding Mary Hartwell as she crowed with delight and splashed the cool water with fat baby hands. ". . . in the name of sun and summer and of bitter wind and winter rain . . ." The old grief and dislocation flooded all through her. "I remember the day we baptized you in the bird-bath, Mary Hartwell," she said. "Like yesterday. *Yesterday.* How can it be?"

"Birdbath?" Mary Hartwell held her aunt at arm's length, gazed at her for a moment, and then kissed her again. "It's so *good* to see you," she said. "You look *well*. Now, come on, my dear" — with an arm around her, gently urging her toward the house — "let's sit down on the porch and talk."

Martha shook her head. "No privacy. Howie's prowling around in there like — like a hungry cat. And Mrs. Crawley, in the kitchen — guarding their saucers of cream. Let's see. Yes. We'll go out in the back garden where we can't be overheard. Harper, maybe, but that won't matter. I don't care what Lucas says, I trust Harper."

She stopped and looked around at her niece. "But am I right? Can I? And you? Can I? That's the point we're driven to."

"Aunt Martha! You must try to stay calm and tell me quietly . . ."

"I *am* calm," Martha said. "All right. Let's walk on. No — this way, Mary Hartwell. For some unknown reason Howie rooted up the old walk that went around the side there. Scup-pernong arbor's gone, too, you notice." She shrugged. "One could expect things like that — if that were *all*. But *this* . . ."

She stopped and faced her niece. "I haven't even seen Lucas today. Harper told me last night he was still here. But they wouldn't let me go down to him this morning. Said he was still sleeping. And I'm not strong enough, Mary Hartwell, to *force* them to — all by myself. And you can see my position, if I were to try — they could make me look mad, *mad*. And he looked so pale and shaky last night . . . Oh, what's happening? What are they doing to him?"

"Aunt Martha! I'm *here*. We'll look after Lucas."

"Yes! Of course you are. Everything will be fine now. Come." She set out again, hurrying, talking as she walked. ". . . kept him in my room all day yesterday — lying on the bathroom floor, you know, because that way at least we could be sure if *they* came in, they wouldn't find him. And Howie did — but he's not all that bright, you know, Mary Hartwell (Howie)." She laughed drily. "I managed to . . . Although how he thought Luke could have walked downtown after what they must have given him . . . And the seals. I kept the machine talking all day so they wouldn't hear us. The seals swimming all along the continental shelf . . . And it worked . . ."

Mary Hartwell's voice when she answered was quiet — controlled and reasonable. "Try to tell me what you were so upset about on the phone last night," she said. "What's going on here? I'm listening. I want to help you."

"I *am* telling you." Without speaking again, Martha led her to a bench under the elm tree at the corner of the yard and they sat down together. She looked up into the branches. "I'm afraid this old tree is going to go," she said. "Dutch elm disease? Has it gotten to us?"

"There is something wrong with the elms in Memphis," Mary Hartwell said, still in a quiet and reasonable voice. "I've been noticing it for a year."

"Maybe they'll let us alone here for a while," Martha said. "They've been peeping out the window at me every ten minutes since breakfast. Afraid I would run away? Or sneak around the house to get to Lucas? But I knew better. I just sat quietly, Mary Hartwell, and waited for you. No one knew you were coming. But where have you been? I thought your plane got here at eight forty-five."

"I stopped by to see George," Mary Hartwell said. She did not elaborate.

"And he's been telling you . . . But never mind. You were going to have to hear all that sooner or later. But Lucas! I'm so worried about Lucas!"

"Aunt Martha, try to listen to me and understand what I'm saying. You're getting more and more excited. Try not to worry about Lucas. I know we can help him. Hold in your mind that — that — however, whatever made him do it, it was like a dream. It was not him — not really. And . . ."

Whatever made him do it! A warning bell clanged in Martha's brain. For a long moment she could say nothing. She felt a weight of exhaustion seeping, seeping, as if into her bones, as if she were sodden with mineral-laden water that slowly, slowly, turned each separate cell to stone. Saw herself lying age after age, bleached and stone hard, at the bottom of some clean creek bed, cold water rippling over, until the earth heaved, folded on her, ground her to sand, and washed her into the sea. That wouldn't be so bad, she thought.

". . . tell me *quietly, slowly,* all about yourself — all about everything . . ."

Who was this aging woman, gray-haired, and so professionally competent that one might take her for a good — a conscientious — nurse? I scarcely know her, Martha thought.

"I never should have called you," she said. "I suppose you're 'in with them' too — without even knowing it. I know now what Ethel Crane means when she talks that way — 'in with them.' Nothing paranoid, nothing senile about it. Is there?

Well . . . Well . . ." She sat gazing at the ground, at the dry browning grass of August, the scattering of fallen elm leaves. "I can't give up so easily," she said in a low voice, as if to herself. "Can't despair. I have Lucas to think of."

"*Tell* me."

"These are the facts," Martha said. "There is nothing wrong with Lucas. He did not attempt to rape Lucy. He *did* see Howie with her, as he says he did. They do keep Mrs. Wheeler in a cage. They *have* drugged Lucas to keep him quiet."

"See Howie? Cage?" Mary Hartwell was puzzled. George's account of what had happened had been general: Lucas, he said, had made "wild accusations about the staff out there — something about burning people with cigarettes and God knows what else." She took the beloved old lady's hand. "This is what I think would be the best thing for you to do," she said. "Come home with me. Plan an indefinite stay. If Lucas is unhappy, dissatisfied here, he should leave. I'll help him find a little apartment, if he would like me to. Let everything simmer down. If you and he still want to marry — then in three months, six months, I'll go along. I'll do all I can to help you. Fair enough?"

Martha held herself erect, the old back straight, fists clenched. She *would* go on. She would not give up — not yet. "Mary Hartwell," she said, "you haven't asked me what *I* think is the best thing for me — us — to do. We've talked here ten minutes." With a flash of malice she added, "Have you had time to *evaluate my condition?* That's probably what Newton suggested you do. Ten minutes, and already you're telling me what *you'll* make possible. Doesn't it cross your mind that *I* have some ideas about my life? *Listen!* If you were a sane person shut up in a madhouse and if I came and found you there, don't you think I would just take an ax and break in the door and say, 'Quick, come out and go on about your business'?"

Mary Hartwell was contrite. "You're right," she said. "I'm too hasty. I'm going to stay a few days. We'll try to work out a way — within reasonable limits — to do what *you* think best."

"Nobody has to work anything out. There is no need to temporize. All I want to do is *leave*. This minute. To be let alone. To go with Lucas. And — 'within reasonable limits' (of time) — to have my house returned to me."

To this Mary Hartwell at first made no reply.

Then she said, a bit sternly perhaps, "Don't you see, Aunt Martha, that no matter what has happened, George and Albert have your best interests at heart? That I can't just dismiss everything they say as if they were — at best stupid and deluded, at worst scoundrels? That we have to — temporize, as you call it? Can't you go along with me until we — ?"

"Until we get me tied hand and foot? And Lucas, too? Luke! What are they doing to him?" The clenched fists trembled as with a fever. A deep congestive flush dyed the brown wrinkled face.

It may be that Mary Hartwell was alarmed at this surprising — this unreasoning — show of passion. In any case she got up somewhat hastily. "I'll go get him," she said. "Maybe if you have him right here with you, if the three of us can talk it over together . . . All right?"

Martha nodded. "If *they* will let you," she said.

When Mary Hartwell had gone, she got up from the bench, moved slowly around the elm tree, and stood with her back against it, feeling under her hands the deeply grooved, lichen-covered bark of the massive trunk. She looked up into the gently moving masses of green leaves above her head, saw there vague bird shapes darting, hesitating, flickering against the brilliance of the morning sky. Grackle voices complained. A faint

roar like the sound of the sea in a shell washed over the birdcalls.

A new sound (the creak of rope against limb?) struck her
ear, and she looked up to see bearing down on her out of the
green leaves the shape of a child — a young boy in knickers and
knee socks, brown hair flying, foot in the loop of a long rope
swing, face rapt in the joy of flight.

CHAPTER 17

HARPER HAD COME to work that morning and, when he entered Lucas's room after a gentle knock, had found him still lying in bed, feigning sleep, his breakfast tray untouched. He spoke softly. "Dr. Alexander?"

Lucas swung his legs over the side of the bed and sat up rustily. "I thought you would never get here," he said. "Didn't want to eat that stuff" — he pointed to the tray — "or seem too alert."

"Well, I'm here, I'm here," Harper said. "I came. Brought you something, too." From the pocket of his white waiter's jacket he brought out a chocolate bar and an orange. "That's energy," he said, "and that's vitamins. I was afraid your tray might be gone by the time I got here." He looked down. "You can eat that toast and bacon, Dr. Alexander," he said. "You got to use your head, you know. Just leave the coffee and cream and orange juice alone." He picked up the orange juice glass and coffee cup, dumped their contents in the toilet, and flushed it. Then he rinsed the glass, filled it with water, and brought it back.

"Of course. Of course."

Harper took out a pocketknife, cut the orange into quarters, and laid it on the tray. He put the chocolate into the drawer of the bedside table against later hunger. "You go ahead and eat while we talk," he said. "She or he might be coming in to check on you, so we got to get our talking done as quick as we can. Are you feeling O.K.?" He looked closely at Lucas. Then: "We *can* talk," he added. "She was right about that — up in the attic. Only it's turned around now. Anything you say I said, I can say you are lying." He gave a short laugh.

Lucas picked up a piece of orange and took a bite from it. "You're going to help us," he said. "Aren't you, Harper? Between us, we can teach these folks a lesson they won't forget."

"Now wait a minute, sir, wait a minute. Hear me out, please, Doctor. I lay my cards on the table — all right? — and maybe we can figure out something that'll work for everybody. But we got to be *careful.*"

"All right," Lucas said. "I'm listening." He picked up his piece of toast.

"Here's what I got to thinking last night after I talked to Lucy. I got to do what's best for us — for my children. Nobody but me to look after them. Nobody. Therefore I *got* to think first about them. Wait! Maybe what's best for us might turn out to be best for you. Let's figure on it." He spoke as calmly as if they were discussing the best route for a trip.

"Harper! No compromise here! How can Lucy compromise on this? Either she's with them or she's with me — us."

Harper laid his finger on his lips, stepped lightly to the hall door and listened a moment, then went over to the closet and began laying out clothing. "We'll just be doing this," he said, "in case somebody comes in. These people are *going* to have their way," he went on. "Don't you see that? It won't do you — or her — any good to talk about 'no compromise.'"

"Speak up," Lucas said. "I can't hear half you're saying."

Harper brought a pair of socks, a shirt, underwear, and shoes, laid them on the bed, drew up a chair, and sat down. "I'm helping you dress," he said. "You got to listen to me, sir. You got to listen and *hear* — to understand what I have to contend with. Lucy says she won't go along with me. She won't quit. She says if you didn't *do that*, you might have."

Lucas stared back bleakly at him. "I know. I know."

"She says she's got to take this opportunity and I got to go along with her unless I want to ruin her."

Lucas shook his head slowly, continuing to stare into Harper's face.

"Don't blame her, Dr. Alexander. Don't feel bitter toward her, because, you know, she's trying to make it in a hard world. And . . . and some way in my absorption, I must've failed her . . . Or is she — could she be — one of those miserable blunderers going to end up saying, 'Why me, why me?' "

"What?" Lucas said. "*What?*"

"It came to me in the night," Harper said, "that you and Miss Martha and me and mine are all in the same boat now. We all got to fall back and look for new caves."

"Caves?"

"You never had to hide, Dr. Alexander," Harper said, "but you got to learn now, if you're going to get out of this place and live your lives out, and I'm the one can teach you."

"Talk sense, Harper," Lucas said. "We both know what's necessary. Are you trying to tell me you won't help me, won't tell the truth?"

"I don't think the truth matters," Harper said, "and *that's* the truth. You *still* got to listen to me, if I'm going to help you. Put yourself in my place, please. Can you do that?

"Now the way I see it, I've got three choices. I can keep my mouth shut, close my eyes, and never say a word, except 'I never saw nothing. I don't know nothing.' No use wasting our time talking about all the reasons — Lucy and you and Miss Martha

— it would be hard for me to act like that. But I *could* do it. Might have to. Choice two: I could come over onto your side and sneak you out of here and wire up your car (Yes, they took the ignition wires loose — you didn't know that. And you probably don't know how to put them back) and go to a lawyer with you and tell him whatever it is you want me to tell him — the truth, I mean. I feel like it would be the truth.

"Now, how can I do either one of those things? How can I? One would be as bad for Lucy as the other. The only good thing for Lucy and me and the children to do is to get *out*. To find a new hiding place (I'm right about all of that, after all). But Lucy won't do it.

"Well, I could take the other kids and abandon Lucy, couldn't I? At least that way they wouldn't be tainted with — I was going to say, with this crazy white peoples' business. But I reckon I got to mean *human* business, if I'm going to be consistent. That's what I worry about most. Andrew. Matt. My baby girl. Are they going to get sucked into this destroying world when they see Lucy with fine cars and gold bangle bracelets?

"And then, too, it would mean Lucy would have a place to run to, if — *when* — she came to her senses. I've got to think about that. But where can I go — at my age? Used to be, I would think about the country. But now? A young man like Andrew, handsome, light-skinned, smart — stands out in the country like a neon sign. Nothing left there but old people and girls with their babies. Where to go? How to live? How to keep the human race going? It's not so possible as people might think. Can we do it? The times close in."

Lucas stared at him as at a lunatic, but Harper went on.

"I'm not young anymore," he said. "Tired of listening. Tired of having every day to be alert, never to miss a thing.

And Andrew says, Andrew wants — this and that. Of *course* Andrew wants his rights as a man, wants to go to school, to be a success. All those things are waiting for him that I couldn't waste myself dreaming of when I was young — and couldn't have got if I had. He's an eagle — that boy — as my mama would have said. Maybe he'll fly up and see the whole world below him and spot his own green wood, his own field, his own mossy spring, and come down there. And under a bayou bank, down in a deep ravine under the roots of an oak tree, he'll find his cave. But I . . ."

Lucas, half-crazy with impatience, broke in abruptly. "I don't know what all this means, Harper," he said. "I feel as if I've come in on the third act of a play. Is it some kind of double-talk, meant to tell me without telling me that you won't help us? If it is, I haven't time for it. I've got to get up and get dressed and get Martha out of here and get a lawyer."

Harper shook his head. "I brought you a chocolate bar and an orange," he said. "I brought you food last night, and you can tell by the way your brain is working, it was all right. (I saw you a minute ago taking your pulse.) Now you got to listen to me, because I'm the only one who can tell you the truth about everything. And I find . . ." — he gave a cluck of disapproval and an impatient shrug at his own weakness — ". . . I find I can't abandon you.

"*Listen! We* have to get out and *you* have to get out. Now I know I can get us out some way. The problem is *you*. Is it going to be any better for you and Miss Martha than it would be for me to try to fight these people? You think there's any way in the world you can win?" He shook his head. "Not a chance. At your age — this late — you got to learn to survive. You have to become like us. Best you — the two of you — can do (*like us*) is to disappear. You haven't had any practice at disappearing, but I can tell you how to do it.

"You got your social security and she's got hers. You got your little farm and she's supposed to have the house. (Yes, I know that, too, you see.) But forget all that to begin with. Forget right and wrong. Forget teaching 'em a lesson and all that. You can't afford it. Get up there this morning and tell 'em how mixed up you were. Eat mud. Tell 'em you're as crazy as they want to think you are. Go on acting like you're half-asleep. Like *we* been doing for some generations."

During this speech Lucas had got up from the bed and begun walking up and down the room, shaking his head. Now, he threw off his pajama jacket and began to put on his shirt. "For what?" he said. "For what?"

Harper went on methodically with his program with only a "You know for what.

"Get Miss Martha to do the same thing. Then, as soon as they settle down, pack your things, get out of the house as quietly as you can. I *could* wire up your ignition, but that's not a good idea. It would expose me — and anyhow you're not strong enough to drive as far as you need to go. Here's what to do. I'll get you your suitcases out and get them to the bus station. You call a taxi to meet you on the corner of the freeway service road and Clarke Street. You and Miss Martha walk on down there, get in the taxi, drive to the bus station, and get on the bus for New Orleans. Here's the schedule. Taxi to meet you at one-fifteen this afternoon. Bus leaves at one fifty-seven. It's a through bus. Get you to New Orleans in three hours. I believe you'll be there and out of the bus station before they miss you. They're used to you taking long walks and all.

"Now, when you get to New Orleans, don't call that niece and nephew of yours. Chances are they're gonna come down on the side of these folks."

Lucas had stopped dressing to listen to these specific instructions. "They're in Europe, anyhow," he said. "I couldn't get them if I wanted to. But I don't. I can manage my own affairs."

"Now, next, here's the name and telephone number of a cousin of mine in New Orleans. I called him on the telephone last night and he says he'll do this for you. He's got the Mandingo blood like me, *but* . . . Well, he's not the student I am, but he's a sharp fellow, he knows how to cover his tracks, and he can always use a little extra money. He'll rent a car for you and he'll drive you to Atlanta, if you pay him enough to make it worth his while. Atlanta. I believe that's the place to go. It's a big city. It's far enough away. But it's not too cold and it's close to the country. You don't have any connections there that I know about. Do you?"

Lucas shook his head. "I'm not going to do all that, Harper," he said. "I might be all right for you. But I *refuse* . . . !"

"I know it may sound wrong to you," Harper said. "You're accustomed to operating in another way. But, believe me, if you don't do something this drastic, they're going to get you. *Believe* me. Trust me long enough to hear me out."

"All right. But hurry up," Lucas said.

"Next," Harper said. "Settle down there — in Atlanta. Live on your social security. *Quietly.* Better go on and get married, I reckon. You'll lose one check, but Miss Martha'll be a little bit better protected, if they find you. And they are going to find you in the long run."

Here he broke off and for a moment watched Lucas who had sat down in a straight-backed chair and was pulling on his shoes, at the same time shaking his head impatiently, although he honored his promise and did not interrupt.

"I see it this way. They're gonna find you, so you better find them first. You've got to risk that. You got to establish a kind of delicate balance where they can feel like they're helping you — being *magnanimous*, you know, where you're not getting in their way or being a nuisance to them, and where you're getting enough money to live. Here's a thought for you. Make some kind of claim on 'em that'll make 'em feel good. Write 'em and tell 'em you're settled, you realize you were hasty to leave, you did wrong, and all that, but now you're satisfied and you want 'em to send Miss Martha an allowance." He interrupted himself. "Oh, it's dangerous — dangerous! And you can't be sure what'll work."

"Allowance!" Lucas glared at Harper and shook his head violently. "And her house?"

"Forget the house. Just ask for that little allowance. And then, the end of this year, when you're getting ready to rent your farm for next year, maybe you ought to sell it. Get Newton to handle the sale for you. Newton's not a bad man, Doctor. He doesn't want to cheat you. He doesn't even want to get you in his power — I don't *think*. He just doesn't want you to get in his way and be a nuisance. He'll do right by you with the farm. I believe he will. And he and the rest of 'em will be glad to make themselves easy by sending Miss Martha a little bit of money every month — if it's not too much. I believe you'll be amazed how soon they'll settle down and forget completely all about you and Miss Martha."

"You believe! You think! That's why you people are in the mess you're in right now. That kind of — of backing off. That kind of — *cowardice!*"

Harper's face, open and animated as Lucas had never seen it before, closed like a slammed door. "I reckon you want us all to come and cut yo' th'oats in the night," he said. "Like we could — if we chose. Not me, Doctor. Not me. I'm not a killer."

"Matthew!" Lucas called his name as a man lost in a swamp might call the name of the brother who sought him. "I'm sorry. I didn't mean it. Wait!" Something else struck him. "Don't you see how important it is for you to help Lucy get out of this?" he said.

"I'm thinking about Lucy," Harper said. He gave Lucas a venomous look.

"This is different. The past is over," Lucas said, almost without thinking. "Nobody is forcing her. You know it's different."

"Maybe." Harper rose and took up the breakfast tray. "Anyhow, regardless of what happens to you, I intend to be around to help her when she needs me — if I'm alive."

"I *said* I'm sorry," Lucas said. "I have to think. Let me think. Temporize . . ." He gave Harper a halfhearted smile. "We're doing what you want us to already. Maybe you're right. Maybe we'll have to keep on. But . . . If we were to get away from here," he said, "we'd *have* to have my car." He broke off and was silent a moment as Harper stood and watched him, pity flickering in his dark eyes.

Then, "Ridiculous!" Lucas said. "Absurd! How can we do it? Hopping around the country like Bonnie and Clyde. No! Lived here all my life. Damn well live here until I die. I won't let them do this to us."

At this point there was a knock at the door and he heard Mary Hartwell's deep soft voice, so like Martha's, asking if he were still asleep.

CHAPTER 18

MARTHA STOOD with her back to the tree, palms pressed flat against the bark. George? Crash into me? Into the tree? She moved quickly to one side, held out her arms to catch him and break his headlong downward swing, but he flew lightly past her, grazed the tree trunk, and continued his pendulum course out and back. Don't get in my way, he called as he swung by again. She moved aside, backed slowly out of the line of his swing, hearing underfoot the crackle of first leaf fall.

Fall, fall, a cardinal whistled from far off, and, *Winter,* the grackles rustily creaked. Winter, coming.

All right, she said. *I* still know the seasons change — Lucas and I. Everybody else is shut up inside that airless, changeless climate of the tomb. She knew that she was moving, heard the rustle of elm leaves, turned slowly, as in a dream, toward the flagstone walk that ran along the edge of the ravine. Far away, in the center of the yard where the birdbath had stood — the small leaden boy, knee-deep in periwinkle, holding up his scallop shell — she saw vague shapes moving, misted over by a fog that drifted inward from all sides — from the ravine, from the house, even rising in wisps and tatters from the wall of cane beyond the garage.

Sister? she said. Is that you?

No one answered.

She continued to move slowly toward the edge of the ravine until she was standing on the walk. She stopped there and stood, as it seemed to her, for a long time. At this point a series of flagstone steps, curving downward toward the bayou, were set into the steep slope of the ravine. Ferns grew here, and in the spring trillium put up its delicate trefoil bloom from drifts of leaves left undisturbed. A wisteria vine thick as a man's thigh twisted upward into a Spanish oak. Now she saw, lodged in a twist of the vine not high above her head, the deep grassy nest of an orchard oriole. The male shook his bright tawny feathers, cocked his black head, and sang, a burst of joyous trills and chirrs. She felt something brush electrically against her leg, sparking and prickling. Looking down, she saw a cat, smoke brown, sleek, and elegant, with a small dark head and large, smoke brown eyes, around its neck a collar plaited of golden threads. The cat crouched in the crisp leaves without a sound, without stirring a leaf, and looked at the nest and the oriole. The end of its tail vibrated with excitement.

Scat! Martha said. Get! Get!

The cat rubbed softly against her leg. Well, she said, all right, all right. As long as you don't worry the birds.

But now the jays began to scream in the elm tree and, looking back, she saw sitting on the bench she had just left another, this one a calico with a fierce smile, tattered, a great patch of hair missing from its tail, one eye closed, and a long scratch across its face. It contrived, she thought, to look both fat and hungry, both battered and strong. And it leaped from the bench and crossed the yard in her direction, no ordinary cat. She looked about her for a stick.

I'm not afraid, she said.

While she looked, the smoke-brown set its claw to the wisteria vine and began to go up. The oriole cocked his head, shook

his black-barred tawny wings, and sang, as orioles do, his seductive song of chirrups and liquid trills.

Don't you see that cat?

She found, leaning against the birdbath, a stick that suited
her purpose — a root, it appeared to be, cut the length of a
walking cane. Its gnarled top fitted her gnarled hand as if made
for her. She took it up.

All the garden was as still as winter night, even the jays silent
now, as the calico advanced across the yard and she swam toward it through a sea of air as palpable as water.

The child swung on his rope, mouth open, in a whistling silence. George, she called to him, look out. Danger! Stay
where you are. I'm going to run these cats away. She gripped
the stick as tightly as she could in trembling hands and advanced
slowly toward the wisteria vine, keeping her eyes on the ground.
For, she said, at my age I have to be careful.

Now, in the fern bed just below the rim of the ravine she saw
three more nestling among green fern fronds: one white, as big
as a possum, with blue eyes and a sly face; one sleek, blue gray
and round faced, with a diamond collar; one a long-headed gray
tabby that looked peaceful enough. It was not until the white
one spoke that she realized it was Albert. Well, sweetheart, he
said, don't worry. We want only the best for you. We're going
to look out for you. He sprang, still agile as a young tom, up
onto the bank and up the wisteria vine where the smoke-brown
was sitting above and peering into the nest, and with his soft,
sheathed claws scooped out a scrawny featherless nestling. We'll
clear out these vines and other nuisances and spruce the place
up, he said.

The calico gave a moaning yowl. Martha's heart beat so
heavily that she was conscious of the pounding against her ribs
and of the surge of blood through the big arteries in her neck.

Lucas says that's the basal, and in front the carotid, she said.
She laid her hand against her own cheek, felt the fire of blood
under the crinkled-paper skin, a throbbing behind her eyes and
a needle of pain far inside her head. Everything appeared now
in a new light. She looked all around her and then raised her
eyes and looked into the burning misted sky.

Sister? she said. Mama?

The neatly dressed father oriole sang: *Chirrup.*

She drifted toward the middle of the garden past two low
mounds of blooming lantana and a plum thicket to a bench near
the birdbath, where she sat down to think.

There are five of them, she said. They are behind me. She
noticed then that she was sitting under a crape myrtle tree that
she had never seen before. Where am I? she said. She looked
up into the tree, heavy with its burden of white panicles, and at
the ground, starred with white petals, and recalled that this was
a variety of crape myrtle Elizabeth had always liked. Did she
plant it? But I need to think about the cats. Five of them. I
have turned my back on them, but they are still there, waiting.
I will have to get up soon and look at them again. Has Albert
killed the orioles? Why? Where am I? she said again. A terrible sickness of anxiety took her by the throat like nausea.
Lucas? she said. Are you coming? She sat looking straight
ahead, her back pressed hard against the back of the bench, her
old hands gripping the gnarled root.

Across the yard, at the edge of the scuppernong arbor three
more cats appeared. They did not walk out of the arbor, but
appeared, confident and unafraid, on the very spot she was gazing at. Two were yellow half Persians, one was a black alley
cat with long legs and a high rump. They may have come up
out of a hole in the ground, she said. There is a spot over there,

where the stump of that old sycamore rotted away . . . She knew now that the cats had surrounded her. More of them were lying concealed, bellies to the ground, in the cane thicket, under the house, in the garage, watching her, waiting. She could not bear to think of the soft electric touch of their fur.

Then she heard a new noise. Upstairs in the house, Howie threw open his study window, leaned far out, and looked down at her. He held his cigar clamped between his teeth, and the smoke curled up and drifted into the still garden air. His teeth were plainly visible to Martha as he spread his lips in a queer wide grin, the cigar wagging up and down in his mouth. He wore a short-sleeved sport shirt and the sun glinted in the reddish hair on his forearms.

Would you like me to come down and help you? he said. I have everything under control in here. He indicated the house with a sweep of his hand and she saw that except on his end the outside wall was missing, so that she could see a cross-section of every room — as if it were a dollhouse. The floors were bare of furniture. A few chests and chairs and beds were painted in *trompe-l'oeil* on the walls. Ethel Crane moved stiffly about her empty room. Mrs. Aldridge, insubstantial as a ghost, retreated, dragging her walker, down an endless hall.

No, Martha said. Don't come. She closed her eyes, but not for long. As soon as she closed them, she began to hear soft movements all around the garden. The hair rose on her trembling arms and when she opened her eyes again she was under the scuppernong arbor with Lucas. Clusters of bronze fruit hung down heavily. They stood together, reaching up to gather it. The wild sweet taste and prickle was on her tongue. Albert's out there, she said. The others too, I think.

Those are Howie's cats, he said. He took a bunch of scuppernongs from her and dropped it into his basket. He was young, his mustache dark. The slate blue eyes pierced her with love. No one can get to *us*, he said.

You don't understand. George is on the swing and — the others — God knows what the others are doing. No one feeds the cats anymore. We always did, but things have been so difficult lately. Do they belong to Howie?

Yes, he said.

The mantel slants, Lucas. The clock won't run. I am winding down. The spring in my heart is broken. *They* think it's my head. Not so. Even though the needles are probing at my brain, everything is clear to me. But my *heart* — probably this time it won't mend.

Then she heard a terrible mewing and screaming, as if a hundred cats were fighting, and she turned around bravely. The first five cats were gone, she saw, and the sound of the fight came from below the edge of the ravine.

High up in the Spanish oak jays rasped, *Cree, cree* — kill, kill, kill. The father oriole sang. Albert and the smoke-brown looked at each other across the nest. She was standing on the edge of the ravine again and heard below her a pattering and rustling of feet on the dry leaves, but she saw nothing. Lucas? she said. Harper? The calico bolted out of the ravine and leapt up the twist of wisteria vine.

Come, now, Harper, Martha said. I need you.

Again Howie leaned out of the upstairs window, whiskery and smiling. He waved his cigar at her. I'm coming, he said. Don't worry. I'll help.

The three cats met in the birds' nest and began to scream. She saw them tear the featherless nestling apart, saw its scrawny neck and gaping beak, and heard the crunch of teeth on its hollow bones. She stood on her tiptoes and whacked with her twisted stick, but instead of the cats, she struck the father oriole and he fell to the ground at her feet, his head at a crazy angle to his body, his black and tawny wings beating against the ferns. She bent to pick him up, but the other cats came clawing and roaring out of the ravine. She stood up straight, gripped her stick, and faced them.

It's all right, children, she said. Sister. Don't be afraid. I'm here.

In the middle of the battle that followed Howie climbed out of his study window and down the trellis that stood against the wall. She knew he was coming, although she had no time to look around. She had to keep turning, turning, and swinging the stick, for the cats came clawing in from all sides.

I have to hide, she said. No use. Too many for me. As soon as she said the word "hide," terror overwhelmed her and she staggered down the steps toward the cattail bed beside the bayou and began to claw her way into it. Hide, she said again, forcing her way through the thicket. She saw red blood trickling down her arms where the razor-edged leaves tore her flesh. Standing still in a tiny clearing, walled in on all sides by ranks of green leaves, scarcely breathing, she listened, waited. Howie touched her on the shoulder and she could feel his icy hand through her thin summer dress. He nodded and snapped his fingers. The big calico jumped down out of the air. She felt it land on her shoulders, soft and furry, and bury its front claws in her scalp, and heard herself moan with pain and terror. Everywhere around her now she heard the cats calling to one another with horrible singing yowls. They appeared in the clearing, tumbling over one another, clawing at her legs, climbing up her skirts, wrapping their tails around her neck and face so that when she breathed, the hairs stuck in her throat and choked her. She was tired — the stick heavy in her hand, her voice a hoarse whisper.

Help me, Lucas, she said. Harper?

One last feeble whack and she tripped over her stick and fell. She lay still, her eyes open wide, every narrow cattail leaf clearly visible to her. She saw the repeated curves of the leaves outward from the straight stalks, and the brown candles at the top of each, and followed the passage of a black-spotted orange ladybug along one leaf. The cats were silent, sitting, waiting. She brushed her hand across the cool damp earth and touched the body of the father oriole, lying close beside her, still warm, but dead now. She took him up and held him gently in her hands. Oh, she said. Oh.

She lay, as it seemed to her, a long time without saying anything more, and then she fell asleep for a little while. After her nap, although she could not get up (her left leg persisted in giving way under her), she felt strong and well. She called out several times for Mary Hartwell and Harper, but they were still in the house and did not hear her. The cats had vanished. She was lying close to the edge of the ravine under a loquat tree. Above her head a mockingbird lit and sang, as if for her, its most passionate moonlight song. She quietly listened and thought to herself that it would be wise for her to wait until Mary Hartwell came back to help her up. I won't make any more of this than I have to, she thought. The main thing, *still*, is to get out of here.

Not more than ten minutes had elapsed between the time Mary Hartwell went into the house to get Lucas and the time they came out together and found Martha lying there, lucid enough by then. "Nothing is broken," she said. "I'm all right,

Luke. I just can't get up by myself and I waited for you to come help me."

Mary Hartwell called Harper and together they helped Martha to her room, got her into her bed, and called Dr. Blanks.

While Mary Hartwell was on the telephone, Lucas got a quilt from her closet, covered her, sat down beside the bed, and took her left hand in his. "Squeeze as hard as you can," he said, and she obeyed.

"No strength," she said.

"It's all right, Martha," he said. "All right." He pushed a strand of hair back from her face, looked carefully into her eyes, and counted her pulse. "You fainted," he said firmly. "You'll be all right."

"Dreams . . ." she said. "Our dreams are true." Then, "I know what's the matter with me, Lucas. Not necessary for you to lie. Never been — your habit. Don't start."

His slate blue eyes filled with tears. "I'll get you out of here," he said. "I will."

CHAPTER 19

"SOME PROBLEMS have a way of solving themselves," Howie said to Newton later that same day. "It never pays to be in too big a hurry. With a little patience, we'll have everybody happy again in no time."

All was quiet at Golden Age.

Lucas had sat a long time, stupefied, as it seemed, by Martha's bed; had stared blankly at Mary Hartwell, coming and going in the sickroom and busying herself with the trivial necessities of illness; had then, without protest, allowed himself to be led down to his own room. There, he stirred the food on his luncheon tray, emptied his coffee cup into the toilet, and lay for a long time on his narrow bed, his eyes thoughtful and his face composed, staring sometimes at the ceiling above his head, sometimes out the open door into the garden.

Two or three times during the afternoon he emerged from his room to climb the stairs and sit again by Martha's bed. He held her hand lightly on his palm and kept his finger on the pulse. Once he brought his sphygmomanometer and took her blood pressure. Afterward, returning to his room, he muttered to himself: For what? For what?

She was drowsy and weak — spent most of the afternoon sleeping. Toward suppertime a light drizzle of rain began. She roused to find herself alone in the room with him, her hand in his. She turned her head, seeming more to listen than to look out the darkening window, and then turned back to him.

"Raining! We'll find meadow mushrooms next week," she said slowly. "Maybe even chanterelles?"

He nodded. "If it keeps up long enough."

"Are you all right, Lucas?"

"Yes," he said. "I have a plan for us. Don't worry."

At eleven that night Lucy came to work as usual. She made her rounds upstairs and found everyone sleeping. Downstairs she looked about her. All the doors opening on the corridor were closed. She opened the first one on her right at the foot of the stairs and stepped in. By the night-light she could see that Mrs. Wheeler was sleeping. Miss Carrie lay with open eyes staring at the ceiling. The drawsheets on both beds were dark with urine. "Change y'all later. If I do it now, you'll just pee again." In the hall again, she glanced at Lucas's closed door. "Locked. Won't be long before we fix that." She continued on her way and stopped for a moment at her desk to check charts and instructions. At the other end of the hall the Strange brothers' door was closed and no light shone above it. She did not look in. "Keep me talking half the night," she muttered.

Barring an emergency, there would be nothing more to do now until she made her rounds at two. She went to Howie's door and knocked lightly.

Twenty minutes had gone by with the hall quiet and empty when the door to Lucas's room swung noiselessly inward and he stepped out, dressed in his bathrobe and slippers. He too looked about him. Earlier, as he made his plans, he had rehearsed the geography of the house, particularly of the lower floor: at his end of the U-shaped building, his own room and bath, reached by a short corridor branching off the main hall; at the foot of the stairs and opening on the main hall, Mrs.

Wheeler and Miss Carrie; next, an empty room waiting for Mrs. Crane, whose son had now consented to her being moved downstairs; beyond this, the nurse's station in a jog in the wall; then, last room on the main hall, the Stranges; opposite their door, the other short arm of the U leading to Howie's room and bath. Two night-lights shone dimly — one above Lucy's desk, the other at the far end of the hall. Lucas listened but heard no one stirring. He moved along the hall and, stopping at the desk, tried the deep bottom drawer.

It slid open. If it had been locked, he would have gone back to his room; he had an alternative and more complicated plan that he could have executed the following day, but it would have meant writing prescriptions for himself and getting them filled at several drugstores. This way was quicker and easier. He had been almost sure, moreover — had *known*, even after all that had happened — that there was more than a chance the drawer would be accessible. "So sure of themselves," he muttered. He closed it without touching anything inside. It would be prudent, he thought, not to get what he needed here until he had done one thing more.

He returned to his room, picked up his flashlight from the top of his chest of drawers, went outside, and walked quickly along the flagstone path toward the garage, flashing the light ahead of his footsteps and breathing deeply. He felt the fresh damp air at the very bottom of his lungs. No emphysema tonight. His muscles worked as freely as if he were twenty-five years younger.

Outside the garage he allowed himself to pause, cutting off the flashlight to look about him. Clouds obscured the night sky and the air was weighted and sultry, but the drizzle of rain had stopped. The high old trees moved quietly, dropping the last-held raindrops to the grass below. Deep in the ravine a chuck-will's-widow called. The sound vibrated in the very center of his belly — a call from the green world.

Then: No stopping. Weakness! Don't think. Act!

He snapped on his light, made his way into the lean-to shed off the garage, found the gallon tin of gasoline that Harper kept for the lawn mower, and, taking it up, returned to his room. Inside, he looked at his watch. Twelve-fifteen. He checked the hall and, finding it still empty, went to the desk, opened the drawer, and selected from the jumble of pillboxes and bottles there a bottle half-filled with colorless liquid and one of capsules, and a couple of five-cc syringes. These he took to his room and left on the chest with the flashlight.

That's all. Have to be enough. Now, Martha.

Her name sounded in his mind like thunder and he felt himself stagger as if a stone had struck his heart. As if, he thought, deep in anesthetized sleep, when the heart failed and the self dissolved, I felt some ruthless surgeon jolt me with fist and shock to life.

For a moment he came to himself: Am I doing this?

I swear by Apollo the physician . . . into whatsoever houses I enter, I will go into them for the benefit of the sick.

He closed his mind and continued on his way.

Upstairs he went directly to her room and awakened her. She looked at him in confusion, then smiled, held out her hand to him, and squeezed his. "Getting stronger," she said indistinctly. "I'll be all right tomorrow."

He nodded. "I want you to come to my room for a little while, Martha." He had already gotten her housecoat from the closet and now he helped her out of bed and got her into it. "Can you walk?"

"Weak on the left side," she said. "But I think, if you help me . . ."

"Come on then. Quietly. Lean on me. Like this." They made their way out of the house and around to his outside entrance, he supporting her, whispering encouragement and reassurance.

Outside his door she looked at the night sky swirling with thin clouds that half veiled the gibbous moon, then, wonderingly, at him. "Dreaming," she said. "Dreaming again. This time more real than it's ever been. You, too? Are we in this dream together?"

"Yes, Martha." With his finger tips he touched her cheek, brushed back a strand of hair escaped from the thick white braid. "We're dreaming," he said. "But this time a good dream. No more nightmares. All right?"

In his room he settled her in the armchair on one side of his fireplace and gave her two capsules which she swallowed without question. More? I *can't*. Not yet. Put that off . . .

"Sit there," he said softly. "See — the door is open." Quickly he stepped outside, pulled a sprig of mint, crushed it between his fingers, and, inside again, laid it on the table beside her. "Can you smell the mint bed?"

She nodded drowsily.

"The clouds are lifting," he said. "Tomorrow will be fair. We'll sit by the bayou and . . ."

Her eyes closed. He bent over her and brushed her forehead with his lips. "Good night," he whispered.

Upstairs again, he did not think except of the immediate task. He walked down the hall to Ethel Crane's room, knocked, and, when she spoke, went in, identifying himself in a low voice as he opened the door. "Lucas Alexander, Ethel. May I talk to you for a few minutes?"

She had turned on the lamp by her bed and lay propped on her pillows, gray hair straggling about her shoulders, her long skinny body outlined under the sheet. She looked curiously at him.

"I'm sorry to have to waken you." He was matter-of-fact, alert, attempting, as he crossed the room and drew up a chair beside the bed, to assess her condition. Was she in one of her spells? Would she take in what he had to say? If not, what? Force? No! Pretend she misunderstood me? Think about that if I have to.

"I don't sleep much," she said. "I was awake. They say the older you get the less sleep you need. Don't they?" She shrugged. "I *need* it — need not to be lying here thinking. But it won't come."

She's all right, he decided. For our purposes: mine — and hers. He drew a deep breath. "Ethel, do you remember when you hit yourself on the head with your cane?" he said.

"Yes. I remember *before* — remember wanting to do it, planning . . ."

"I saw it happen, you know. Harper and I picked you up and took you to your room."

"Ah," she said. "Did you? Well?"

"You wanted to die."

"I wasn't strong enough," she said. "I've given up now. There's not even a window high enough to jump out of. Unless . . ." She broke off and a look of cunning came into her eyes. "Why are you talking to me about that? In the middle of the night. What do you want? Do you think I have anything *you* can take?"

He shook his head emphatically. "No! I don't want anything. But I knew you wanted to die. I know about things like that, too. And I wanted to be sure you remembered."

"Yes," she said. "Sometimes I remember everything that has ever happened in my life."

"Do you still want to? Tonight?"

"Yes."

He found that he was trembling uncontrollably, his hands knotted in his lap. He felt cold sweat trickle down his scalp and under the collar of his robe. His teeth chattered. *I will abstain from every voluntary act of mischief and corruption.*

"Are you cold?" she said.

"I can help you," he said. "If you still want to." He unclenched his hand, groped in his pocket and drew out the bottle of capsules. "I have these." He showed them to her. "Surer than a cane. All you have to do is swallow them. I'll give them to you, if you will do as I ask without any questions."

"Why?" she said. "Why are you saying this to me? You're trying to trick me."

"Other people want to die, too," he said. "We all come to an end. If we help you, you have to help us."

"Ah," she said again. "I see." She held out her hand for the bottle.

"Only if you do as I tell you. We have to do it right. Not much medicine, and we have to be *sure*."

"All right. All right."

"Come downstairs with me. That's all you have to do."

Again, out of the house, down the hill, and in at his outside door. Martha was asleep in the armchair by the fireplace. He settled Mrs. Crane in his bed, gave her a handful of pills and a glass of water and watched her gulp them down. After half a dozen she gagged. "It takes a while," he said. "No hurry." Then, "That'll do."

They looked at each other. There was nothing for him to say about her life. Nothing. "I have things to do," he said. "I have to go now. Just sit quietly — no one will come in here. All right?"

She was far away, but she roused. "Thank you, Lucas."

He looked at his watch. It was now five minutes to one. Hurry. I have to hurry. Darkness and confusion coiled through his brain, settled on every tiny throbbing circuit like a rope of oily smoke. He felt it seeping, sinking lower, clutching his throat, constricting his precious breath. Lightly! Relax! He clenched and relaxed his fists, shook his hands gently at the end of limp wrists, watching Martha's peaceful sleeping face beside his fireplace.

What next? Don't think. Act!

Mrs. Wheeler and Miss Carrie. He slipped rapidly, silently down the hall and into their room, closing the door behind him. Silently he untied the net from the corner of Mrs. Wheeler's bed. She lay sleeping, mouth slightly open, a small moaning snore issuing with rhythmic regularity from her mouth. A drool of spittle slid from the grayish yellow whiskers on her chin.

He reached into his pocket, drew out the bottle of Demerol, and looked at it. How much left? Not fifteen cc's. Will there be enough? Taking one of the syringes from his pocket, he plunged the needle through the rubber cap and withdrew as much as it would hold. No telling what they've been giving her — how much tolerance she's built up. But just so she gets enough to keep her sleeping. No pain. There's been pain enough.

He glanced up. Miss Carrie Stock lay on her bed across the room. Her eyes were open, looking toward him. A low formless sound escaped her. He nodded. "I'll be with you in a minute, Miss Carrie," he said. "Don't worry, it's just me, Lucas Alexander."

Gently he pulled Mrs. Wheeler's nightgown up to expose her slack, almost fleshless buttock. She moaned and stirred.

"James?"

Without a moment's hesitation he plunged the needle in. She opened her eyes and gave a squeak of astonishment.

"It's all right, Mrs. Wheeler," he said. "All right. Dr. Alexander. Go back to sleep now."

She nodded kindly at him, unsurprised by any suffering that might come her way. "Thank you," she said in her low pleading voice. "If you would sit with me a little while now . . . Please . . ."

"All right," he said. "I will. I have just one or two more things to do and then I'll join you."

He crossed the room to the other bed. "Do you understand me, Miss Carrie?" he said. "Do you know me?"

She blinked.

"Are you blinking once for yes?"

She blinked.

"I'm going to give you something to help you sleep," he said. *I will give no deadly drug to anyone, though it be asked of me, nor will I counsel such.* "Do you trust me?"

She blinked.

"We haven't time to talk about what I'm doing," he said. "Trust me. Only I can help you." He bent over her, took up the flaccid arm. "I *told* them," he said. "I told them you knew . . . No one cared."

The tiniest tremor at the corner of her mouth and a faint croaking sound.

"I'll be back," he said. "Now, sleep. Tomorrow will be different."

As he left their room, he saw by the night-light that it was now five minutes to one. Next? How long do I have? Lucy? Will she come out before two? The Stranges? What are we going to do about the Stranges? He retreated to his room.

No thinking. Images. Keep to what I see. Do what I see my-self doing. This house, this particular hell, my corner of hell.

In his mind again, a map of the house. The location of the registers for air conditioning and heating in every room, the louvered lower halves of the doors for circulation, the return in the hall. He saw a kind of smudge fire below the return in the hall. Smoke coiled through the ducts and began to drift into every room.

Suffocate in their sleep. Easy! But Lucy and Howie are awake. Notice it. I've already thought of that. Wasting time! Didn't I decide how I was going to do it?

He saw a smooth, dark slender arm reaching out to him, gold bangles flashing against the narrow wrist, the wrist strong for embracing, the long hand smooth and graceful, the pulse trembling below the thin dark skin. Saw flame sear and shrivel and char the flesh . . .

Lucy! Will I kill her? No! Howie? What did I decide? And Martha? Can't bear . . . Act!

Again the map in his mind. He saw it crumpled like a sheet of discarded paper, saw himself put a match to it, saw it consumed.

Windows for a draft opening from the hall into the back garden. The door from the hall into my room and, in the wall opposite, the outside door. Martha and Mrs. Crane between. Open? Or shut? Shut the door and leave the window open. The grating will keep them from getting in — long enough. The stairs on this end opening into the main hall — like a flue to draw the fire into the upper story. I have to remember to keep that door shut. Confine the fire to us. Will it work? The Stranges in their room at the other end. Howie can get them out. I've done the best I can.

Harper. The thought pierced him like a knife. He saw the

studious yellow face with its look of austere compassion: "You have to become like us. Disappear."

Never!

Lucy? He felt his chest slit open and the clamps separating his ribs, felt the hand of the ruthless surgeon lift out his beating heart.

He got up from the chair where he had been sitting staring at Martha's peaceful face, moved stiffly across the room, and picked up the gallon tin of gasoline that he had brought in from the toolroom. He noticed that there was a curious numbness in his hand. He could not feel the pressure of the grip on his fingers. He set the can down, opened it, and sniffed the seductive fragrance of the gasoline. Breathed it in deeply. He picked up a folded newspaper from the table beside his bed and, holding the can against his chest and still breathing its fragrance, moved stiffly out into the hall.

He went first to Mrs. Wheeler's room and found both women sleeping quietly. He touched Miss Carrie and knew that she was dead. (No tolerance. They've never bothered to give *her* anything.) Mrs. Wheeler still snored softly.

He laid his fire neatly under the painted wooden chest that stood next to their open closet. Crumpled the newspapers, took out a couple of dresses and wooden coat hangers from the closet for kindling and arranged them on top of the papers, opened a drawer of the chest, poured a little gasoline on the clothing inside and a little more on the papers below. Quickly he closed the can, stepped into the hall, and set it down. Then he struck a match, opened the door a crack, tossed it on the pile of paper and kindling, and closed the door on a whoosh of flame. He opened the window in the hall.

Back in his room.

How much start should I let it get before I finish? Time? He raised his arm and held it stiffly before him, gazed at the face of his watch. Have the hands moved? Time no longer moving past? Did I once feel it rushing by me like a wind? No longer. All is still. Dead? Am I dead? Is this death? To be destroying, to be suffering, to be dissolving, but without sound or motion — still, still, still?

He heard the mantel clock strike once as loud as the cathedral bell and then a thunderous ticking in his ears. Stood up. Did I fix it? Time?

I *will* finish. Now.

He opened his door and looked down the hall. Black smoke drifted through the louvers of Mrs. Wheeler's door and down the hall toward the return. He heard the hot crackle of burning wood.

Have I waited too long?

With stiff fingers he laid two piles of kindling — papers and wooden hangers — in his own room, one under the chest against the wall by his outside door, one under a chair which he dragged across the room and braced under the knob of his inside door. He locked both doors.

Now I must call Howie.

He saw Howie naked on his bed, the hairy reddish skin of his legs and arms glowing in the firelight, Lucy dark and cool beside him, her long brown leg against his. Ground his teeth and shivered. If I don't call him, the others will burn — will waken burning. He picked up the telephone from the table beside his bed and dialed Howie's inside line.

He heard the answering "hello" as from an immense distance, then his own voice, quavering and uncertain: "Listen carefully, Howie. I have . . ." Gathered all his strength and spoke as strongly as he could. "I have set fire to this house. Don't hang up! You don't know where the fire is or who is in danger. Lis-

ten to what I have to say. First: the upstairs is not burning yet.
Next: no use to worry about Mrs. Wheeler and Miss Carrie —
you can't get to them and anyhow they are both already dead.
As for Martha and me, we are safe. Now, as soon as I hang up,
get the Stranges out of their room. They are the only ones in
danger right now. At this moment the fire is confined to the
downstairs. Understand? The Stranges! Don't panic, Howie.
I hadn't the guts after all to destroy *you* — only your lair. You
and Lucy and the Stranges can get out. Then call the fire department. Stranges first! Get them and you'll be a hero. Then,
upstairs . . ."

The receiver slammed up in his face. He crossed the room
quickly with his precious gasoline tin, poured a little on his kindling by the inside door, struck a match and lit the fire. No more
hesitation. The rest has to be done. He lit the fire by his outside door, took up his syringe and drew into it the last drops of
Demerol. *Martha.*

How did I decide who was to die and who to live? *With purity and holiness will I pass my life and practice my art.*

༒

But the upstairs was burning. The closet in Mrs. Wheeler's
room and the closet in Mrs. Cathcart's room directly above
were both built in the old dumbwaiter shaft, a natural flue that
went all the way up into the unused attic bedroom. The makeshift floor in Mrs. Cathcart's closet that served also as ceiling
to Mrs. Wheeler's closet was burned through in a few minutes by the flames drawn upward through the shaft. Above,
the fire burst into the attic, roaring and crackling through ancient bone-dry studs and joists, and in minutes had burned
through the cedar shakes of the roof. Flames shot up into the

hot August night. Showers of sparks set the shakes to burning all over the roof.

Matthew Harper, on the other side of the bayou in his snug little house — five blocks from Golden Age by the street, but only a hundred yards by the footbridge that crossed the bayou below the cattail bed — was not asleep. Earlier, he had sat a long time on his front porch, scarcely hearing the shouts of the children playing on the sidewalk, his thoughts a tangle of grim confusion.

"We got to get our minds right about all this. That's the first thing," he muttered to himself once. But he did not believe that this confusion would yield even to his careful mind.

Shortly after one o'clock he sighed, shrugged, and went into his house to prepare for bed. In his kitchen he stood in front of the sink, a glass of water in his hand, gazing as in a trance at his own reflection in the glass of the back window. His head was backlighted by the reflection of the naked light bulb hanging from the middle of his kitchen ceiling, so that he appeared to himself to have a halo — an effect which he found fleetingly amusing. Then he saw, appearing at first to be part of the reflection of the light bulb, showers of sparks and a bolt of flame before his eyes. He whirled, for an instant the sensation of heat and flame, the very sound of crackling, at his back. But his kitchen was empty and silent. The naked bulb glowed steadily at the end of its cord. He turned again to the window, stared out. Fire? Yes. Where? He hurried out onto his back porch and stared into the darkness. Saw through the tall trees on the opposite bank of the bayou the leap of flame and the showering of sparks. It could be nothing but Golden Age.

Lucy!

Without an instant's hesitation he ran to his telephone and dialed Operator. "Fire!" he shouted into the phone. "Fire at

Golden Age Acres, lady! Twelve twenty-four Clarke Street. A big one. Call the fire department quick! And then call Mr. Newton Clarke. Understand? Newton Clarke. It's his house."

Lucy!

He threw down the telephone and set out down his side of the ravine, stumbling and cursing in the darkness.

That was how Newton and Harper happened to get to the scene of the fire so quickly — even before the fire trucks, whose sirens they both heard, as they approached the house from opposite directions. Newton had flung out of the house in pajamas and robe, shouting to his father to follow, and now he leaped out of his car, climbed the front steps three at a time, and, running toward the house, met a little group stumbling down the front sidewalk in dazed confusion: Mrs. Aldridge, Miss Rebecca Steinman, Mr. Howard, and Lucy. The Strange twins sat side by side on a bench under the big Spanish oak. The house and yard were lit up by the burning roof, and the faces of the people fleeing the house gleamed in the flickering darkness.

"Where are the others?" Newton shouted.

Everyone stared at him. Mr. Howard gestured vaguely toward the house. "Well . . ." he said. "Well . . ." and then, "My cars — they'll be burned!"

Newton grabbed Miss Rebecca Steinman by the shoulder and shook her. "Aunt Martha? Howie? Where are they? Quick!"

Even she, usually so alert, the black eyes always sharp with curiosity, could only shake her head. Then she raised a wavering hand and pointed to Lucy. "She . . . She says you . . . you can't get to Mrs. Wheeler's room. The fire's too far gone downstairs. Nobody knows where Martha and Ethel Crane are. They weren't in their rooms — weren't anywhere upstairs. Howie . . ." She drew a deep shuddering breath. "Howie's gone back to try and get Mrs. Cathcart out. We . . . We couldn't get to her."

"Lucas? Has anybody checked his room?"

The howl of the fire siren drew nearer.

Lucy, hair wild and disheveled, uniform half-buttoned, stood with one bare foot on top of the other, tears streaming down her face. Her teeth clicked and she shivered as if it were December. "Grandpa," she said. "He come in and . . . and then we . . . we was all coming out, and he said maybe the doc . . ." She broke off and stared in terror at Newton. "Grandpa!" she screamed. "Where is my grandpa? He hadn't come back."

She started toward the house at a run, turned down the sidewalk that went around to Lucas's outside door, and disappeared into the darkness, Newton running behind her.

Outside Lucas's closed door they both stopped. They could see, through the barred window, the flicker of rising flames, as if the fire there were just beginning to catch. Newton tried the knob, then hurled himself at the door. Lucy shrank back, then started, as Harper stepped out of the deep shadows and touched her on the arm. They looked silently at each other. He laid his finger on his lips, shook his head warningly, and drew her back into the darkness as Newton hurled himself at the door again and again.

"Grandpa! I thought you was dead, thought you gone in there and . . . and I thought you . . ."

He spoke in a whisper in her ear. "They're in there," he said. "I already tried the door myself, and then I looked in the window and there they were, her sitting in her chair, eyes shut, and him standing looking at her. And then he sat down across from her where he always sits. Fire hadn't even started good, but they just sat there, like they were satisfied."

"Grandpa! I thought you was . . . dead!"

Newton drew back from the heavy six-paneled cypress door and kicked out with all his strength, bursting in the panel next to the doorknob, reached in, cursing the heat, and turned the knob, releasing the night latch. He threw open the door.

Behind him, Harper drew Lucy deeper into the shadows. "Just sat there," he whispered. "Like they were satisfied. And so I let 'em be."

When Newton flung open the door, the air sucked inward and the fire leaped up in the doorway, blocking his entrance. Beyond it they could see Martha and Lucas still sitting in their chairs, Martha asleep, as it appeared. Mrs. Crane lay on Lucas's bed. The gasoline can was beside his chair. The fire had spread by now from the two piles of kindling: the bed had begun to burn; the wall smoldered and, while they looked, burst into flame. Newton kicked aside the pile of burning hangers and clothing, ran into the room, and crossed it through smoke and flames to his aunt.

Lucas rose, the tall thin body insubstantial and wavering in the midst of smoke and flame. "Get out!" he shouted. "Too late, Newton. Out!" He saw Newton struggling to pick up Martha's inert body. "No! For God's sake let us alone." Staggered, shaken by a paroxysm of tearing coughs, across the room, and seized Newton by the arm. But Newton shook him off, gave him a shove that sent him reeling against the inside wall, took Martha's body under the arms, and, holding his breath and keeping his eyes almost closed, dragged her out of the room and away from the house. He dropped her, without a glance, left her lying, one arm twisted under her, on the rain-wet grass, and turned again toward the burning house.

Harper, stepping out of the shadows, bent down to her, straightened her limbs, and raised her head. Lucy, still weeping and shivering in the hot August night, sat down and took her in her arms, holding her close, as if they might keep each other from the cold. Martha opened her eyes, gazed about her into the night, and said something unintelligible. Harper took her hand. "Mama?" she said. "Children? Lucas? Is everybody all right?"

Before the gasoline can exploded and filled the room with flame, Lucas, himself now surrounded by fire, saw Newton twice more approach the doorway, twice shrink back. The second time, as the smoke cleared for a moment, he saw Harper step forward and, looking briefly and without expression into the room, drag Newton back.

Still he stood like one anesthetized, seeming not to feel the fire. "Too late," he shouted. "Too late, Newton. We're dead. You can't do anything more for us . . ."

Then, vaguely aware of a prickling in his legs and thighs, Lucas looked down and saw that his bathrobe was on fire. Somewhere far away and above his head he heard a sound he knew well — the voice of a woman screaming with pain. For a moment agonizing doubt, more terrible than fire, shriveled his soul.

Wait! Wait! Could I have set it wrong? And then: Our lives — all our lives — to end like *this?*

The fire leaped up and he was gone.